TALLGRASS

SANDRA DALLAS

TALLGRASS

ST. MARTIN'S PRESS ❧ NEW YORK

www.stmartins.com

Design by Greg Collins

Library of Congress Cataloging-in-Publication Data

Dallas, Sandra.
　　Tallgrass / Sandra Dallas.—1st ed.
　　　p. cm.
　　ISBN-13: 978-0-312-36019-1
　　ISBN-10: 0-312-36019-3
　　1. Japanese Americans—Evacuation and relocation, 1942–1945—Fiction. 2. Teenage girls—Fiction. 3. World War, 1939–1945—Colorado—Fiction. I. Title.

PS3554.A434 T35 2007
813'.54—dc22

2006051271

First Edition: April 2007

10　9　8　7　6　5　4　3　2　1

For

LLOYD ATHEARN

And in memory of

FORREST DALLAS (1903–1973)

Two awful good men

ACKNOWLEDGMENTS

In February 1942, just two months after the Japanese bombing of Pearl Harbor, President Franklin D. Roosevelt signed Executive Order 9066, authorizing the federal government to relocate all people of Japanese ancestry who were living on the West Coast. At great financial and emotional sacrifice, more than 100,000 people, many of them native-born Americans, were uprooted and sent to ten desolate inland camps. Some 10,000 went through the gates of Amache, located near Granada, Colorado.

I first heard about Amache on a pheasant-hunting trip with a friend in southeastern Colorado in 1961, a little more than fifteen years after the camp closed at the end of World War II. My friend, who'd grown up in the area, took me to see what remained of Amache—concrete slabs and roads bladed into the prairie. The buildings had been carted off when the camp was shut down, and in researching the camp not long after I first visited it, I discovered that my journalism classes at the

University of Denver had been held in a former Amache barracks.

I did nothing with the information I'd collected on Amache until I read Robert Harvey's superb book *Amache: The Story of Japanese Internment in Colorado During World War II,* with its interviews with former evacuees. I was disturbed by what I read, and not just because it exposed the shameful way America deprived its own citizens of their civil rights during World War II. The Iraq war was under way at the time I read the book, and the news was filled with disturbing stories of men being held without charges at Guantanamo Bay. I could not help but wonder if there were a corollary between the Japanese evacuation of World War II and the detainment at Guantanamo. That concern led me to write *Tallgrass*.

It is the story of a Japanese relocation camp in southeastern Colorado and the effect it has on both the evacuees and the townspeople. The book is entirely fiction, which is why I renamed the camp Tallgrass. I am not Japanese, so it would have been presumptuous of me to write from a Japanese point of view. Instead, the story is told from the perspective of Rennie Stroud, a young girl whose farm is adjacent to the camp.

Despite its dark theme, *Tallgrass* was a pleasure to write because I love the characters, particularly Loyal Stroud, Rennie's father. Originally, he was to have been a good man but a shadowy figure. As I wrote, however, I realized that Loyal was my father, Forrest Dallas, who died in 1973. Not only does Loyal use my father's expressions, but he drives Dad's truck, Red Boy, has Dad's sense of humor, and, most important, he has my father's strong moral core. I'm grateful to my sister, Mary Cole, and brother, Michael Dallas, who shared their memories of Dad.

In researching *Tallgrass,* I drew heavily on Robert Harvey's book and on personal conversations with the author. Carl Iwasaki, my friend of nearly fifty years, shared his experiences at Heart Mountain, the Wyoming relocation camp. Bill Hosokawa, who was at Heart Mountain, too, suggested additions. Uncle Bob Glendon gave me permission to use Red Boy. I couldn't write this or any other book without the support of my friend and writing buddy, Arnie Grossman. Danielle Egan-Miller and Joanna MacKenzie at Browne & Miller Literary Associates insisted that I go back again and again to refine the story, and my editor, Jennifer Enderlin, and copy editor, Carol Edwards, at St. Martin's Press suggested additional ways to strengthen *Tallgrass.* Thanks to all of you.

Most of all, I want to thank Bob, Dana, Povy, Lloyd, and Forrest. You are my moral core.

TALLGRASS

I

THE SUMMER I WAS thirteen, the Japanese came to Ellis. Not Ellis, exactly, but to the old Tallgrass Ranch, which the government had turned into a relocation camp. Tallgrass was a mile and a half from Ellis, less than a mile past our farmhouse. It was one of the camps the government was building then to house the Japanese. In early 1942, the Japanese on the West Coast had been rounded up and incarcerated in places such as the Santa Anita racetrack. Those destined for Colorado waited there until streets had been bladed into the yucca and sagebrush at Tallgrass, guard towers and barracks thrown up, and the camp fenced off with bobwire. Then they were put on a train and sent a thousand miles to Ellis.

I remember the crowd of townspeople at the depot the day the first Japanese arrived. The arrival date was supposed to be a secret, but we knew the evacuees were coming, because the government had alerted the stationmaster and hired bus drivers, and guards with guns patrolled the station platform. I'd sneaked away from my parents and gone to the depot, too, because I'd never seen any Japanese. I expected them to look like the cartoons of Hirohito in the newspaper, with slanted eyes and buckteeth and skin like rancid butter. All these years later, I recall I was disappointed that they didn't appear to be a "yellow peril" at all. They were so ordinary. That is what I remember most about them.

The Japanese gripped the handrails as they got off the train because the steps were steep and their legs were short, and they frowned and blinked into the white-hot sun. They had made the trip with the shades in the coaches pulled down, and the glare of the prairie hurt their eyes. Most of the evacuees on that first train were men, dressed in suits, rumpled now after the long ride, ties that were loosened, and straw hats. Some had on felt hats, although it was August.

The few women wore tailored skirts and blouses and summer dresses with shoulder pads, coats over their arms. They pulled scarves from their pocketbooks and tied them around their heads to keep the hot wind from blowing dust into their hair. Some of the women had on wedgies or open-toed spectator pumps and silk or rayon stockings. Each evacuee carried a single suitcase, because that was all they had been allowed to bring with them.

The adults stood quietly in little groups, whispering, waiting to be told what to do. I expected one of the guards to take charge, to steer the people to the school buses lined up along the platform or tell them to go inside where it was cooler. But no one did, so they waited, confused. I wanted to point the evacuees to the drinking fountain and the bathrooms in the depot. They must have needed them. But I didn't dare speak up.

Some of the men took out packages of Camels and Chesterfields and Lucky Strikes and lighted cigarettes. None of them chewed tobacco, and none of the women smoked. Several children, cooped up for days, seemed glad to be out in the open, and they squatted down to examine the tracks or ran around, jerky as Mexican jumping beans. A little boy smiled at me, but I turned away, embarrassed to make a connection with him. I wondered if the kids were supposed to be our enemies, too. Then the mothers called to them, and the children joined their parents, fidgeting as they looked at us shyly. Only the children took notice of the group of townspeople on the platform staring at them, many hostile, all of us curious.

A man who stepped down from the last car removed his hat, an expensive one that did not have sweat stains like the hats the farmers wore. He smoothed his hair, which appeared to have been slicked back with Vitalis or some other hair oil, because every strand was in place, despite the wind. Holding the hat in his hand, he rubbed his wrist across his forehead. Shading his eyes, he squinted at the prairie grass that glinted like brass in the sun and asked the man beside him, "Where are we?" The second man shrugged, and I suddenly felt sorry for the Japanese. What if the government had taken over our farm and sent us far away on the train, and nobody would tell us our destination? But we weren't Japanese. We were Americans.

"Ellis. You're at Ellis, Colorado," a woman near me called out.

Her husband shushed her. "Don't tell those people where they're at. Don't you know nothing?" He rubbed his big face with a hand that the sun had turned as brown as a walnut. The man had shaved before coming to town. You could tell by the tiny clots of dried blood where he had nicked himself and the clumps of whiskers the razor had missed. They stuck up in the folds of his skin like willow shoots in a gully.

The Japanese man looked into the crowd, searching for the woman who'd spoken. She kept still, however, so he put his hat back on, tightened his tie, and buttoned his suit jacket as he leaned down to whisper something to a girl about my age. I admired her saddle shoes, thinking she must be rich, because saddle shoes cost more than the plain brown oxfords Mom bought me. I wondered how long her shoes would stay white in the dirt of Tallgrass. It wasn't likely that she'd put shoe polish into her small suitcase. The girl shook back her hair, which was long and black and glossy. I had never seen such hair. It was as if coal had been spun into long threads. She unfolded a scarf splashed with pink flowers and put it around her head, tying it at the back of her neck, under her hair.

"Silk. Real silk," a woman near me muttered, but I could not tell if she was jealous or just stating a fact.

A man beside her observed, "I thought they'd have buckteeth. They don't have buckteeth."

"You got buckteeth enough for all of 'em," called one of the boys at the back of the crowd. The man turned around and searched the faces, but he couldn't identify the kid who'd spoken.

I could. He was Beaner Jack. I knew because Danny Spano stopped chugging his Grapette long enough to slap Beaner on the back and say, "Good one." Beaner and Danny were always together, except for the time when Danny was in the army. He'd been in an accident at Camp Carson, near Colorado Springs, and hurt his foot, and the army didn't want him anymore, so he'd been mustered out. Now he was back in Ellis. Both Danny and Beaner were eighteen, the age of my sister, Marthalice, who had gone to Denver to work in an arms plant after she graduated in May. I didn't know whether she'd done it because she was patriotic or because she was blue after her favorite boyfriend, Hank Gantz, quit school to join the navy. My brother, Buddy, who was twenty-one, had left college to enlist in the army the week after Pearl Harbor.

"Haw haw," said Marlys, one of the high school girls who were standing beside the boys. She smiled at Danny, because he was tall and had curly black hair like a movie star. Beaner, on the other hand, was squat, with hair as thin as corn silk. He'd be bald one day, like the rest of the Jacks. And mean, too. I didn't understand how people could be as mean as the Jacks. It was just their nature, I guess. They had meanness in their bones. I couldn't imagine my telling a grown-up that he had buckteeth, but I wasn't surprised that Beaner did.

The bucktoothed man glared at Marlys.

"Beaner's a bushel of cow pucky," whispered Betty Joyce Snow, who was standing on the platform next to me, and we both giggled. With Marthalice gone, I was especially glad that Betty Joyce was my best friend. We told each other everything. Betty Joyce and I got along as squarely as anybody. She'd sneaked away from her father's hardware store to come to the station, and I knew she'd have the dickens to pay if her dad found out.

Then Lum Smith observed, "I don't see nothing wrong with them. They don't even hardly look like Japs, some of 'em anyway." He was a small, henpecked man with no chin, like Andy Gump in the comic strips. His wife, Bird, frowned at him. Bird Smith's hair was in pin curls, covered by a red bandanna that was tied at the top of her head. The ends of the scarf stuck up like rabbit ears. Stout, with legs the size of Yule logs, she didn't look much like her name. She didn't sound like it, either. Mrs. Smith was one of the dozen members of Mom's quilting group, the Jolly Stitchers, which meant they considered themselves friends, but Mom didn't seem to care much for her. I was glad that at thirteen, I didn't *have* to be friends with anybody.

"That's why they're so dangerous," Mr. Rubey said. "You'd not hardly think they was the enemy. But it's a fact. Some of them have a shortwave with a direct line to Tojo." He jerked back his head for emphasis, sticking out his chest, which made his overalls pull up over his big hams.

"Shortwave radios don't send signals that far," his son Edgar told him.

"Was anybody asking you, mister?"

"No, sir." Edgar was the smartest boy in my grade, but he was a twerp. Once, I said New York City was the capital of New York State, and Edgar asked if I wanted to bet on it. I was so sure I was right that I bet a quarter. But I was wrong, and Edgar lorded it over me, saying only a dummy would bet against him. He'd known all along that the capital was Albany, because he'd visited his aunt and uncle there. That wasn't fair, and I didn't have a quarter. But I wasn't a welsher, so I paid off Edgar at five cents a week. Then he made me pay him three cents' interest.

The guards moved among the evacuees then, pointing to school buses that Ellis folks still call "the yellow dogs." The Japanese picked up their suitcases, the women moving about like hens as they gathered their children and scurried toward the open doors.

"They ride on a machine, while I ride my horse to town," said Olney Larsoo, who ran the filling station. His face was raw, as if it had been scoured by sand, like paint on a frame house in a storm. "I'm a World War One vet, and they're a bunch of damn foreigners." He leaned over the edge of the platform and spit out his wad.

"Aw, they can't help being born that way," someone said.

"I believe the government ought to make them go back to where they come from," Frank Martin said, loudly enough for one of the Japanese men boarding the bus to hear. The evacuee turned around, and Mr. Martin leaned forward and repeated louder, "Ought to make them go back where they come from."

A man made his way through the crowd then and said just loudly enough for all of us to hear, "Those folks came from California. Where at is it you're from, Frank?" People laughed because Mr. Martin had moved to Ellis from Italy after the Great War, and he ate spaghetti and sold dago red to the high school boys for fifty cents a jar. His real name was Martinelli, and some people said that meant jackass in Italian. Mr. Martin sent a reproachful look at the man who'd spoken.

I couldn't see him, but I recognized the voice. It belonged to my father, and he came up beside me and took my arm. "We've been looking for you, Squirt. We thought you were with Granny. I reckon there's chores to do." He glanced over at Betty Joyce, who'd begun studying the splintery boards of the platform, but he didn't say anything to her. If Betty Joyce's father thought I should go home, he'd tell me in a second, but Dad wouldn't discipline another man's child.

"I wanted to see the Japs," I said, my face red. I knew Dad was disappointed that I'd come to the station. He'd said on the way into town that Ellis folks should have the decency to leave the evacuees alone. He hadn't exactly told me I couldn't go to the depot, but that wouldn't be much of a defense if Dad decided to scold me. He'd accuse me of fuzzy-headed logic, and he might feel he had to start telling me what to do again, as if I were still a little kid. Since Buddy and Marthalice had gone away, Dad had trusted me to make more of my own decisions. But at least he wouldn't smack me the way Betty Joyce's father smacked her.

"I believe they are called Japanese."

"Yes, sir."

"These here are Japs, Loyal. Can't you see that?" Mr. Rubey asked my father, scratching his stomach through his overalls.

"All I see are some unlucky Americans. By Dan, I dislike the enemy as much as the next fellow, but I don't see any enemy here," he said as Mr. Rubey turned his hands into fists. People stepped back a little. Dad wasn't a big man, just average in height and size, and his dark hair had begun to creep back on his forehead. He didn't look like a fighting man, but folks around Ellis knew enough not to take him on.

Once when I was in third grade, Ralph Muggins complained to the teacher, Mr. Gross, that someone had stolen a boiled egg from his lunch bucket. Mr. Gross told us all to open our lunch pails. I had a giant boiled egg in mine, and the teacher ordered me to admit I'd stolen it and apologize to Ralph. When I wouldn't do it, Mr. Gross made me stand in the dark cloakroom. At first, I wasn't scared, just humiliated, knowing that the drone in the room meant my classmates were talking about me, accusing me of being a thief. When the bell rang, dismissing classes, and the room grew quiet, however, I wondered if I'd have to stay there all night. The closet was stuffy, and the closeness made me sleepy, but I was afraid to sit down, for fear of rats. Dad was in town that afternoon and heard the bell and decided to give me a ride home. He ran into Mr. Gross as he was leaving the school. "Oops, I put Rennie in the cloakroom to punish her for stealing, and I forgot about her," Mr. Gross told Dad, giving an apologetic shrug. "Good thing you came along, Mr. Stroud. I sure wouldn't like to have to come back all this way to let her out." Dad rushed to the classroom, grabbed me, and carried me outside. Then he slugged Mr. Gross so hard that the teacher fell to the dirt, breaking his glasses. Dad would have killed him, but Mr. Gross refused to stand up, and Dad wouldn't hit a man who was down. Although he apologized to me in class the next day, Mr. Gross didn't come back the following year, and folks said he should have known all along that Mom had put the boiled egg in my lunch that morning: Mom's eggs were the biggest in Bondurant County, and the Muggins raised guinea hens. I never liked closed, dark spaces after that. And people were careful not to cross my father.

Dad stared until Mr. Rubey put his hands into his pockets; then Dad said, "Good day to you, sir." He turned and, pulling me behind him, went back through the crowd, people parting to let us through. I looked over my shoulder to tell Betty Joyce good-bye, but she was watching the yellow dogs lumber onto the washboard Tallgrass Road. The yellow dogs sent up plumes of dust, which settled over the people at the depot. Men took out bandannas to wipe their faces, which were grimy with dust and sweat. A woman pulled her long apron up over her head. I'd seen pictures of California vineyards and orange groves, and I thought how bewildered the Japanese would be when they saw their new home carved out of the treeless prairie. Some would live there for three years, until V-J day.

As Dad and I jumped off the platform next to the depot, a man with a pencil and a pad of paper got up from the running board of a car where he had been sitting, watching, and came over to us. "Seems like folks aren't too happy about the Japs being here," he said. Dad stared at the man until he explained who he was. "Jeff Cheever, *Denver Post*. I'm doing a story on the Tallgrass Internment Camp. Like I say, it seems that you wheat farmers aren't too happy it's here."

Dad didn't answer at first. Instead, he pulled out the makings, sprinkled tobacco onto a cigarette paper, rolled it up, and licked it shut. The reporter took out a lighter, but before he could flick it,

Dad struck a kitchen match on his overalls and lighted the cigarette, which was twisted at the ends and bent a little in the middle. Dad glanced over at a second man, who was fitting a flashbulb into a big square camera. "Sugar beets. This is sugar beet country. You better get that right, son."

The reporter shrugged. "So how do you feel about the Japs?"

Dad inhaled and blew smoke out of his mouth. "There's some would like to talk to you about it. I'm not amongst them. Good day to you." Dad touched his straw hat to the man and started off.

"Hey," called the reporter, "don't you want to see your name in print?"

Dad stopped, and I hoped he'd changed his mind. Getting our name in the paper would be exciting. People would read what Dad had said and remark on it. Kids would say, "Hey, I read about your dad in the *Post*." I'd cut out the story and paste it in my scrapbook and get extra copies to send to Buddy and Marthalice.

But Dad hadn't changed his mind. "Are you hard of hearing, young man?" he asked.

Before the reporter could reply, Mr. Smith interrupted. "Well, I'm not so particular. I've got a piece to say, if you want to listen. I think they ought to 've shipped them to Japan, and the governor with them. If the governor had ran for office right now, he wouldn't get my vote or anybody else's." When the government announced it was evacuating the Japanese from the West Coast, most states made it plain they didn't want them, but Colorado governor Ralph Carr said it was all right to send them to Colorado. He was never elected to office again.

The reporter wrote all that down, asking, "And what was your name?"

"Lum Smith. That's Lum for Columbus, father of our country," Mr. Smith said. He grinned while the photographer took his picture. I wondered if Christopher Columbus was the same father of our country as the first president of the United States, Mr. George Washington.

Now that the buses were gone, people crowded around the reporter, probably hoping to get their names into the paper, too. Dad and I started toward our wagon.

"You should have talked to him, Loyal. You could have told him there's some of us here that don't hate the Japanese. That reporter's going to write us up like we're a bunch of rednecks," said Redhead Joe Lee, who was standing at the edge of the crowd. He ran one of the two drugstores in Ellis, the one where we traded, because Mom didn't like the way Mr. Elliot, the owner of the other, patted her on the fanny once when she went in to buy a bottle of Mercurochrome. That was okay with me, because I didn't like Mr. Elliot's son, Pete, who was a friend of Beaner and Danny. The Lee Drug had perfume and dusting powder on the counters and a marble soda fountain and tables with wire legs and wire chairs. Someday, I'd have a boyfriend who would take me there, and I could sit with one leg under me, the way Marthalice did, and lean my elbows on the table while I drank a Coca-Cola through a straw and flirted. Maybe he'd buy me a blue bottle of Evening in Paris cologne for my birthday. Sure, I thought, right after I win first place on "Major Bowes' Original Amateur Hour."

"You're the fellow that can give it to him straight," said Mr. Lee, who was in shirtsleeves and had on a vest that was buttoned wrong, maybe because he'd been in a hurry to take off his white coat and get to the depot. He was almost as handsome as Dad, and Mom called him "Ellis's most eligible bachelor." That didn't mean much, however, because most of the other bachelors were hired men.

Dad smoked his cigarette down to his fingers, then dropped it in the dirt and ground it out with his foot. "I'm straight as a string, all right, Red. I sure am good-looking, too." Dad paused. "Isn't that right, Mother?"

Mom had come up behind me, and I turned and saw her look Dad up and down before she replied. "You got that string part right."

"Oh, she thinks I'm good-looking as a barber. She can't hardly keep her hands off me," Dad told Mr. Lee, grinning at Mom so openly that she shook her head and looked away. Mom was tall, and instead of being nicely plump like she used to be, she'd lost weight since Buddy had joined up. Her face had become gaunt, and she seemed tired all the time. There was gray in her blond hair, too. But Dad still told her she was the prettiest thing since strawberry ice cream, and he believed it. I suppose I knew that there was something special about my parents, although I never thought much about it. They never criticized each other like the Smiths, never argued the way Betty Joyce's parents did. They respected each other—and me, too—and I was still hoping they wouldn't say I'd let them down by coming to the station to watch the Japanese. There wasn't anything as hard to take as my folks' disappointment; now that my brother and sister were gone, I had to bear all their disappointment.

"Oh, go on. Don't talk so, Loyal," Mom said.

"Red here thinks I should say something to that reporter over there, tell him we don't all hate the Japanese. What do you think?"

"I think you ought not to stir up trouble. Who knows what the Jolly Stitchers would say to that?" Then she told us to come along because Granny was waiting and might wander off.

"And how is the old lady?" Mr. Lee asked, scratching at his

head. He had only a fringe of hair, and his freckled bald head was always peeling, even in the winter.

"Granny forgets. And she frets about that. But then she forgets she forgets." Dad sighed. "There's things I'd like to forget right about now, so I guess she isn't in such a bad way."

My grandmother had forgotten most of what had happened in the past forty years. I loved Granny, who was sweet and smelled like cinnamon and lavender powder, and sometimes wandered into my room and slept with me. That was because when my sister went off to Denver, Mom moved me out of the big bedroom we'd shared and into Granny's room, giving Granny the front bedroom. It was sunny, and Granny could sit by the window, piecing quilt tops. "I'm making this one for Mattie," she'd told me last week. Mattie was her sister, who'd lived in Mingo and died there in the early part of the century. Sometimes Granny forgot she had moved into the front bedroom, and then she'd go into her old room, curling up like a kitten in the bed beside me and keeping me warm. From time to time, she would snap out of her dreamy world and recall something that had happened a long time ago—or as little as a month or two ago. "I didn't make Buddy a quilt to take off to war, because soldier boys now have good warm blankets. Remember, Buddy wrote that in his letter," she'd said one night at dinner.

Dad said good-bye to Mr. Lee, and as we walked away, Dad asked Mom if she'd bought the yellow material she'd had her eye on.

"I can put that quarter to better use," she told him.

Dad said he didn't guess we'd lose the farm for two bits. Besides, with the war, crops were going sky-high, and we'd be rolling in money. "Might be we could sell a little something to the Tallgrass Camp. They're going to need eggs."

"Lord, Loyal, I'd hate to make money off the Japanese. I don't know what's people to think if we did that."

"Somebody has to provide them with eggs, and if we do it, those folks'll eat choice. It wouldn't surprise me if the government's giving them the powdered stuff," Dad told her. "Squirt and me will wait in the wagon with Granny whilst you buy your cloth."

"Perhaps I will, then. Granny favors yellow." Mom didn't really believe the Depression was over, and it pained her to spend money on herself, so she had to be convinced that it was going for someone else.

"You might pick up a nickel's worth of licorice, too," Dad said. He and I were crazy about licorice, although nobody else in the family liked it.

Mom went off to the dry goods—she walked slower now than she used to—while Dad and I headed toward the wagon. We had a truck, but we drove the wagon when we could to save on gasoline and tires. We were so close to town that we might have walked if it hadn't been for Granny.

"How do you feel about the Japanese, Squirt?" Dad asked as we reached the wagon, where Granny sat with her piecing. One good thing about being the only kid left at home was that Dad asked my opinion more often. He listened, too.

I thought hard how to answer him, because I wanted to say something that Dad would be proud of, that he would repeat at the feed store. He'd say, "You know, my daughter says..." But the truth was, I didn't know how I felt. The Japanese at the depot didn't seem like alien enemies working for the downfall of America, but how would I know? The government wouldn't have sent them to Tallgrass if it hadn't believed they were dangerous. That made me uneasy, and I wished the camp were someplace else.

"Somebody at the depot said they were spies and that we ought to lock them up," I said.

"If you locked up people for minding other folks' business, the jail would be full." Dad gave me a sly glance. "They'd have a cell just for your mom's quilt circle."

I thought some more, and then I said slowly, "I think the Japanese are bringing the war home to Ellis."

Dad nodded, looking off down the Tallgrass Road. The dust had settled, and there was no sign of the evacuees or the yellow dogs. Maybe he did repeat what I said at the feed store. He told Mom, and years later, he reminded me of it. Tallgrass did indeed bring the war to us, brought it more than the shortages or rationing or the news on the radio. It made the war as close to us as what happened to Buddy. I grew up during World War II. When the war started, I was a little girl. By the time it ended, I'd become a young woman who had seen much of sorrow and sadness. Tallgrass became our own personal war.

2

WE DIDN'T SEE MUCH of the Japanese at first, because they were busy getting the camp ready for the rest of the detainees, who would be shipped in over the next weeks and months. "They've been handed the wrong end of the stick," I told Betty Joyce. "The government makes them move to Tallgrass, and then it tells them to build their own jail."

"Yeah, but it beats living in a hardware store," she replied. She was embarrassed that she lived with her folks in rooms in the back of the hardware. If I went there at night, I had to pound on the front door of the store and hope somebody would hear me. Even worse for Betty Joyce was that she had to have dirty old Mr. Snow for a father. He took a bath about once a year, less than that when we had the drought.

Another reason we didn't see the evacuees was that while they could get passes to go into town, most of them stayed at the camp for the first months. They were as scared of us as we were of them.

But we knew the Tallgrass Camp was there. At night, the searchlights illuminated the sky like a harvest moon. Big flatbed trucks loaded with lumber and pipe and storage tanks passed our house hour after hour, sending up clouds of dirt, which settled on the leaves of the trees and on the washing Mom hung out on the line. All day long, the sounds of construction broke the peacefulness of our farm. The noise drove me stark raving crazy sometimes, and I'd climb into the hayloft with one of my Nancy Drew books to try to get away from the sound. Quiet was one of the things I'd always liked best about the farm. Before the camp went in, I could sit in the haymow, looking out the big door at the clouds, and not hear a thing except for a calf bawling or the scat sound of insects. It was as if I were the only person in the world, and I could dream about being a girl investigator with a roadster, like Nancy. Mostly, however, I built air castles, in which I was grown up. Now, the camp made more noise than a crew of beet workers, and even in the haymow, I could barely concentrate on my book.

Having the camp down the road changed me, too. I'd always felt safe on our farm, but now, I'd begun to have nightmares. When that happened, I'd get up and look out into the yard at night and see shadows that scared me. Once, sirens woke me and made me go downstairs to Mom and Dad. They'd heard the sirens, too, and said it wasn't anything, but I feared that somebody had gone under the bobwire surrounding the camp and was going to break into our house and kill us. Maybe Mom was afraid, too, because she began locking the doors at night, something nobody in Ellis ever did, even when they went away on vacation. We'd see the yellow dogs filled with new inmates on their way to the camp, and the Japanese would stare at us when they passed our farm. People in Ellis didn't gather at the depot to watch the evacuees get off the trains anymore, but many of them glared at the newcomers to show them that they weren't welcome.

Dad walked down to Tallgrass, where he got a tour of the camp, which was about a mile square filled with row after row of barracks and surrounded by barbed-wire fences. The bobwire, which was deeply resented by the Japanese, was there to mark the boundaries of the camp, not necessarily to keep the evacuees inside. Armed U.S. troops in high watchtowers set several hundred yards apart made sure the evacuees didn't leave. An armed soldier at the entrance cleared Dad to enter the camp. He returned sad and troubled. "We treat our hired man like a king compared to the way the government treats those folks. You wouldn't let your chickens live that way," he told Mom, putting his straw hat on a hook beside the door. The hat had left a line around his damp head, as if he'd been wearing a rubber band.

Entire families were crowded into twenty-foot-square rooms made of unpainted gypsum board, Dad said. They hung sheets across the room for privacy. The barracks were thrown up so quickly that dust sifted in through gaps in the siding and cracks around the windows. The women dusted, and the dirt blew right back in. "It doesn't take more than thirty minutes before there's enough dust to write your name in," Dad said. He predicted that come winter, people would get pneumonia from wind and snow blowing in on them as they slept.

The rooms were so hot and airless that the people couldn't stand to be indoors. But if they went outside, they stood in the hot wind on dirt streets, because neither grass nor trees had been planted where the sage and chamisa had been bulldozed. And the Japanese had to take showers in bathhouses down the street, with one large room for men, another for women. "They say the old women don't wash themselves until the middle of the night, when nobody's around to see. Just imagine Granny stripping buck naked in front of the choir," Dad said. I didn't like getting undressed in front of anybody, even Betty Joyce, and I'd be as dirty as Mr. Snow if I had to bathe that way.

Everybody ate in a dining hall, the kids sitting with one another instead of with their families, which was no way to raise children, Dad said, and the food was heavy and coarse. "I think the government's cornered the market on beef hearts for them," Dad told us, and I stuck out my tongue and put my finger down my throat. I'd rather have eaten alfalfa than organ meat. Many of the Japanese, he added, were used to eating fish and fresh vegetables, and they'd gotten sick from the food, as well as from the heat and the crowding. "There's not a hospital yet. They say a woman gave birth on a bare table, with no doctor to attend to her. Lord knows what will happen if there's an epidemic or a catastrophe. The fire truck is a hose wrapped up on a spindle on wheels. And they don't have a library. There's not much of a school, either. You'd think with the way we uprooted them like pigweed, we could at least offer them a little education."

"That's not asking too much," Mom agreed.

Dad studied her for a moment before he sat down at the kitchen table and poured himself a glass of iced tea from a pitcher that was damp on the outside with sweat. He sipped and frowned because he liked his tea sweetened, but we'd agreed to drink it plain to save on sugar. We raised sugar beets, but when it came to getting refined sugar, we were in the same boat as everybody else.

Dad shrugged and finished the tea, then looked at Mom slyly. "Might be you could teach," he said.

Mom, who'd been sprinkling the laundry, using a green

Coca-Cola bottle filled with water and plugged with a stopper that had holes in it, rolled up a damp shirt and put it into the basket before she wiped her hands on her apron. The apron was made from flowered feed sacks and had been washed so many times that the print was faded to almost nothing. She looked up at Dad. "I couldn't teach a bird to find a worm. Besides, the only thing I know is chickens, and you told me yourself they don't raise chickens out there."

"Come winter, when the rest of the Japanese women get here, you could teach them to quilt."

"Go on! Anybody can quilt. You've just to do it. Besides, why would they want to quilt? I didn't see any of those women climbing onto the yellow dogs with scrap bags in their hands."

Dad said the Japanese would need quilts to keep them warm in winter.

Mom sat down then and poured her own tea, thinking. "Oh, I don't know, Loyal. Where's the time to come from? Granny's getting worse every day; you know how she wanders. She's perfectly fine one minute, remembering the names of the men who worked the harvest last year, and the next, she doesn't know her own name. And with Marthalice and Buddy gone away, Rennie and I are hard put to get the work done."

Mom was right about that. I didn't have time to read much or make doll clothes now, although I'd gotten too big for dolls. Instead, I was doing more chores around the house. I guess this was what was meant by growing up, and I wasn't sure I liked that part of it. Mom was so grateful for my help, however, that I didn't resent the extra work. I wished Marthalice were around to make it more fun, however. We'd always shared the housework. She'd taught me dance steps as she vacuumed, and when we did the dishes, she'd tell me about the boys at school who draped themselves over her locker or left notes in her desk. She'd finish by saying, "Of course, you'll have twice as many boyfriends as I do." Fat chance, I'd think, but it was nice of her to say so.

Mom brushed a strand of hair out of her face with her wrist. "What would people say? That I'm aiding and abetting the enemy? I'd be an abettor, whatever that is." She gave a nervous laugh. "I'd not want to stir up trouble with the Jolly Stitchers. So many of them's against the camp."

"You wouldn't have to say you're teaching," I suggested. "You could just tell the bees you're busy with the chickens." Dad had dubbed the members of Jolly Stitchers sewing circle "the bees" and Mom "the queen bee."

Mom gave me a stern look. "That would be a lie."

I looked down at my arms folded on the oilcloth that covered the table. "Not a real lie." I raised my arms, which were sweat-glued to the oilcloth, and they made a squishing sound as they came loose. "You really are busy with the chickens." If Mom taught at Tallgrass, she'd want me to go along to help her, which meant I'd see the camp close-up and even meet some Japanese. None of the kids I knew had been inside Tallgrass.

"Rennie," Mom warned, and I looked down at the wet place where my arms had been. That wasn't even fuzzy-headed logic. It was a lie, and Mom couldn't abide a liar.

Dad got up and straightened the strap of his overalls, then took his hat from the hook and put it on. Dad's face was two-toned, the bottom half tanned, but his forehead was as white as milk from where that hat had shaded it from the sun. "There's a job of work that needs done. I got to go aid and abet the cows," he said. He told Mom to do what she wanted, and she said in that case, the teaching was out. The screen door squeaked open, then slammed shut when Dad let go of it, and I felt comforted that the door would announce anybody who tried to sneak into our house, at least anybody who came through the side door.

Mom set up the ironing board and lifted the basket of clothes she'd sprinkled onto the table. She plugged in the iron, and after a minute, she licked the tip of her finger and tested the iron's heat. I got up and poured cream into the big glass jar that served as a churn and began to turn the paddle, watching the cream thicken and turn yellow as the wooden blades went around. After a while, Mom said, "I'd be stirring up trouble just as sure as you're stirring up butter." I knew better than to bring up the subject of her teaching at the internment camp again.

IN THE SPRING OF 1942, the government had bought Tallgrass, an old ranch that had been named for a patch of tall grass that grew in the middle of our short-grass prairie. A few weeks later, hundreds of men arrived to build the internment camp, and folks in Ellis talked about the relocation of California Japanese to Colorado every bit as much as they talked about Pearl Harbor and the price of sugar beets. They didn't discuss much whether it was right or wrong to force those people, many of them born on American soil, as Dad pointed out, from their homes and into camps. If you pressed them, people said we were at war, and better be safe than sorry. Besides, white people were making sacrifices, too, they said. Our boys were losing their lives in the service of their country, and that was a lot more serious than a Japanese family giving up a farm or a fishing boat in California.

No, the talk around Ellis was about what Tallgrass would do to the community. At first, local people hadn't minded the idea of a camp going in. They'd gotten construction jobs, and skilled workers had moved into Ellis, some renting spare rooms, although most lived in tents out near the campsite. There'd never been so much money in town, even before the Depression. The drugstores stocked up on first-aid products and tobacco and men's magazines—and some said on rubbers, since a few hussies had moved into Ellis and rented the rooms above Jay Dee's Tavern. I wasn't absolutely sure what rubbers were, but I heard boys joking about them and knew better than to ask my mother. And since I shared Marthalice's letters with Mom, I knew it wasn't anything I could write about to my sister.

The cafés stayed open until 2:00 A.M. to serve supper to the evening shift from Tallgrass. The owner of the dry goods said he could have sold twice as many pairs of work pants and hard-toed shoes, but with all the factories turning out uniforms for the soldiers, he couldn't get them. The bars never closed, even on Sunday, although you had to go in through the back doors to buy a drink on the Sabbath. Prohibition had been over for a long time, but the bootleggers did a thriving business anyway, because some people preferred the stronger homemade stuff. Frank Martin doubled the price of dago red and still sold all he could produce. I found his empty jars, which boys threw out of their car windows as they drove along the Tallgrass Road, and once, I came across a jar that was full. I was tempted to taste it, but if I did, I was sure I'd die a terrible death. Or worse, one of the Jolly Stitchers might smell strong liquor on my breath, and my soul would be in danger.

By the time the Japanese arrived late in the summer of 1942, the talk in Ellis had changed. Most of the electricians and plumbers and carpenters had been drafted or had moved on to other jobs, building defense plants, and the Japanese were left to finish construction.

So the bottom dropped out of the war business in Ellis, and people turned sour. "If we had a real prison, we'd have wives and kids coming in on visiting day, staying in the tourist courts and eating at the restaurants. But who's going to come and see a Jap?" asked the man who ran Tom-Tom Motor Court, which had eight cement wigwams with poles sticking out of their tops. "There ain't nobody fool enough to come to Ellis on a vacation when we got five thousand Nips a mile away."

"What tourist ever picked Ellis for a vacation anyway?" Dad asked. He pointed out the contractors and salesmen and government officials visiting the camp were going to bring in more business than the few motorists who passed through Ellis on their way to Denver or Colorado Springs, and that the Tom-Tom ought to put up a neon sign and build half a dozen more tepees to accommodate them.

"Besides, everybody's hoarding gasoline, so there aren't any tourists," I piped up. Dad sent me a stern look that told me not to be smart. But later, he said I was right about that.

Some people turned hateful. Mr. Elliot, who ran the other drugstore, put a sign in his window with a cartoon of a Japanese man with teeth like a beaver and slanted eyes. NO JAPS SERVED was written on it. Folks came in and pointed to the sign and shook Mr. Elliot's hand.

One night, somebody broke into the Elliot Drug and stole money out of the cash register, as well as the packs of Sen-Sen and cartons of Lucky Strike. Then he tore the sign in half. Mr. Elliot claimed that proved he'd been robbed by a Japanese person who'd sneaked out of Tallgrass. Sheriff Henry Watrous said the robber might have destroyed the sign so the camp would be blamed. In fact, the sheriff went out to talk to Beaner Jack about it, but Mr. Jack said unless he'd come to arrest Beaner, Sheriff Watrous could just get off his property.

"I don't understand Beaner," Dad said when he told us the story. "Why would that boy do such a thing?"

"It's because he's a Jack, and they're meaner than red ants," I said.

Mom frowned, because she didn't like me saying unkind things about a person, even a Jack. But Dad agreed. "I reckon that's about right."

Then someone set fire to the railroad trestle about five miles from Ellis. The fire burned a long time before it was spotted, and the damage held up the trains for two days. The FBI came, looking for espionage, but the agents couldn't find any proof of that. "Just vandalism," one of them concluded. Dad said it wouldn't hurt to talk to Beaner Jack, but the agent told Dad vandalism wasn't his department. Most people thought one of the Japanese had burned the trestle, and folks in Ellis were even more resentful about the internment camp.

Then that *Denver Post* reporter who'd been at the depot the day the first Japanese arrived came back to Ellis and wrote a story about how fine life was at Tallgrass. Only half of the inmates were expected to work, he wrote, and even I figured out that didn't mean anything, because the other half were children and old folks. The Japanese had white people waiting on them in the mess hall, the article claimed, and folks in Ellis were plenty mad about the government coddling the Japanese with good food and feather beds, while their own sons ate rations in foxholes overseas. Dad had told us what the food was like, and I'd seen some of the inmates cutting prairie grass to fill their mattress ticks. The reporter hinted that the government was sending the most dangerous Japanese agents in America to Tallgrass.

"My dad says that's a fact," Betty Joyce told me when we talked about the article. I wondered how a dope like Mr. Snow knew anything, when all he did was sit behind the counter every day selling nails and screws and yelling at Betty Joyce and her mom. But I wouldn't tell my friend that. Betty Joyce had enough troubles without having to defend her father for being a knothead.

After that article was printed, the tension in Ellis got so bad that the mayor called a meeting at the school and invited the head of the camp, Mr. Halleck, to talk to us. Mom tucked Granny into bed and let Mr. Hale, the hired man, stay in the house and listen to the Philco radio, so that he could keep an eye on Granny while Mom and Dad and I went to the meeting. Just before we left, Mr. Hale took Dad aside, and the two of them had a long conversation, Dad nodding and looking serious. Then Dad said, "Good luck to you, sir," and slapped Mr. Hale on the back and shook his hand.

"What's that jawing about?" Mom asked as the three of us got into the truck.

Dad said it was too much work to hitch up the team at night, and slow going in the wagon besides. Our Nash automobile was up on blocks because Dad couldn't get parts for it. So we took the truck after dark. It was a beat-up old truck, which Dad had painted with red house paint and named "Red Boy." I loved to ride around with Dad in Red Boy. He kept a little sack of hard licorice in the glove compartment for the two of us. Once, when I was waiting for Dad outside the feed store, I ate all the licorice. Then I got out of the truck and picked up black pebbles and put them into the licorice sack. I waited for about five years for Dad to discover what I'd done. Finally, he came into the kitchen one day and said, "I just broke a tooth eating a piece of licorice." He let me squirm for a full minute before he grinned and said it was the best trick I'd ever pulled on him.

Now, as we drove into Ellis, Dad said, "He's just got his draft notice, Mother. And the two Romeros went into town this afternoon and signed up. They're all three of them going to war." The Romero brothers lived in a shack across the field and had worked our beets for the past three years. Betty Joyce said they made dago red, too, because her dad bought it from them. I asked Dad if they did, and he said, "If I knew the answer to that, I'd have to tell your mother, and she'd be likely to shoot them. Now you wouldn't want Mother to go to jail because you're nosy, would you?" That was too complicated for me to follow, but I knew if I let on to Mom about the Romeros making wine, she would spend the rest of her life in the state penitentiary in Cañon City. And I'd have to drop out of school to take care of Granny and do all the work around the house. I kept my mouth shut.

After Dad told Mom about Mr. Hale and the Romeros, the two of them were silent for a minute, and I knew they were wishing Buddy hadn't enlisted, so that he could help with the beets. I did, too. I loved our farm, and a bad year or two might make us lose the place. "Bud would have been drafted by now anyway," I said.

"We'll make do." Mom used to say that when our region was part of the dust bowl. Back then, the dirt and wind ruined our crops, and we barely held on. "With the Lord's help, we'll make do, Loyal," she'd say.

When Dad told her the Lord could do His part by bringing rain, Mom said not to blaspheme. The rain finally did come, and Dad said he supposed the Almighty was better late than never. Mom replied if he went to church once in a while, the Lord might not treat him like a stranger. It wasn't fair that the dust bowl years, when men tramped the country looking for jobs, ended just before the war. Now there was plenty of work but nobody to do it. I'd told Dad I thought God's timing wasn't too good on that score, either, and Dad had laughed and said not to let Mom hear me say that. He'd ruffled my hair with his knuckles. Now that Buddy was gone, I was Dad's pal.

Folks came from all over the county to attend the meeting, which was held in the biggest classroom in the school. Not everybody could find seats, so some of the men stood up along the wall and little kids sat on their mothers' laps or on the tops of the desks. Government officials showed up, too, trying to act like local people. But you could tell who they were because they wore suits and ties, and instead of chewing toothpicks, they smoked cigarettes in holders clinched in their teeth, like President Franklin Delano Roosevelt. If I ever smoked cigarettes, I'd use a holder, a long black Bakelite one, set with rhinestones. Yeah, I thought. I'd take it with me when I went to the White House to visit Mrs. Roosevelt. I glanced at Dad, who was lighting a roll-your-own, and tried to think of him using a cigarette holder. The idea was so funny that I had to hold back a laugh. It came out as a snort, and I sank into my seat, hoping nobody had heard me.

After the Methodist preacher gave a prayer thanking God for backing our troops in the war, we stood and recited the Pledge of Allegiance. Then Mr. Halleck, who'd been brought in by the government from Kansas City to run the camp, went to the teacher's desk, where a lectern with a seal of the U.S. government on it had been set up, and he began reading facts about Tallgrass—the number of inmates, the number of guards, the amount of money spent on construction, "which some of you folks here got the advantage of," he said. The camp was designed like an army base, with an administration area and a barracks area, he told us. "The rooms are nice, but I'm here to tell you no one's being coddled." He'd read the *Denver Post* article, too. Nobody smiled, so he cleared his throat. "We got a four-strand double barbed-wire fence all around the place for your safety." He paused to let that sink in, but instead of being reassured, people looked disgusted, because there wasn't a boy in Ellis who couldn't get under bobwire. "Sixteen-foot watchtowers, too," he added. "And guards assigned to them with rifles." A few men nodded at that, but I thought about the girl at the depot who was my age, the one in saddle shoes. I figured she must feel awful living in an encampment with guards ready to shoot her. I thought the government ought to let her go back home, along with the rest of the women and children. But maybe they wanted to be with the men. If Dad were locked up someplace, Mom and I would want to go with him.

"You got a jail there, do you?" someone called out.

"We don't need one. We think these are peaceable folks. We don't expect one bit of trouble out of them," Mr. Halleck said.

"Then why not leave them in California? How come you shipped them all to Colorado and locked them up?" asked Redhead Joe Lee. "If they're so all-fired trustworthy, why didn't you let them go about their business and save the taxpayers a lot of money?"

Dad laughed at that, but Oscar Kruger shifted in his little-kid seat and told Mr. Lee to shut up. "Ain't you never heard of Pearl Harbor?"

"I guarantee you none of those folks out at Tallgrass dropped the bombs," Mr. Lee said.

"A Jap's a Jap," Mr. Kruger told him.

"I guess that means a German's a German. Maybe we should have a camp for Germans," Mr. Lee taunted.

Dad touched Mr. Lee's arm to cool him off, but I knew he wanted to say "Good one!" I gave Mr. Lee a thumbs-up sign. He ignored it, of course. Why would he care what I thought?

I wrapped my fingers around my thumb so that if anybody had seen me make the sign, the person would think I was just messing around with my hand.

"Nobody can't say I'm not one hundred percent American," said Mr. Kruger. When he stood up, he bumped his knee against the desk and muttered something in German.

Then Mrs. Kruger said, "We don't even like sauerkraut." Everybody laughed, and she pulled her husband back down onto his chair.

"We just can't be too safe with the Japanese. We haven't found any cases of espionage yet, but some folks, including Mr. Walter Lippmann, the newspaper columnist, think that just proves how sneaky they are. Myself, like I say, I don't believe it," Mr. Halleck said. He told us that in time the camp would have a hospital so that the Japanese wouldn't have to use the facilities in Ellis, which made everybody laugh, too, because Ellis didn't have a hospital. I thought that government people weren't very smart. When I mentioned that to Dad later, he said I was pretty good at figuring things out.

"Are their kids going to school here? Where'd we put them?" someone asked.

"I don't want my kids playing with Japs," a woman called out.

Mr. Halleck explained that the government was finishing a school at Tallgrass. "It'll have a gymnasium and a science laboratory," he said.

I spotted Betty Joyce and mouthed "Wow!"

When Mr. Halleck ignored Mr. Kruger's hand waving in the air, Mr. Kruger yelled out, "How come they's to have a science laboratory when we don't have one ourself? Seems to me if the gov'ment's so anxious to spend our money on a school, they could spend it on a school for our kids. We'll just be training a fifth column." When there were murmurs of agreement, Mr. Kruger looked smug and added, "You tell that to the gov'ment." He folded his arms across his chest.

"I certainly will," Mr. Halleck said. He asked if anybody else had a question, then sighed and glanced at his watch when several people raised their hands.

"I hear the Japs got all the sugar and steak they want, while we go 'thout," Mrs. Larsoo complained. She and her husband were large people, like all the Larsoos. There was never anybody as hungry as a Larsoo. "These days, all I got to put in Olney's sandwich is a can of Spam."

"You take it out of the can first?" Dad asked real loud, and people laughed. Mom sent Dad a look that told him to be still, but she also put her hand over her mouth so no one would see that she was smiling.

I dug my elbow into Dad's rib and muttered, "Good going." Lately, I'd begun to think of Mom and Dad and me as the Three Musketeers, or maybe the Two-and-a-Half Musketeers. So I felt I could let Dad know when he said something funny. He grinned at me.

A man standing in the aisle on one foot, the other braced against the wall, asked what would happen if one of the Japanese committed a crime in Ellis. "Same's as if you did," Mr. Halleck replied. Others worried that the water wells at the camp would cause our own wells to go dry. They complained about the searchlights and the traffic. They asked whether the government would compensate them if their property values went down. Mr. Halleck said he didn't expect they'd go down, but I wasn't so sure about that. Our beet workers were leaving, and if we couldn't harvest the beets and Dad had to sell out, who would buy a farm that was less than a mile from the camp?

I got fidgety and glanced around until I saw Susan Reddick, who lived down the road from me. She'd had polio and now had trouble walking. When she caught me looking at her, she rolled her eyes and put the top of her crutch over her head and yanked her neck to show she wished somebody would come and yank Mr. Halleck out of the room. I turned back and saw Danny Spano staring at me, and I looked away quickly, embarrassed. Although I thought a lot about boys at school, I felt strange around Danny and his crowd. I didn't know how to act with them. I'd ask Marthalice the next time I wrote to her, because she used to joke around with Danny.

The talk droned on and on, and people began shuffling their feet and moving around in the seats, which were too small for the men and most of the women. Kids escaped from their parents and wandered up and down the aisles. A baby cried. As far as I could tell, the only reason for holding the meeting was to give people a chance to gripe, because Mr. Halleck didn't answer many questions. Mostly, he just said that the government was taking care of things and that he'd pass along our concerns. For all the good it did us, we could have stayed home and called him up on the party line.

Then Dad stood up. "I'd like to know if I can get some of those Japanese fellows to help harvest my sugar beets. My hired man just got drafted, and my beet workers joined up." Mom stared straight ahead, and I wondered if Dad had talked this over with her. He usually got her advice before he made a big decision, but he hadn't said anything on the drive into town. If Dad had asked me about hiring them, I'd have said no go. It was bad enough having the Japanese in a camp just down the road, but I didn't want them in our fields, swinging those long, ugly beet knives. Dad didn't usually ask for my advice about farming, however.

The room grew still. "Why don't you hire a white man, Stroud?" someone asked.

"What white man's that?"

"It's un-American to hire Japs," someone else called.

"Seems to me it's un-American to leave the beets in the field to rot. Last I heard, our boys in the army like a little something sweet to eat. This harvest's for my son, by Dan." His hands clenched, Dad looked around the room as if challenging anyone to disagree with him.

Danny smirked at me. Although I didn't want Japanese workers in our fields, I mouthed "Yeah!" at Danny to show him I backed up my dad. And maybe I did at that. There'd been a depression on most of my life, and I knew you could lose a farm after only one or two bad harvests. I'd rather the Japanese harvested our beets than nobody at all, I thought.

Mom pulled at Dad's pant leg to tell him to simmer down, but he ignored her.

A woman in front of us turned around and told Mom, "Your husband's a troublemaker, Mary, if you ask me."

Mom sat up straight and adjusted her hat and said, "Did anybody ask you?" When Mom saw people staring at her, she flushed and began picking at her fingers. But I glared at the woman, my tongue poking through my lips just a little.

She sniffed at me and muttered, "Mind your manners, little girl."

Then Mr. Gardner, who grew sugar beets, too, said, "I believe Mr. Stroud's asked a good question. I haven't heard the answer."

Mr. Halleck stretched his neck. "It's our intention to have those Japanese boys help the farmers. That's what the government wants. Many of our inmates come from the agricultural fields in California. But we haven't worked out the details yet."

"I reckon you better look into it pretty quick, because the beets'll freeze in the ground. Mine are about ready to be dug now," Dad said.

"We need a straight answer and none of your government flimflam, either," Mr. Gardner added.

Mr. Halleck nodded at a man in the first row, who clamped his teeth around his cigarette holder and took a pad of paper out of his pocket and wrote something on it. "Name's Gardner, young man," Mr. Gardner called to him.

"Now, if there are no more questions—"

"I got one." Mr. Spano interrupted, and Mom and Dad exchanged glances.

Several people had gathered up their coats and hats to leave, but when they heard Mr. Spano, they stayed put, because whatever he said, it was liable to cause a stir. Mr. Spano got to his feet and slowly turned to glance down the row on either side of him to make sure people were paying attention. He was an oddly proportioned man, his arms reaching barely below his waist and his head too small for his big body. Dad had said about him once, "Little head, little wit." Mrs. Spano was crudely made, too, so folks wondered where Danny got his looks. He got his wits from his father.

"Who's going to protect the womenfolk if you let them Japs out of the camp to work Stroud's place?" Mr. Spano asked.

Mr. Halleck's eyes bugged out and he leaned forward over the lectern. "Sir? I don't believe I understood you."

"I believe you did," Mr. Spano said. He stood up and put his thumbs inside the straps of his overalls and worked a quid around in his mouth. "But I'll say again: Who's to look after my wife and daughters if you loose them yellow devils on this community? You can't tell me Tojo ain't told them to go after a white woman if they got the chance." A few of the women gasped, but Mom kept on looking straight ahead. I wondered if she was afraid. I was, although Mr. Spano'd probably made that up. Old Tojo wouldn't have called up Mr. Spano on the long-distance telephone and shared his plans with him.

The government man in the front row craned his neck to see Mr. Spano, then glanced at another government man, who gave a slow nod like some kind of a signal before he took out a cigarette and fitted it into a holder.

"I say keep the Japs locked up and let them as doesn't have hired men do their own harvest," Mr. Spano said, and a few men muttered agreement.

"Not everybody's got a son at home to help," Dad said, and some of the men grunted to back *him* up. Besides Danny, Mr. Spano had three other boys at home, two in school and Cleatus, who was so feebleminded that the draft board didn't want him. Only Audie, Danny's oldest brother, was in the service. The Spanos kept two blue stars in their window, although Danny had been mustered out after the accident at Camp Carson. "If you let me hire a few of those Japanese boys, I'll be responsible for them," Dad said.

"Maybe you don't care about what one of 'em does to your wife and girl, Stroud," Mr. Spano said slowly, then spit onto the classroom floor. Danny Spano looked at his hands then, but Beaner Jack, who was sitting next to Danny, gave a sharp laugh. If Danny hadn't been such a jerk, I might have felt sorry for him. But Danny'd always been a jerk. It was an awful thing to be born a Spano.

Mom grabbed Dad's hand then and dug her nails into it. She didn't like it when Dad spoke out, and I was hoping he would sit down, because I was afraid Danny and Beaner would give me a hard time later on. But Dad didn't pay Mom any mind. "If

I thought my womenfolk were in danger, I wouldn't let a Japanese man or any other man on my place," he said. "Right now, I'm worried about harvesting my beets, so I can keep a roof over my family's head."

"Well, I wouldn't let no Japs within a mile of my wife and daughters," Mr. Spano said. I had to swallow a laugh at that, because Mrs. Spano could play catch with a bail of hay and the Spano girls didn't live in Ellis anymore. They'd married and moved away before they finished high school. "Maybe you don't care about your women, Stroud."

Dad clenched his jaw, and his hands balled up into fists. I prayed he wouldn't start something, because I knew I'd be mortified. And Mom wouldn't be able to face the Jolly Stitchers then, either. Before Dad could reply, however, Mr. Lee jumped in front of him, blocking his view of Mr. Spano, "Mr. Halleck, we sure do want to thank you for coming out this evening."

Mr. Halleck looked up, surprised but glad that Mr. Lee had given him a chance to end the meeting. He said quickly, "Glad to do it. I'll just stay here a little longer in case any of you folks have more questions. I know it's past bedtime, and most of you have to get up with the chickens. I'm a farm boy, too." He laughed, but nobody else did, because we weren't so dumb that we didn't know when somebody was talking down to us.

Mom stood up and shooed Dad and me in front of her. "Only a fool fights a fool," she said, just loudly enough for the three of us to hear.

"I'm not a fool," Dad told her. He was stubborn and not nearly as anxious to leave as Mom.

"I didn't say you were, Loyal. But you would be if you mixed it up with John Spano."

"Come on, Dad," I said, grabbing at his hand, which had about as much effect as talking to a chicken.

A few men came up and spoke to Dad, but more gathered around Mr. Spano to shake his hand and clap him on the back. The room seemed hostile then, and I didn't know how people who had been our friends all of our lives could suddenly be against us, glaring at Dad—and at Mom, too, although she hadn't said anything. I hadn't, either, but people still looked me up and down, which made me think again about the Japanese girl at the depot and how she must have felt with people staring at her.

"Glad you spoke up, Loyal," Mr. Gardner said. "I couldn't hire hands if I paid them ten dollars a day—even if I could afford ten dollars a day."

"That's the truth," Dad said. He and Mr. Gardner talked for a few minutes. Then Mr. Lee told Dad to come around to the drugstore on Sunday while Granny, Mom, and I were at church, and that he'd treat him to a chocolate soda. The others who'd spoken to Dad left, along with one or two of the government men, and I got nervous when I looked across the room at the people still standing around Mr. Spano. Susan Reddick's father was among them, but Susan and her mother were still seated, both of them staring at the floor.

Every now and then, one of the men with Mr. Spano turned to stare at us with narrowed eyes, as if they were talking about us. Some dope had drawn a cartoon in chalk on the blackboard of a Japanese man and underneath it was a misspelled caption: "Your a sap Mr. Jap." One of the government men took a swipe at the picture with an eraser, leaving a swath through the face like a black-and-white rainbow.

Dad and Mom and I went outside into a night that had turned cold, and Mom buttoned up her coat around her neck. "I sure could use that Persian lamb jacket you were going to buy me," she said, trying to get Dad's mind off the meeting. The two of them had joked as long as I could remember about Dad buying her a fur coat, but so far she'd never even had a fox-fur scarf.

"I'm working on it," Dad said, squeezing her hand, and I thought how nice it was that Mom and Dad liked each other.

We got into Red Boy and Dad turned on the motor, and we started down the Tallgrass Road. Although it was dark, the sky was bright from the spotlights at the camp. I wondered what it would be like to be a Spano, which made me shiver. Being a Spano meant sharing a house with rats, sleeping in a bed without sheets, and eating antelope. The only thing worse was being a Jack. Either possibility was too horrible to contemplate.

Mom had been thinking about the Spanos, too, because she said, "That Mr. Spano is mean enough to step on baby chicks." That was the worst thing Mom could say about a person, since baby chicks were helpless, and Mom loved them almost as much as she loved Buddy, Marthalice, and me. If the weather was cold, she'd take the chicks inside, two dozen or more little balls of yellow fluff, and put them into a box next to the oil stove.

"Oh, don't worry about John Spano and them. They perform like a circus; they're all show," Dad said, patting Mom's knee. He was silent until after we reached the turn into our farm. He slowed the truck, downshifted, and straddled a hole before coming to a stop. I got out and opened the gate; then Dad drove through and waited for me to latch the gate. Instead of getting back into the truck, I stood on the running board and put my hand through the window to hold on to the backseat, because I'd have to open the barn door. Our dogs, Snow White, the collie, and Sabra, the mutt, came out and barked, then ran along beside us. We heard a clucking from the henhouse, and Mom said she thought there might be a coyote somewhere about and that she ought to take down her shotgun. Mom loved most living things, but she hated a predator, and she'd kill one if she had to. She was a good shot, too. Dad kept a picture on the dresser of Mom that had been taken when she was a little girl. She was sitting on a chair in front of a quilt, with her dog and her gun. Dad said that pretty well summed up Mom.

I leaned my head against the roof of the truck and heard Dad say, "It may not be a Spano, but I'm afraid somebody's going to make trouble over this camp, Mother."

"You stay out of it, Loyal, and don't embarrass me in front of my friends."

"What about you, Mary? You feel the same way I do about the Japanese."

Mom laughed. "But I'm not the one who goes looking for trouble."

"You, Squirt? How do you feel about tonight?"

Dad stopped the truck, and I jumped down to open the barn door and didn't answer, because I couldn't make up my mind about the Japanese. I agreed with Mom and Dad that they'd gotten a rotten deal by being sent halfway across the country to live in a camp. But still, I wished they'd been sent someplace else.

THE NEXT WEEK, DAD and Mr. Gardner went to Tallgrass to talk to Mr. Halleck about hiring Japanese boys for the harvest, but Mr. Halleck hadn't worked out the system yet.

"It's a durn shame. Those young men want to work, but the government has them sitting there playing cards," Mr. Gardner said. "I believe cards do more to weaken the mind of a boy than an honest day's work."

"I have to agree with you on that," Dad said. After Mr. Gardner left, Dad teased Mom. "You hear what he said about cards, Mother?"

Mom, who loved to play pinochle, sniffed. "He said boys, not women. And don't tell me you don't play poker on Sunday mornings down at Red Lee's place."

Dad laughed and slapped her on the bottom as he went out.

"Behave," Mom told him, but she smiled, and I pretended I hadn't seen them. Sometimes my folks embarrassed me.

SO THE JAPANESE DIDN'T help with our 1942 sugar beet harvest, but Dad and Mr. Gardner found some Mexicans, young boys and old men, who worked the beets for us. "They aren't very fast, but they make up for it by charging more," Dad complained. Still, he didn't have much choice, so he hired the fellows, and we got our beets in.

I stayed out of school to help Mom with meals for the crew. Despite the hot, hard work, harvest was one of my favorite times. The kitchen smelled of homemade bread and pies. The table was stacked with plates and platters, silverware, dishes of butter, salt and pepper shakers, pitchers of iced tea. Mom treated me just like one of the women she'd hired in years past, assigning me chores and nodding her approval when I did them right. There weren't any women to hire that year, what with so many of them working the fields in the place of sons and husbands who'd gone off to war. So we had to make do with family. Granny still pitched in. Her mind always worked fine when it came to farm work. She'd fixed meals for harvest crews from the time she and

Gramp started farming in Ellis fifty years earlier, and even before that, as a girl in Fort Madison, Iowa.

"You got to figure a pie feeds four men, five if you have to, although a man might think you're trying to skimp him," she told me as she took four pies out of the oven and set them on the Hoosier cabinet. "I've found they like apple above all others, but you better not give a man a dried-apple pie. Mattie used to tell me, 'I loathe, abhor, detest, and despise dried-apple pies. Give me pneumonia or poke out my eyes, but never give me dried-apple pies.'"

"Betty Crocker has a recipe for pumpkin pie that looks real good," I told her.

"Betty Crocker." Granny thought a minute. "There was a Sam Homer Crocker up north of here. I don't recollect his wife's name. Mattie will know."

"Who's Mattie?" asked Betty Joyce. Because it was Saturday, she had come over to help, and she was carrying tin cups and plates and utensils out to the tables, which were planks of wood laid across sawhorses.

"Mattie's my sister. She lives up to Mingo," Granny said.

I didn't tell Granny that her sister had died a long time ago; I just looked at her and worried that I'd be like her one day. She deserved better. It wasn't fair that God had let her mind wear out before her body. I figured maybe she'd get worse and I'd have to take care of her all the time. As much as I loved Granny, I didn't want to be her nurse. For a minute, I felt sorrier for myself than I did for her. Since Buddy was in the army and Marthalice lived in Denver and had a job, I did their chores and took care of our grandmother. Sometimes Granny's mind was as clear as the Methodist bell, but most of the time, she couldn't remember anything that had happened since the *Titanic* sank to the bottom of the ocean. I was worried that maybe I'd have to leave school one day and look after her full-time. Girls did that. Dropping out of school was the worst thing I could imagine. But I knew Mom would never allow that. She and Dad expected me to go to college, although they hadn't insisted on that for Marthalice. I didn't understand why they treated us differently.

Mom came in then. She wore slacks instead of a housedress, and her hair was tied up in a bandanna because she'd been hauling water to the workers. She wiped her face on a dish towel and took over at the stove, where I was frying pork chops and potatoes. "I don't know which of us has got the worst of it, Granny, me with the bucket and dipper under that sun, or you in here over a hot stove."

Granny smiled at her and said, "You rest, Mattie. I'll fix the rest of the dinner."

"I thought your Mom's name was Mary," Betty Joyce whispered.

With my finger, I made a circling motion near my head to show that Granny was a little nuts, which made Betty Joyce snicker, but Mom frowned and shook her head. I knew better than to make a joke at Granny's expense. I glanced at Betty Joyce out of the corner of my eye, but she was so used to being yelled at that she didn't pay attention to Mom's reproof.

Mom cut into a chop to see if it was done, then began piling the meat onto a platter, the potatoes into dishes. Betty Joyce drained green beans and put them into dishes, too. Then we all carried out the platters and bowls of food, the pies, and a dishpan full of sliced bread.

Mom rang the dinner bell, and in a few minutes, the Mexicans came in from the fields and sat down. They crossed themselves before they piled food onto their plates, and in a few minutes, they had eaten everything, including the pie. Some of them sat at the tables then, drinking iced tea or coffee that we poured from a gallon pot. A few said, *"Gracias,"* but most of them didn't look at us. Some of the men sprawled on the grass under the trees, smoking or resting with their hats pulled over their faces, their long, narrow beet knives by their sides. Half an hour after the Mexicans sat down, the crew boss stood up, and the others followed him back to the field.

Dad, who'd come in after the men, went into the kitchen and turned on the tap in the sink, putting his head under the water faucet, then shaking it just like our collie, Snow White, did. "Those jaspers aren't so bad after all. Sure beats me how they can work like that in the hot sun," he told us. "Squirt, your mom's peaked. You let her stay in here where it's cool. Then after you girls help Granny with the dishes, you can carry the water bucket." Mom started to protest, but Dad was firm. He'd never told her to stop work before, and I wondered if she was feeling poorly. Dad reached into his pocket and said, "Here's you a little something to buy stamps for your war-bond books." He handed both Betty Joyce and me a silver dollar.

"Gee, thanks, Mr. Stroud," Betty Joyce said. "Do we have to buy stamps?"

Dad grinned. "It's your money. You can buy anything you want."

Betty Joyce looked relieved. If her dad found out she had savings stamps, he'd cash them in and keep the money, even if it was only a dollar. Betty Joyce wouldn't have told me that about her father, but she didn't have to. Some things I figured out on my own.

"It's okay. You don't have to pay me," I told Dad when he handed me the dollar. Even with the Depression over, money was tight. He didn't pay Mom and Granny, so I didn't expect money from him.

"You do your part, Squirt. I don't know what we'd do without you." That made me feel good, because Dad didn't hand out many compliments, and this one was better than the silver dollar. I decided to spend the money on war-bond stamps. Then Dad added, "Don't know what to do *with* you, either."

Betty Joyce and I filled the bucket and carried it to the field, setting it down at the end of a row. Then we stood in the shade of a tree, watching the Mexicans. One man drove a two-wheeled horse-drawn lifter down the rows, loosening the beets. The workers followed, yanking the beets out of the earth and knocking them together to remove as much dirt as they could. With their long knives, they topped the beets. Then they sliced off the roots, some of them seven feet long, and threw the beets into piles. Finally, using seven-tined forks, the men pitched the white beets into a wagon that Dad pulled with a tractor. When the wagon was full, Dad drove it to the receiving station in Ellis, where the beets were dumped and weighed and the sugar content of each load was calculated.

"I wouldn't want to be a beet worker," Betty Joyce said.

I shuddered at the idea. "It's the hardest work there is."

"Too hard for Beaner Jack," Betty Joyce said, nodding toward the fence that separated our farm from the Tallgrass Road. Beaner was leaning against the fence, joking around with Danny Spano and Pete Elliot. While Danny was tall and handsome and Beaner was squat, Pete was sort of in between, neither short nor tall, average in every way except that he had a scar from the edge of his mouth to his cheek, which made his mouth look twisted up on one side. He was a dope, too.

"Hey, wetbacks," Beaner called to the men in the field.

The workers ignored him, all but one Mexican, who glanced up, then quickly looked at a sugar beet and whacked off its top.

"Yeah you, greaser," Danny called, and the boys with him laughed. When the Mexican didn't pay any attention to him, Danny yelled, "You got a seester?" Beaner cracked up at that and pounded his fist on the fence post. The boys were laughing so hard that they didn't see Dad move along the fence until he was only a few yards away from them.

"You fellows have business here, do you?" Dad called. Beaner had come looking for a job just before harvest started, but Dad turned him down. Beaner wasn't known as much of a worker, and Dad was afraid he'd start fights with the Mexicans. "I wouldn't hire Howard Jack's son if he worked for free," he'd told Mother.

"Now don't be visiting the sins of the father on the son," Mom'd said.

"I expect that boy has a sin or two of his own."

Now Dad continued along the fence toward the three boys and repeated, "You have a reason to be here, do you?"

Pete glanced off down the fence past Dad, while Danny kicked at a clod of dirt with his boot. But Beaner gave Dad a surly look. "Seems like all you hire are damn foreigners. Somebody's got to keep an eye on them."

"Last I heard, we weren't at war with Mexico," Dad told him.

Danny looked up and laughed, then said, "Good one," and for a moment I thought Dad might smile, but he didn't. Beaner frowned at Danny, who turned his back to the fence.

"Now you boys just go about your business. You hear me?" Dad said.

"Yes, sir," Danny replied, and Pete mumbled something. But Beaner was defiant. "I guess we're not breaking any law."

"You're standing on my property."

"Yeah?" Beaner raised his fists.

They hadn't seen the beet knife Dad carried beside his pant leg. He lifted it, resting it on the top rail of the fence. It was for show. In a million years, Dad wouldn't have attacked a man with a beet knife, but he wouldn't have hesitated to use his fists if he had to.

"Come on, Beaner. Let's us go get us a beer," Danny said.

Pete gave Dad that weird scar-face smile and started off. Danny followed him. But Beaner took his time. He slapped the fence rail with his fists, then spit into the dirt at Dad's foot. "Yeah, maybe we'll go into town and find us some one hundred percent Americans."

3

BY THE TIME THE beet harvest was over in the fall of 1942, we knew the war was going poorly and would last a long time. Every night after supper, we listened to the war reports on the Philco, to accounts of the Germans invading Russia and our soldiers fighting at Guadalcanal in the Solomon Islands. Whenever Dad went into town, he brought back news of Ellis boys who'd been called up or had enlisted before they could be drafted. Several joined right after the harvest, saying that fighting Germans or Japanese couldn't be any worse than spring hoeing.

"That's a fact," Mom told Dad.

"I hope you're right," he replied.

At school, we had air-raid drills and newspaper and scrap-metal drives. I saved every piece of paper that came into our house and scoured the farm for useless iron tools and broken machinery, trying to do my part. I even helped Betty Joyce swipe rusted iron pieces that her dad stored outside the hardware, so

that our class could win first place in the drive. All that made me
feel as if I were helping Buddy. People invested their beet money
in war bonds, just as I had when Dad gave me the silver dollar. I
wanted the war to be over so that Buddy could come home—
and so that the government could close down Tallgrass. I wanted
the searchlights turned off and the yellow dogs to stop going up
and down the road, and mostly, I wanted the Japanese to move
back to California, so that we could return to normal.

Reminders of the war were everywhere. We faced shortages—
of gasoline, farm equipment, shoes, clothes. There were fewer
fabrics for Mom and Granny to choose from for their quilts, and
food staples disappeared from the grocery store shelves. When it
came to food, we were luckier than city folks, however, because we
grew much of what we ate. Dad slaughtered pigs and butchered
steers, and we produced more butter and cream and eggs than we
needed. In the summer, I'd helped Mom can quarts of tomatoes
and green beans and peaches, and we made pickles and sauerkraut. Still, Granny cooked her jams with honey and apple juice
for sweetener, I no longer made sugar and butter sandwiches, and
Mom stopped preparing desserts such as chess pie, which were
mostly sugar. We tried vinegar cake and syrup loaf but decided to
do without. That was a sacrifice I didn't mind making.

What brought the war home to me most, besides the camp,
was that Buddy and Marthalice were gone. When I complained
to Dad that the war had taken away my brother and sister, he
said, "Why, Squirt, you know Strouds are free as birds. Those
two wouldn't be here anyway. It doesn't matter where they are."

But it mattered to me. Buddy had been attending Colorado
A&M in Fort Collins when he joined the army, and Marthalice,
who'd turned eighteen in June, would have gone to beauty
school or even college if she hadn't moved to Denver to live with

Cousin Hazel, who was the granddaughter of Granny's sister Mattie. But if they'd been in school, my brother and sister would have come home for the summer and taken time off to help with the harvest and visited us during vacations. I hadn't seen either one of them since they went away, and I'd been lonely, especially for Marthalice.

She wasn't around to talk to about little things like whether I should cut my hair in bangs or if I looked better in red than in blue. For as long as I could remember, Marthalice had done nice things for me. When I started first grade, she stitched a crayon case out of a remnant of material. It had a pocket for each crayon, and you rolled it up and tied it with a piece of ribbon. For Christmas one year, she lined a cheese box with fabric to make a jewelry box for me. She sewed rickrack on my skirts and taught me how to use bias seam binding. When I turned twelve, the year before she left, Marthalice washed my hair every week and set it in pin curls, then brushed it out.

If she'd been at home, Marthalice would have told me how to deal with the arithmetic teacher, who wouldn't call on me because he said it was a waste of time to teach math to girls. I wrote to Marthalice about that, but she forgot to answer. Her letters told of the movies she'd seen or the drugstore soda fountains where she ate. Sometimes she sounded like an adult instead of my sister, telling me to help Mom all I could and how lucky I was to have Mom and Dad for parents. Well, I knew that. Marthalice's letters were short and a little vague, but still I read them over and over again, sharing them with Mom and Dad, and with Betty Joyce. I kept them in a cigar box that Mr. Lee had given me, and sometimes I took them to school in my notebook. Not many girls received letters from anybody besides their grandmothers.

Mom took the train to Denver just before we finished up the beet harvest, because Marthalice had gotten sick. I wanted to go along, but Mom said I'd already missed too much school due to harvest. That wasn't fair, because so many kids took off for harvest that school all but shut down. Mom said someone had to help Dad keep an eye on Granny, who wandered around the house at night and sometimes unlocked the door and slipped into the yard. If anybody from the camp had wanted to get into our house, all he'd have had to do was look for Granny outside in her nightgown.

Mom spent two weeks in Denver, and when Marthalice was better, Mom helped her move out of Cousin Hazel's house into a sweet little room in an old mansion not far from downtown, which they were lucky to find, because apartments in Denver were as scarce as hen's teeth. Mom said that maybe after Dad signed the beet contract with the sugar company in the spring, I could visit my sister. If the war didn't end before then—and we all knew it wouldn't—beet prices would be sky-high. I was excited about seeing Marthalice, who was as pretty as the pictures of Snow White, tiny, with black hair and white skin, while I looked like Dopey the dwarf, only taller. At thirteen, I was five four, with brown hair that was neither straight nor curly and brown eyes. I figured if I ever did become a movie star, as Marthalice predicted once, saying she had this feeling about me, I'd be Mickey Rooney.

Buddy had been good to me, too. He teased me and told me I was a nuisance and shouldn't follow him about the farm when he did his chores, but he didn't really mean it. When I stepped on one of Mom's chicks and cried because that meant I was mean, Buddy told me, "It only counts if you do it on purpose, you knucklehead." Then he held the chick in the cup of his hands while I pumped water on her, and after a while, the chick came around. Buddy named her Hopalong because her foot was crushed. He and I kept that chicken in a box by the stove for a week before we turned her loose, and when the chick turned into a chicken, I wouldn't let Mom slaughter it. Hopalong died of old age. When he went off to war, Buddy told me I was responsible for looking after Sabra, the dog he'd found by the road as a pup and raised. Every Sunday, I cut out "Terry and the Pirates" from the funny papers and sent the comic strip to him.

I saved Buddy's letters in the cigar box, too, and I wrote to him. I told him who had joined up or been drafted and who was trying to get out of serving his country. I wrote to him about going with some of the Jolly Stitchers to take a Christmas basket to Helen Archuleta, Susan Reddick's sister. Helen's parents had turned her out after she quit high school and got married. Mr. Reddick said she'd shamed the family by marrying a beet worker—and a Mexican one at that. Bobby Archuleta had been drafted right afterward, and Helen lived in town with a widow who was on a pension, doing housework in exchange for room and board. She was pregnant now, and although she worked for Mr. Lee at the drugstore, she didn't have much money for the baby. So the Jolly Stitchers got together baby clothes and blankets and arranged them in a pretty basket tied with a red ribbon. They put other things into the basket—diapers, a box of chocolates for Helen, two dollars. The women didn't talk about the basket at the Jolly Stitchers' meeting because Mrs. Reddick was a member. Mom said she was sure Helen's mother knew what was going on but that she could ignore the basket if nobody mentioned it.

A few days before Christmas, Mom took me and two of the nicest Stitchers to call on Helen. "We hoped you could use these things," Mom told Helen.

Helen didn't invite us in, just stood in the doorway, proud, her arms folded, her eyes darting from one woman to another. I leaned against the edge of the porch, kicking at the snow and wishing I weren't there. We'd embarrassed Helen, maybe even shamed her. She had so little.

The women didn't seem to feel that way. "It would give us such pleasure to see a little baby have them," Mrs. Gardner told her. She was a jolly lady, with hair so blond that it was almost white and blue eyes like the sky on a sunny day.

"You will let us come and hold the baby once in a while, won't you? My fingers itch to hold a little baby," said Mrs. Rubey. Her only girl had died of scarlet fever ten years before. "I hope you have a girl."

"Well, I don't know," Helen said. "I've already got so much." If I'd been Helen, I wouldn't have wanted people to know I took charity. It would be an awful thing if folks knew you accepted other people's leavings, that you were one of those women they dubbed "less fortunate."

Mom knew that, and she wanted Helen to understand that the things in the basket were presents, not just hand-me-downs. "Afton Gardner made a layette with Scottie dogs on it," Mom said, "and there's a cunning little quilt we pieced."

Helen bit her lip. One tooth was crossed a little over the other.

We all stood there, none of the ladies knowing what to say, Helen looking off into the distance. I'd been feeling lonely with Marthalice gone, but I had Mom and Dad. Helen had nobody. Her folks had kicked her out, her husband was gone, and Susan was crippled from polio and couldn't walk into town to see her. "Susan worked on one of those quilt squares," I said suddenly. "Mom let me make one, and I told Susan, and she said she wanted to stitch on it. I thought you'd want to know." My face felt warm, and I looked down at the porch floor and the Stitchers' feet. The women had worn their good boots, not old galoshes. They wanted Helen to believe they were there on a social call, not there to hand out a charity basket.

"Susan?" Helen asked.

"I know I wasn't supposed to tell her, but she was so excited you were going to have a baby." I looked at Mom then, wondering if I'd said the wrong thing. I squirmed, hoping she wouldn't scold because I'd let Susan know about the quilt.

But Mom was smiling at Helen. "We all are. Nobody's had a baby in a long time."

After a pause, Helen asked, "Which square?"

"The worst one. I'm not very good."

"I'll look for knots. Susan's the worst there is for getting her thread tangled up. I'm always having to straighten it for her. I mean I *was*." She paused. "I guess it wouldn't be nice if I turned down a quilt Susan helped make. I wouldn't want to hurt her feelings." The women smiled at Helen, who added shyly, "I think I have some tea bags."

"We wouldn't want to rob you," Mrs. Gardner said.

"It's no trouble."

Helen stood aside, and the ladies walked in, Mrs. Rubey exclaiming, "Why, isn't this the dearest place," although the room was plain, with so few chairs that I'd have to sit on the floor. Mom patted my shoulder as she passed me and gave me a look that said she was glad I'd come. I was, too. I didn't always say the right thing, but that day I guess I did. And I'd learned from the Stitchers that there was a nice way to give a present, especially when somebody needed it.

———

JUST BEFORE NEW YEAR'S, Buddy came home. We hadn't
expected him, and I was the first to see him, because I was outside sweeping snow off the side porch. Our house was two stories, with a parlor and bedroom on the first floor, three bedrooms
upstairs, and a one-story ell in the back of the house for the
kitchen and a dining room big enough for a round oak table
plus a sofa and rocking chairs. Nobody used the parlor door in
the front of the house—or the parlor, either. People always came
around to the side, where wide steps led up to a porch. Unless
the preacher called or the Jolly Stitchers met to quilt, visitors sat
in the dining room.

As I pushed the snow through the spindles at the edge of the
porch, using a broom instead of a shovel, because the snow was
dry and as powdery as baking soda, I saw an old Plymouth stop
and a soldier get out on the passenger side. I started down the
steps, thinking he wanted directions. But the soldier headed for
the side porch, and then Sabra went tearing past me, barking
and hopping up into the air, wild with joy, and I knew the soldier was Buddy. He came up onto the porch and hugged me,
which wasn't something we did in our family. But he was that
glad to be home. And I was that glad to see him. I hugged him
back, holding my face against the rough wool of his coat and
smelling the cigarettes and hair oil. I could have held on forever,
but Bud said, "There now." I let go, and he looked me over. "You
grew up while I was gone."

"You did, too," I told him, and it was true. Buddy was taller
and bigger, and in his uniform with the heavy coat and smart hat,
he looked like a man. I grabbed his hand and pulled him through

the door, yelling, "Everybody come a-runnin'! I've got a surprise for you!" I felt important that I'd been the first to see Buddy.

Mom emerged from the kitchen, her hands wrapped in her apron, and said, "Oh my stars." She put her hand over her heart and slid into a rocking chair.

Granny was right behind her, and she rushed past Mom and grabbed Buddy and said, "Our soldier boy is home." Buddy looked at me as if to ask if she knew which soldier boy he was and from which war, but I couldn't tell, so I just shrugged.

Buddy knelt beside Mom and took her hands, and gazing at Buddy, she said, "Rennie, you better go get your father."

I went out to the barn, where Dad was milking Lottie, and for a few seconds I watched the rhythmic pull as the milk squirted into the bucket. Dad's hands were like weather-hardened leather. I hopped from one foot to the other, waiting for him to look up.

He didn't, but finally he asked, "Was that a car I heard?"

"Yes, sir. There's a man inside to see you."

"Who?"

"Some soldier."

Dad looked up quickly then and searched my face, and I realized he was afraid that the soldier might be someone with bad news about Buddy. "He hitched a ride from the depot," I said quickly, and grinned.

When Dad saw the grin, he asked, "Is he a young soldier, as handsome as me?"

"Nobody's that good-looking."

"By Dan, you're right about that."

"He's smarter than you are, though."

Without breaking his rhythm, Dad squirted milk at me. "I reckon it's not your brother, then."

"You won't know unless you go in there." I slid onto the edge of the milking stool, pushed him aside, and took over without so much as missing a beat. Dad had taught me how to milk after Buddy went to college, and he told me I was pretty good at it, but I figured he'd said that because he wanted me take over the milking for him. Still, I *was* pretty good.

Dad got up slowly, squeezed my shoulder, and said, "You're not worth much, Squirt, but I sure am glad we've got you at home yet. I guess we'll keep you awhile longer."

It might have been the nicest thing he'd ever said to me, and it told me that although Bud had come home, Dad and I still were best pals. I swallowed and waited a long time, so that my voice didn't crack, before I asked, "You milked June yet?"

"All done."

The back door slammed then, and Dad glanced up with a dopey look on his face and said, "Well, I'll be. He's not so bad-looking at that."

Dad stood by Lottie's stall, letting Buddy come to him, and they shook hands, and for a minute Dad didn't speak. Then he put his arm abound Buddy and said, "Son." That was all. The two of them went inside, and although the barn was so cold that I kept on my mittens while I finished the milking, I felt as warm as Christmas morning. My family wasn't much for hugging and kissing and paying compliments, unless they were backhanded ones, but we all knew we loved one another fiercely. I wished I could bring Marthalice home and keep us all together, safe until the war was over. I knew we couldn't go back to what we'd been before the war, with Buddy and Marthalice in high school and me a little kid building a fort out of tables with quilts over them. But still, I wanted us to be together again. I wished that every day until the war ended.

THE NEXT DAY, BECAUSE it was school vacation, Buddy asked me to ride into Ellis with him while he picked up a carton of cigarettes at the drugstore. Dad had told him to take Red Boy, and I climbed in beside Buddy, shivering in the icy cold, my hands underneath my thighs to keep them warm, since the truck had no heater. The wind battered us as we drove over the frozen dirt ruts of the road, past fields covered with snow. But as we reached town, I rolled down the window so that I could wave and yell "Buddy's home." I wanted the whole town to hear.

"I'm not the first soldier to come back to Ellis on leave, you know," Buddy said the third or fourth time I called to someone.

"Yeah, but you're the best one."

"I guess that's about right," Buddy agreed, sounding just like Dad. In fact, he was a lot like Dad, the same size, the same thick hair. Both squinted when they smiled, and Buddy had Dad's ears, which stuck out a little too much. I didn't have their hair, but at least I didn't have the ears, either.

Buddy parked Red Boy at an angle in front of the Elliot Drugstore, but I told him that Mom and Dad didn't trade there anymore. "Mom doesn't like Mr. Elliot, and Pete Elliot's still a dumb duck. Besides, Mr. Elliot put up a hate sign about the Japanese."

Buddy backed the truck out into the street and drove another block to the Lee Drug. "Does everybody here hate those people in the camp?"

"I don't guess everybody. Dad doesn't." I shrugged.

"How about you?"

"I've never met any of them. They don't come into town much." I jumped down out of Red Boy, but instead of rushing ahead of Buddy into the store, I waited by the door so that I could walk in next to him and people would know we were together. I took his hand, something the old Buddy wouldn't have let me do, but my soldier brother didn't seem to notice.

Inside, Redhead Joe Lee was stacking round blue boxes of Evening in Paris dusting powder in a showcase. "Well, look who's here. We're proud as Punch of you boys," he said, coming from behind the counter and holding out his hand and shaking his head as he looked Buddy up and down. "I suppose your dad won't be fit to live with for the next month, what with you coming home looking like a soldier in a Pepsi-Cola advertisement."

"You know, I fell off old Pumpkins, our horse, when I was a kid and landed on my head. Dad said I wasn't any good for nothing after that. He says if I'm the best the army has to offer, we might as well surrender." Bud laughed.

"That's your dad's way of complimenting you, all right."

Buddy shook Mr. Lee's hand. Then Mr. Lee extended his hand to me. I wiped my hand on my overalls and took it.

"Half of Mom thinks I'm going to be a war hero, and the other half wants me to spend my enlistment as a supply clerk," Bud said.

"And which half's going to win out?"

"I couldn't say. They don't ask me. If they did, I'd defend my country in Hawaii, protecting the palm trees and the hula-hula girls."

"That's choice work," Mr. Lee said, then turned serious. "My advice to you is, don't go looking to be a hero. Your folks don't care about you getting a Purple Heart."

"I don't intend to get one," Bud said. I stared at him wide-eyed, thinking how awful it would be if he got hurt. He rubbed the top of my head and said, "Don't look so glum, kiddo."

"Danny Spano got wounded," I told him. "He was in a truck accident at Camp Carson, and he got discharged. He limps."

"Danny Spano fell off a bar stool, but don't tell nobody you heard it from me," Mr. Lee said. He chewed on the end of his mustache, which was not really red, but orange, and raised an eyebrow at Buddy.

"Taken in the line of duty," Buddy said, and they both laughed. I didn't get it and thought then that men and women didn't always find the same things to be funny. Men had a sense of humor meant just for men, like the Jolly Stitchers had one for one another.

Mr. Lee straightened the jars of Pond's Vanishing Cream that were sitting on the counter. "Old Man Spano acts like Danny won the Medal of Honor, although you and me know Spanos weren't in the front of the line when courage was passed out. Danny didn't get no good-conduct medal, I can tell you that," Mr. Lee said.

"Oh, Danny's not so bad, at least that's what Marthalice said once. I wouldn't know myself. Beaner Jack's another thing," Buddy said.

Mr. Lee left us to find a hot-water bottle for a woman who wore a Christmas corsage of silver bells and red ribbons pinned to her coat and complained she couldn't keep her feet warm at night. Buddy and I wandered around the drugstore, examining eyewash and Ipana toothpaste, Buddy stopping to talk to people who shook his hand and wished him good luck and said they were proud of our boys in uniform. Mr. Spano came in for a tin of chewing to-bacco and nodded at Buddy but didn't speak to him. Looking through the window, I saw Beaner with Pete Elliot, lighting cigarettes under the corrugated iron awning across the street. Beaner turned his back to the wind and cupped his hands around his cigarette, and when he turned back, the tip of the cigarette glowed red.

"You want a Hershey bar or a Baby Ruth?" Buddy asked me, looking at the stacks of candy bars next to the cash register, and

I told him a Hershey. Buddy took one from the display, then reached under the counter for a Whitman's Sampler, the big cream-colored box with a design on top like Granny's cross-stitched picture that hung in our living room. "Mom and Granny will like this," Buddy said. Whitman's was my favorite, too, because there was writing inside the lid that told you about each piece of candy, so that you could avoid the coconut and the caramels. And when the candy was gone, you could use the box to store things. He put a carton of Lucky Strikes beside the candy, paid the girl at the cash register, and we sat down on stools at the green marble soda fountain, where Bud ordered Coca-Colas for us. I wondered if people would think I was on a date. Sure, right after they recognized me as Betty Grable.

The girl poured the Cokes into cone-shaped paper cups stuck in metal holders. "Sir," she said, setting down Buddy's drink in front of him. "Ma'am." Nobody'd ever called me that before, but then, I'd never before sat at the counter of the Lee Drug with a man in uniform. I sipped my Coke through two straws, but Buddy drank from the cup, sucking on the ice when he was finished.

Two high school girls came into the drugstore and fussed over the face powders and rouges and lipsticks, twisting the tubes up to see the colors. They sat down on stools next to Buddy, and one of them, Marlys, leaned forward, her elbows on the counter, and said, "How's tricks, Rennie?"

That took me by surprise, because Marlys had never spoken to me. I knew she didn't care about tricks, however; she wanted Buddy to notice her. When he'd joined up, Buddy was just another farm boy, but grown up and dressed in his uniform, he really was as handsome as a Pepsi-Cola model. Buddy looked at Marlys and nodded, then began crunching his ice. Mr. Lee came over and picked up the green check that the counter girl had torn off a pad and set down in front of us. He crumbled it and said, "Your money's no good here, Bud."

Buddy thanked him, and I whispered, "Do people always buy things for you?"

"Only when I'm with a pretty girl." He grinned at me, and I smiled back. This was one of the great days of my life.

We'd finished our Cokes, so Buddy picked up his cap, which was lying on the counter. Just then, Marlys sucked in her breath and said, "Oh my. Who let them out?" We swung around on our stools and saw three little Japanese boys who looked like brothers. The camp gave the Japanese passes to go into town to shop, and we saw men and sometimes women walking past our place in groups of three or four. They kept to themselves in town, doing their business quickly, quietly, nodding if someone spoke to them, but not going out of their way to be friendly. They shopped at the dry goods or the Lee Drug, but not the Elliot Drug, because of the sign. Some of the older Japanese boys had gone into the pool hall once, but the regulars made it clear that they weren't welcome, so the Japanese hadn't gone back.

I looked around for the boys' parents, but they weren't in the drugstore. The two older boys examined the candy bars and boxes of chocolates, but the youngest, who might have been eight, stared at the soda fountain through steel-rimmed spectacles. When he saw us looking back at him, he turned his eyes to the floor, then moved behind one of his brothers.

"We just got invaded by Japs," the second girl said. They both looked at Buddy as if they expected him to pull out a tommy gun and mow them down.

"Dad says they're Japanese, not Japs," I said, loudly enough for the two girls to hear me. The one who'd asked about tricks rolled her eyes, but I didn't care. Those little boys weren't going to hurt anybody.

"What if you have to fight the Japanese?" I whispered to Buddy.

He put on his cap and stood up. "It won't be those three." As we passed them, Buddy patted the little one on the head, ruffling the boy's beetle-colored hair, and said, "Hey, soldier." The boy glanced up at Buddy, his eyes big behind the thick lenses of his glasses.

Buddy and I were almost to the door when Mr. Lee asked the boys where their parents were. The oldest boy shrugged. "Sneak out, did you?" Mr. Lee asked. Sometimes Japanese kids crawled under the bobwire at the camp to chase jack rabbits or hunt for arrowheads. They usually didn't come into town. When the boy didn't answer, Mr. Lee told the three they'd better get back to camp before somebody spotted them.

"Yes, sir," the boy said.

"Just a minute now," Mr. Lee said. "You boys like ice cream?" They nodded, and Mr. Lee told the fountain girl to give each of the kids a double-decker cone.

We went outside, where Pete and Beaner were leaning against our truck. Pete blew two streams of smoke out of his nose, then dropped his cigarette onto the ground. He pumped Buddy's hand. Beaner slapped Buddy on the back and asked him what it was like being in the service. Then Beaner lowered his voice and said something I couldn't hear, and Buddy shook his head while the other two laughed. That was more men's humor. I was sorry those boys were there, because I didn't want to share Buddy with them. But it was Buddy's choice to be friendly, not mine. He asked when they were going to join up.

"Heck, we ain't got our draft notices yet," Pete said.

"I'm thinking I don't want to turn out a cripple like Danny. He got hit by a truck," Beaner added.

Buddy glanced at me, as if warning me not to say we knew what really had happened to Danny, but I wasn't that dumb.

"Speak of the devil," Pete said as Danny crossed the street. His hair hung in his face and a cigarette dangled from the corner of his mouth. I thought he was hoping somebody would say he looked an awful lot like John Garfield. But John Garfield didn't have a gimpy leg, and he wasn't a Spano.

"You killed anybody yet?" Danny asked.

"I haven't seen any action yet, unless you count a fight with a couple of soldiers from Texas. I showed them what a Colorado boy can do." Buddy got out his keys and told me it was time to go.

"Yeah, I hear you. Well, when you get shipped out, kill one for me," Danny said. "Right, Beaner?"

"You do that," Beaner said, and Danny grinned, letting the cigarette drop out of his mouth.

Buddy said good-bye, and we were getting into the truck, when the Japanese boys came out of the drugstore holding their ice-cream cones. "You might could start with those, Bud," Beaner said. "Slap a Jap."

"Little boys?" Buddy asked.

"Like the man says, nits breed lice."

Buddy asked if the boys came from the Tallgrass Camp, although he knew they did. Pete nodded.

"I didn't enlist to fight Americans," Buddy said.

Pete sneered and said, "Look who's getting up on his high horse, just like his old man."

"Strouds always was pantywaists," Beaner said.

I felt my hands make fists and wanted to say something smart, but I knew if I did, I would make Buddy look worse, because girls didn't defend boys, and besides, I'd get pounded by those three. They expected Buddy to slap Beaner a good hard one, but Buddy only slid into the seat and started the motor.

"We got big trouble if Bud Stroud's America's finest," Beaner called.

Buddy acted as if he didn't hear, and I was disappointed. Bud was as strong as Dad, and he could have licked Beaner easy, maybe even with Pete and Danny thrown in. I'd have been proud of him for standing up for himself, and his winning a fight with Beaner would have rubbed off on me. The kids at school would have asked me about it, and I could've said how tough Strouds were, that there weren't any flies on us. But now the kids would think Buddy was chicken, and maybe he was. "How come you let them talk to you like that?" I asked, turning around to watch Beaner, Pete, and Danny stare after us. Buddy stopped the truck at the dry goods a block away to pick up some things for Mom, and I thought the three might follow us, but they didn't.

"What good would that do?"

"They insulted you." Maybe Buddy really was a coward. There was a tiny cold feeling in my stomach when I thought about that. What if my brother wasn't brave after all? Maybe he'd turn out to be a bad soldier. What if he got into battle and froze or ran away? He could get court-martialed, like the soldier I'd heard about on the radio. That would be a terrible thing for us to live down, I thought, then rolled my eyes. A Stroud wouldn't run from his duty just because he didn't stand up to Beaner Jack.

Buddy might have guessed what I was thinking. "You can't rid the world of bullies. Besides, if I'd smacked Beaner and them around, they'd have been mad enough to take it out on those little Japanese boys from the camp. I don't suppose you noticed those kids got away while we were talking, did you? Besides, you know what Dad says: 'When a man fights, it means a fool's lost his argument.'"

"That doesn't stop Dad from fighting." Buddy wouldn't have been a fool if he'd licked Beaner, but I didn't tell him that.

We did Mom's shopping, then drove home. Just before the turnoff to our farm, we passed the three little Japanese boys walking back to camp. They were still licking their ice cream. Buddy stopped and offered them a ride. The sky was the gray-white of ashes, and dry snow had begun to fall again. But the boys were suspicious, and the oldest one said, "No thank you, sir." Bud saluted him, and the three kids stood up straight, their necks stretched out, and saluted him back.

The Japanese boys made it past our farm, but they didn't get home free. Three men drove along the section road to intersect with the Tallgrass Road just beyond our place. We found out about it when Sheriff Henry Watrous stopped to ask Dad if he'd noticed anybody along the road making trouble.

The boys were less than half a mile from the camp, he said, when a truck pulled up behind them, and three men threw snowballs at them, calling the boys names. The men got out of the truck and pelted the boys with dirt clods. Then as the boys ran down the road, the men threw rocks at them, threatening to break their necks. A rock hit the smallest boy in the head, knocking him to the ground, and his brothers dragged him along as the men laughed and told them they'd better hurry up or they'd sic dogs on them. The boy who fell had a concussion. A guard at the camp called Sheriff Watrous, but the parents didn't want things to go any further, for fear of stirring up trouble. Besides, the boys said they hadn't seen their attackers' faces and couldn't identify the truck, which Sheriff Watrous said was bunk, because boys were boys, and they knew motors. After all, they'd told him that when Bud offered them a ride, he was driving a 1933 red Ford pickup with a cracked back window and crumpled left rear fender.

Buddy said he was sure it was Beaner and them, and Sheriff Watrous said he knew it was, but there wasn't any proof. He asked Buddy and me to drive back down the road with him to see if we could spot anything that would help him identify the bullies. But all we saw were half a dozen cigarette butts, a pair of broken spectacles, and an ice-cream cone frozen in the dirt.

THAT NIGHT AT SUPPER, Dad told us there had been other rock-throwing incidents. "Every time something's in the news about our soldiers going into battle in the South Pacific and even in Europe, people here want to take it out on the folks in the camp. Hen Watrous says some of those Japanese out at the Tallgrass Camp get hot under the collar about being held responsible for every American who gets killed, but most of them just want to be left alone."

"You can't hardly blame Ellis folks," Mom said. "Two boys up to Mingo already got killed in the Philippines. Their pictures were in the paper last week, just kids. It could have been Buddy." Her face went rigid then, because we never talked about the danger Buddy might be in, and she glanced at him and said quickly, "Bud, I swear they don't feed you in the army. You eat enough for two men."

"Me and Kilroy, that's who I'm eating for," Bud said, and we all laughed, because even in Ellis, we'd learned about Kilroy. Some kids had soaped KILROY WAS HERE on the window at the

Vogue Dress Shoppe, along with that funny cartoon of the GI. Betty Joyce had had to explain to me about Kilroy, because I thought the drawing was of Frank Martin, who had a nose like an Idaho spud.

"You better finish these boiled potatoes, or we'll just have to fry them up for breakfast." Mom handed the bowl of potatoes to Bud, and Granny passed the cream gravy. Bud took half a potato and a dab of gravy. "Now save room for dessert. We've got apple pie. I don't know why everybody's so crazy about apple pie. I'd rather have rhubarb any day of the week, but we won't have rhubarb until May, maybe April if there's an early spring." Mom talked about food when she got nervous.

Dad wasn't nervous, and he asked Bud how he felt about the camp.

Bud mashed the potato with his fork, but he didn't eat it. "It doesn't bother me, but I don't have to live next to it. You might be in more danger because of Tallgrass than I'll ever be from anything in the army."

Dad tore off a piece of bread and wiped his plate with it. "Oh, I don't believe we're in any danger, unless the Japanese march into town and throw sugar beets at us. They're just ordinary people up there, farmers most of them, like me and you." He shoved the bread into his mouth.

I held my breath, waiting for Bud's answer.

"No, sir," Bud said slowly. "They're Japs—all right, Japanese."

"They're not any more Japanese than the Krugers are Germans."

"You don't know that for a fact," Mom said.

"No, I don't. I don't know for a fact that water won't run uphill, either. But I've never seen it do that, and neither's anybody else. None of those people at the Tallgrass Camp have ever been caught spying." Dad snorted. "What's there to spy on in Ellis?"

"That's not the point. They're not spying in California; that's the point," Mom said. She told Buddy, "Your father's made some enemies talking like this."

"It's not right to lock up those people. I wish we hadn't done it," Dad said.

"Well, I wish we could fly like birds, too," Mom retorted, then calmed herself. "I agree with the Jolly Stitchers when they say we're better safe than sorry."

"Is that what they say?" Dad asked.

Mom gave him a look that said she didn't appreciate the remark.

"How'd you feel if we got locked up?" I asked her. The question just popped out, probably because I was upset about the little boys. At first, I thought Dad would tell me not to be smart, but maybe he decided I had the right to ask. Or perhaps he was curious about the answer. He cocked his head and looked at Mother as if to say, Well?

Mom pushed back her chair. "Oh, who'd lock us up? We look just like everybody else."

I got up and helped clear the dishes, listening to snatches of conversation between Dad and Bud as I walked back and forth to the kitchen. I'd rather have sat there and listened to them talk, but Dad wouldn't have stood for it if I didn't help Mom, especially since she'd been feeling peaked lately. He asked how the boys in the service felt about the internment camps.

"We don't pay much attention to them, but I don't suppose any of the soldiers would object. You see one of those Japanese on the street, and you ask yourself whose side he's on. Maybe Mom's right about being safe instead of sorry."

"It doesn't bother you that their rights have gotten taken away?"

Buddy leaned back in his chair and put his feet on the center pedestal of the big oak table. He pushed his plate toward me, but I was slow in picking it up. Then I rearranged his knife and fork on it because I wanted to hear his answer. "No, sir. They're not the only ones. Besides, their rights are only being suspended. Our boys who've been killed, now their rights are gone for good."

Dad asked about the rights of the three boys who'd been beaten up.

"Oh, come on, Dad. We're not talking about little kids. I'm sorry for them. But you said yourself there are angry men in that camp. Who's to say they wouldn't help Hirohito if they had the chance? What if I'm sent to fight the Japanese? Wouldn't you feel better knowing all those people are locked up? How come you're so hot around the collar anyway?"

Dad thought a minute, putting his hands together so that they formed a little church, his index fingers a steeple. "It might have been that colored boy who was lynched up near Limon when I was a kid. You remember that, don't you, Granny?" He looked over at Granny, who nodded, and I knew she did remember. "They said he raped and murdered a white girl." Dad glanced up at me, and I was afraid he'd wait to continue until I left the room, but he didn't. "They burned that kid to death, tied him to a stake and piled up brush around him. The girl's father lit the match. Folks danced and laughed while that poor boy screamed, his flesh melting off the bones. Hell's fire itself couldn't have been any worse for him."

I shuddered and held on to the chair. I'd never heard that story and couldn't imagine anyone doing that. "Was anybody from Ellis there?" I asked.

"I hope not," Dad replied, but he didn't sound sure.

"You saw it, did you?" Bud asked.

"No, I was just a tyke. Besides, your grandparents didn't hold with lynching. Isn't that true, Mom?"

Granny, who was staring at her hands, which were folded in her lap, didn't look up. "There was a newspaper man in New York City who wrote colored people weren't any freer in Colorado than they were down south," she said softly. "I was ashamed to say I lived here."

"Folks talked about it for years. Some of them were kind of proud of themselves. I heard one man say the boy smelled just like a pig roasting on a spit. He went to church every Sunday, too. That's one reason I don't. But there were some, like your Granny and Gramp, who never could come to terms with it. Isn't that so?"

We all looked at Granny, but she was still staring at her hands, and I wondered if her mind had begun to wander off. Mom said once that Granny's mind was like an old crazy quilt, where some of the pieces were bright but others were worn through. Now her mind seemed as thin as shoddy.

Dad continued. "Aunt Mattie—she was a righteous woman, just like all the McCauleys." He reached over and patted Granny's hand. "Aunt Mattie said if it'd been a white boy who'd killed a colored girl, some of those folks would have put up a statue to him, and what a shame that would have been. Maybe those words stayed in my mind because they were just about the last ones Aunt Mattie ever said to me. She died right afterward. I've thought about that poor Negro boy lots of times over the years, and it's never set right with me, there being different rules for different people, based just on how they look. I didn't hold with prejudice. I never held much with statues, either."

"It's different now, Dad. We're at war," Bud said.

"Yes, son, we are." Dad slowly twirled the castor set, the silver stand we kept in the middle of the table that held crystal bottles of vinegar and oil, salt and pepper. I reminded myself I had to fill them. It felt like I'd never remember all the things I was supposed to do. Taking on a woman's responsibilities wasn't easy.

"How about you, Rennie? What do you think?" Bud asked.

I stopped clearing the dishes, Bud's plate in my hand, as Dad and Bud stared at me. I shrugged.

"No, you tell us what you think, Squirt," Dad said. "You haven't done that."

I looked down at the potato left on Bud's plate. The truth was, the people at Tallgrass were different from us, and they still scared me. So did the lights and the dust and the noise and locking our doors at night. I didn't like the war and how it took away Buddy and Marthalice, how it changed our family. But what upset me right then was the meanness toward those three little boys. It wasn't the Japanese who frightened me the most; it was us. I didn't understand what made somebody from Ellis hurt little kids just because they were Japanese. "I don't think right and wrong change just because we're at war," I said.

Dad and Buddy exchanged a look, and Dad said, "Out of the mouths of babes . . ."

I bristled. I wasn't a babe. Babies didn't clear the table and milk the cows and clean the chicken coop. Dad had told me at harvest that I did my part, but maybe he hadn't meant it.

"Maybe not such a babe," Bud told him.

"Maybe not."

They were silent while I finished carrying the dishes into the kitchen and Mom and I brought in dessert. She set a piece of pie in front of Dad, and he said, "That looks awful good, Mother. Bud, your mother makes the best apple pie in the county, maybe in all Colorado."

"Why stop there?" Mom asked, sitting down.

Dad started in on his dessert. "They say they're good workers, the Japanese at the Tallgrass Camp."

"How do you know?" Bud asked.

"It's a fact. They had farms all over California." Dad cut a bite of pie, but instead of eating it, he left it sitting on his fork and looked Bud in the face. "I've been thinking about hiring a few of those boys to help with the beets. The government's giving them work passes in other places where they've got camps."

Dad put the pie into his mouth, and the rest of us ate in silence for a minute.

"Maybe if you bought a new drill and a better tractor, Loyal, you wouldn't have to hire anybody," Granny said. When it came to farming, Granny's mind was always strong. She and Gramp had run our place for years before he died and she turned it over to Dad. Granny'd worked the beets more than half of her life and knew as much about them as anybody.

"I would, but where am I to get them? With the factories turning out tanks and whatnot instead of tractors, there's no farm equipment to be had."

Granny knit her brows together. "Don't hire those boys hanging out by the fence last harvest."

"You mean the white boys?" Dad asked her.

Granny nodded.

"Why's that?" Mom asked her.

"I don't know, but I don't like them." Granny was confused now, and she lapsed into silence.

"I don't like them much myself," Dad said. He turned to

Bud. "She's talking about Beaner Jack and them. I wouldn't hire them, but I won't hire those Japanese fellows, either, if you don't want me to."

Bud had finished eating the apples out of his pie, and he began on the crust. He was one of those people who ate all his corn before he started on the potatoes, and he ate those before the meat. He looked at Dad, surprised. "Since when do you ask my advice?"

"Since you grew up. This'll be your farm one day, and I don't want to cross you. Besides, with you in the army, you don't need to worry about things at home."

"I wouldn't worry about the Japanese so much, but I might worry about what people around here would do if you hired men from the camp. Folks can get mean, you know. I wouldn't put it past Beaner to take a sledge to your equipment."

"Oh, I think I can handle those boys all right. Mom's bees, now they're another thing. We wouldn't want them cutting her dead."

"I guess you wouldn't have to worry about them," Mom said.

"They might make knots in your thread or take great big stitches in your quilts," Dad said, teasing her.

"If they do, Rennie and I will just take them out." I knew we would, too. We'd done it before, after the Stitchers had worked on her quilts.

"Well, that's a worry off my mind."

After we'd finished dessert, Mom and I carried the plates and forks into the kitchen, where she put the remains of the supper into the icebox while I filled the dishpan with soapy water. "What do you think about Dad hiring those Japanese?" I asked her, scrubbing a plate and putting it into the dish drainer.

Mom glanced over her shoulder into the dining room, where Dad and Bud were talking. Granny had taken out her needlework and was lost in piecing a quilt block of an airplane. "If it was up to me, I wouldn't do it. But if it was up to me, we wouldn't be in any war, either." She paused, then picked up a plate and began drying it. "Still, there's the beets to think about. We've got to get them planted in a few months. There's nothing more important than that. This is not a matter of my choosing." She paused. "What do you think about it, Rennie?"

I'd never been asked my opinion so much in my life. "Like Granny says, they'd be better than Beaner. But aren't you worried about the Jolly Stitchers?"

"Not one bit," Mom said quickly. Then she added, "I've never been one to care what other people think."

"Huh?" I said.

After I went upstairs to bed, I reread all of Marthalice's letters. It didn't take long, because there were only six of them, and they were short. And Marthalice wrote with a big hand. Then I opened an old tin Whitman's Sampler box that Granny had given me and took out a pencil and sharpened it. I removed some sheets of Santa Fe Railroad stationery that Mom had picked up on the train home from Denver. I wrote Marthalice a long letter, telling her all about Buddy's surprise visit, because I wanted her to be part of it. And I asked when she was coming home. When Marthalice answered my letter, she said she'd give anything to see Bud in his uniform. But she never said a word about coming back to Ellis.

THE SNOW, WHICH HAD started before Christmas, continued all night, a hard, stinging snow brought by a wind that swept a thousand miles across the prairie. The wind pounded on the north side of the house, rattling the window sashes, and I felt it, although I slept in a wooden bed with a high headboard and footboard. Snow drifted in through cracks, dusting the covers over me like flour from a sifter. I had so many quilts piled on top of me that I could hardly turn over, and I ached from being curled up into a tight ball, my feet tucked inside my flannel nightgown to keep them warm against the cold, stiff sheets. My bedroom was above the kitchen, and there was a grate in the floor to let the heat rise, but the room still was freezing. I didn't mind, however. I liked lying there in the cold, exploring the sheets with my toes and listening to the murmur of voices below me. I felt as if I were inside a cocoon.

When I finally got out of bed, I grabbed my clothes and hurried downstairs to dress by the oil heater in the dining room. I loved icy winter mornings, when there didn't seem to be anything in the world but our farm. Although I knew the place would go to Bud one day, I still couldn't imagine ever living anywhere else. I wanted to attend college, and thought maybe I'd get a job and a sweet little apartment in Denver like Marthalice's, but in my heart, I hoped I'd marry a beet farmer one day and live on a farm like ours.

The snow had stopped, and the sun shone lukewarm through the gray sky, which promised another storm. Huge drifts, polished to a shine by the wind, were pushed against the fences. Mom had fixed breakfast for Dad and Bud, and they'd gone to check the livestock. She was in the henhouse with the chickens.

"There's flannel cakes," Granny said, stirring the makings left in Mom's green batter bowl. Granny turned on the flame under the frying pan and spooned in bacon drippings from the grease can. After the drippings sizzled, Granny poured batter into the pan and made a test cake, and when it was done, she threw it into the garbage pail for the chickens. Then she poured batter into the pan, and we watched until bubbles formed and created holes; then she flipped the pancakes over and let them cook for a few seconds on the other side. When they were done, she set them on a plate that had been warmed in the oven. Granny had kept the bacon warm, too, and the syrup was hot in a pan on a back burner. We did things nicer than most folks. When I spent the night at Betty Joyce's house, we ate cold fried eggs and side meat that had congealed in its grease, because Betty Joyce's dad said his wife wasn't making two breakfasts. If we wanted hot food, he told us, we could get up at dawn with him.

While I ate, Granny took up her piecing, using tiny stitches to attach the tail onto the body of the airplane on her quilt square, and I thought how much things had changed since she was a girl. She and her sister had come across the prairie in covered wagons. Now Granny could look up into the sky and see airplanes, or at least she could if one ever flew over Ellis, which in my memory it never had. I wondered if things would change as much during my lifetime. They'd gotten a good start.

Dad and Bud came up onto the porch, stamping the snow off their feet and taking off their galoshes before stomping into the kitchen. Dad's face was red, and he took off his plaid wool hat with the earflaps and rubbed his ears to warm them. "It's colder out there than an old maid in December," he said, going to the stove and turning on the fire under the coffeepot. "Remember there was a man up north got caught in a storm and froze his hands and feet? He wasn't much good after that."

"Well, what's your excuse? You never got froze," Granny said, and Dad squeezed her shoulder, happy that her mind was with us that morning. I was, too. It was such a fine morning that Granny deserved to enjoy it.

She reached into the dish drainer for green glass coffee mugs for Dad and Bud and took her china cup and saucer out of the cupboard. When Granny leaned over to set down the cups, I smelled cinnamon along with talcum powder, and I knew she'd already mixed up the yeast batter for cinnamon rolls for dinner. There wasn't sugar for icing, but they'd be just as good plain.

While I finished my breakfast, the three of them sat at the table with me, drinking their coffee, chatting about the storm and how glad they were for the moisture. They talked about the little things that needed doing, the way farm folks always did at the start of a day. I loved the comfort of that talk. Bud said he'd climb up on top of the barn and fix the lightning rod that had come loose in the wind. Granny mentioned she'd sure like a new cream separator, and Dad reminded her gently that he'd bought one just that fall. Mom came in, and they asked how the chickens had weathered the storm. The talk warmed me as much as the pancakes, and I thought there wouldn't be anything nicer than having that conversation around my own kitchen table one day. I hoped my farm wouldn't be too far away from Bud's, and that perhaps Mom and Dad would live with me, and we'd remember when Buddy went off to war and how worried we were, and then he'd come home without a scratch. "Why, we worried for nothing," I'd say, and Mom would agree. Then I thought I was getting kind of sappy.

Mom turned on the fire under the teakettle and spooned fresh grounds into the basket of the coffeepot, and after the water boiled, she poured it into the pot and let the coffee drip. She was taking her cup from the drainer when we heard someone on the porch stamping snow off his feet. Dad leaned back, balancing his chair on two legs, and looked through the window in the door to see who it was. The light shone through the jewel-like panes of colored glass that framed the window, casting a rainbow of colors onto the floor.

"Come on in, Mr. Watrous. Door's open," Dad called before the sheriff could knock.

Sheriff Watrous opened the door and stood there a moment, kicking one overshoe against the other, but he didn't get rid of all the snow, because after he came in and stood beside the door, a puddle of water formed on the linoleum, which was faded where Mom and Granny had scrubbed it over the years. "Cold as a witch's behind out there, Mr. Stroud," he said. "Ladies." He touched his Stetson to Mom and Granny but didn't take it off.

"Here's some hot coffee. I must have known you were coming." Mom handed him a cup. "How you doing, Mr. Watrous?"

"I'm doing pretty good," he replied, sipping. You could tell the coffee was scalding hot by the way he drew in his breath after a taste.

Dad asked Sheriff Watrous if he wanted a saucer to drink his coffee from, which surprised me, because Mom said drinking coffee out of a saucer was trashy. But she also said polite people made their guests feel at home.

Mr. Watrous declined and took small sips of the coffee, and in a minute, he had drunk most of it.

"What brings you out on a day like this? I thought you'd be sitting at the jail with your feet up on the oil stove," Dad said. Dad sounded casual, but I knew from the look on his face that he was anxious. The sheriff never stopped by to visit the way other folks did. I thought maybe some other Japanese boys had been beaten up. "Best sit down, Mr. Watrous," Dad said.

"This might not be something for Miss Evelina and the girl." Mr. Watrous cocked his head at Granny and me.

"There's nothing Granny hasn't heard, and Rennie knows considerable about the world these days."

I sat up a little straighter, trying to act worldlier, although I'd just been thinking how nice it was that my whole world that morning was the white winter farm. I was pleased, however, that Dad didn't tell me to go into the other room, that he felt I was old enough to know what was going on outside our place.

The sheriff took a deep breath and laid his hat on the Hoosier cupboard. "Well, it's like this, then." He eyed Granny and me, but he didn't say any more about us. "You know the little Reddick girl that lives on the other side of Tallgrass? Susan, her name is."

Dad barely nodded. I glanced at Mom, who put her hand on my shoulder but didn't look at me. I knew she was thinking about our visit to Helen Archuleta, Susan's sister, not long before Christmas. I hadn't heard anything about the baby being born and wondered if something bad had happened to Helen. I wondered if the sheriff had gotten the names mixed up and he meant Helen instead of Susan.

The sheriff glanced at Mom out of the corner of his eye, but he spoke to Dad. "They found little Susan out in the field this morning, tore up pretty bad and frozen in a haystack."

"Lost in the storm?" Dad asked. He leaned forward and put his hands flat on the oilcloth of the table, waiting for the answer. I thought about Susan losing her crutches in the wind and crawling around on the cold ground, trying to make her way back to the house. She would have reached the haystack and known she'd gone in the wrong direction and crawled into the hay to keep warm. Susan wasn't brave, and I shivered, knowing how terrified she must have been. Shoot, I'd have been terrified, and I could walk just fine.

"No, sir. I wished that was the cause of it." He paused and chewed his bottom lip. "The little girl was murdered. And along with it, I'm sorry to say, the poor little thing had got ravished."

4

"OH," MOM SAID, GLANCING at Granny, and then at me as she sat down hard in her chair. Granny was sewing placidly, not paying attention to the sheriff. His words had made no impression on her. But they had on me. I stared at him, barely breathing, and I prayed Mom wouldn't find some chore for me to do upstairs. I needed to stay. Susan was my friend. I had to know what had happened to her. Mom made a halfhearted waving motion at me to tell me to be still, but I hadn't been about to say anything. I wasn't absolutely sure what the word *ravished* meant, but I had a pretty good idea. I pulled my elbows into my sides and stared at the table.

Susan was a warm, sweet girl, like a bunny. How could anybody hurt her? I wondered. Just a few days before, I'd gone to her house, and we'd worked a thousand-piece puzzle she'd gotten for Christmas. The picture on it was of Cliff Palace at Mesa Verde, and Susan said it made her want to visit a cliff dwelling.

She asked if Cliff Palace had an elevator, and we laughed. It was nice that Susan wasn't self-conscious about her crutches. She had invited me back the next day, but I didn't like puzzles much. Then Buddy came home, and I forgot about Susan. Maybe she stayed up late last night working on the puzzle, I thought, and somebody saw her through the window. If I'd finished the puzzle with her, she'd have been in bed, safe. I'm sorry, Susan, I said to myself. Although I was in the safest place I knew, the kitchen of our farm, with Buddy and Dad to protect me, I was scared. I'd never been so scared in our house before.

"That poor thing," Mom added. "I'll bake a cake." Like all farm women, Mom's reaction to bad news was to take food to the bereaved. It helped them, and it gave her a chore that made her feel useful. I wished I had something to do.

"She was an awful nice little girl. What happened to her, Hen?" Dad asked. Dad looked almost ready to cry—at least I thought he did. I'd never seen him cry. He glanced at me, and I knew what he was thinking, because I was thinking it, too: What if that had happened to me?

"I guess I'll set down." Sheriff Watrous unbuttoned his coat but didn't take it off. He dropped into a chair while Dad got up and poured himself coffee, then put the pot on the table. The sheriff waited until Dad took his seat before he spoke. "It looks like the little girl woke up in the night and went outside to use the backhouse. She got the polio a few years back, you know, and was crippled up and couldn't manage the stairs, so her folks had her to sleep in a room near the kitchen door. This morning, when Elmo Reddick got up, he found the door wide open and the snow blown in. The storm was over by then. At first, he thought his girl was outside, but then he saw the snow was piled up on the floor,

and there wasn't no footprints in it. So he figured she'd gone outside in the evening and hadn't latched the door good when she
came back in. You know how the wind was blowing last night,
hard enough to take a door right off the hinges." He shook his
head for emphasis. "Course, it wasn't like that storm two years
ago, or was it three?"

Mom cleared her throat, prodding the sheriff to forget about
the storm and get on with what had happened to Susan. She
poured herself more coffee, although she just held the cup and
didn't drink. "Go on, Sheriff Watrous," she said. I stared at him
without blinking, hoping he'd get the hint to move along.

"When Elmo looked in the bedroom, the girl wasn't there.
So the two of them, Elmo and Opal, went outside looking for
her. They were afraid she'd gone out and got lost in the storm.
You know how these prairie blizzards can be awful bad."

We all nodded. Plains storms were deadly. With the snow
swirling around, you could lose your sense of direction and
freeze ten feet from your back door. Men put up ropes between
their houses and the barns in the winter so they wouldn't get
lost. "And they found her?" Mom asked, agitated that Sheriff
Watrous was back on the weather.

"Opal found her back of the barn, covered with hay. She
thought Susan'd crawled in there to keep warm. She was about to
wake up the little girl, but then she saw the blood. Even then,
Opal said, she didn't believe her girl was dead, because she looked
so peaceful." The sheriff leaned back on two legs of his chair,
thought better of it, and eased the chair back down. "Then Elmo
went to pick her up, and they saw little Susan's throat had been
cut, like it'd been sliced with a sickle, and her legs was . . ." The
sheriff looked at Mom and said, "Well, she was disarranged. And

she didn't have on her nightdress. She was froze to the hay with her blood. Naked she was." He pronounced the word *necked*.

I looked at the table, embarrassed for Susan. What if I'd been murdered and Mom and Dad had found me naked, and the sheriff had come and looked at me? My insides got all balled up as I thought of Susan outside in the storm without any clothes, her arms and legs and back icy with the cold, how she couldn't have gotten away from the man because she couldn't run with her crippled legs. My own hands grew cold as I wondered who had taken her out there and what he'd done to her. I started to cry. Buddy put his arm around me and squeezed my shoulder. Without looking at me, Dad reached over and put his hand on top of mine.

The sheriff watched me a minute, maybe hoping I'd get up from the table. When I didn't, he continued. "Elmo stayed with her, and Opal came for me in that big old truck of theirs—don't know how she made it over the roads, but she did—and me and the coroner was the ones had to tell them for sure that their little girl'd been"—he looked at Granny, who was still sewing—"been taken liberties with, you might say."

"Been raped," Dad said, looking over the sheriff's head.

"Yes, sir." Beads of sweat stood out on the sheriff's face, although it was not hot in the room. "It brings a lump to a fellow's throat."

"Any idea who did it, sir?" Bud asked. Everyone looked at the sheriff then, including Granny.

The sheriff shook his head. He picked up his cup, which was empty, and reached for the pot, but it was empty, too. Mom got up to make fresh coffee, turning on the water in the sink to fill the teakettle and rattling things around more than was necessary. "I wish I had cookies left, Sheriff Watrous, but Bud's eaten every last one of them. You know how these boys are. They don't feed them so good in the army," she said.

"Yes, ma'am. Thank you. I can't say as I'd care for food just now."

"Oh, those were real good cookies. We gathered the black walnuts ourselves last fall. October, I believe it was. Granny and I."

Dad said, "Hush, Mary," and she was quiet.

"You ask who done it, and I tell you I've got no idea a'tall," the sheriff told Bud.

"They have a hired man," Dad said.

"It wasn't him, 'cause he was in town all night. One of the girls upstairs over Jay Dee's Tavern vouched for that. We asked her right after we took the body to town. No, sir, somebody else was in that yard, and the poor little girl must have bumped into him when she went out to do her duty."

"How come she went outside instead of using the chamber pot?" I asked.

Sheriff Watrous jerked up his head, then looked at me so fiercely that I stared at the oilcloth again and began tracing a flower with my fingertip. "That's a good question, young lady. You know, I wasn't thinking right. A man, now he'd get up, but a little girl like that would use the thunder mug under the bed, especially in a storm. Her father said he believed she'd gone to the backhouse, and I never stopped to ponder it." His head went up and down few times. "You know what that means, don't you, Mr. Stroud?"

"It means somebody came in the house after her," Bud said before Dad could answer.

"That's about right," the sheriff said. It was a horrible thought, a person coming right into the Reddicks' house to get Susan. What if someone had come into our house after me?

"I bet somebody'd been watching her, and he knew where she slept," Bud said.

"And knew Reddicks don't lock their doors," Dad added.

"Well, that's not much of a deduction. There's only some that lock their doors, even now, with the camp open. Besides, it wouldn't matter if they did. You can get into most any house around Ellis with a skeleton key." The sheriff took out his pack of ready-mades and asked Mom if she minded if he smoked. Dad got out the makings and offered them to Bud, who shook his head. Then Dad rolled his own cigarette, struck a kitchen match, and lighted the sheriff's cigarette and his own.

"Who'd be watching her?" Bud asked.

"That's the question, ain't it?" the sheriff said. "That's why I stopped to talk to you folks." He turned to me. "You ever see anybody watching little Susan, somebody who oughtn't to be?"

I thought that over, wishing I had an answer, hoping I could come up with something more important than an observation about a chamber pot. I hadn't seen any tramps around, and none of the boys at school paid much attention to Susan. I shook my head.

"Didn't think so," the sheriff said. "Mr. Stroud, anybody coming from town last night would have gone right past your place on the Tallgrass Road."

"Unless they took to the section roads," Dad told him.

"Not last night. Those roads was too drifted over."

"We didn't see anybody," Dad said, looking around the table. We all shook our heads. "Hearing's something else. There are folks driving up and down that road all hours of the night, even last night. I wouldn't have known who it was."

Then Bud asked about Beaner, and I could tell by the way Dad nodded that he was wondering about Beaner, too.

"First name I thought of." The sheriff said he'd gone over to the Jack place right after talking to the girl at Jay Dee's and had had to wade from the road through three-foot drifts. "They were pure driven snow. Nobody came in or out of that farm since the storm started, and Beaner was inside the house. Besides, mean as Beaner is, I don't know as he'd do something like this. He's a bully, but he's not a killer."

Bud asked about Pete and Danny, but the sheriff said they were snowed in, too. "Besides, the only time they get into trouble is when Beaner puts them up to it," he added.

"I can't see any local boy doing this," Mom said. "Maybe there's a workman left in town, somebody who came in to build the camp."

"The camp," the sheriff said slowly.

Dad said, "Hen, I don't reckon—"

"I don't like to think it, either, Mr. Stroud, but it's the only thing that makes any sense, ain't it? Somebody's been looking out at that little girl, waiting for a chance at her, and the Reddicks live as close to the camp as you do."

Mom said, "Oh!" and looked at me, and I knew she was thinking that if it were somebody at the camp and he'd looked east instead of west, he would have come to our farm. I hadn't considered the Japanese when Sheriff Watrous asked me if anyone had been watching Susan, and I tried to recall if I'd seen any Japanese near her farm. But the Reddick place was in the opposite direction from town, and the Japanese didn't go that way. And because Susan was on crutches, she wouldn't have walked down the road past Tallgrass. Besides, the Japanese looked away when we passed them on the road. But what if it was a Japanese boy, and he's hiding in a gully, watching our house right now? I thought. Perhaps he knew Buddy was here, and that was why he went to Susan's place instead of ours. He might be marking time until Buddy leaves. Or is the person who killed Susan a white man, someone I know? He couldn't be. Nobody in Ellis would do such a thing. I wondered what I would do if the bad man come after me. I wasn't crippled, so I could run, but maybe I'd be so afraid that I'd just curl up and die, too.

"I was hoping you could tell me something so's I wouldn't have to go out to the Tallgrass and question those folks. That'd sure stir up trouble." Sheriff Watrous sighed and got up, touching his hat to Mom. He said he had to return to town to take care of things at the jail, since his deputy had taken off for Denver for the holidays. The sheriff was planning on going back to the Reddicks' in a couple of hours, and he wanted Mom and Dad to ride out with him. After that, he'd stop at the camp and ask around. "Mr. Stroud, you have a level head about those folks. I'd like it if you was to come along."

"I reckoned you'd say that," Dad told him.

Dad turned to Bud, who raised his hands before Dad could speak and said, "I was planning on staying right close to home today."

"I'd be glad for it," Dad said.

BY THE TIME THE sheriff came back from town, Mom had baked a layer cake—which I iced with caramel frosting—fried up a chicken, and gone to the cellar for a jar of green beans that we'd bottled last summer. With the side roads so bad, Mom said, women might not be able to get to the Reddick farm for another day, and she didn't want Mrs. Reddick to have to worry about cooking. "Maybe if there's food, they'll eat a little. It'll keep up their strength."

"I expect Mrs. Reddick'd appreciate the aid and comfort a woman'd bring her," the sheriff said.

"You sure you feel up to it, Mother?" Dad asked, and the two of them exchanged a glance.

"Of course, I do." She explained to Sheriff Watrous, "I've been a little tired lately is all."

Dad studied her a moment then turned to the sheriff. "Reddicks are awful fond of Rennie," he said, and I jerked up my head, because I hadn't asked to go with them. I wasn't even sure I wanted to. It would be creepy. But I figured maybe I owed it to Susan. Ever since the sheriff had told us about her, I'd felt guilty that I hadn't gone back to her house to finish the puzzle. I turned to Mom and waited for her answer.

Dad and Mom exchanged glances, then Mom nodded, and the sheriff said, "Bring her along."

"We'll be back after a bit," Dad told Bud.

Dad drove Mom and me in Red Boy, behind the sheriff's car, and when we turned into the Reddick farm, Mom sighed and said, "There's no cars and not many tracks here. I was right, Loyal. Nobody's come yet to grieve with them."

"The Reddicks don't have a phone. Maybe nobody knows what happened," I said.

"And that fool sheriff never thought to call the neighbors. What's come over the man? These folks could starve to death, with nobody to bring them a meal. If you ask me, Sheriff Watrous ought to find another line of work. He's got no more common sense than a rooster."

"Now, Mother," Dad said, but he and I both knew she really wasn't blaming Sheriff Watrous. She was just blowing off steam. She'd been so busy fixing food that she'd hadn't thought to call, either, but I didn't mention that.

"Oh, I know, Loyal. I can't recall but a single murder he's had to deal with, and that was a Jack, the one who was killed in a fight at Jay Dee's. I don't suppose this is easy for him, either. He's more at ease with cattle rustlers than child killers. Still and all, it wouldn't hurt for him to have a little compassion."

As Dad drove to the back door of the house, I glanced around for the haystack where Susan had died, turning to look out the back window of the truck. Mom frowned and shook her head, and Dad told me, "I believe they found her out beyond the barn. There wouldn't be anything you'd want to see."

"No, sir," I said, embarrassed that they'd caught me, but I was still disappointed that I couldn't see the murder scene.

"Don't ask any questions. Just act as natural as you can, whatever that is," Mom said. "It might do them good to know one of Susan's friends is grieving for her."

Dad parked beside the house, and by the time we got the food hamper out of the bed of Red Boy, Sheriff Watrous had opened the back door. The snow on the stoop was muddy, and spikes of dried grass stuck up next to the cement. "Folks, you home? I brung company. Strouds is here," the sheriff called.

"Well, of course they're home. Did he think they'd gone to the picture show?" Mom muttered. She walked past him, with me behind her, and set the food on the table. In a minute, Mrs. Reddick, a small woman with a lined face and hands covered with liver spots, stood in the kitchen doorway, her hand clutching the frame, and said, "Mary."

"Opal," Mom replied, with as much emotion as I'd ever heard anyone put into a single word. But she didn't need to say more. Mom put her arms around Mrs. Reddick and led her into the parlor, where the two of them sat down on a horsehair sofa. Mrs. Reddick began crying softly, her hands over her eyes, tears seeping out from between her fingers. Her long hair, which she usually pinned on top of her head in a bun, hung loose down her back.

I sat down on the other side of her, sliding a little on the slick horsehair, which poked my legs. "I'll miss Susan. I liked her a lot." I thought that was a pretty stupid thing to say, and I wished I'd come up with something better, but Mom nodded her approval, and Mrs. Reddick reached down with a wet hand and clutched my arm.

"She liked it when you came to play. Not many girls visited," Mrs. Reddick said, making me feel even worse that I hadn't returned to help Susan with the puzzle.

Mr. Reddick came in then and said, "It's the first time the woman's cried. She's in need of it." He broke into great sobs. Mr. Reddick always reminded me of a rooster, strutting around with his neck stretched out and his chin raised. Now he was just a small, fat, bedraggled man who hadn't shaved. "Oh Lord! Oh Lord! You took both my daughters. What have I done to deserve this?" he cried. Dad put his arm around Mr. Reddick and took him outside, and through the doorway, I could see Susan's father on his knees in the snow, wailing, the weak sun glinting off his bald head. In a minute, he began cursing God.

"He ought not to do that," Mrs. Reddick said, sniffing back tears.

"I think the Lord will forgive him. He's placed a heavy burden on you," Mom said.

I'd begun to shiver. There was no heat in the parlor, but more than that, Susan's death and her parents' grief made me cold all over. The only people I'd known who'd died had been old, and they'd just gone to sleep. Mom told me to go into the kitchen and build up the fire in the cookstove, then boil water for tea. "Tea will keep your strength up, Opal. The worst isn't over," Mom said.

I got kindling out of the wood box and blew on the coals until the wood caught, then went to the pump in the kitchen sink and moved the handle up and down until the kettle was full of water. The sink had black spots where the porcelain had been chipped, and the varnish on the tongue-and-groove wall in back of the sink was stained and warped where water had splashed on it. The kitchen was ugly, cold and brown. Susan must have been lonely living in that house after her sister moved out. I should have been a better friend. I looked over at the little table under the kitchen window where we'd worked the puzzle. The table was there, but the puzzle pieces were spread all over the floor, as if Susan had gotten mad and brushed the puzzle off the table. But Susan never got mad, and she'd loved that puzzle. She wouldn't have destroyed it. I raised my eyes to the ceiling and whispered, "I'm sorry, Susan. If I'd known, I'd have come over." That was a dumb thing to say. If I'd known, I'd have told the sheriff, and Susan wouldn't have gotten killed.

I found a teapot in the cupboard and poured tea leaves into it. Then, as I waited for the water to boil, I stood in the doorway of Susan's bedroom, staring at the rumpled quilt covered with Sunbonnet Sues that Mrs. Reddick had pieced. The Jolly Stitchers had quilted it. They'd worked on it at our house, because the quilt was a birthday present for Susan, and Mrs. Reddick wanted it to be a surprise. She'd given it to Susan at a birthday party, then taken a Kodak of all Susan's friends standing around it. Susan had asked me to pose in front of the quilt with her. Now the quilt was lying on the bare board floor, as if it had been torn from the bed, and peeking from beneath it was Susan's nightgown with blood on it. I'd cleaned enough chickens to know what blood looked like. How could the sheriff have missed it? I wondered.

Maybe, since he'd thought Susan had been murdered on her way to the outhouse, he'd never gone into her bedroom.

I stared at the quilt, imaging the bad man coming through the back door and grabbing Susan out of bed. She would have been terrified, waking up to find a stranger in her bedroom— that is, if he was a stranger. She might have awakened when he tore off her nightgown. Or maybe he knocked her out while she was asleep, and she never knew what happened. I stepped around the quilt on the floor and sat down on the edge of Susan's bed, put my head in my hands, and cried. Life had been so unfair for Susan: She was crippled, her sister had left, and now she'd been raped and murdered.

The Reddicks didn't need somebody else crying, and I got up and wiped the tears from my face with the backs of my hands. I went to the cookstove, poured the boiling water into the teapot, and let the tea steep. As I was getting out the cups, the sheriff came into the kitchen, and I whispered that Susan's nightgown was under the quilt. I pointed out the puzzle pieces lying on the floor, too. "Well, I'm damned," he said.

Dad came in with Mr. Reddick, who smelled like whiskey, and the sheriff told Dad, "You've got an awful smart young lady here, Mr. Stroud."

"Oh, not so smart," Dad said, smiling at me for the first time since the sheriff had arrived at our house. I tried not to feel important. After all, my friend had been murdered. But I couldn't help being glad I had noticed things the sheriff had overlooked. It made me feel as if I'd made it up a little to Susan for being such a crummy friend.

Mom led Mrs. Reddick into the kitchen then, and while the sheriff searched Susan's room, the rest of us sat at the table, drinking tea and eating Mom's cake. Mr. Reddick mashed his down, while his wife took small bites and chewed and chewed, but she couldn't seem to swallow. Mom told them she'd brought a chicken and not to worry about meals because she'd take care of them. She'd left enough for the next couple of days, she said, and as soon as we got home, she would call the Jolly Stitchers and arrange for them to bring more food.

The sheriff came out of the bedroom, eyeing the cake, and Mom cut him a piece. "You hear anything in the night?" he asked the Reddicks.

The couple looked at each other. Then Mrs. Reddick shook her head, while Mr. Reddick replied, "Only the wind. It was fierce. We didn't hear Susan go out, but you already asked us that."

"I've been thinking somebody must have came in after her. Is this her nightdress?" He laid the nightgown on the table, then put his hands into his pants pockets, jingling coins. With its dark red stains, the nightgown was spooky.

Mrs. Reddick's hands trembled and she sagged in her chair. Mom, who was sitting beside her, reached over and took her hands, stilling them.

"You sure about that, her being killed right inside the house?" Mr. Reddick asked the sheriff.

"I don't know anything for sure, only what looks likely. The Stroud girl here saw Susan's nightdress. And I was wondering about that puzzle that got knocked all over the floor."

Mr. Reddick turned his head aside and slammed his fist on the table. "I should have heard him. I hear good, you know. I can hear a calf bawling all the way from the barn. I should have heard my own girl call out."

"That is if she did call, Elmo," Dad said. "This could have happened while she was asleep."

"Besides, if somebody came in, he'd have been real quiet. You couldn't have heard him, especially with the storm and all," the sheriff added.

"But I should have. Oh Lord, did my girl cry out for me and I didn't hear?" Mr. Reddick scrunched up his face, but he didn't cry. "I've been a sinner, broke one of His commandments, and the Lord, for a fact, is punishing me."

I leaned forward to hear which commandment Mr. Reddick had broken. My bet was on coveting his neighbor's property, because the Reddicks didn't have much. But before Mr. Reddick could confess, Dad said sharply, "Now we'll have no more talk like that. I don't know any Lord who plays tit for tat." I wasn't aware that Dad knew any Lord at all, because he never went to church.

Mom did, however, and I wanted to ask her if God punished people for being bad. But it didn't make sense to me. If God punished bad people, he'd have to reward the good ones. Mrs. Reddick was as good a woman as Mom, and Susan's death wasn't any reward to her. It seemed to me like God wasn't paying much attention.

"I have committed adultery," Mr. Reddick said, clicking his false teeth. That's the last commandment I would have chosen for him to break, because he was about as good-looking as a gopher, and he smelled like rotten hay. I glanced at his wife, but Mom was talking to her, so Mrs. Reddick hadn't heard her husband. Maybe she already knew. Mom gave me a hard look, as if to tell me I wasn't to repeat anything I heard in that kitchen. I already knew that. But Lord, I wanted to tell Betty Joyce!

"Hush," Dad told Mr. Reddick harshly.

I hoped he wouldn't, because it wasn't every day that somebody confessed in my presence that he had lain down in sin, but just then, there was a knock at the back door, and before anyone could open it, Mrs. Gardner pushed her head inside and said, "Yoo-hoo." She stood in the open doorway a moment, and we heard the creak of chains as the wind blew the porch swing against the house. Mrs. Gardner shut the door and went over to Mrs. Reddick and put her arms around her. "I came as soon as I heard about Susan." I wondered how she'd found out, but I wasn't really surprised. The Stitchers always seemed to know about problems. "I just put together a few things from the cupboard that'll do you if you're hungry." She waved her hand dismissively at the basket she'd set on the floor, but I could see a bread pudding sitting on top of a stewpot and knew she must have brought her own family's dinner. "Hello, Mary, I should have known you'd be the first out in time of need."

"Hello, Afton." Mom gave up her chair to Mrs. Gardner. Mrs. Reddick didn't seem to notice the change, nor that the rest of us stood up then. Mom said she'd stop by in the morning, and Dad and the sheriff asked the Reddicks if they needed any help with the chores. They didn't answer or even look up.

"My boy will be by to do the milking," Mrs. Gardner called as we opened the door.

"No need," Mr. Reddick said, pulling himself together. "If I don't do chores, I can't know what to do with myself."

Mom and I got into the truck, while Dad went to the sheriff's car with Mr. Watrous so that the two of them could drive together to the Tallgrass camp. Mom started the motor, but before she put in the clutch, she locked her door, then reached over and locked mine. On the way home, I asked if Susan's dying meant that the Reddicks would be kinder to Helen, maybe ask her to move back in with them. That would be a nice thing for God to do for Mrs. Reddick, I thought.

"Her mother will want her to come home, but Mr. Reddick's a stubborn man. You wouldn't think it, but sorrow just makes some people harder, and my guess is, he's one of them."

DAD AND THE SHERIFF didn't stay long at the camp. As Dad said, "There isn't the slightest bit of proof one of those jaspers is guilty."

"There's plenty of folks who think so," Mom said. She'd just called the last of the Jolly Stitchers, arranging for them to take food to the Reddicks. Every one of the women had asked if a man from the camp had murdered Susan.

"Maybe you ought to have called the missionary circle instead," Dad said.

"Oh, they'd be just as bad. Besides, they'd pray for Susan's soul instead of fixing covered dishes. Prayer's not going to do the Reddicks any good if they starve to death."

"Might not do them any good if they don't, either." Dad slid his eyes over to me, then looked back at Mom and asked, "Have you seen any signs around here—" But Mom cut him off with a shake of her head.

"It's best to keep a look out. Maybe you better talk to Squirt," Dad said, biting his lip. Mom told him she already had.

She hadn't said much, however, only that bad men sometimes lurked around the barn or peeked in windows, and I had to be ever vigilant. I pointed out that I slept upstairs, and that anybody who came into the house would have to pass her and Dad's bedroom on the first floor to get to me. Mom told me men sometimes tricked little girls in other ways. "Don't ever let anybody pull up your dress. . . ." She paused, embarrassed, but I had a good idea of what she was talking about. Like all farm kids, I'd seen bulls mount cows, and I thought it was something like that with men and women, although I couldn't understand why anybody would do that with a little girl like Susan. I wished I could talk to Marthalice, but since I let Mom read all of my sister's letters, I didn't dare ask her to write to me about that.

When Bud came in from milking, Dad told us what had happened at the camp. By the time he and Sheriff Watrous got there, the guards knew all about Susan's murder, so they'd been sure the sheriff would be along. They'd already made up a list of the men who'd had passes to leave the camp the day before, but all of them had been back by nightfall. "Of course, someone could have sneaked out," the sheriff remarked.

"Who would that be?" Will Tappan, who was in charge of camp security, asked.

The sheriff leaned an elbow on the counter of the guard shack and scratched the back of his neck. "Anybody been causing trouble? Anybody been caught cutting the fence at night?"

Mr. Tappan shrugged. "They're model people—or prisoners, I guess you'd call them, since they're locked up against their will."

"You know what Walter Lippmann said. The fact they haven't got caught is proof they're up to something," Sheriff Watrous told him.

"The next person who tells me what Walter Lippmann said can eat my shoe. You got any proof one of these boys is responsible, or are you just trying to throw suspicion on them because you're too dumb to find the real killer?"

"Now hold your horses, bub." The sheriff held up his hands. "A little girl's got ravished and killed. We never had any of that in Ellis before the Japanese got here."

"You never had twelve straight days of snow the last of December before they got here, either. Are you going to blame the Japanese for that?" Mr. Tappan took a few seconds to calm down. "Sheriff Watrous, you know you don't have an ounce of proof, or you'd have told me when you walked in here. If you keep talking like that, things'll be rougher'n a cob around here. You'll have half the farmers patrolling the Tallgrass Road with shotguns."

"I know that, and it might not be such a bad thing. Maybe if we'd had patrollers, Susan Reddick wouldn't be lying in a box at the funeral home," Sheriff Watrous said.

Then Dad broke in. "I think the sheriff's hoping to eliminate your boys, Mr. Tappan."

"How's he going to do that, Mr. Stroud?"

Dad suggested the guards check the fence around the camp to see if it had been cut. That could mean someone had crawled under the barbed wire.

"That wouldn't tell you who. We already know kids have been sneaking out. How do you think those three little boys who were scared so bad down by your place got out? Maybe you're thinking they went after the girl."

One of the guards laughed.

"You'd not make a joke of it if you'd seen what was done to little Susan," Sheriff Watrous said.

"Nobody's making a joke of it," Mr. Tappan told him. "I'm just saying if you blame any of these Japanese without you've got proof, there'll be bad trouble in Ellis about it. Folks around here are itching for a reason to go after the Japanese, and you know it. You tell them one of our boys is responsible, and all hell's going to break loose. Now if you've got the proof, you tell me, and I'll bring the boy in here so's you can talk to him. But if you don't, you better go on into Ellis and keep your people from committing a criminal act of their own. This is federal property, and they wouldn't want to get mixed up with the FBI."

When Dad finished telling us about the camp, Bud said, "There's nothing the sheriff can do to calm people down if they get riled up."

Mom nodded. "From what the Jolly Stitchers say, they already are."

BURYINGS WERE ALWAYS A big draw in Ellis, no matter who the dead person was. Mom said people attended services because they wanted to show respect for the deceased and sympathy for their loved ones, but Dad thought it was a way to ensure a big crowd at their own funerals. "Folks take attendance. They remember you weren't at their grandfather's funeral, so they stay away from yours," Dad said. "Most measure a man's importance by how many show up at his service." He might have been right, because I'd heard Mom say that forty-seven, or sixty-eight, or, one time, ninety-seven people had attended a funeral.

That was not the reason so many people turned out for Susan's burying three days after the Reddicks found her in the haystack. Some went because they loved Susan and her folks—well, at least they loved Susan and Mrs. Reddick. That's why Mom and Dad and Granny and I were there. Bud would have gone, too, but his furlough had ended, and he'd had to return to the army. But others wanted to look at poor Susan in her coffin and gawk at her parents. The service was held in the cemetery, and folks drove in from all over the county—Mom counted 147 persons. There were families with kids, couples, and several women standing alone. I wondered if one of them had broken the commandment with Mr. Reddick. My bet was on the woman who was wearing pumps instead of boots and had a half a dozen ermine tails lined up and attached to her coat with a clasp. She was the prettiest lady at the funeral. But why would a woman who looks like that commit adultery with porky Mr. Reddick? I wondered.

As we drove down the road to the cemetery, Dad stopped to pick up a woman who was walking by herself—Helen Archuleta. She hadn't had her baby yet, and she looked tired, but maybe that was because her face was red from crying.

"Your folks are over there," Mom said after Dad parked the truck and we were making our way through the graves.

Helen took Mom's arm and whispered, "They don't want me. Can I stay with you?"

"Maybe all's forgiven," Mom told her.

Helen shook her head. "They didn't even tell me about Susan. I heard what happened at the store." Helen had worked at the soda fountain at the Lee Drug until she started to show. Then, since customers didn't want a pregnant woman waiting on them, Mr. Lee found work for her to do in the back room. "A woman was talking about it, and at first, I didn't even know it was Susan. When I heard, I just cried my eyes out. Mr. Lee had to tell me to go home and rest up. I thought he'd dock me, but he didn't." She turned her head toward her parents, but when her father looked over the crowd, Helen drew her arms close to her sides and stared at the ground.

I felt so sorry for her. What if I'd died, I thought, and my folks wouldn't let Marthalice come to my funeral? I couldn't even imagine that.

"I have a right to be here. She's my sister, after all. It's all right for me to be here, isn't it, Mrs. Stroud?"

"Of course it's all right," Mom told her.

"If the baby's a girl, I'm going to name her Susan."

"Why, I would, too," Granny said. "And if I had a boy, I'd name him Loyal."

"You already did." Dad put his arm around Granny. It was not one of her better days.

I took Helen's hand, which was bare and cold, and said, "Susan missed you. She told me so." I didn't make that up. We'd talked once about how nice it was to have big sisters and how we wished they were still at home. I added, "She was glad I told you she worked on that quilt square. She wanted you to know. She said after your baby came, she was going to ditch school to go see you."

Helen held my hand a minute before putting her own back into her pocket and squeezing her elbows to her sides. "I'm dreadful cold," she whispered, more to herself than to us.

Snow had fallen all day, and the wind stirred it up as we waited for the minister to begin. Men stomped their feet and coughed into their hands. Women tightened the wool scarves tied under their chins. One snuggled her hands deeper into a muff that looked as if it were made from old men's beards. I flattened my earmuffs against my head to keep my ears from stinging. We all wished the funeral would get under way and that it wouldn't last long. I hoped they wouldn't open the lid of the coffin for a viewing. I didn't want to look at Susan's dead face, snow falling onto it. I shivered at the thought, and Mom put her arm around me and drew me close, but it didn't help. The temperature was below zero. It was so cold that the grave diggers had used dynamite to blast a hole in the frozen earth for the grave.

The aching cold might have been the reason the service was indeed short. Or it could have been that the minister didn't know what to say about a little girl who'd been ravished and murdered. He said Susan was brave and good and told us the Lord had His reasons for taking her, which we would understand in the fullness of time. I asked Dad what the fullness of time was, and he said it was when God got around to it. Mother told us both to be still.

I wondered what he would have said if I'd been murdered instead of Susan. That I won the three-legged race with Betty Joyce on field day the year before and came in second in the seventh-grade spelling bee? Or that I did my share of chores without complaining and that I was a good milker? I was glad I wasn't dead, because Mom and Dad would be embarrassed that there wasn't anything more to be said about me. And I'd have hated for people to come across my tombstone and read "Good milker."

We sang "Jesus Loves Me"—Dad, too, and I was surprised that he knew it. I asked Granny once if Dad had gone to church when he was a boy, but it was one of her bad days, and she replied, "I don't know your daddy, dearie."

We finished the service with "Going Home"; then everyone pushed forward to tell the Reddicks how sorry they were. Some wandered to other graves, ones that had been decorated before Christmas. The wreaths and evergreens were brittle now, and the red ribbons were limp from the snow. Helen turned toward the road, and Mom told her to wait in the truck and that we'd drive her to town. I was glad they didn't lower the coffin into the grave then. I couldn't bear to see Susan put into that cold, dark hole and have dirt piled on top of her.

As we walked past Susan's coffin, a woman said, "Why doesn't somebody open the lid? I wouldn't have come all this way if I'd known the lid was going to be closed. I surely would like to see what the Jap did to that little girl." Mom gave her a stern look, and the woman said, "Well, wouldn't you?"

"No," Mom said. "And how do you know who did it?"

"Well who else would? Nothing like that happened around here before the Nips came." The woman looked around to see if anyone agreed with her, and several people nodded.

"It's already started," Dad said after we shook hands with the Reddicks and were walking back to the car.

"What else are people to think, Loyal?" Mom asked. "There are thousands of men in that camp, so there's bound to be a few bad apples, just like with people anywhere."

The five of us crowded together in the cab of Red Boy, and we drove Helen back to the drugstore. Then we went to Fellowship Hall behind the church, where mourners were already waiting for cake and coffee. The cakes, which had been dropped off before the service, were lined up like Christmas packages—devil's food with chocolate icing, white cakes with pink or yellow icing, lemon, caramel. There must have been a year's supply of sugar rations on that table. Mrs. Rubey had brought a German chocolate cake—"It's called a Victory cake now," she whispered to Mom—and Mrs. Jack had made her beet cake. I knew better than to eat that one. Besides, Dad and I always chose Mom's cake because we knew how embarrassed she'd be if nobody ate it. She'd used Granny's recipe to make a Scripture cake. It called for six cups of Jeremiah 6:20 and two cups of Numbers

17:8 and about ten other ingredients that you had to look up in the Bible. But Mom used the recipe so often that she knew that six of Jeremiah 17:11 meant six eggs, and a pinch of Leviticus 2:13 was salt.

Mom put on an apron and stood behind the table, cutting slices of cake and setting them onto plates. I took a piece of cake for Granny and led her to a chair, then went back to the table to help Mom.

People were crowding into the hall, filling it with the smell of wet wool. They stamped their feet, leaving puddles of melted snow. Women took off their scarves and fluffed up their hair. A few men blew their noses. At first, people talked quietly, mumbling greetings and whispering. A man laughed and was hushed. But after a while, the voices rose and folks began to speak in normal tones. As they pointed to the cakes they wanted and the ladies sliced them, they complained about the cold, telling how thick the ice was on the water trough that morning, and more than one claimed that it was so cold, the thermometer got stuck.

"Cold as a witch's tit," Mr. Jack said in a loud whisper, nudging the man next to him. He was as big a jerk as his son.

"What's that, Mr. Jack?" Mom asked.

"Why, I'm just saying I never seen it so cold," he replied, then told her he wanted two kinds of cake. As Mom cut them, I saw that Mrs. Jack's beet cake was still whole. Even her husband wouldn't eat it.

"That man's dumb enough to haul water in a sieve," said Mrs. Gardner, who was standing next to Mom.

Mr. Lee stopped in front of Mom and asked which cake she'd made. Mom pointed to an empty plate. "It's gone, but there's an awful good beet cake here," she said.

Mr. Lee leaned over the table. "Don't try to fool me, Mrs. Stroud. I got some compounds at the drugstore that taste better than that."

When the last people in line had gotten their refreshments, Mom said she thought she'd take a slice out of the beet cake.

"Really?" I asked. Beet cake was slimy and tasted like pig slop. Besides, you would die in agony if you ate something out of the Jack house.

"Duty does not demand that you do so," Mrs. Gardner told her.

"Maybe not, but courtesy does," Mom replied. She cut a piece so big that it looked like three slices had been taken out of the cake. Mom took a bite, pursing her lips a little. Then, looking around to see if anyone was watching, she used her fork to push the cake into the garbage pail.

"Here, Mary. I never could stand a martyr." Mrs. Gardner raised an eyebrow as she handed Mom a piece of lemon cake.

I began picking up dirty plates, carrying them into the kitchen, where women were washing dishes and putting them away. A man handed me his coffee cup and asked if I was the Stroud girl. I told him I was, and he said, "Your dad ought to send you off to school in Denver so's what happened to the Reddick kid don't happen to you."

I stared at him, my mouth open, because that was a terrible thing to hear, especially from someone I didn't know. Maybe that man killed Susan, and I'm next, I thought. I wondered if murderers stalked their victims the way some wild animals did.

"You're as close to that camp as the Reddicks, you know," he continued. It frightened me that he knew where I lived.

"Don't scare the little girl. You don't know for a fact who did this," another man told him.

"Don't I?"

Before the second man could answer, the room became still, and I looked over at the door, where the sheriff was standing, his big felt hat in his hands. He looked uncomfortable at the attention and started for the cake table.

"You got anything to tell us, Sheriff Watrous?" someone asked him.

"When I got something to tell, I'll tell you," he said.

"I guess that means he ain't figured out which Jap done it," Mr. Jack said in a loud voice. "Some sheriff we got here."

Sheriff Watrous took a plate from Mom, then slowly turned to face Mr. Jack. "You think you can do a better job, do you?"

"Shoot, my boy Cleatus could do a better job. If I's you, I'd line up one Jap a day and shoot him, until the son of a bitch confesses."

The minister stepped forward then and said, "Mr. Jack, please remember that you are in the house of God."

Mr. Jack gave him a flinty-eyed look and stomped out, followed by his sons. Others began to leave then, and Mom told the women in the kitchen to go along and she and I would finish cleaning up. In a few minutes, we were almost alone in the hall. Redhead Joe Lee fidgeted and looked at the door, saying maybe he'd best be going. "Take a seat, Red. It's fine to see you. It's fine to see you anytime," Mom said. She offered the men second helpings of cake.

"Looks like it's up to you to find out right quick who murdered Susan Reddick, Hen," Mr. Lee said.

Sheriff Watrous gave him a long look. "I guess I'm the cat in the flypaper right about now."

Mr. Lee shifted in his seat and added, "Oh, I'm not saying you don't know your job. I've done some thinking on this, if you want to hear it."

"You and everybody else." He swiped his hat against his pants leg. "This evening, right after the funeral, somebody drove past the Tallgrass Camp and put a load of buckshot into one of the barracks. Everybody was to dinner and it didn't do no considerable damage. But some lady's never going to use her pretty little teapot again."

5

IN FEBRUARY, SIX MONTHS after the first evacuees arrived at
Tallgrass, Dad went to the camp to find a crew of Japanese men
to help with the sugar beet planting. He and Mom had talked
about hiring some of the inmates ever since the fall harvest, and
she didn't like the idea any better now than she had then. She
knew the Jolly Stitchers would complain about it, especially
since Susan Reddick's killer hadn't been caught. But it couldn't
be helped, Mom said; the beet seed had to go into the ground.
I wasn't keen on Japanese men working on our farm, either.
What if Dad hires the one who attacked Susan and he comes after me, maybe in the barn when Dad's in the fields and Mom's in
the house? I thought.

I wished we could find white men, workers like our old hired
man, who'd taught me to whittle and to snap my fingers. When
baby birds hatched in spring, he'd brought me their broken
shells, which I kept in my room, along with other things I'd

found around the farm—arrowheads, a hornet's nest, a rock
with a leaf impression in it, a gold coin that Dad had picked up
while he was plowing. But the hired men had all gone off to
war. And Mom was right: We had to plant.

Dad talked to Mr. Halleck at the camp, and when he got
home, he told us that three Japanese would be at the farm the
next morning. Mr. Halleck had handpicked them. More would
come for hoeing and harvesting. "They'll be good workers, because the government wants the other farmers to give the Japanese jobs, too. Mr. Halleck hopes I'll spread the word. He said,
'We provide you with stoop labor, and you give our fellows a
way to make money, so they don't hang around the barracks
playing cards and smoking cigarettes.' It's a good thing for them
and for us, too."

"It is if all hell doesn't break loose," Mom said, adding, "Excuse my French. Rennie, would you get my sewing?" I left the
room, found her sewing basket, and, as I returned to the kitchen,
I heard her say, "Just as soon as they know they're to stay out of
the house and away from her, because—" I stepped back into the
kitchen, and she stopped talking, and I knew I'd been sent off on
one of those errands that would get me out of the room so that
Mom and Dad could discuss something. It was obvious she was
telling him those men were to keep clear of me. But that was
okay. I didn't want anything to do with them.

The next morning, the three Japanese showed up just after
breakfast, before I left for school. "There they are," Mom said,
leaning forward to see them from the kitchen window. She
turned to Dad with a surprised look on her face. "Why, Loyal,
they're nothing more than boys. You didn't tell me they were
just young boys." Dad waited while Mom debated with herself.
"They'd better come inside just this once." Dad had known all

along that if Mom took little chicks into the kitchen to keep them warm, she wouldn't let three boys stand out in the cold. Mom knew what he was thinking and said, "Now you watch it, Loyal Stroud."

Dad went to the door and called to the boys, and Carl Tanaka, Emory Kuruma, and Harry Hirano walked up to our back door. When I saw them, I was relieved. They weren't much bigger than I was, and I bet that if they caused me any trouble, I could knock them down. I didn't get into fights the way I had when I was a little kid, but I knew how to punch somebody if I had to.

"They're slight," Mom observed. "The wind could blow them away."

"They're sizable for Japanese, and they know about farm work, at least farm work on the West Coast. I don't see that it's much different from here in Ellis. One of them worked in the lettuce fields and another in a greenhouse. The oldest one, Carl, studied agriculture at college before he got yanked out and sent to the camp." Dad and Mom exchanged a look that said, Imagine if that had happened to Bud.

Mom's hands were in dishwater and she shook them and reached for a towel. She leaned past Dad and called, "You boys come on inside now and get warm."

So the boys came into the house and shook hands with Dad. They bowed as Dad introduced them to Mom, Granny, and me. Mom fluttered around, pulling out chairs and telling the boys to sit down and she'd get hot coffee from the stove. "Or there's tea. Maybe you'd rather have tea," Mom said, speaking each word distinctly and a little too loudly, as if the boys were deaf.

"Coffee's fine. I don't like tea," said Carl, the tallest of the three. He had black eyes and black hair as straight as hay. It stuck out in all directions.

"Oh, you speak English. I'm glad, because I surely don't know Japanese," Mom said.

"Me, neither," Carl told her.

"We're from California," Emory added. "We were born there. All of us." Emory was heavier and a little shorter than Carl, and his eyes looked as if they'd been chiseled into a face that was as smooth as marble. Harry, the third boy, nodded. He was small and wiry and reminded me of a bull calf. He had spaces between his teeth, although none of the boys had buckteeth like the Japanese in the propaganda pictures. By now, I was used to seeing Japanese in Ellis, but these were the first I'd ever talked to. I stared at them.

Mom cleared her throat, and when I looked over at her, she shook her head to tell me to mind my manners. She reached for coffee mugs, thought better of it, and got out cups and saucers. "Did you boys have your breakfast?" she asked.

They nodded. Mom looked around and spotted the tin of divinity she'd made earlier in the week, then passed it around. The divinity was special because Mom had used our sugar rations to make it.

"Little early in the day for candy, isn't it?" Dad asked.

"They'll work it off soon enough under you," Mom told him.

"Wow!" Carl said, biting into the divinity, which looked like clumps of snow. "I never had this. I wish my mother would make it."

"I'll give her the recipe," Mom said. She looked embarrassed then, and she told me later that she should have realized the women in the camp didn't have cooking facilities and ate in a mess hall. "Even if they did have kitchens," I asked, "where would they get sugar to make candy?"

The boys didn't take offense, however, and Carl said, "Thanks, ma'am."

Dad seemed amused and sat there watching Mom chat with the boys. When she got up to make another pot of coffee, Dad finally said, "If you don't mind me breaking up your coffee klatch, Mother, I ought to take these fellows out and show them the beet fields."

"Now don't you let him work you too hard," Mom said as everybody got up. My jaw dropped at that, because Mom had never been soft on hired men. She'd never been soft on me, either.

"Well, they're just boys," Mom said.

As the three followed Dad outside, Carl asked Mom where to set the sacks with their lunches.

She frowned. "I certainly hope they don't think at that camp that we'd let our hired hands make do with a cold dinner," she said. "You come on in at noon, and I'll have a hot meal waiting." As she spoke, Mom gripped the back of a chair and eased onto it.

Dad looked worried, "You sure you're up to it, Mary?"

"Well, of course I'm up to it. Since when can't I cook for farmhands?"

Dad started to protest, but Mom waved him off, telling him that Granny would help.

"You'll eat awful good, then. Mrs. Stroud's as good a cook as there is," Dad told the three.

"Oh, go on, Loyal," Mom said, but she was flattered.

"Good-bye, Miss Mary, Miss Evelina," Harry said, bowing to Mom and then to Granny. Then he bowed at me. "Miss Rennie."

Nobody had ever bowed to me before or called me "Miss" anything, and I liked those three even better. I still wasn't so sure about the camp, but I knew our boys, as we came to think of them, wouldn't hurt anybody.

"You just call her Rennie," Dad said, to my disappointment.

As they went out the door, Mom leaned forward, her hand gripping the table, and called, "*Sayonara,* boys." I think she'd learned the word from a moving picture.

Carl turned back, grinned, and said, "*Sayonara* yourself, ma'am."

AFTER THAT, THE BOYS stopped in the kitchen each morning for coffee before heading out to the fields with Dad. They were just like Ellis High School kids, talking about movies and cars and how they would spend their wages. Sometimes, I had to stop and remember that they were Japanese and that they lived in a prison and couldn't own automobiles or go to the pictures whenever they wanted to and that most of their pay went to help their families.

Not long after the three came to work for us, Mr. Gardner hired a Japanese crew to work his beet fields. Other farmers did the same thing. Still, many people in Ellis were skeptical of employing the Japanese. Others were more than skeptical. They were just plain mean. Mom found a dead cat hanging on our gate, which made her cry, because she hated it when anybody was cruel to an animal. It was a wild cat, but she made Dad dig a hole and bury it anyway. Somebody pitched manure into the bed of Red Boy when it was parked in town, and a man at the feed store called Dad a "Jap lover."

"What did you reply to that?" Mom asked.

"I said, 'Well, bub, we got a difference of opinion.' He was just beating his gums, so I went about my business."

"Didn't you fight him?" I asked. Bud and I were proud of how Dad always came out on top. He had shown me a thing or two with my fists, and I was pretty good, too.

Dad blew out his breath and hooked his thumbs in the straps of his overalls. "Squirt, I reckon my fighting days are over. Socking a fellow gets his attention, but it doesn't do much to change his mind. I hope you'll remember that." He glanced at Mom, who looked skeptical. "I expect after a bit they'll forget about the boys," Dad added. "Things might be better if they caught the fellow who killed the Reddick girl, though."

Mom agreed with that, and so did I. At night, I shut my window so that nobody could get in, and when I walked to town, I looked behind me every so often to see whether anyone was following me. I even checked the stalls in the barn before I did the milking.

After we hired the boys, Doris Davidson, one of the Jolly Stitchers, refused to meet at our house, telling Mom she didn't want to fraternize with the enemy. Mrs. Davidson was short and round, with white curls like bedsprings.

"Does she mean the boys, or the rest of the bees?" Dad asked.

"I couldn't say." Mom laughed. "Doris does try my Christian forbearance sometimes. Maybe it's good for me. After all, the Bible says, 'Tribulation worketh patience.'"

"What's that mean?" Dad asked.

"If you went to church, you'd understand."

"Oh, so you don't know, either."

The Stitchers met at our house anyway, and Mrs. Davidson stayed home. Mrs. Rubey told Mom, "Aren't you the lucky one, Mary. Now you won't have to take out her toenail stitches." *Toenail stitches* were so big that you could catch your toenail in them. Mom was a good quilter and proud of her work, and she always examined her quilts after the Stitchers went home. More than once, she had handed me a pair of scissors and told me to rip out Mrs. Davidson's stitches.

I had my own problems. I didn't tell anyone that Dad had hired the boys, but the word got out right off. I found a cartoon of three evil-looking Japanese men with thick glasses in my desk at school, with the words "Shut your traps to the Japs" printed on it.

One morning, Edna Elliot, a high school girl and Pete Elliot's sister, backed me up against the slide in the school yard. Edna didn't like me, although I'd never figured out why. When we were little kids, Edgar Rubey called Edna "bacon face" and then made oinking sounds, because Edna was as fat as a hog for slaughter.

Edna cried, and I told Edgar he stank and to take it back. Edgar was mean to tease Edna, but mostly, I was still mad at him for charging me interest on that bet on the state capital of New York.

"You going to make me?" he'd asked.

"Yeah."

So Edgar punched me, and I bloodied his nose, and we both got sent to the principal's office, and the word got around that Edna was too fat to defend herself. Maybe she blamed me instead of Edgar for calling attention to her size, and she'd been waiting all these years to get even. I guess that morning in the school yard, she figured her chance had come. "Your dad's cheap enough to skin a skunk to save a scent," Edna said.

"Oh yeah! He is not!" That wasn't the cleverest thing I'd ever said. Comebacks usually hit me when I was going home from school.

"He is, too. That's why he hires Japs. Those dirty Japs killed Susan Reddick."

"Says who?" You could fill a book with my brilliant remarks that morning.

"Everybody knows it except a dope like you." Edna's friend Marjorie grabbed my lunch box and opened it. "I bet the Strouds eat seaweed and raw fish." She threw my sandwich on the ground, then turned over the lunch box and spilled the rest of the contents, stepping on each waxed paper–wrapped packet. I was mortified, wondering if everybody on the playground was watching me. Dad had done the right thing in hiring the boys, but part of me wished he'd tried harder to find some white men to work the beets. It wasn't easy having people hate us.

As I looked down at my lunch, deciding I'd go hungry before I'd stoop to pick up the smashed food, Edna suddenly socked me in the chest. She wasn't very coordinated, but she was fat; if she really had been a pig, she'd have rendered out a year's worth of lard, but I didn't dare tell her that because she packed a wallop. She hit me again, knocking my head against the slide, and I fell to the ground.

I looked around for Betty Joyce. Her father had gotten kicked in the head by a mule when he was loading a roll of barbed wire onto a wagon and was laid up, however, so she'd missed a good deal of school. Now I was on my own. I knew I could take on the three of them, because they were flabby and uncoordinated and I was good with my fists. But I remembered Dad saying he'd given up fighting, and I knew he'd be disappointed if I hit Edna. "What'd you do that for?" I asked, rubbing the sore spot on my head and brushing dirt off my coat as I got to my feet.

"Give that to your old man," Edna said, looking at her friends, who laughed and said, "Good one, Edna."

"Yeah, tell your dad if he doesn't get rid of his Jap workers, there's more where that came from," Ardis, another fat girl, said. The three of them were like coyotes, which weren't worth much on their own, but they built up courage when they were in a pack.

Marjorie added, "Your mom chews, too." She giggled.

"She does not!"

"Her old man thinks he's such a big shot, but he's nothing but a lousy beet farmer," Edna told them, then turned back to me. She took off her coat and handed it to Marjorie. "Come on, put up your dukes, you little traitor." She made awkward fists with her hands. The others did the same thing, although they stood behind Edna.

"You're a coward," Edna said.

I couldn't let her get away with that. Still, I didn't slug her. Instead, I grabbed Edna's braids, one in each hand, and yelled, "You take it back or I'll snatch you bald-headed!" Edna dug in then, so pulling her was like tugging at a stubborn calf. As I yanked, the barrettes fastened to the ends of her braids came off in my hands. I let go to throw the barrettes on the ground, and Edna almost fell over. But I grabbed the braids again. "Take it back!"

Edna's friends looked at each other, either too surprised or too scared of me to come to Edna's aid. Finally, Marjorie spotted a teacher and yelled, "Miss Ord. Rennie Stroud's beating up on Edna, and Edna didn't do anything to her. Rennie started it."

Ardis added, "Yeah, her father's a Jap lover, too."

"She stole a boiled egg once," Edna called. Turning to me, she added, "I think she's going to lock you in the closet with crawly things. That's what I'm thinking."

My mouth felt sour as I remembered having to stand in a closet in grade school for the egg I hadn't stolen. I didn't know Miss Beatrice Ord. She'd come to Ellis in January to replace a teacher in one of the older grades who'd joined the WACs. But the other girls knew her, so I was sure she'd take their side.

The new teacher came over to us and said, "Rennie, you can let go of Edna's hair now."

"She started it," Edna said. Her friends nodded. "She called me a name."

The teacher looked hard at me, but I didn't say anything, because I figured she wouldn't believe me. It was three against one. I wondered if I'd get detention or be suspended from school. Miss Ord might send home a note telling Mom I'd been fighting. My folks wouldn't punish me, but they'd feel I'd let them down, and that would be worse.

Miss Ord said, "Rennie must be awfully brave to take on three girls who are big enough to whip her." She cocked her head and ran her tongue over her teeth as she studied Edna. "Especially after one of you knocked her against the slide and she banged her head."

Edna gave the teacher a self-righteous look. "My dad says we have to protect ourselves against people who are un-American. My dad's on the school board." Her sash had come loose, and she yanked at the two ends, pulled them straight, and retied the sash behind her back. But she did it the wrong way, and the bow was vertical. She took her coat from Marjorie and put it on. The sleeve was folded in on itself, and she pushed to get her arm through it. There was a ripping sound.

"I know he's on the school board," Miss Ord said. "Doesn't that mean you ought to be an example for others?" She smiled.

"No such thing. I don't have to do anything," Edna said, pouting.

Miss Ord turned starchy. "Go to your classroom, Edna, and take your friends with you. If I see any one of you picking on a younger girl again, I'll report you to the principal. Rennie, you come with me."

As Miss Ord turned away, Edna stuck out her tongue at me and said, "Now you're going to get it." She turned to Marjorie and Ardis. "Come on, girls. We don't want to have anything to do with her."

I followed Miss Ord to the fence that surrounded the school yard, where she stopped and turned, her hand resting on the mangled wire. She was too pretty to be a teacher. She had a figure like a pinup, wore her blond hair in a peekaboo style, and her gray eyes sparkled in the sunlight like polished silver. "Your father hired some boys from the camp to help with the beets, didn't he?" Miss Ord asked.

"Yes, ma'am." I figured she'd pick up where Edna had let off.

"How do you feel about that?"

"It's okay." I didn't want to discuss it with her. It was bad enough taking on a stupid girl like Edna. If I argued with a teacher, I'd get detention for sure. Still, I wouldn't let her put down my dad, and I was ready to talk back if I had to.

"I'm from California. I grew up with Japanese boys and girls. They're hard workers."

I nodded, running my hand along the wire fence, stopping to test a broken end with my thumb. I wondered whether I was being set up.

"They'll do a good job for your father, and because of that, other farmers will hire them. I understand a few have already."

I looked up at her. She was standing with her back to the sun, and I had to squint to make out her face. "Don't you think he's aiding the enemy?" I asked.

"Why no. Do you?"

I shaded my eyes as I took a good look at Miss Ord. She was the only teacher I'd ever seen who wore lipstick and rouge. "No, ma'am. You're about the first one who doesn't."

"Mr. Stroud's a fine man. If there were more like him in Ellis, we wouldn't have such acrimony. Do you know what that word means?"

I didn't, but I nodded. Later when I asked Dad, he replied, "It rhymes with matrimony." He grinned at Mom, who swatted him. I didn't think it had anything to do with matrimony.

Miss Ord thought for a minute. Then she said, "Here's what I want to tell you: Your father's stood up to a good bit of criticism lately. Do you know that several men have called him names?" I nodded. "He's taken it without resorting to striking them, although I have an idea he's pretty good with his fists. You will hinder his good work if you fight with bullies like Edna Elliot."

I looked over to where a little boy had grabbed hold of one of the rings hanging on chains from a circular apparatus that looked like a backyard clothesline. He made it to the second, then the third, and finally the fourth ring before he fell onto the dirt. I rooted for him to get up and try again, but he didn't. I turned back to Miss Ord. "I didn't start it."

"I know that. I was watching. And I understand why you grabbed Edna's hair. I was hoping you wouldn't, but I probably would have done the same thing. In fact, I've been tempted to do something similar with a few of the teachers here." She smiled when I gaped. I couldn't believe that teachers fought. "Now, can you understand, Rennie, that you will be much more effective if you just walk away?"

"Kids will think I'm yellow."

"They'll think you have principles. They might even respect you. You and your dad." Miss Ord thought that over and laughed a little. "No, that's saying too much. A few might respect you, but not all of them. Still, I believe you'll have less trouble if you just keep your chin up and don't get lured into fighting everybody who calls your father names. Nobody's thought the less of him because he's refused to fight. I believe he would not want you to fight, either. Am I right?"

I shrugged. I wasn't sorry I had pulled Edna's hair, but I was glad now I hadn't socked her.

"I thought you'd agree."

The first bell rang, and kids started for the building, but both Miss Ord and I ignored it. "Why do you care?" I asked.

I thought she would tell me then that she wanted what was best for all little boys and girls, or that it was her job to mold future citizens, the kind of thing teachers always said. Instead, she replied, "Oh, someday, I'll tell you a little secret." She smiled. "Someday, when the war is over. For now, I want you to understand that there are people in Ellis who are on your father's side—and on yours. I count myself among them."

I smiled to show Miss Ord that I appreciated what she'd said. Then I told her, "It probably doesn't matter. Dad says people will get over the evacuees pretty quick now."

BUT FOLKS DIDN'T GET over the Japanese. Late one night, a couple of weeks after my fight with Edna Elliot, the traffic on the Tallgrass Road woke me up. I was used to cars and trucks driving along the road at all hours, but this was more traffic than usual. I went to the window, but I couldn't see anything on the road, although I could smell the dust the tires sent up and hear the engine noise. When I realized the cars were driving without their lights on, I started to go downstairs to tell Dad.

He was already awake. His voice came through the register in the floor of my room. "I tell you, Hen, it seems like twenty or thirty cars have come past here in the last ten minutes, and you know each one's got three or four men in it. I don't know for sure they're stopping at the camp, but this time of night, driving with their lights out, they're up to no good. What's that?" Dad paused. "Of course Tallgrass has got guards. You know that. But they're just young boys. Halleck and Tappan are both in Denver. I saw them at the depot this morning and told them right there that with the way the town is all riled up, they ought not to leave at the same time. I think it'd be a good idea if you came out. The camp jurisdiction just goes to the fence. You're the law on the road." He listened a moment. "I appreciate that. I'll take the shotgun and cut across the field to meet you there." Dad was silent, then said, "No, don't call Reddick. He's most likely in on it. And, Hen, my womenfolk are all asleep, so don't turn on the siren." He pronounced the word *si-reen*.

I knew if I asked Dad to let me go along, he'd say no, so without a sound, I dressed in the dark. After Dad left the house, I sneaked downstairs and started off after him, keeping far enough behind him that I could barely see his dark bulk. Halfway across the field, I stumbled over a clod of dirt and went tumbling into a gully; our farm was sliced with them. Dad turned and looked around, but I lay still, so in a minute, he started up again. I followed a little farther back now, because I could see him easily in the light coming from the camp's floodlights.

I saw the cars now, too, maybe two dozen of them, parked on either side of the road. There really had been no reason for the drivers to keep their lights off when they drove to the camp, because we could see the cars as plain as day—and the men, too. They were getting out of the cars and gathering in the middle of the road in front of the entrance to Tallgrass. A car door slammed, and somebody said, "Damn!" and a man called, "You hush up back there."

They didn't hush. Instead, the men talked in low voices, sounding like bees swarming. There was the sound of broken glass, and an angry voice said, "Now see what you've gone and done. You've made me break it."

"Here's you another bottle, then," a second voice said.

"Hell, Frank, this stuff's sour. You saving the good stuff for the high school kids?"

"The good stuff goes to them that pays."

"Anybody got a cigarette?" a man asked. "I can't think without I got a cigarette."

"Moocher." The men laughed.

A voice said, "Take this smoke and shut up. We ain't at the pool hall."

Dad had stopped inside the fence across from the gate, his shotgun in the crook of his arm. I slid down beside a fence post, where he couldn't see me. Nobody saw Dad, either, which was a good thing. Dad could fight one or two or even three men, but he couldn't stand off half the male population of Ellis. When I looked up at the guard towers and saw faces peering out of the windows, I realized Dad wasn't alone. But there weren't enough guards to take on all the men in the road.

The men quieted down then. They began talking together in voices so low that I couldn't hear them. I wondered if they had a plan, or if coming to Tallgrass was just whiskey talk. Maybe somebody had started talking big at the pool hall and they'd all piled into cars and driven out to the camp. Whoever it was might have known that both Mr. Halleck and Mr. Tappan were away, and he'd made the rounds of the pool hall and Jay Dee's, gathering up men. They milled around the cars now, not sure what to do.

At last, someone in the crowd called up to the guards. "You send out the boy that killed the Reddick girl."

"Which one's that?" a guard yelled. His voice sounded young and high-pitched and scared.

The men talked for a few minutes, and one called back. "I guess you better figure that out right quick."

"We don't want to hurt you up there, boy," added a man who sounded like Mr. Jack. "There's more of us than you.

"You're responsible for the women and children in there. Any one of them gets hurt, it's on your head," called a man who wore a white cowboy hat. I knew that hat. It belonged to Mr. Elliot.

"We got reinforcements coming," a guard yelled. "You men go about your business."

"Protecting our families against the Japs *is* our business," a man yelled back.

"Just ask Reddick here," Mr. Jack added.

Dad moved a little closer to the fence. I wondered what would happen if one of the men shot a guard. Would Dad shoot him? I didn't like Mr. Jack, but he was our neighbor, and I'd never heard of anybody shooting a neighbor. Dad wasn't scared of anything, but I couldn't see that he'd shoot a man, no matter the circumstances.

"I guess we better go on in there and look around for ourselves," a man said. There was a murmur of voices and the sound of shells being chambered. Then the whole group started toward the gate.

"You men stand aside," a voice yelled down from the guard tower. "We'll shoot if we have to." I doubted that. I'd seen the guards in town, young men mostly, not much older than Bud.

They hung out at the drugstores and the pool hall and probably knew the men who were swarming toward the gate.

Dad straightened up and took his gun in his hands, and I guessed he'd figured out what he was going to do. But before he could take a step, a voice called, "Yoo-hoo, Mr. Davidson. How's Doris doing? Is she over the flu yet?"

The men stopped, and one of them—Mr. Davidson, it had to be—turned around and asked in an incredulous voice, "How's that?"

"I asked how Doris is getting along. I meant to take her a cake, but the time got away from me." Mom's voice trembled a little, but she stood firm, her hands out to her sides as she stood alone in the field. The men turned to stare at her.

"Why, Mr. Smith, hello there. I just saw Bird at Quilters. My, that woman can sew!" Mom sounded as calm then as if she were calling to friends after church.

"Uh, yeah," Mr. Smith said, shaking his head, bewildered.

"You give her my regards," Mom said. "And Mr. Reddick, oughten you to be home with Opal? I know she doesn't like to be by herself in the house at night."

Mr. Reddick put his hands on his head and didn't reply.

Mom called to half a dozen men, naming each one, as if it were the most normal thing in the world for her to be standing in a field in the middle of the night, her hair in pin curls, a coat over her nightgown.

"You better get back home, Miz Stroud," a man told her.

"This is my home," Mom said firmly. "These are my fields. I came out to see what the ruckus was all about. I wouldn't like anything bad happening here."

The men looked at one another. Some kicked at the dirt with their shoes. "Why doesn't she git?" a man muttered.

"You get her out of here," another man told him.

Then someone ejected the shells from his shotgun.

"Ah hell, let's go," one of the men growled at last. He left the group and went to a car, then started the engine.

"Wait up," someone called, hurrying off and climbing into the passenger seat. Slowly, the men went to their cars, grumbling and slamming doors. They turned on the engines and the lights. One of the cars went on past the camp and pulled off at the Reddick farm, but the others turned around and headed back toward town.

Both Mom and Dad stayed where they were—and so did I—until the troublemakers were gone and a man emerged from the darkness. "That was mighty fine, Mrs. Stroud," Sheriff Watrous said. "I wasn't sure myself just how we was going to diffuse the situation. I guess you took it in your own hands."

Now that the men were gone, Mom looked unsteady, and Dad hurried over and put his arm around her. "Whatever made you do that, Mary?" he asked.

Mom gave a queer little laugh. "I don't know myself. I heard you on the phone, so I just came out to see what was going on. It hit me that if I named them, they might be ashamed enough to leave. Men in packs are one thing. But they aren't so brave when they have to stand by themselves."

"You're right about that," the sheriff told her. "I guess there are some young boys up there in those guard towers that are awful glad you came along. I'll give you folks a ride back to the house. I'm parked just down the road a little," the sheriff said. I shivered, thinking I'd have to walk back across the fields by myself and sneak into the house.

"We'd appreciate that," Dad told him. He put his arm around Mom and started toward the fence. But Mom stopped and looked around, and then she held out her hand to me. Dad looked startled when he saw me, and Mom said, "If I hadn't heard Rennie leave the house behind you, Loyal, I might not have come."

DAD WAS PLEASED WITH the way the boys took over the planting. He said that all he'd had to do was explain how to prepare the fields, and the boys had gone to work and done it—and done it better than any hired hands he'd ever had. They didn't loaf when he wasn't around. If he went to town and came back two hours later, they'd put in two hours' work.

Each morning, Dad and the boys planned the day as they drank coffee at the kitchen table. They always bowed to Granny when they came in and asked about her health. Carl explained to us that the Japanese honored their old people. Granny didn't always know who the boys were, but she beamed whenever they said "Good morning, Miss Evelina." Sometimes they talked about the war news or asked if we'd heard from Bud, who'd gotten shipped off to Europe not long after Christmas. We hadn't been happy when he wrote to us about it, because we'd hoped he'd manage to stay in the States. But at least Bud hadn't gone to the South Pacific. Dad didn't have to say how much that would have complicated things at home. I wondered if he would have hired the boys if Bud had gone to fight the Japanese.

Although the boys sometimes talked about the hostility at Tallgrass, they spoke mostly of everyday things, such as how people were adjusting to their close quarters or what craft classes were offered at the school. They never talked about Susan's death, which Dad said must have had a big impact on the camp, or the Ellis men who'd gathered at Tallgrass that night. If they knew Mom had scared away the men, the boys didn't mention it. And although we knew that some of the Japanese men at Tallgrass who were considered troublemakers had been sent off to one of the tougher internment camps in California, the boys never said anything about that, either. We didn't find out until long afterward that Emory's father was one of them.

They did talk about the evacuees who had joined the army, however. Harry said once that he sure would like to join, maybe after the beet harvest, but Emory asked why he'd want to fight for a country that took away his rights. "We're second-class citizens, and no mistake," Emory said. Carl told him to shut up.

One morning, Dad was explaining how he wanted the boys to operate the beet drill. "We'll plant four pounds of seed per acre. That means you have to keep your speed right at two and a half miles per hour," he said.

"Mr. Gardner says he plants six pounds at three miles," Carl said. Then he explained, "My cousin works for him."

"Some like to make time, but I find this works best for me," Dad said.

Harry asked how they could tell the speed of Dad's old beet drill.

"You walk alongside the drill for twenty seconds. Make your strides long, thirty-five inches. You count how many you take in that twenty seconds, then divide by ten. That gives you your speed."

"We better let Carl do the walking. He's got the biggest feet," Emory said, and he pounded Carl on the back.

"And you do the talking, because you got the biggest mouth," Carl replied.

Mom laughed along with the boys, then got up to get the coffeepot. She sat back down suddenly, her hand on her chest.

"Loyal." She took a deep breath. "Help me to my bed, Loyal. It's my heart," she gasped.

Dad grabbed her before she could slide to the floor, then half led, half carried her into the bedroom.

Mom had been tired a lot, since before the camp opened, but she'd never had a spell like that. Suddenly, I wondered if she was sick, really sick, and she and Dad had been hiding it from me. I loved Mom more than anything in the world. She had always been our family's strength. We wouldn't have made it through the Depression without her. She'd scrimped so that we could pay the bills that kept the farm going, and she'd built up Dad's spirits when he was ready to quit. What if something happens to her? I thought. How could Dad and I could go on without her?

I looked at Granny, but she was licking her spoon, not paying attention. So I stared at the bedroom doorway, stared so hard that my eyes hurt. I clenched my hands and let my fingernails dig into my palms. Finally, Dad came back to the kitchen and sat down at the table, his head in his hands. He ran his fingers back through his hair, which had streaks of gray in it. I hadn't noticed them before. Without looking up, he said, "Your mother didn't want to tell you, Rennie, but you're old enough to know what's going on. She's got heart trouble, had it for a while. She visited with a doctor last fall when she went to Denver to see Marthalice, and he wanted her to take to her bed right away. But you know your mother. She wouldn't hear of it. She was afraid you and Granny would have to do all her work." Dad looked up at me with sad eyes, eyes too old for him. His face was strained and wrinkled.

Emory got up and poured coffee into Dad's cup, and I thought it was a measure of how much the boys had become part of our family that Dad would talk about Mom's health in front of them.

"She doesn't have to cook for us. We can start bringing our lunch," Harry offered, and the other two nodded.

"Mrs. Stroud wouldn't like for you fellows to have to eat a cold dinner," Dad said. He picked up his coffee cup, looked into it, and set it down without drinking. He told us he'd been thinking of hiring a neighbor lady to come in, maybe one of the Jolly Stitchers. "But who's got time to spare during beet season?"

We sat there thinking, when suddenly Granny jumped up and said, "Oh, I forgot all about my cake." She rushed to the stove and opened the door, but the oven was cold, and there was no sign of a cake. "Somebody ate it." She began crying.

"It's all right, Granny. Mary put it in the cupboard," Dad said. But Mom hadn't put it into the cupboard, because there hadn't been any cake.

"There's Granny to think about, too." Dad sighed. "It seems like her mind wanders out of her head more and more now. I don't know what we'll do."

I did, and I knew what I had to say. But I was silent for a long time, trying to get up the courage. There was no other solution. So in a rush, before I could change my mind, I blurted out, "I'll stay out of school to help. I'll go back when Mom's better." That was the hardest thing I'd ever had to say in my life. I knew if I quit school, I wouldn't go back. Girls never did. I'd seen so many of them leave high school and sometimes even grade school to raise younger brothers and sisters or take the places of mothers who were sick or who'd died. Sometimes girls married when they weren't much older than I was, just to get away from that drudgery. Still, nobody had to tell me that we were more important as a family than we were as individuals. Farm kids knew the farm mattered more than they did. If Mom and Dad needed me, school came second. I felt tears forming and squeezed the backs of my eyes so that I wouldn't cry. I didn't want Dad to know how awful I felt.

He sighed and looked at me a long time before he spoke. "Not on your life," he said at last. "Your mother would shoot me. She's got plans for you." Looking toward the bedroom, he reached over and squeezed my hand. "But you're a good girl to offer, Rennie, an awful good girl."

I tried not to let him show how relieved I was. "Maybe Marthalice could move home for a little while," I suggested.

"No," Dad said quickly. "No, that wouldn't do."

The boys had finished their coffee, and Carl took their cups to the sink, washed them, and put them into the dish drainer.

"I'll think on this. It's time to get to work," Dad said, standing up and reaching for his plaid wool jacket on a hook beside the door.

Before Dad could put on his coat, however, Carl said, "Mr. Stroud."

Dad looked over at him.

"My sister could help out."

"Your sister?" Dad frowned. Carl had never mentioned his sister. I hadn't thought much about the boys having families. I guess I felt their lives centered around us.

"She's got a job in the laundry at the camp, but I know she'd rather work for Mrs. Stroud. Daisy works hard. She used to clean houses on Saturdays. She can cook, too."

"Well, I don't know," Dad said.

Carl added quickly, "Not just Japanese food. Ham and eggs, meat loaf, sardines and crackers, stuff you people eat." Carl walked close to the living room door and said in a loud voice, in case Mom was listening, "She sews real good."

"Maybe she can join the Jolly Stitchers," Dad said, and looked at me out of the corner of his eye.

Carl looked confused, because he'd seen the Jolly Stitchers the day they met at our house. "I don't think so, Mr. Stroud. Daisy's eighteen. She's not an old lady."

"Don't say that too loud, son," Dad told him.

SO DAISY CAME TO work for us. Mom and Dad fussed about it for a week before Mom agreed to give Daisy a try. She wasn't keen on the idea. It was one thing having the boys working in the fields, even coming into the kitchen of a morning. But what would her friends think if she had a girl from the camp right in the house? "Henrietta Kruger will say we've been invaded by the Japanese," Mom said.

"Why don't you tell her the Japanese are all right but that you have doubts about the Germans?" I suggested, and Dad snorted. He was sprawled in an easy chair he'd dragged into the bedroom so that he could sit beside the bed where Mom was resting. If we sat with her every few minutes, she was less liable to get up.

Then Mom said she didn't like the idea of another woman in her kitchen, but Dad scoffed. "You'll get used to her just like you did the boys. I never heard you say you were crazy about washing dishes anyway."

"The money—" Mom said, but Dad interrupted.

"I pay the boys nineteen dollars a month. Daisy'll get fifteen. But if that's too much, I reckon we could always keep Rennie out of school."

"Over my dead body," Mom said. I looked at her, startled, and Mom laughed and said, "That's a joke, Rennie." Mom had assured us that she wasn't going to die, that she only needed rest, but we still worried about her.

"Daisy'll be here only until you're feeling better, which, bless God, won't be too long," Dad said.

"I didn't know you were acquainted with the Lord."

"How can you be a farmer and not believe in something? Besides, I've got to have somebody to blame for not sending rain."

Doc Enyeart said hiring Daisy was a good idea. "I guess you don't have to rest if you don't want to get well, Mary," he told her one afternoon. "But if you're planning on living awhile longer, you'd best find a hired girl." He'd come to see Mom after going to Betty Joyce's place, and Mom asked how Mr. Snow was doing. Betty Joyce was still missing school to help in the store.

"Sometimes the cure is worse than the affliction."

"What are you saying, Doc?"

"I'm not saying a thing. Illness is hard on the best of men."

"I know that, and Gus Snow isn't the best of men," Mom said. "Illness is hard on women, too."

"Women bear up better, in my experience."

"They haven't got a choice. If you ask me, Tessie Snow has the worst of it, running that hardware store with next to no help. She's all in."

"Gus helps when he can. They live behind the store, you know. He sits in the back room and tells her what to do."

"I'd consider that less than no help."

When the Jolly Stitchers found out Mom was ailing, they brought their casseroles and cakes, their cabbage rolls and carrot puddings. Mom drew strength from the women, even those she didn't like so much, because their calling on her showed they cared. I learned a great deal about women during that time, about how in tough times, they pulled together, looked out for one another. They brought their first daffodils to Mom and sewed on their quilt squares while they gossiped and assured her she'd be all right. As the women took turns sitting in the easy chair next to the bed, Mom told them she was going to hire a girl from the camp. If they heard about Daisy from her, she thought, they might not be as critical. Mom was wrong about that.

"Mary Stroud! Have you forgotten poor Susan Reddick?" Bird Smith asked. "It's a day that should always be remembered." Mrs. Smith was a stocky woman who wore a black wool coat and anklets with her high-heeled oxfords. Her clothes were too small for her. She told the Jolly Stitchers once that she always ordered them from the Montgomery Ward catalog, and that she'd been the same size since Woodrow Wilson was elected—the first term.

"Do you mean the same size as Woodrow Wilson?" Mrs. Gardner had asked. Mrs. Smith had sent her a stern look, but the other Stitchers had giggled.

"Of course I haven't forgotten about Susan Reddick," Mom replied, scratching at the tail of a piece of floss that had come loose on her embroidered pillow. Mom was propped up against a design of windmills and Dutch girls. "I don't see what my hiring a Japanese girl has to do with Susan getting killed." Mom looked directly at her, and I wondered if Mrs. Smith knew her husband had been one of the men at Tallgrass. If she did, she didn't mention it. But then, nobody ever talked about that night.

"It was a Jap that done it. Everybody knows that."

"It certainly wasn't a Japanese *girl*."

"It could have been a Jap girl that left that door unlocked." Mrs. Smith's mouth was a thin, straight line, and she clutched her pocketbook against her coat. I hadn't offered to take her coat because I knew that Mom didn't want her staying long. If Mrs. Smith settled in and took out her stitching, she'd be there till the second hoeing.

"The Reddicks didn't employ any Japanese."

"Oh," Mrs. Smith said. "I think that's beside the point. But it's your fudge. I guess I'll let you cook it."

Mom lay back against the pillows and sent me a pleading look. So I went to her side and said, "The doctor's going to get mad again if you don't rest up."

Mrs. Smith stood up. "I just came to cheer you, Mary. That's all."

"And you have, Bird, you and your liver pudding. How can I ever thank you?"

When I walked her to the door, Mrs. Smith told me, "That pudding's for your mother, little girl. You're not to eat it."

"Oh, no, ma'am. I wouldn't eat it in a million years."

Mrs. Reddick came after that. When I told her that Mom was asleep, she asked, "Will you let me just sit by her side? It gets so I can't stand to be at home sometimes." So Mrs. Reddick sat in the easy chair, her little spotted hands folded in her lap while she stared at the roses on the wallpaper; then she lifted her eyes to the ceiling, which was papered in a brown-and-white feather design. After a while, she began piecing a Sunbonnet Sue block, just like those in the bloodied quilt I'd found in Susan's room. I couldn't imagine why she'd make another quilt in that design, but she must have had her reasons.

"Rennie should have woke me," Mom said when she opened her eyes.

"I told her not to. There's nothing that heals like sleep," Mrs. Reddick said.

"Do you sleep, Opal?"

Mrs. Reddick shook her head, then said brightly, "I brought you an apple brown Betty."

"In the midst of tribulation, you are thinking of others." Mom patted Mrs. Reddick's hand and studied her a moment before saying that a girl from the camp was coming to work for us. I thought Mrs. Reddick wouldn't approve of that, but she said, "Why, that's fine, Mary. Elmo hired me the little Jack girl, the one who's so slow. He told her he couldn't pay her much, and she said that was okay, since she didn't work much."

"And was she right?"

"Oh, yes," Mrs. Reddick said. "I don't mind. I like having someone there. It just gets so lonely." Her lip trembled, and she bit down on it. Then she took Mom's hand and said, "I wish I had one of my girls."

"Elmo won't let Helen come home?"

"He won't let me even mention Helen. He says she's not worth it, that she shamed us by marrying Bobby Archuleta, who's no good. He's right, of course. Bobby scared me a little, and maybe he scared Helen, too. Just a year ago, I had two daughters. Now I've got none." She stood and squeezed Mom's hand. "It's turkey one day, feathers the next. But when I'm in town, I sneak into the drugstore to see Helen. She works there. She has a little girl now, named for Susan."

I was getting to feel like a regular stationmaster by the time Mrs. Larsoo called. She was as big as a silo and old, and she carried a handkerchief because her nose ran for no reason. She touched the wrinkled square of cotton to her face and asked Mom how she was feeling, but before Mom could reply, Mrs. Larsoo said, "That Jap girl isn't to sew with the Jolly Stitchers. She might stitch some secret message into the quilt."

Mom, who was resting on the sofa with an afghan over her, chuckled and asked, "Now what could a girl from the camp know that she could relay to anybody?"

Mrs. Larsoo sniffed. "You can't be too careful." She, too, took out a quilt square, a V for Victory design done in browns and blacks, and began embroidering around the *V*s with heavy black floss in a chicken-scratch design.

"We're not making quilts for Tojo, Iris. The next one, that Lady in the White House quilt, goes to the minister at the church."

"There you are. The girl's probably a Buddha or something. She'll stitch a message from the Antichrist into it."

"Daisy's family is Methodist," Mom told her.

"You are making a mistake, Mary. I am wiser than you. I am seventy-six years of age." She looped the floss around her needle and made a big black knot like a squashed fly.

Mom sighed. "Why tell me, Iris? I don't have anything to do with your age."

THE DAY BEFORE DAISY went to work for us, I came out of the A&P and found Beaner Jack sitting on the bench near the door, cleaning his fingernails with his pocketknife. "I hear you got a Jap sister now," he said. I was sorry he knew about Daisy. Why does everybody seem to know about our business? I wondered.

"She's going to be the hired girl."

"You think she can see the dirt with those slanty eyes?" asked Danny Spano, who was hunched over beside Beaner, his forearms on his thighs.

"Careful the yellow don't rub off on your dishes," Beaner said, and they both cracked up.

"Good one, Beaner." Edna Elliot came out of the store just then and stood so close to me that I had to move aside.

Beaner looked up at Edna. "Well, I'm damned. Did you say something, fatso?"

Edna's face fell, and her lower lip trembled. She glanced at me out of the corner of her eye, but I decided lightning would strike her dead before I'd defend her again. Then Danny said, "Ah, can it, Beaner. She's okay."

"You want her, you take her." Beaner pinched Danny's arm so hard that Danny flinched. "So long, boy."

Danny got up and stood a little ways apart.

I started for home down the Tallgrass Road, and after a few minutes I had a feeling that someone was behind me. I turned quickly, thinking it was one of the Japanese from the camp. Instead, it was Danny, and he yelled, "Hey." I kept on going, hoping he'd turn back. "Wait up," he called. He reached me and took hold of my arm. "When's your sister coming home?" Marthalice had gone to the pictures and to school dances with Danny, and sometimes she'd flirted with him at the drugstore. But Mom and Dad never liked her dating Danny, because they said he was wild, and they were glad when she started going out with Hank Gantz.

I shrugged.

"What's her address in Denver? Maybe I'll look her up the next time I'm there."

"I don't remember."

"Don't remember, or won't tell me?"

With my foot, I nudged a rock out of the road and kicked it into the ditch.

"You're just as stuck-up as your sister." Danny tightened his grip on my arm until I looked him in the face. His eyes weren't mean, but they were dark, blacker even than Carl's eyes, and he scared me. "Aw, you can both go to hell."

I SUPPOSE THAT WE expected Daisy to have tiny bones and long, straight hair, to move about silently, talk in whispers, and treat us deferentially. I thought she'd dress simply, maybe wear a kimono. Or that she might even turn out to be the girl with the saddle shoes. Whoever we had expected, she was not the Daisy who showed up with Carl.

She was taller than her brother. Her hair was cut in a page-boy, and it was as dark as midnight. Daisy wore rouge and red fingernail polish. She had on a plaid pleated skirt and a cashmere sweater set with rhinestone scatter pins across the left shoulder.

Daisy wiped the bottoms of her shoes on the boot scraper beside the back door, then came inside "hell-bent for election," as Dad said. She pushed her glasses up on her nose as she grinned. Before Carl could introduce her, she put her hands on her hips and announced, "Hi ya, I'm Daisy. Everybody here doing good?"

Dad leaned back in his chair and smiled at Mom, who was sitting at the kitchen table in her housecoat. She gaped at Daisy as Dad said, "Yes, ma'am. And how about yourself?"

"A-okay." Daisy pinched her thumb and dog finger together before she turned to me. "You've got to be Rennie. How's the world been treating you, Rennie? Okeydokey?"

"Okeydokey," I repeated.

"That's good. You going to help me with the breakfast dishes, or do you have to go to school?"

"I have to go to school."

"I've got your number." Daisy laughed and turned to Mom. "You want me to scrub the kitchen floor? These boys tracked in a whole lot of mud. Boys!"

Carl looked at Dad, then Mom, then back at Dad again. "Daisy's pretty snazzy for a Japanese girl," he said uncertainly.

"We grew up in Los Angeles. She likes to jive."

Dad laughed, and when Mom nodded at him, he said, "That's fine, Carl. She'll do."

Carl and Daisy exchanged glances, and Daisy began picking up the breakfast dishes. "Oh, you can wait on that, Daisy," Mom said. "You might as well have a cup of coffee with us first. The boys always do. I'll show you how we fix it." Dad told Mom to sit still, but Mom waved him off and stood up. "Women are the only ones who can brew a decent cup of coffee. Men!" She said it the same way Daisy had said "Boys!"

Dad slid a glance at me, and I grinned at him. We both thought Daisy was okeydokey.

After Mom showed Daisy the way she rinsed the pot with hot water, and how she measured the coffee and boiling water, Dad helped Mom back to bed. When he returned, Dad told me, "Your mother's an easy touch."

"No such a thing!" Mom called from the bedroom.

FROM THE BEGINNING, DAISY made us glad she was there—me especially, since every morning when she showed up, I was grateful I hadn't had to quit school. She arrived with the boys, full of jive talk, and chattered until she left. But when one of the Jolly Stitchers called, Daisy went outside and hung up laundry or washed out the fruit cellar or cleaned the chicken house. If there was nothing else to do, she just quit for the day and went on back to the camp. Mom said she didn't like the idea of Daisy going across the fields on her own, but Daisy said she could take care of herself.

One afternoon, Mrs. Smith called with a butterscotch pudding the color of hog wallow. Daisy took it from her, but I could tell Mrs. Smith didn't want to give it up. "Girl, are you honest?" Mrs. Smith asked in a loud, slow voice.

Daisy blinked at her and said, "Yes, ma'am."

"That pudding's for Strouds, not for you."

Mrs. Smith spotted me. "You make sure your mother gets that."

Daisy put the pudding into the icebox and whispered, "Even if I was the Thief of Baghdad, I wouldn't steal this."

I studied the pudding. "I wish you would." We giggled, but I felt sorry for Daisy, thinking how awful it was that somebody would treat her like a thief just because she was Japanese.

Daisy put on her coat and went out the back door, while Mrs. Smith watched her from the bedroom. Then she told Mom, "I couldn't rest easy with the enemy in my house." She sat down on the edge of Mom's bed, making the springs sag.

"It's nice to have somebody to talk to, almost like having Marthalice around."

"What about the old lady? You can talk to her."

"Granny's mind isn't there so much now. She doesn't know who Mrs. Roosevelt is."

"Well, I wish I didn't," Mrs. Smith said.

Mom ignored her, because we thought Mrs. Roosevelt sat on the right hand of God, and God, Dad said once, was Mr. Roosevelt. "When I mentioned the war this morning, Granny told me it was about time we freed the slaves. She was a little girl in time of that war, you know."

Mrs. Smith sighed. "It's a burden you carry with Mr. Stroud's mother, Mary." Mom always called Mrs. Smith a "foul-weather friend," because she liked to talk about troubles.

"Oh, I don't mind. She's a dear soul. But it is nice having a young person around during the day."

"At least Miss Evelina speaks English. That hired Nip girl, it's a wonder you can understand her."

Mom had gotten tired of explaining that Daisy spoke English, and that in fact, Daisy understood only a little Japanese, so she smiled and said, "We manage."

Mom and Daisy did a lot better than manage. When I got home from school, I'd find them at the kitchen table drinking Postum and playing bridge or listening to "Portia Faces Life," which was the only soap opera Mom turned on.

"That poor girl," Daisy would say, shaking her head, sometimes wiping a tear from her eye.

"It's only make-believe," Mom would tell her, but she'd sigh and take a handkerchief out of her pocket and blow her nose, then say, "Now Rennie, don't you dare tattle to your father that we've been listening to this." I wouldn't, because I liked to listen to it, too.

Daisy borrowed my Nancy Drew books to read at the camp and brought me her movie magazines when she was finished with them, and we talked about our favorite film stars. "Why, it isn't anything to see famous people when you live in Los Angeles," she told me. Daisy and her girlfriend had stood outside a movie theater in Hollywood during a premiere once and seen Clark Gable and Carol Lombard. Daisy knew somebody who'd sold razor blades to Andy Devine and nail polish to Marion Street. And one time, she'd been waiting for the streetcar when Velma Burgett drove by in a Cadillac convertible. "She was wearing a diamond engagement ring the size of a Chiclet," Daisy said.

When Marthalice sent me records, Daisy put them on the windup Victrola and taught me the fox-trot and the jitterbug. She brought us her high school yearbook, which the principal had sent to her at the camp, to show us a picture of herself. She was jitterbugging with a partner in the school gym, a crowd of kids gathered around them, clapping. Most of the kids were white. So was Daisy's partner.

6

AFTER SCHOOL WAS OUT, Mom and I took the train to Denver to visit Marthalice. The coaches were jammed with servicemen filling the seats and standing in the aisles—"sad sacks," Dad called them as he helped us up the steps, then set our bags down inside the car. Some of the men did look tired and lost, as if they had been riding the train so long that they didn't care where they were going or whether they got there. But others were excited, just like Buddy had been when he'd left us after his December visit. Several stood up and offered us their seats. I sat next to a soldier who told me I reminded him of his sister and gave me half of his Mr. Goodbar. I told him about Buddy, and the soldier said he'd keep an eye out for him.

In the afternoon, when the air in the compartment grew stale from too much cigarette smoke and sweaty uniforms, we stood outside on the observation platform and looked out over the prairie. You could see about a thousand miles. There wasn't anything prettier than a prairie in the late spring. We passed a little farm, where a dozen hens scratched in the dirt, and Mom told a soldier standing next to us, "Chickens always remind me there is a God."

"Yes, ma'am." He lighted a fresh cigarette from the butt of an old one. "They always remind me God's got a sense of humor, too." He looked at Mom out of the corner of his eye, not sure whether he'd offended her. But when she laughed, he grinned and told us he was from a farm in Nebraska. "I guess there's a God, 'cause somebody's got to look out for chickens. I never saw anything so dumb as a flock of hens." Mom loved chickens, but she'd never said they had brains, and she laughed at that, too.

We changed trains, traveling all day, and arrived in the evening at Denver's Union Station, which was about the size of downtown Ellis. Negro porters pushed baggage carts through the tunnels that ran under the tracks, then took them into the waiting room, which was busier than a county fair midway. Soldiers, sailors, and marines lined up two and three deep at a soda fountain that charged a whole dime for a Coke. They slept on the high wooden benches that filled the room—back to back, in long rows—or sat on their duffel bags, slumped over with their elbows on their knees. Some lounged against the walls near a sign that said USO — ALL SERVICEMEN WELCOME, talking to pretty girls who wore rayon dresses with short skirts and sling-back, high-heeled shoes.

A few people, most of them older folks, stood in front of a booth that advertised war bonds, and there were long lines at the brass grilles, where men wearing green eyeshades and garters on their sleeves sold railroad tickets to anyplace you wanted to go—that is, if there was room on the trains. A drawn-out voice announced trains that were arriving or departing and the number of the tracks they were on. The voice boomed across the room, echoing back and forth.

We went out onto the street, where two newsboys were yelling the names of the papers they hawked, chanting in a kind of rhythm—a long *"Rocky Mountain News,"* then a staccato *"Post."* *"Rocky Mountain News." "Post."* Over the sound came a drawn-out "Mare-eee." Both Mom and I swung around, and there was Cousin Hazel. She came up to us and said, "Mary, my dear, welcome. Even after that tiring ride, you look merry as a marriage bell." Cousin Hazel embraced Mom, then turned and held me at arm's length so she could study me. "Dear little Rennie. Marthalice will be so happy to see you. She drew the evening shift this week, but she has the weekend off." Cousin Hazel smelled like violets. "Does everyone tell you how much you favor your sister?" I loved Cousin Hazel for saying that, because I favored Marthalice like ducks favor wild swans.

"I knew you'd be tired, so I brought the car. I'll take you on the trolley another time, Rennie." Cousin Hazel pointed to the big yellow streetcar that had just roared past us on its tracks, its bell clanging, the long pole attached to overhead wires making a prickly *scat* sound.

Cousin Hazel picked up one of our suitcases, and as she led us down the sidewalk, a Japanese man dressed in a suit and tie touched the brim of his straw hat to her. "Good evening, Mrs. Dunn," he said, so softly that if she had wanted to ignore him, she could have.

"Hello, Mr. Hayashi," she replied. The man went on his way, and she explained who he was. "The Hayashis own a jewelry store on Larimer Street. It's not far from here. We used to trade there. We still do." When Mom didn't say anything, Cousin Hazel added, "I'm not altogether sure how you feel about the

Japanese, Mary, although I know you employ some of them. But the Hayashis are nice folks. It hasn't been easy for them, what with the way people feel. Someone smashed their front window last spring." She cleared her throat and said, "Why, here's the car. You can see why I take the trolley. This thing burns more gasoline than a Sherman tank."

She stopped in front of a Packard as big as a combine and put the suitcases into the trunk. Mom got into the front seat, and I started to climb in, too, since I always sat up front in the truck, which had only one seat. But Mom told me to get into the back. There was room enough in there for me and all the Dionne quintuplets.

"Marthalice wanted you to stay with her, but she has just a single bed," Cousin Hazel said as she pulled the big car into traffic and started up Seventeenth Street. I didn't see what difference that made, since Betty Joyce and I shared the sofa when I stayed overnight with her. Heck, when I spent the night with the four Willis girls once, we slept five in a bed, end to end, three with our heads at the top of the bed, two with their heads at the foot, like clothespins mixed up in a bag.

Cousin Hazel drove us to a big brick house two miles from the station, where Cousin Walter was waiting for us. He kissed Mom on the cheek and shook my hand and said, "How do you do, young lady? They told me you were a little girl, but I can see that you're all grown up." I got along fine with Cousin Walter. He taught me to play Chinese checkers and took me to the movies at the Hiawatha Theater, and gave me the olives in the martinis he and Cousin Hazel drank each evening.

We sat in the living room for an hour while our cousins drank their martinis and were not struck dead, as some of the

Jolly Stitchers, who said liquor was the drink of the devil, might have prophesied. Mom and I had apple juice. After we finished, Cousin Hazel led us into the dining room. "This won't be as tasty as that good farm food you brought, Mary," she said. "You should see it, Walter—chicken and steak. You wouldn't know there's a war on."

"I brought butter, too, if you don't mind," Mom said.

"Mind?" Cousin Walter said, slapping his knee. "Your home-made butter's better than the creamery kind any time of the day."

By the time supper was over, I was so tired that I barely made it up the stairs to my bed, which was covered by a quilt just like one of Granny's. That was because it had been made by Cousin Hazel's grandmother, Mattie, who was Granny's sister. I slept until late the next morning, when a voice said, "What's up, snooks?" It was Marthalice. She was sitting on the bed next to me.

MY SISTER HAD BECOME a woman. When I opened my eyes and looked up at her, I suddenly felt shy, because she was so swell. It wasn't just the lipstick and the hair that hung over her face like Veronica Lake's, except that Marthalice's hair was black. Her face was heavier, her eyes deeper. Her figure was fuller, less like a high school girl's. But she was still Marthalice, and I hugged her as hard as I had Buddy when he came home on furlough.

"Hey. You're going to bust me wide open," she said. She laughed, and her voice was richer.

I sat up in bed and folded back the ironed sheets.

"Can you believe this room?" Marthalice asked. "It sure is a lot sweller than anything in Ellis. That's for sure."

"Then how come you moved to your own apartment?"

Marthalice shrugged. "I like Hazel. I *love* Hazel, but I wanted my own place. Nobody tells me what to do there. Of course, it isn't anything like this room. My room is a dump compared to it, if you want to know the truth. But I like it. Besides, Hazel didn't invite me to live here forever." Marthalice stood up. "And while you're here, we've got all kinds of things planned. Maybe I can show you Elitch's. I go there dancing sometimes." She lifted her arms in the air and spun around. "It's an amusement park, too. I'll bet you a nickel you throw up on the roller coaster."

"I never throw up." It was one of the things I was proudest of. The minister could say that about me in his eulogy.

"We'll see."

"How come you call them *Hazel* and *Walter*? Mom will kill you if she hears you." We'd been taught that calling grown-ups by their first names was rude.

She shrugged. "They told me to. Besides, I'm an adult. Now get up. I'll wait in Mom's room." She started for the door.

"Marthalice," I said.

She stopped.

"We saw a Japanese man yesterday. He was walking down the street just like anybody. Cousin Hazel said he ran a jewelry store by the depot."

"So?"

"Do the Japanese here live anywhere? Don't they have to live in camps?"

"They can live wherever they want to."

"Aren't you scared of them?"

Marthalice shook her head.

"Don't you know about Susan Reddick, about what happened to her?"

My sister turned and came back to the bed. Her face was sad. "I know about her."

"Everybody thinks one of the Japanese men did that to her."

Marthalice sat down on the edge of the bed again and took my hand, putting her palm against mine, spreading my fingers against hers. She was wearing nail polish, but she had bitten her fingernails down to the tips of her fingers. She'd never done that before. "What do you think?" she asked.

I pressed my hand against hers. "The Japanese who work for us, they're great. I like them as much as anybody. But since the camp went in, I don't feel as safe as I used to. Sometimes I hear noises in the night and can't sleep. I go downstairs and make sure the door's locked. I don't like to go into the barn by myself after dark, because I'm scared that whoever killed Susan might come after me."

Marthalice looked down at the bedspread. "Maybe you should be afraid of white people instead of the Japanese. Don't ask me why, but I just know." She gave a short laugh, more of a snort really. She added quickly, "I mean that when you live in a big city like this, you get to know a lot of people, and some are good and some are bad, and you can't tell which is which just by looking at them. I know that much."

MOM RESTED ON HER bed with an afghan spread over her while Marthalice and I took the Colfax trolley to Grant Street. Marthalice's apartment was called a studio, which meant it was one room. There was barely space for a single bed shoved against a wall, a chair, a bureau, and a table. She shared a bathroom with three other girls, but she had a corner sink in her room and a hot plate, which was good enough to fix hen scratch, she said. She showed me the rest of the house, a mansion built by a silver king. "Sometimes I pretend I'm one of the rich ladies who owned the house in the old days," she said, and looked away, embarrassed. But I thought that was swell, because if I lived there, I'd have pretended to be the maid.

We left the apartment and walked to the Pencol Drug, where we sat at a little table and ordered grilled cheese sandwiches for lunch.

"Helen Reddick works at the fountain at the Lee Drug. She's Helen Archuleta now. She has a baby," I told Marthalice.

"I know. She married a beet worker. He's no good. Mom wrote that her folks were pretty mad."

"They were so mad, they threw her out of the house. The Jolly Stitchers brought her a charity basket. She almost wouldn't take it."

"Even girls like Helen, who've been ditched, have their pride."

"She wasn't ditched. Bobby Archuleta got drafted." Ice cream from my soda got stuck in the straw, so I sucked it out of the bottom.

Marthalice cocked her head and studied me. "I don't think he got drafted, honey. I think he just took off."

"Can he do that?" I held the straw in the air, and melted ice cream dripped onto the table.

"Men can do anything they want to, especially after a girl gets in the family way." I looked startled, and Marthalice gave me a sad smile.

"That's not very nice. The sheriff ought to go after him," I said.

"Maybe he did. Maybe he didn't." She picked up a pickle chip and bit off a tiny piece of it. "Men don't think it's such a big deal. They aren't always so responsible, especially beet workers. Bobby Archuleta got his draft notice, so he left out. Helen knows it.

Everybody in Ellis knows it. I guess she's trying to save face by saying he's in the army. I bet she doesn't have the least idea where he's at." Marthalice finished her drink and shook the ice in her bulb-shaped Coke glass. "Helen'll be all right. He was a jerk. She's probably glad he's gone. Maybe I'll write her. There are lots of jobs for women in Denver, and she can find somebody to take care of the baby."

"Her mom wants her to move home, but her dad won't let her. Mr. Reddick says Helen is dead to him. I heard Mrs. Reddick say so."

"Mr. Reddick can go to hell."

"What?" Nobody in our family talked like that.

Marthalice didn't reply. Instead, she stared into the mirror above the soda fountain, which was decorated with pictures of a banana split and an ice-cream sundae. A list of sandwiches was written in black crayon along one side of the mirror. She reached into her purse and took out a package of Chesterfields and a book of matches that had *Killarney Inn* printed on it. She shook out a cigarette and lighted it.

"Does Mom know you smoke?" I asked.

Marthalice raised her chin. "I'm grown up. I can do anything I want to." She blew smoke out of the side of her mouth, then tapped ashes onto her plate, although she had eaten only half of her sandwich. "Oh nuts!" she said, flicking a piece of ash off her blouse. "But don't tell her, okay?"

I nodded. "Can I try it?"

"You're out of your mind!"

I sucked the end of the straw again, embarrassed.

"Mr. Reddick's a hard man. You may not know it, Rennie, but Dad is probably the nicest father in the whole world."

She didn't have to tell me that.

"Can you imagine him throwing one of us out of the house for marrying a beet worker?"

"He'd give him a job," I said.

"Shoot, with the trouble he has getting hired hands right now, he'd probably promise his daughters to anybody who'd go to work for him." My mouth dropped open. Marthalice was saying all kinds of crazy things. She said, "That's a joke, snooks."

"Well, I hope he doesn't hire Danny and Beaner," I said.

Marthalice, who was getting money out of her pocketbook, jerked her head up to look at me, but she didn't reply. She put some coins on the table, then stuck the package of Chesterfields back inside her purse and clicked it shut. She snuffed out the cigarette next to the remains of her sandwich. "Remember, don't tell Mom I smoke." She bit at a fingernail, saw what she was doing, and put her hand in her lap.

"How come you do that, bite your fingernails?"

She jiggled her shoulders. "How the hell do I know?" Marthalice stood then, saying she had to go to work. We went outside and started up Colfax, because we were close enough to Cousin Hazel's to walk. A boy followed us out of the drugstore. He'd been sitting behind me, and maybe Marthalice had been staring at him, because he grinned, gave a low wolf whistle, and muttered, "Hubba-hubba." He was nice looking, probably a high school boy, not a soldier or a beet worker. I thought Marthalice would smile back, maybe flirt with him. Instead, she said, "Shove off, buster." Then she drew her arms to her sides and turned and almost ran down the side street, as if she were scared, rabbity scared.

ONE AFTERNOON, WHILE COUSIN Hazel took Mom to a doctor's appointment, I played with Emilie Brown, the little girl who was visiting her grandparents next door. "I'm staying with Grandmother Varian for the summer because my mother and father adopted my sister last year, and she's purely a handful," Emilie told me.

We were sitting in Cousin Hazel's backyard on a swing that had two seats facing each other, and we moved back and forth in tandem, one of us leaning forward a little as the other leaned back. There wasn't much to talk about, because Emilie was a just a little kid, but that was okay. I liked sitting there, smelling the sweet odor of the Chinese lilacs that formed a hedge between the two houses. Cousin Hazel's Negro maid, whose name was Cattie, came out and gave us each a bottle of Coca-Cola.

"Did you used to be a slave?" Emilie asked her.

I stared at Emilie, thinking that was the rudest question anybody had ever asked, but Cattie only replied, "Not me. You think I'm that old?"

"Where I come from, there's lots of coloreds used to be slaves way back yonder in time. We got one works for us. He's older than Moses."

"Moses lived a thousand years ago. There ain't nobody that old that lives yet. Besides, there's no slaves no more."

"I know that. But I bet when we beat the Japs and the Germans, they'll be our slaves."

"You're only seven. How come you know about the war?" I asked her.

"Everybody knows about the war. My daddy works for Miss'sippi war relief."

"You got a camp of Japs out where you live. I heard Mr. Walter say so," Cattie told me.

Emilie stared at me. "Aren't you scared they will kill you dead in your sleep?"

"They live behind barbed wire, and we have guards with guns to make sure they don't hurt anybody. I'm not scared."

"Would the guards shoot the Japs if they got out?" Emilie asked.

"Probably not. We've got some working in our beet fields."

"I hear you got one works right in your house with your mother," Cattie said. "I heard your mother say it to Miss Hazel."

"You lock her up at night?" Emilie asked. "I'd do it anytime in the world if one of 'em worked for me."

"She goes home at night."

"I'd be afraid she'd stick a knife in my back when it was turned. You ask me, all is confusion out there, but I ain't going to worry my head about it," Cattie said. She pulled out a knife and cut branches of lilac, throwing them onto the ground, while Emilie and I swung back and forth silently.

Then Emilie said, "If you've got Japs working for you, I expect they can't all be all bad."

"I guess not."

"How do you tell the good ones from the bad ones?" I thought that over, swinging so hard that the swing began to squeak, and Emilie said, "Slow down. This noise pesters me."

"Maybe there aren't any bad ones. Did you ever think of that? Maybe we made a mistake locking them up."

"You think that, you think I'm Eleanor Roosevelt," Cattie said, gathering up the lilacs and starting for the house.

When Cattie was out of earshot, Emilie leaned forward and whispered, "There's not anybody going to mistake *her* for Mrs. Roosevelt."

AFTER EMILIE HAD GONE home, I went inside and took out one of Cousin Walter's *National Geographic* magazines, which was about Pygmies in Africa, and was sitting in his chair with its back to the doorway when Mom and Cousin Hazel returned. They sat in the dining room drinking iced tea, and they must have thought I was still outside, because after a while, I realized they were talking about me. I wished I'd been paying attention instead of studying midgets.

"I can't tell one and not the other. It wouldn't be right. She's still a young girl. I want to protect her awhile yet," Mom said.

That wasn't fair. I wasn't a young girl when it came to taking over Marthalice's chores or offering to quit school.

"Are you going to tell them the doctor said you're fine, then?"

"I couldn't do that. It would be a lie."

I forgot about being offended over Mom calling me a young girl and began to shiver, although it was hot in the living room. I wondered if maybe Mom had gotten bad news from the doctor and she was going to die. I leaned as close to the edge of the chair as I could to hear them.

Cousin Hazel said, "Of course, you'll be all right, Mary." Her voice sounded too cheerful, as if she were trying to reassure Mom. She didn't reassure me.

"You heard what he said. The prognosis is good."

I repeated *prognosis* to myself so that I could look it up in Cousin Walter's big dictionary, which sat on a stand beside the bookshelves. I hoped I could spell it.

"What will you tell them?"

"That I'm not well yet, that I need rest. She just doesn't need to know the seriousness of it. You've seen her, Hazel. What good would it do to burden her with this? She's fragile."

But not too fragile to do the milking or cook for a beet crew, I thought. I carefully closed Cousin Walter's magazine, disappointed and ashamed that my mother considered me too young to know what was going on. Mom and Dad hadn't shielded me from Susan's death or the internment camp. Mom ought to be square with me about her health, I told myself.

"Is there more tea, Hazel? Oh, don't get up. I can get it. I'm not a complete invalid. You don't have to wait on me."

"Now stay put, dear." A chair moved softly on the thick carpet, and in a minute, there was the sound of ice dropping into glasses. "Cattie makes it with a sprig of lavender. It's a nice touch, don't you think?" Cousin Hazel said. "It's extravagant of me keeping her on, but the fact is, she can't get another job. You'd think with the need for defense workers, they'd be glad to hire a Negro. I can't imagine that the soldiers out there care what color the hands are that put together their equipment. But I guess somebody in the government does." The two of them were silent, drinking their iced tea. "You must have learned plenty about prejudice in Ellis since this war started."

"More than I'd like to. It makes you question the things you've always believed in."

Cousin Hazel chuckled. "You've never had a problem with right and wrong, Mary."

"Loyal certainly hasn't. You've no idea how people are about that camp. It's all but broke up my sewing club. Some have got so high-and-mighty about Tallgrass, they won't hardly speak to those of us who've hired the Japanese. Loyal says a bird can't fly so high that it doesn't have to come to the ground to eat. But I don't know, Hazel. I'd like to go back to the time when I could quilt for a contented heart. The Jolly Stitchers, we call ourselves. We're not so jolly anymore, I tell you."

"I don't see there's much you have to be jolly about these days, what with Marthalice coming here and Bud overseas, and, of course, you getting sick and then that awful rape and murder of the child you wrote me about. They haven't caught the man, have they?"

"The sheriff has somebody in mind, but he can't prove it, so he won't say anything. I wish to goodness he'd hurry up. It's got everybody on edge. I get up two or three times a night to make sure Loyal's locked the doors. Loyal does, too, sometimes."

That made three of us, and I wondered that we didn't bump into one another in the dark.

Mom lowered her voice then, and I strained to hear, since I hadn't been told anything about the sheriff knowing who'd killed Susan Reddick. But I couldn't make out her words. I'd be easier in my mind if I knew, I thought. But I couldn't ask Mom later, because then she'd know I'd been snooping. They talked in low voices. Then they were silent. In a minute, Mom said, "You've done so much for us. How will we ever thank you?"

"Nonsense. You've no idea how much it means to be useful."

"There was nowhere else to turn."

"That's what families are for."

Outside, kids screamed. They were playing softball, and a boy yelled, "You are, too, out!" I used the noise to snuggle into the chair so that if Mom or Cousin Hazel came into the room, I could pretend I was asleep. The afternoon was warm, with a breeze that brought the smell of the lilacs into the living room. Off somewhere in the house, Cattie sang a song soft and low. I wondered if maybe I really would fall asleep. Fat chance.

"Marthalice could have stayed on here. Walter wanted her to. We could have kept an eye on her," Cousin Hazel said.

"You know we agreed it was best she get her own place. I think she's adjusted. She's more grown up."

And smokes and cusses, I thought.

"Marthalice will be all right, Mary."

"She wrote she caught sight of Alberta Hern from Ellis last year, right in downtown Denver. Alberta's the worst woman for gossip in two counties." There was a pause, and Mom added something I didn't catch. Then she said, "Her husband killed himself with a shotgun on their wedding night."

"On purpose?"

I didn't know that and leaned toward the edge of the chair to catch her reply, but Mom must have answered with a shake of her head, because she didn't say anything. I wondered if it would be okay to tell Betty Joyce about that.

"What an awful thing to live down."

"She never has. Any time her name comes up, somebody adds that piece of information in the next breath—just like I did. It's not very Christian, is it?"

"I don't think you have to worry about not being Christian."

One of them pushed back her chair, and I hoped they would not come into the living room. I knew I'd really get it if Mom knew I was listening. Mom despised snoops almost as much as she did liars. Still, I was glad I'd heard what they had said. It wasn't just overhearing things I wasn't supposed to. I liked listening to the way the two women confided in each other. Mom and Dad were as close as any married people, but I sensed that there were things Mom couldn't talk about with Dad, things he would brush off or say were silly. There was a closeness among women. They understood one another in a way that men didn't. If Mom told Dad her feet hurt, he'd tell her to soak them in Epsom salts or change her shoes. But if she complained about her feet to even Bird Smith, who was her least favorite Jolly Stitcher, Mrs. Smith would cluck and know that all Mom wanted was a little sympathy because she'd had a hard day.

I was learning that when women liked each other the way Mom and Cousin Hazel did, they formed a bond that was different from what either one had with her husband. It didn't mean Mom was disloyal to Dad for being that tight with women. That closeness was in addition to what she had with Dad. He would always be the center of her world, but her women friends eased her life. Betty Joyce and I had that kind of friendship, or at least we'd started on it. We told each other things we wouldn't tell our folks or that we'd never tell our boyfriends, if we had them. Sometimes we didn't even have to say things out loud. I knew that Betty Joyce was relieved to get away from the hardware and spend time on our farm. And I think she knew I knew.

"I might as well help you rinse these glasses. I'm not much good for anything else," Mom said.

"Oh, let's sit a bit longer. Besides, you're company."

"I'm no such thing. I'm a nuisance and no denying it," Mom said.

"I'll tell you when you're a nuisance. Sometimes I get so starved for female companionship, I could just cry. I envy you your sewing circle, even if you don't always get along. When that business with Walter happened, well, the only way I could stay sane was to confide in you, Mary. Mrs. Varian next door is the dearest woman in the world and my closest friend, but I couldn't tell her. She sees Walter every day. I can't imagine what you thought when I unburdened myself in that letter, probably that I was an awful woman."

"I thought no such thing. Hazel. You weren't to blame."

"Who's to say? I haven't been such a good wife. It's no wonder he took up with her. You know what a temper I have. And I still get those awful headaches. Who wants to be married to a woman who spends so much of her time lying down in a dark room with a washrag on her head?"

"The headaches aren't your fault." There was a clink of ice. "At any rate, the girl's gone."

"Girl!" Cousin Hazel sniffed. "You might as well call a mutton lamb!" She took a minute to get control of herself. "But yes, she joined the WAVEs, thank the Lord, and Walter's come to his senses. He says he doesn't know what got into him. He liked her very well, but I don't think it was love. He's begged me a hundred times to forgive me, and I have. Still, you forgive, but you don't forget. He's forgotten, I think, but I just can't, not in the middle of the night, at any rate. I start thinking about the two of them together and . . ." She gave a nervous laugh. "It's like shivering over last year's snow, but I can't help it."

"Some things you never forget. I expect this is one of them. But you deal with them. That's what women do."

I sagged into the chair, heavy with the secrets I'd heard. Cousin Walter, that nice man who fixed drinks for his wife every evening, had committed adultery. I'd thought it was foul-smelling men like Mr. Reddick who went to bed with women who weren't their wives, that it was part of their nature. Was adultery part of Cousin Walter's nature? Why hadn't Cousin Hazel walked out on him? She could have gotten a job, but doing what? Working at the war plant with Marthalice or in a drugstore like Helen Archuleta? Maybe Cousin Hazel didn't have any choice but to stay with Cousin Walter and make the best of things. I wished I could ask Marthalice about all that.

"You didn't mention it to Loyal."

"No, of course not. It's not his business. And he wouldn't understand anyway. Men don't, you know. They understand it's wrong, but they don't know how the pain lingers, how it hits you at the oddest moments."

"You do understand, then. If I didn't know better, I'd think it had happened to you."

"Oh, no," Mom said quickly. "But I had a friend who went through it. More than one friend, in fact."

"In Ellis?" Cousin Hazel laughed. "Oh, Mary, you do me a world of good."

I think they might have hugged then, but I didn't dare look around the edge of the chair to see. I'd overheard more secrets in the last few minutes than I had in my whole life.

After a moment, Mom said, "I wonder where Rennie's got to. I'm glad I don't have to worry about that one."

They pushed back their chairs and took their glasses into the kitchen, and there was the sound of running water. Then the two of them went upstairs, and I opened Cousin Walter's dictionary, but I'd forgotten the word I was going to look up.

MOM SPENT MOST OF the week resting, while Cousin Hazel and I rode the streetcar downtown. She took me on my first elevator ride, to the top of the Daniels & Fisher Tower, and introduced me to a doorman who was seven feet tall. I found postcards at Kress to send to Betty Joyce and a record at Wells Music for Daisy, and Cousin Hazel bought fabric for Granny's quilts at Joslin's. We went into the hat department of Neusteter's and bought a hat for Mom, because "nothing makes a woman feel better than a new hat," Cousin Hazel told me. We talked with the saleslady about the colors and the shapes and the style. Then we decided on a brown felt hat with a maroon bow and a dark brown feather. "It will broaden her face, and the color's right. It's not as fancy as what she ought to have, but she won't be embarrassed to wear it to church," Cousin Hazel said. I thought again how lucky Mom was to have women who loved her. Dad would have bought her a hoe. From time to time, I peeked at Cousin Hazel, looking for some sign that she was a wronged woman, but I didn't know what to look for.

"Is Mom really sick?" I asked after we had finished shopping and were eating ice-cream sundaes at Baur's.

"Why do you ask that, Rennie?"

We were sitting at the counter, and I twisted around a little on the stool. "Well, she's been sick since last fall, and you took her to the doctor."

Cousin Hazel nodded. "I don't think it's anything for you to worry about."

"No, ma'am." I wasn't going to get information out of Cousin Hazel.

She stirred her ice cream and chocolate sauce together. "It's not my place to talk about your mother's health. I think you should ask her." She took my hand and squeezed it. "She told me you'd offered to stay out of school to care for her. That was a generous thing to do."

I shrugged.

"You like school, don't you?"

"Yes, ma'am."

"She didn't know if Marthalice was college material, but it

would break your mother's heart if you didn't go. She says you're the smart one. Your parents think the world of you."

THE DAY BEFORE MOM and I left, Cousin Walter drove all of us, including Marthalice, up to Lookout Mountain in the Packard for a picnic. After I heard that he'd cheated on Cousin Hazel, I didn't know if I could look him in the eye. But I did, because he was Cousin Walter, and I liked him, and I kept forgetting he was a sinner. When he thought nobody was looking, Cousin Walter pinched Cousin Hazel's bottom through her slacks, and she giggled. I didn't think Mrs. Reddick would want Mr. Reddick to pinch her.

Cattie had fixed a lunch basket, and we ate it at a picnic table under pine trees. "We sure are going to miss you people, and not just because of the chicken," Cousin Walter said, holding up a drumstick.

"You'll have to make this an annual visit," Cousin Hazel said.

"I wish you folks would come and visit us," Mom told them.

"I'd like that. Do you think we could do that, Walter?"

"Loyal'd put me to work."

"He might at that. Yes, he might," Mom said. She glanced at me out of the corner of her eye, and I knew we both were trying to imagine Cousin Walter bending over the sugar beets in his suit. "You could bring Marthalice with you." Mom turned to Marthalice. "We sure would like to see you at home for a visit, honey. Your dad would, too. He misses you."

Marthalice bit the nail of her index finger. "I know, Mom. I'd like to, but I have to work. It's hard getting time off. The work we do, they need us. It's for the war effort."

Cousin Hazel said, "Mary, couldn't Loyal come here and see Marthalice? Surely those boys could work the beets for a day or two without him."

"Oh, you know Loyal and the beets."

A chipmunk ran up a rock near us, and Cousin Walter pinched off a piece of chicken skin and threw it to him. The chipmunk ate it and ran off. Cousin Walter threw another piece to a black-and-white bird; then another bird flew down, and the two of them began squabbling. "Hold on there," Cousin Walter said, but he didn't throw any more food.

Cousin Hazel took out a cake with white icing and cut big pieces. The cake was red inside. "Ooh, look at that," Mom said.

"Red velvet cake. It's only food coloring. I'll give you the recipe, Mary."

"Just wait until the Jolly Stitchers see that."

"They'll think you're a red Commie," said Cousin Walter, teasing Mom.

"Well, yes, they might. They might at that."

After we ate the cake, Marthalice closed her eyes and turned her face to the sun and smiled. Cousin Walter asked her, "You meet any nice young fellows at that place where you work, Marthalice?"

"Nope. There aren't many fellows who work there, mostly girls." Marthalice opened her eyes. "But I met a boy at the ballroom at Elitch's a couple of weeks ago. He's in the Army Air Corps. I'm going to see him again Saturday night."

Mom looked surprised. "I don't like the way that sounds."

"It's all right, Mom. That's where everybody meets. Maybe he won't even show up." She gave a nervous laugh, which didn't sound like Marthalice at all. She used to be sure of herself around boys.

We all sat in the sun after that, letting the lunch settle, until the clouds came over. Cousin Walter said it was going to rain, that it always rained in the afternoon in the mountains. We packed the leftovers in the basket, and Cousin Walter carried it to the car. Mom and Cousin Hazel followed him, while Marthalice and I folded the tablecloth.

I'd been thinking about Marthalice coming home, and I said, "Maybe you could ask if you could get time off to help with the beets. That's war work, too, you know. You could ask."

Marthalice laughed and kicked at a rock, sending it skidding down the mountainside, with a stream of dirt behind it. "Maybe I don't want to. Have you thought about that? Maybe I don't want to go back to Ellis."

I *hadn't* thought about that. I couldn't imagine Marthalice never coming home.

MOM AND I GOT a seat together on the train going east, and she went to sleep right away. When she woke up, we unpacked Cattie's lunch, but Mom wasn't hungry.

"Cousin Hazel said you asked her if I was really sick," Mom said.

I didn't reply.

"Well, I'm not going to die."

"Are you pretty sick?"

"I could be. My heart's weak. The doctor says if I want to get well, I'll have to stay in bed and rest up, more than before. And I intend to do that. Lord knows how your father would get along by himself."

"Me, too."

"It's all right, Rennie. I don't intend for either one of you to have to. It's hard work to die, and I haven't the time for it." Then Mom added, "I don't like putting the burden on the two of you, especially on you."

"I don't mind. Besides, Daisy does a lot of the work."

"Not all of it. I couldn't manage without you, Rennie." She squeezed my hand. "You mustn't let on to Marthalice how sick I am. I wasn't going to tell either one of you, but I decided you have a right to know, since you'll be taking over so much of the responsibility for me. You can handle it, but your sister's different. She's not very strong, and I don't want to upset her. You mustn't write her about me."

Suddenly, I knew that it was Marthalice, not me, who was too fragile to deal with Mom's heart trouble. I squeezed her hand in return, relieved and happy that Mom had confided in me. "I won't."

"You're getting awful big now. You do your part and more. And there's not many girls your age I'd trust with keeping secrets." She put her head against the window then and closed her eyes, and I stared out at the sky, which was streaked with pink and rose, like the marble soda fountain at Baur's. The train whistle sounded long and low over the prairie, and I watched as the light faded and the sky turned black. And then I realized Mom knew I had overheard her conversation with Cousin Hazel. And she knew I'd keep it to myself.

SOMETIME IN THE NIGHT, the conductor came through the car calling out "Ellis," and Mom shook me awake, and we gathered our things. A soldier sitting across the aisle helped Mom take down the suitcases and then carried them to the door of the car. When the train came to a stop, there was Dad waiting for us, and the soldier handed down our baggage to him.

We were the only ones who got off at Ellis. I went down the steps first, and Dad grinned and grabbed me. When he set me down, he said, "Well, hi there, Squirt. I wondered where you'd got to." Then the conductor helped Mom down. When she stepped off the little stool, she hugged Dad so hard that he took a step backward and said, "Here now. What's this all about? Here now."

1

BOTH MOM AND DAD were quiet as we left the station. Smoky Blessinger, who ran the depot at night, sold tickets, helped passengers up the steps to the trains, loaded freight onto the big carts, and wrote down the telegraph messages, waved when he saw us and called, "Miz Stroud, I'd like to say—"

Dad cut him off. "Not now, Smoke. Can't you see Mrs. Stroud and the girl's just got home? And they're plenty wore-out." Then Dad hurried us to Red Boy, while Mr. Blessinger stood on the platform, his arm still raised in greeting.

"How's Granny?" Mom asked.

"She didn't even know you were gone. But I did. I got awful lonesome."

"That's good, I guess. You left her alone?"

"Only for a few minutes. I waited till I heard the train whistle. She was asleep. There's not time enough for her to get into trouble."

Mom managed only a little smile, because she was tired from the long trip, her face hollow and as gray-white as the freight wagon that stood out bleak and splintery in the light that puddled in big circles around the electric poles beside the tracks. When she got into the truck, Mom sagged against the seat and laid her head back on the worn wool upholstery. Dad seemed worried about her, anxious to know what the doctor had said, but he wouldn't ask her about it just then, because he didn't know that her condition was not a secret from me. He kept glancing at her as we turned onto the Tallgrass Road. After the noise of Denver, the countryside sounds were comforting—a dog barking, a coyote yelping, the knocking of the engine, dirt crunching under the truck's tires. As the headlights swept the fields beside us, I saw the long rows of sugar beets, which seemed to have grown a foot since we'd been away. A cat ran in front of the truck, and Dad braked and swore softly. "Dad blamed thing!" But he didn't hit it.

Mom opened her eyes, startled, and looked around until Dad explained. "Somebody's fool cat near got itself killed, by Dan. Cats!" It seemed as if he was taking out something on them.

"Hazel's neighbor's got a cat," Mom said. "The woman had its claws taken out. So's now it can't protect itself, and it has to stay in the house all the time. She talks to it in baby talk, like it's a regular person. I never understand why people's so crazy to treat animals like they're human."

"Unless they're chickens," Dad said, and smiled. But the glance he gave Mom was raw with hurt. He must have been plenty worried about what she'd learned from the doctor. I wanted her to tell him right then that she was going to be all right, that all she needed was rest. But it wasn't my place to speak up.

Mom closed her eyes and didn't see his look. "Oh, hush up."

"Chickens are different, all right," Dad said. He patted Mom's hand, leaving his palm on top of it until he had to shift gears.

"I saw a polar bear when we were in Denver, a stuffed one, a polar bear and a cub at the natural history museum," I said. "And we went to Elitch Gardens, and I rode a roller coaster. I didn't throw up, either."

Dad didn't reply right away, and I thought he hadn't heard me. Then he said, "Why don't you tell me about it after a bit, Squirt."

I was disappointed that Dad didn't want to hear about our trip. He'd probably worked hard while we were away and was tired, too. I wondered if maybe there was another reason that he was upset. Something could have gone wrong with the beets, or a bad thing might have happened with the boys. I thought perhaps someone at the camp had caused problems. Then I wondered if the sheriff had caught the man who'd killed Susan. I hoped so. That would make it a good summer. Everybody would feel easier about the camp, and people wouldn't be so edgy about the Japanese. They'd say Dad had been right all along to hire the boys, and kids at school would admire me for not fighting. But if Susan's killer had been caught, Dad would have told us right away. Perhaps there was an attack on the camp or another murder, and Dad didn't want to let us know about it. The awfulness came back to me.

I leaned against the cold metal of the truck door and shivered despite the summer warmth, looking off into the fields, which were dark after the headlights passed them by. At Cousin Hazel's house in Denver, the night was always brightened by porch lights or the streetlamps at the corners of the blocks, but here in the country, the fields were a comforting, velvety darkness, illuminated only by the stars and then the glow from the camp. I put my head back against the seat, like Mom, and thought about Susan until Dad stopped the truck. I reached for the door, but Dad said, "Stay put," and he got out and opened the gate, then drove through, got back out and closed the gate, and drove to the back of the house.

I opened the truck door, and Dad came around to help Mom down, but she said, "Loyal, I'm not dead yet. I guess I can make it to my own house."

Still, he took her arm, and she didn't resist. He walked inside with her, holding on to her all the way to the bedroom. Then he and I carried in the suitcases and the shopping bag of things Cousin Hazel had sent home with us. He asked me to check on Granny, then said, "Daisy left you your supper in the refrigerator. I'll see if your mother wants a bite to eat." And then he did the oddest thing. He went into the bedroom after Mom and shut the door.

I wished he knew he didn't have to shut me out of the conversation about the doctor. But maybe she hadn't told me everything. She wouldn't lie to me, I thought. Mom wouldn't do that, of course, but she might have left out some of the truth. I rummaged around in the shopping bag for Granny's material, then picked up my suitcase and carried it upstairs, stopping at the door to Granny's room and looking in. She was making little gurgling sounds like babies do in their sleep, so I tiptoed in and placed the material on her bed, where she would see it when she woke up. After I put my suitcase in my room, I went back downstairs and got out cold ham and bread and a dish of canned tomatoes. I set them on the table, wondering if I ought to just go to bed and forget about supper. I was tired enough to fall asleep with my head in my plate. Then I saw a rhubarb pie with two pieces gone—Dad's and Granny's—and I thought I could stay awake long enough to eat rhubarb pie.

I stooped and reached for it, and as I did, I heard Mom cry from the bedroom, "Oh! Oh no, Loyal!"

Dad said something that I couldn't understand.

Then Mom cried again, "Oh no! No!" She began to sob. I'd never heard her make those sounds, which were almost like hiccups.

I stood up, staring in the direction of the bedroom, the icebox door open, the cold chilling my side. Something terrible had happened, and it wasn't about Mom's heart. I stood there in the cold from the refrigerator, thinking again about Susan Reddick, when Dad came out of the room and said, "Daughter, get your mother a glass of water." He never used the word *daughter* unless he was angry.

"What?"

"Did you not hear me?" His voice was sharp, and I wondered if I'd done something wrong.

"What happened? And why are you mad at me?"

He didn't answer me, just stood there, and I wasn't sure he'd heard my question. I shut the refrigerator door, took the drinking glass we kept beside the sink, filled it, and handed it to him, and he returned to the bedroom. Since he didn't close the door, I followed him. Mom was perched on the edge of the bed. Her hat was on the dresser, along with her earrings and watch, and she'd taken off her stockings and shoes and was sitting in her dress, barefoot. Her face was weary with fatigue, and it was as white and bleak as a winter morning.

Dad sat down next to her, making the bed sag and the springs squeak. He held the glass while she drank in small sips, but she had trouble swallowing, and the water trickled out of the sides of her mouth. She wiped her face with her hand. Then she sniffed and reached for her pocketbook, took out a handkerchief, and blew her nose. She saw me then and reached out both arms. We weren't much of a hugging family, and I walked to her slowly, confused, wondering what was wrong. "Tell her," Mom said to Dad, her voice breaking.

Dad opened his mouth, but he couldn't speak.

"Is it another murder?" I asked. "Is it another girl?" Then I saw the yellow telegram on the dresser, the lines of type all in capital letters, and I remembered Mr. Blessinger calling to Mom at the station. I took the final steps to Mom and sank to my knees, burying my head in her lap, just as I had when I was a little girl and I was scared. "It's Buddy, isn't it? Is Buddy dead?"

"Oh, no, Squirt," Dad said quickly. He patted my arm awkwardly with a hand that was calloused and rough. There was a line of pinpoint scabs on his wrist, maybe where he'd scraped it on a barbed-wire fence, and a trace of Mercurochrome. "He's not dead. Our Bud's missing."

"What?" I'd thought about Buddy getting killed or even hurt, coming home with a broken leg and having to hobble around on a crutch or with his arm in a sling. I'd even considered that Bud might lose an arm or a leg and thought how I would be proud that he'd lost it fighting for his country. I knew I wouldn't be embarrassed or act the way Billy Lutens did when his dad was discharged from the army because his right hand had been shot off. Billy walked on his dad's left side and turned his face away when he saw the end of his dad's empty shirtsleeve. Big boys teased Billy about things Mr. Lutens couldn't do with his hands anymore, like clap and shift gears, and Billy cried. But I'd have fought anybody who called Buddy a cripple.

Dad reached over for the telegram. "It says here, 'The secretary of war has asked me to express his deep regret that your son, Pvt. Loyal Thomas Stroud, Jr., is missing in action. . . .'" Dad's voice broke, and he put down the telegram and cleared his throat. "There's more, but that's about the gist of it. The telegram came two days ago. I didn't want to call you and Mother in Denver. It wouldn't have been right to tell you over the telephone." He cleared his throat again. "Smokey Blessinger himself brought it out at the end of his shift, instead of giving it to some blabbermouth kid. I said to him, 'Keep your trap shut till the womenfolk get back,' and I guess he must have, 'cause none of the bees have come calling. The telegram tells there's a letter to follow."

"Does Granny know?" I asked, getting to my feet.

Dad shook his head. "I don't see any need to tell her. She'd likely forget, and we'd just have to tell her all over again."

"When they say he's missing, does that mean he's dead and they can't find him?" I thought about Bud half-buried in the mud somewhere or lost in a forest, lying dead under the bushes, just like a dog or a cat that had wandered off when it was hurt. Soldiers would hunt for him, call his name, but after a while, they'd give up. Maybe they'd stop looking for him before Buddy was dead. I began to shake, thinking of Bud dying like that, lonely, his body lost forever. He'd rot into the earth like some wild animal. There wouldn't be a grave, and Mom couldn't go to the cemetery with a jar of flowers. Even Susan Reddick had a grave.

"Oh!" Mom said, as if somebody had slapped her on the back and the air had gone out of her. She made room for me between them on the bed, and I was glad the three of us were together to share our grief. Mom and I couldn't have dealt with it alone. Dad had been right not to call us in Denver, but how had he borne it by himself? "You don't really think he's dead, do you, Loyal?"

"I don't think he is, Mary. The telegram doesn't say so, and they'd tell us if they knew."

"That's it, isn't it—*if* they knew. Maybe they don't know."

"What does that mean, 'missing in action'?" I asked. "How can they miss him?"

Dad took a deep breath and put his arm around me. "It probably means he's been captured."

"By the Germans?"

Dad nodded.

Mom began to cry. She put her hands together and slid them between her knees and looked down at her feet. Her legs were tan, but her feet and ankles were white from wearing socks when she worked outside in the sun.

"Is he hurt?" I asked.

"I don't know," Dad said. "If he's been captured, the Germans have to let the Red Cross know about it. Then the Red Cross will tell the U.S. government. They'll let us know where he's at. I expect that'll take a month or so. Then we'll be able to write him, send him packages. Mother can make him a quilt." He gave a hoarse chuckle.

Mom looked up and said, "Oh, Loyal, how can you joke at a time—" Then she looked at me and said, "And Bird Smith will make him a batch of her awful cookies."

"Fine and dandy," Dad said, and they glanced at each other over my head as if they were making a pact to look on the bright side.

"I'll cut out 'Terry and the Pirates' for him," I said, playing my part in the conspiracy.

"Sure you will," Dad said a little too forcefully.

But if there was a bright side, I didn't see it. I pictured Buddy being guarded by ugly Huns with mustaches, evil men who looked like Hitler, who'd prod Buddy with rifles and yell orders at him in a language he didn't understand. They'd have ferocious dogs they'd sic on my brother and other brave American boys. The Germans would make him sleep on the ground without any blankets, and they'd feed him watery soup, or maybe they wouldn't give him anything at all to eat. Then I remembered Tallgrass and the barracks the Japanese lived in and the mess halls where they ate. And I thought about Mr. Tappan and the men who were employed as guards there and the way they treated the Japanese. I hoped the German guards would be just like them, decent fellows who worked crossword puzzles with the inmates and showed them pictures of their children. Some of the guards rode on the yellow dogs with the football team from the Tallgrass High School and cheered for the Japanese boys. If the German guards were like that, Buddy would be all right. Then something else occurred to me, and I said, "Maybe after a bit, they'll give Buddy a pass to work on a farm," I turned to Mom and said. "Maybe some German farmer like Dad will hire Buddy to work in his fields. Buddy wouldn't have to fight anymore. He could spend the rest of the war working sugar beets."

Dad squeezed my shoulder until it almost hurt. "Why, Squirt, I guess if something like that happened, I don't see but what it'd be all right."

Still, things weren't all right. The world was more dangerous than ever. Susan's killer was still out there, Mom was sick, and now Buddy wouldn't be coming home until the end of the war—or maybe never. After a while, I went upstairs and got in bed, but I couldn't sleep. I looked out the windows at the shadows, watching for any that moved. And then I slipped back down the stairs and tested the doors again to make sure they were locked.

"It's all right, Squirt," Dad called to me from somewhere in the darkness. "I've already checked them."

IN THE MORNING, GRANNY woke me up, whispering, "Buddy came in the night." I was groggy, because I hadn't slept well. I was worried about Buddy, but it had been a hot night, too, and I'd slept with a sheet between my legs to keep my sweaty knees from touching. I thought maybe I'd forget about Susan's killer and leave the window open at night. Whoever had killed Susan didn't seem so important anymore, now that Buddy was missing.

Since Granny sometimes had presentiments, I held my breath for a minute, wondering if a second telegram had arrived, maybe telling us that Buddy's body had been found. Or perhaps she'd awakened and come downstairs and heard us talking about Buddy. "How do you know?" I asked.

"Lookit here. Buddy left this on my bed. He knows I like yellow." She held up the piece of material I had placed beside her.

"How do you know Buddy left it?"

"Buddy's dog's on it." Granny beamed at me.

I looked closer, and sure enough, there were tiny dogs that looked like Sabra among the little figures on the fabric.

"He put it here while I was sleeping," Granny said.

"Are you sure?"

"I knew Buddy was coming. A man from the depot brought a telegram. That's why I know."

"Maybe the fabric's from Marthalice," I said.

"No. It wasn't from Marthalice. Marthalice isn't coming back. I don't think she's ever coming back. I remember . . ." Granny had a far-off look in her eyes. Then she blinked and smiled at the fabric. "I'll save this for a baby quilt." She smoothed the material with her old hand. "Somebody always has a baby."

After she left, I went to the window and opened it, thinking that we would have to write Marthalice about Buddy. It would be hard for her, living alone, to open the letter and read about him. I thought, Maybe Mom should write to Cousin Hazel and ask her to tell Marthalice. I decided to suggest that to Mom.

The day was early yet. Dad's shadow was long on the ground beside the chicken coop, and I could see his shadow hand throwing out feed. He must have told Mom to stay in bed while he did her chores. My chores now, I thought; I'd be taking over the chicken coop. Dad picked up a bucket and went toward the barn to milk the cows, walking slower than usual, and I wondered if he, too, had slept poorly. The barnyard was all long shadows—the two poles and wires of the clothesline at an angle like a parallelogram, the haystack like a black mountain, Sabra's legs so long that she was a shadow colt running across the yard.

The honeysuckle bushes beside the house were in bloom, and their fragrance drifted up to my room. And there were the farm sounds I heard every morning. Calves bawled; hens clucked as they scratched in the dirt, leaving their crazy chicken-feet marks. I sat at the window a long time, winding a cowboy bandanna that Buddy had given me at Christmas through my hands. I'd slept with it on my pillow. I wondered if wherever he was, Buddy was thinking about this farm morning, and I wished he knew that we were thinking of him. But, of course, he did.

After a bit, Dad came back from the barn with the bucket of milk. He kicked at the mean old rooster who went after him. "Get away, you worthless thing, or this'll be your last day." Dad had named the rooster Hitler, because we were going to kill him and eat him, and he said that to Hitler every time the rooster went after him. But on this morning, Dad didn't put much feeling into the words. He shaded his eyes with his hand and looked up at my window.

I waved the bandanna. "Hi, Daddy."

His face was old, and his overalls hung on him as if he'd lost weight in the last few days, but he grinned at me and said, "Make that two worthless things."

"Then how come you missed me so much?" I asked.

"Did I say that?"

"No, but you know you did." I wanted to make him laugh.

And he did laugh a little. "Oh, I might have missed somebody following me around, getting in my way." Dad picked up a stick and tossed it at me, but it fell short of the window. There were voices, and Dad glanced beyond the house, then looked up at me again. "Daisy and them are on the way." His voice was thin now. "You better get down here pretty quick and help me explain about your brother."

"WHAT'S THAT MEAN, 'MISSING in action'?" Daisy asked, just as I had when Dad read me the telegram. Dad told her it probably meant captured, and Daisy and the boys said how sorry they were.

"Hell!" Emory said, and Dad nodded, instead of telling him to watch his language.

"It stinks," Carl agreed.

The four of them knocked on the bedroom door and told Mom they hoped Buddy was all right. Then they stood around the kitchen, looking at the floor, the boys kicking one foot against the other, until they'd drunk their coffee. Even Daisy was silent.

Later, after Dad and Carl and Emory had left for the fields, Harry stayed behind to fix a pipe under the sink. He was always looking for some excuse to hang around Daisy. He told her that "missing" might mean Buddy was dead but that nobody'd found his body. "Sometimes they get all shot to pieces and you can't find enough of them to make a good identification."

"Shut up, smarty," Daisy hissed, glancing in my direction.

"They'd know he was dead. They'd find his dog tags," I said.

"Yeah," Daisy added. "They'd find the dog tags."

"Maybe he took off. Maybe he cut and run."

"He did not!" I said, ready to take on Harry, although I knew he could beat me bloody if he wanted to.

"Hey, I was just kidding."

"It's not very funny. Get out of here," Daisy told him. After he left, she said, "That dope doesn't mean anything. He's just mad. They put us in the camp because we're not real Americans. Then they tell the boys if they don't join up and fight for America, they'll throw them in jail. Harry says that after going through the evacuation, he doesn't have to be loyal. But the next thing you know, he wants to join the army, because it's part of our Japanese culture to help our country. Me, I don't understand it. I tell you, it's like the fellow on the radio says: It pays to be ignorant."

"Maybe you're better off in the camp."

Daisy gave me a long look. "Maybe we'd be better off if we had a choice."

That made me feel smaller than five cents. One minute I was an adult, and the next I was a dumb kid. I tried to think how I'd feel if I'd been put in a place like Tallgrass, if Mom and Dad and I had been yanked off the farm and penned up behind barbed wire, with people hating us because of the color of our skin. But I couldn't even imagine it, because, like Mom said, nobody would do that to us; we were white people.

Daisy punched me in the arm and said, "It's okay, kid. If your brother's lucky, maybe he'll end up in a camp like ours."

"What if he's not lucky?" I asked.

"We'll say a prayer for him," she said, "a Methodist prayer. And Emory will say a Buddhist prayer."

IT WASN'T LONG BEFORE the Jolly Stitchers arrived, one by one, with their cakes and casseroles, their words of encouragement, their prayers. Mom took comfort from them, as she had before. She told Mrs. Rubey, "We do fuss with one another, but in times of trouble, we pull together. I don't know what I'd do without my friends in this hour of need."

I wished I had friends like that to talk to about Buddy, but all I had was Betty Joyce, and I'd barely seen her all summer. Edna Elliot wasn't likely to call on me.

"You know we care, every last one of us. I don't know what it is about women that makes us so ornery, but when times are hard, we can count on each other. Try to remember that," Mrs. Rubey said. She was such a nice lady that I wondered how she could be married to a bigmouthed dope like Mr. Rubey and have that nincompoop Edgar for a son.

They both laughed, and Mom said, "I will try." And they laughed again. Then after she left, Mom put her head against the pillow and tears ran down her face. I knew how she felt. One minute I laughed, and the next I couldn't stop crying. It would be easier if we just knew where Buddy was, I thought.

"The truth is, he might be better off in a prison camp with a roof over his head than sitting in a foxhole in the rain, his feet getting the foot rot, with those Germans and Eye-talians shooting at him," Mrs. Davidson told her, and Mom nodded in agreement. Although Mrs. Davidson had refused to come to our house when Dad hired Carl and Harry and Emory, she told Mom she'd put her principles aside because Mom needed her presence now. Perhaps Mom did.

"And who knows, maybe Bud'll be hired out to a farmer, just like the boys at Tallgrass," Mom said.

"Why, I hadn't thought about that. With any luck, he'll find an employer like Mr. Stroud. Wouldn't that be awfully fine? I'll ask the Lord not to send him to a family like the Jacks." They both laughed.

It seemed to be an unspoken agreement that "missing in action" meant Buddy had been captured. Nobody told Mom that he might have been killed and his body lost, and I never mentioned to her or to Dad what Harry had said about Buddy getting shot into so many pieces that he couldn't be identified, although they both must have thought about that. Neither one of them would have believed for a minute that Bud had deserted. We all knew that Bud wouldn't have done that.

Bird Smith came in the afternoon. She walked through the door without knocking and called in a loud voice, "Are you up, Mary Stroud? I wouldn't want to wake you."

"Tell her I'm awake now," Mom said when I went into the bedroom to check.

"So he's went and got hisself caught. Your boy ain't no coward to surrender. No coward at all," Mrs. Smith announced, taking the pin out of her hat and setting the hat on the dresser. "I'll sit, because my knees don't hardly hold me. It's the arthritis," she added, pronouncing the word *arthur-itis*. Mrs. Smith took a quilt square out of her pocketbook, smoothed it with her fingers, and began to stitch on it. I never knew how someone with hands as big as ham bones could make such tiny stitches.

"I never thought he was a coward," Mom told her.

"That's the spirit. There's not a thing wrong with giving up. Anybody asks, you tell them I said so." Mom's as likely to do that as I am to get drafted, I thought. "I've come to cheer you," Mrs. Smith added.

"You have already, Bird." Mom glanced at me out of the corner of her eye. I thought that what Mrs. Smith had said was so preposterous, it had indeed cheered Mom.

"Have you started you a remembrance quilt? You could make your blocks with jeeps and flags and soldier boys, anything you want. I find piecing takes away the pain," Mrs. Smith said.

"Why, I hadn't even thought about that. Bird, you've made my heart better than anything has since I read the telegram."

Mrs. Smith beamed. "And I brought cookies for you to send to him."

"Of course you did," Mom said. "I can always count on you." After Mrs. Smith left, Mom told Dad, "By the time we figure out how to get a box to Bud in prison camp"—she took a deep breath, as if she had forced herself to say that without flinching— "those cookies will have turned to sawdust."

Dad looked at the waxed-paper packet of cookies on the bed beside mother, untied the string, and bit into one. "They already have," he said. "But the chickens aren't too particular." I was in the kitchen then and heard Mom begin to cry again, then sniff and say, "I've got to get hold of myself. We've put a heavy burden on Rennie."

"I believe she can handle it," Dad told her. "She's the strongest of the lot."

"I'd like to let her be a child awhile yet."

That gave me a start, because I was closer to being a woman than a child. But Dad said, "She's not a child anymore, Mary. She hasn't been for a while yet."

"I know," Mom said. "I wonder if she resents it."

I didn't anymore. With Mom sick and Buddy missing, I didn't mind doing my part.

WHILE THE WOMEN WENT to the house, the men came into the barnyard or stopped along the road near where Dad was working.

"It don't mean he's dead. No, sir, it don't," Sheriff Watrous told Dad, slapping his straw hat against his leg and wiping his forehead with the back of his hand. I was hanging up laundry a little ways away from them.

"I appreciate that," Dad said.

"Funny how the good ones get sent over and the culls like Pete Elliot and Beaner Jack get deferments. I guess Bud could have got hisself a deferment as a farm worker, too, but he's just too patriotic. Course, as an American, I'd rather have Bud fighting for me overseas than them other two."

Dad didn't reply, just leaned against the wagon and inspected a harness. The sheriff squinted off into the distance before he turned his face up to the sun, and the two of them stood there for several minutes. Women got edgy when they weren't talking, but men seemed comfortable with silence. They didn't have to talk unless they had something to say. I couldn't decide which way was better.

A car pulled up, and Mrs. Reddick got out and waved to the men, who called, "How you?" She went inside with a covered dish, walking with her shoulders pulled forward. In the six months that Susan had been dead, Mrs. Reddick had shrunk to the size of Granny and looked almost as old, although she must have been the same age as Mom. I decided to follow her into the house as soon as I finished hanging up the clothes, because she liked to talk to me about Susan. Mrs. Reddick always said the same things, but I didn't mind. I had come to understand how women needed to talk, even if you didn't listen. I guess I needed to talk about Susan, too, and that was why I walked down to the Reddick farm from time to time. Once, Mrs. Reddick slipped and called me Susan, then burst into tears when she realized what she'd done. I told her it was okay, that it might be the nicest compliment I'd ever had.

Dad asked the sheriff, "You know anything more about the Reddick girl?"

I had hung the sheets on the line between the men and me, and I hoped that they'd forgotten I was there. I moved along the clothesline quietly, my mouth full of clothespins, tasting the wood.

"I tell you, Loyal, I could put out a murder warrant for a certain person right now if I had any evidence, but I don't."

"You pretty sure of him, then?"

"Being sure don't do a damn bit of good if I ain't got the facts to give a jury."

"That's about right. You want to share who it is?"

There was a silence, and I bit down on a clothespin, the splintered wood rough on my tongue. I took a shirt from the laundry basket and slid the sleeve onto the line, securing it with the clothespin. It was the last one in my mouth, so I waited, afraid if I reached into the bag, I would rattle the pins and draw attention to myself. I knew even if the sheriff didn't arrest the man, I'd feel better knowing who he was, because then I could keep clear of him.

"I don't believe I better do that. If I'm wrong, I could do a good bit of harm."

"I respect that."

I didn't, and I almost sighed out loud with disappointment.

"You probably have an idea of who I'm talking about anyway."

"I believe I do."

They talked so quietly then that I couldn't hear them. Finally, the sheriff said, "You tell Mrs. Stroud the missus says she'll keep your boy in her prayers. I can't say mine would do him much good. Women know more about that than we do."

"That's about right. She'll thank her for it. I thank her, too."

"You take care of yourself, Stroud. I think he'll come home." I looked out from behind the sheet and saw the two of them shaking hands. Dad said something that I couldn't hear, and the sheriff gripped his arm. Mrs. Snow drove up then and got out of the car with Betty Joyce. The two men exchanged glances, and Dad muttered something.

"Miz Snow, you doing all right?" Mr. Watrous asked. He stared at her so long that she looked away. Both Betty Joyce and her mom looked thin and worn-out, and I knew they'd had to work hard, because Mr. Snow was still laid up. He used to go to Jay Dee's and the pool hall at night or just wander around and not get home until morning. But now he spent his time in bed, so that neither Betty Joyce or her mother could get away. I'd missed Betty Joyce, but whenever I went to the hardware store, Mr. Snow told me to go on home, that Betty Joyce didn't have time to waste on me.

"I expect we're fine," Mrs. Snow said as I picked up the empty laundry basket and went over to her car. Mrs. Snow wrapped her hands in her apron, then realized she had it on and took it off and put it into the car. "I didn't bring nothing for your mother, Rennie. We just come to pay our respects."

"That's okay. We got enough food to feed a harvest crew."

Dad and Sheriff Watrous watched while the Snows passed Mrs. Reddick coming through the back door. I hadn't seen so many people in one place since we left Union Station in Denver. "Come and see me, Rennie," Mrs. Reddick said, and I promised I would. Then she turned to Mrs. Snow. "We miss you at Stitchers."

"There's so much needs doing at the hardware that I ain't got the time to sew." Mrs. Snow held out her arms, palms up, as she shrugged, and I saw bruises, probably from where she had lifted heavy boxes at the store. Betty Joyce looked as if the work had taken its toll on her, too.

When Mrs. Snow went into Mom's bedroom, I whispered to Betty Joyce, "Come on upstairs. I got you something in Denver." I led her to my room and took out a red-white-and-blue rhinestone V for Victory pin from a Neisner Brothers sack.

"It's swell," Betty Joyce said, sitting on my bed.

"Why don't you pin it on your shirt?"

"I guess I could." But she didn't.

"Want me to do it for you?"

"I guess."

"I won't if you don't like it."

"I do. I'm just tired. Mom and I have to do everything, and Dad's never satisfied. He gets so mad at us. The only reason we left is that the doctor gave him something to make him sleep. Mom said she had to get out of there for an hour. If Dad wakes up, he'll be boiling mad."

I sat down next to Betty Joyce. "Why doesn't your father hire some boys from the camp to help at the store? My dad says they're the best workers he's ever had."

Betty Joyce shook her head and said in a low voice, "He says he'll rot in hell first." She looked at her hands, embarrassed that she had repeated such a thing.

"Maybe we could go to the drugstore one night after the hardware closes, my treat," I said.

"I can't." Betty Joyce didn't explain why, but I knew. Her father wouldn't let her.

In a minute, Mrs. Snow called up the stairs, telling Betty Joyce it was time to go. As they left, Mom said from the bedroom, "Tessie, won't you take some of that food the Stitchers brought? We can't eat it all, and it will spoil in this heat. I know you and Betty Joyce are just too busy to cook."

"I wouldn't want to rob you, Mary."

"It would be a favor. I hate to see it go to waste. Rennie, you spoon up a little from each dish onto some plates, and nobody'll be the wiser. Tessie, you saved me from feeding it to the chickens."

Dishing up the food, I glanced at Betty Joyce, whose eyes were wide as she stared at the plates, and I wondered what the Snows had been eating—of if they'd been eating at all. They couldn't be taking in much money, and what did come in probably went to pay for Mr. Snow's medicine. Even in the best of times, Mr. Snow wasn't very successful in the hardware business, because people didn't like dealing with him. He wasn't honest. If you bought a dozen bolts from Mr. Snow, you had to take them out of the sack and count them right there in the store, because chances were he'd given you only eleven. He was selfish, too. When I spent the night with Betty Joyce, Mr. Snow ate dinner first. Mrs. Snow, Betty Joyce, and I finished what was left. Sometimes, Mrs. Snow cooked her husband a steak, while the rest of us ate only vegetables. As I covered the plates with waxed paper and set them in a box, Mom called from the bedroom, "Don't give them Mrs. Smith's cookies."

Mrs. Snow looked at Betty Joyce, and the two of them laughed. It was the first time either of them had smiled since they'd arrived.

———

LATE IN THE AFTERNOON, when she knew she wouldn't run into the Jolly Stitchers because they'd be home cooking supper, Helen Archuleta stopped by the house with baby Susan. She'd walked partway; then Beaner and Danny had given her a ride to our gate. "They were a-goin' someplace. I don't know where, but they stopped. I sure was tired of walking."

"Do you like them?" I asked as I held the screen door open. Beaner's truck pealed off down the road, spinning a tornado of dust behind it.

"They gave me a lift, but . . ." She shrugged. "I think I'll walk back. Beaner asked me to go to Jay Dee's for a beer, but I don't want to. I said I had to take care of the baby." She shifted Susan from one hip to the other and smiled at her instead of looking at me. I was glad the infant had Helen's light brown hair and pale blue eyes instead of Bobby Archuleta's swarthy looks. It wouldn't do the baby any favor to look like a beet worker. I said the baby looked like her sister, which pleased Helen.

"Hi, cutie," Daisy said, coming into the living room and reaching for little Susan.

Helen didn't know Daisy, and she clutched the baby to her, so I introduced them, explaining that Daisy had worked for us since beet season began. Then I told Daisy that Helen was a friend of Buddy and Marthalice. "My sister says you ought to move to Denver. You could find a job easy and somebody to take care of Susan," I told Helen.

She shrugged and said she already had a job and that Mr. Lee was good to her. "Sometimes Mom comes into the drugstore. She's in awful bad shape. I don't know what she'd do if I moved away. Dad . . . well, I don't see him."

"What about your husband?" Daisy asked. She reached for Susan again, and Helen gave her up. Susan touched Daisy's glasses, and Daisy jerked her head to one side and laughed. Then the baby grabbed a handful of Daisy's hair and tugged. I smiled at Susan while I watched Helen out of the corner of my eye, waiting for her answer.

"Oh, he's in the service." What else did I expect Helen to say, to admit to Daisy Tanaka and me that Bobby had dumped her? I wondered if she was better off without him. Marthalice had told me Bobby was a jerk and that she knew for a fact that he'd hit Helen. I couldn't imagine a man hitting a woman.

"Has he seen the baby?" Daisy asked.

"Oh, no," Helen replied quickly.

"Well, he's going to be proud. That's as sure as Cheerioats mean cereal." Daisy bounced Susan on her hip as she carried her into the bedroom, setting her down on the bed. Mom was stitching on a star patch for Buddy's remembrance quilt, using scraps of fabric left from shirts she'd made Buddy when he was a boy. She set her sewing aside and reached for Susan, and Daisy and I went into the kitchen to let Helen and Mom visit. Daisy removed her apron, got out her purse, and gave me instructions for finishing dinner. I asked her why she wasn't going home with the boys.

"I don't wait around for anybody." She took off her glasses and breathed on them, then rubbed them on a dish towel to remove Susan's tiny fingerprints. "I guess I ought to say nobody waits around for me." With the boys working in the far fields near the camp, it was easier for them to go on back to Tallgrass when they were finished for the day than to come to the house to pick her up, she explained. When she'd first started working for us, Daisy had walked home alone, but lately, there had been incidents where boys in trucks had thrown rocks at Japanese who were by themselves on the road or had called them ugly names. Dad said it had to do with the war news coming from the South Pacific.

"Don't you worry about walking back by yourself?"

"Nah. Who's going to bother me?" She took a scarf out of her purse and tied it over her head to keep the dust off her hair when she walked across the fields. Remembering that I'd brought her something from Denver, I went to my room and came back with an Andrews Sisters record.

"Wow! Suits me, sister!" Daisy said. "We'll play it tomorrow, and I'll teach you some keen jitterbug steps I learned. We're up-to-date in that camp." Daisy set the record on top of the Victrola.

Then I gave her a second present. I'd seen it at the cosmetic counter at the Republic Drug when Cousin Hazel and I had stopped there to buy aspirin at the end of our shopping day. I'd already bought the record, but I explained to Cousin Hazel that I *had* to get this for Daisy—a gold compact with an enamel bouquet of daisies entwined with an American flag on the lid. Above the bouquet were the words *Daisies Don't Lie* and beneath the flowers it said *True American*. The compact cost seventy-nine cents, and Cousin Hazel had agreed that it was perfect for Daisy. In fact, she'd insisted on paying for it. "Here." I handed it to Daisy.

She didn't say "Wow!" or anything jive. Instead, Daisy looked at the top of the compact and read the words. She slid her fingernail under the tiny latch that opened the compact and looked at herself in the mirror in the lid, then lifted out the velour powder puff. A piece of cellophane covered the powder. Cousin Hazel had chosen a color she thought would be good for a Japanese girl.

Daisy was quiet so long that I asked, "Do you like it?"

"It's just the nicest thing anybody's ever given me," Daisy said quietly.

I looked away, because that embarrassed me more than if she'd thought it was dumb. "You don't have to say that. It's okay if you don't like it."

Daisy took off her glasses and wiped away a tear that had started down her cheek. "I'm going to use it every morning before I come to work and every night before I go home." She took off the little piece of cellophane and rubbed the puff across the powder, then looked at her face in the mirror again and patted it with the puff. "See. Pretty swell, huh?" Daisy clicked the compact shut and placed it inside her pocketbook. "Now how am I going to keep the boys away?"

"Do you have boyfriends?" I asked.

Daisy grinned. "Three of them. But don't you tell Carl. He'd kill me if he knew."

"Are they all Japanese?"

Daisy looked at me curiously. "Where do you think I'd meet a white boy?"

I squirmed. "Is Harry one?"

"This Daisy doesn't tell." She made me think then of Marthalice, the way my sister teased me by not admitting which boy she liked best. Daisy reminded me of my sister in other ways. She'd taught me dance steps and corrected the spelling in my compositions. When I couldn't understand diagramming, she'd showed me how it worked, and she'd sympathized when I complained about the math teacher at school. Daisy filled a little of the vacant place that Marthalice had left. I wondered if Daisy felt that way about me, if she thought of me as kind of a kid sister. I wanted to ask her if she did, but I didn't know what I'd do if she said no, so I kept my mouth shut.

After Daisy left, I went into the bedroom and sat with Mom and Helen. They didn't talk much, just played with the baby, and a few minutes later, Helen looked at her wristwatch and said it was time to go. As I walked to the door with her, she told me, "Beaner says the sheriff knows for sure that one of the Japanese men killed my sister, but he's too chicken to arrest him."

"How would Beaner know?" It sounded like Beaner was just showing off, but still, I remembered what the sheriff had told Dad earlier.

"Beats me. Mr. Lee doesn't think it was a Jap, but he's always sticking up for them. Beaner says we have to teach the Japs a lesson. Beaner says if the sheriff won't do it, he will himself."

"How'll he do that?"

Helen shook her head. "I don't think he has the guts."

"Except when it comes to beating up little kids."

"I heard about that. He scares me sometimes." We went out onto the porch, but I saw Beaner's truck coming down the road and pulled Helen back inside. She waited until Beaner had passed our farm; then she left and started down the road. I didn't blame her for walking. I wouldn't have gotten into a truck with Beaner Jack for a month's supply of sugar rations.

DAISY KEPT US GOING, chattering away, singing the latest songs, telling jokes from the "The Jack Benny Program" and "Fibber McGee and Molly." We'd already heard them, but we couldn't help but laugh when Daisy repeated them, stumbling over the punch lines, getting one joke mixed up with another. "It's terrible times," Mom told Dad one evening. "What would we do without our friends?"

"You include Daisy among 'em?" Dad asked.

Mom thought that over and shook her head no. "More like family."

Midway through the summer, we got another telegram. Mr. Blessinger didn't deliver it. A boy came by on a bicycle and stopped at the house. I was sitting on the swing on the front porch, shelling peas, and I took it from him. Instead of going inside with it and giving it to Mom, I ran out into the far field where Dad was working and, without saying anything, held it out to him.

He looked at it a long time before he brushed the dirt off his hands and then took it from me. He reached into his overalls for his pocketknife, opened the small blade with a fingernail that was black from where he'd caught it in the beet drill, and carefully slit open the envelope. Then he closed the knife against his palm and put it back into his pocket. He took out the telegram and smoothed it between his hands, glancing at me. I was so anxious that I wanted to grab it from him and read it myself, but I knew why Dad was taking his time. He was afraid of what was in the telegram. So was I.

Almost reluctantly, Dad held it up and read it. He nodded and folded the telegram, returning it to the envelope and sticking it inside the pocket in the front of his overalls. "Well, Squirt, we were right. Our boy's been captured after all. It says here he's a prisoner of the Germans." Dad reached down and gripped my shoulder to keep from crying. "We best go back to the house to tell your mother." He didn't move for a moment, just stood silently, looking off across the fields, and if he'd been somebody else, I'd have thought he was praying. But I'd never known Dad to pray. "He's the first Ellis boy captured in Germany. I guess your Mother'd rather not have that distinction."

So there came another round of visits from the Jolly Stitchers, although their calls had only tapered off a little, never really stopped. This time, they came with boxes of cookies and hand-knit socks and funny cards to send to Buddy. They stitched on the rembrance quilt, too. "We're not good for much of anything but standing around. The womenfolk are better at this than us," Mr. Gardner told Dad. The two of them stood beside the water trough while Mrs. Gardner went inside with a fruitcake for Mom to send to Buddy. She said she'd made a fruitcake because she didn't know how fast the German postal system was, and a fruitcake would keep a long time.

"I don't imagine any of it's going to reach him," Dad told Mr. Gardner.

"Doesn't make much difference. It's the doing of it that matters." He was right. I felt as if I was helping Buddy when I cut out his comic strips or took snapshots of the farm to send to him.

Mom boxed up all the things the women brought, and Dad took the packages to the post office. Once, he mentioned that some German official was going to live high off the hog.

"Loyal!" Mom said. "That's a terrible thing to say."

"Well, it's the truth."

"Don't you ever say that again."

He never did. But he still thought it, and I did, too. I suppose even Mom did.

ONE MORNING NOT LONG after that, Daisy didn't come to work with the boys. "She fell at the camp," Carl explained.

"Was she hurt?" Dad asked.

Carl shrugged. He didn't look at Dad. Neither did Emory or Harry.

"Was she hurt?" Dad asked again.

"She's okay," Carl said.

Mom heard the conversation, and she came in from the bedroom in her bathrobe. "Maybe I ought to go out to the camp and see if she's all right."

"Oh, no, ma'am. She hit her head. They took her to the clinic when they found her. She's got a concussion."

Mom sat down at the table as she asked what had happened.

"She went to the shower house late."

"Maybe she slipped on some soap," Emory suggested.

"Yeah, I never thought of that," Carl replied.

"I hate that camp," Harry said. "They shouldn't make those women go out at night to take a shower. What did Daisy ever do to them? Damn government."

I was sure then that Harry was one of Daisy's boyfriends.

"Loyal, I'd like to call on Daisy," Mom said.

"That's okay, Mrs. Stroud. Daisy'd feel bad about that, you being sick and all. Besides, she'll be back in a couple of days," Carl said.

Dad and Mom exchanged a look, and Mom said, "Whatever you think. Rennie'll make some divinity for you to take home with you."

Daisy didn't return to work for more than a week, and except for a bruise on the side of her face, she looked all right. She told us she'd fallen and banged her head, and that the doctor had made her stay in the infirmary until he was sure she was all right. She pronounced herself "as good as new."

But she was quiet, and I wondered if maybe the fall had hurt her brain. Mom said that being in accidents sometimes made people grow up a little. Daisy stopped chattering and dancing to records. She didn't primp the way she once had, and she no longer powdered her nose before Carl walked her home. But maybe that's because she'd dropped the compact I'd given her and didn't want me to know. I saw it on the table once, scratched, the mirror broken.

Harry thought up reasons to come in from the fields to hang around, but Daisy didn't want him near her. If he had ever been her boyfriend, he wasn't anymore.

One morning toward the end of the summer, Harry didn't show up for work. "He won't be coming back," Carl told Dad. "Harry's joined the army."

8

BETTY JOYCE DIDN'T SHOW up for the first day of ninth grade, and I was afraid she wouldn't come back to school ever again.

Mom sighed when I told her. "It doesn't surprise me," she said. "There's so many that drop out before they get their diplomas." Mom was frying potatoes for supper. As the summer wore on, she had begun feeling better. A good thing, Dad said, since the Jolly Stitchers came calling every day to keep her spirits up, and instead of resting, she was entertaining company. Bird Smith claimed Mom was improving because of the remembrance quilt, and Mom said she wasn't sure but what Mrs. Smith was right. As Mom became stronger, Daisy seemed to get puny, still suffering from the fall in the shower house.

"Maybe Betty Joyce's sick or something. I could stop by after school tomorrow and see," I said. The hardware store had a telephone, but Mr. Snow hung up when anyone phoned for Mrs. Snow or Betty Joyce. I moved my schoolbooks off the table and began laying out silverware on the oilcloth, which had a bright design of roses on a lattice. "It's not fair to make Betty Joyce work in a hardware store all her life. She wants to be a nurse." In fact, Betty Joyce would have waited tables or slopped pigs or scraped beet pulp off the floor at the sugar refinery, anything to keep from being around her father. No matter how hard Betty Joyce worked, her father called her lazy, and he didn't care that she missed classes.

Dad came in then and went to the sink, washing his hands with the bar of harsh soap that we kept there. "What's up at the hardware store?" he asked.

Mom stirred the potatoes, scraping the bottom of the heavy iron skillet with her big metal spoon. "Betty Joyce didn't go to school today. I expect Gus Snow's kept her out to do his work. There's too much of that."

"Always has been."

"Times are better now. Maybe you could talk to him. He's always set store by you."

I set a knife down on the oilcloth, lining it up with a strip of latticework, leaving my hand on the handle while I looked over at Dad. He was prying dirt out from under his fingernail with his pocketknife and didn't answer, but I knew he'd heard. He rinsed his hands, turned off the water, and reached for a towel. "What's for supper, Mother?" He closed the knife and put it into his pocket.

"Meat loaf, potatoes, green beans with bacon. Daisy made corn bread, and there's leftover strawberry pie, if you want it."

"When did I not want strawberry pie?"

"Rennie, you better whip up some cream, then," Mom said.

Dad wiped his hands on his overalls, because he hadn't dried them completely on the towel. Mom and I waited. "Times aren't any better for the Snows. And Gus Snow never set store by me when it came to the hardware. Besides, you can't come between a man and his family, especially that man. He's mule-stubborn," Dad said. "Maybe the preacher ought to talk to him."

Mom harrumphed. "Gus Snow's never seen the inside of a church. He makes you look like a regular deacon."

"Wouldn't want anybody to do that," Dad muttered.

"Betty Joyce is a fine girl, almost as smart as Rennie," Mom said. I jerked up my head at the compliment. Dad grinned, but Mom ignored me. "If she stays in that hardware store, Betty Joyce'll end up just like her mother, all beaten down, bless her heart." Mom gave the potatoes a vicious stir. "She'll end up like Darlene Potts," Mom added for emphasis. Darlene Potts had been the smartest girl in Buddy's class. She'd won the county spelling bee when she was in the ninth grade, and she'd talked about becoming a teacher. The principal said that with her grades, she could easily get a scholarship to teachers college in Greeley. But Mr. Potts asked what good was an education for a girl when he needed her on the farm? He pulled her out of school for spring plowing, and she never went back. He worked her so hard that Darlene ran off and married one of the Jack boys, and by the time she would have graduated from high school, Darlene had two kids. Now she had four and looked thirty-five years old. The Jacks worked her as hard as Mr. Potts ever did.

I finished setting the table, then got out the beater and began to whip the cream. Granny came into the kitchen with a little bunch of purple asters and set them in a vase on the table. "Aren't they pretty? I always did like a bouquet on the table," she said. "Betty Joyce ought to be in school. Mary's right. You should talk to Mr. Snow, Loyal. Girls deserve an education, too." Mom and Dad and I grinned at one another to show how pleased we were that Granny was in good form.

"There," Mom said.

"Please, Daddy," I said.

Dad scratched the back of his head. "Three to one. I guess I'm outnumbered."

"You see what an education did for you, son. You can count," Granny said, pulling out her chair and sitting down. She bowed her head and mumbled, "Thank you, Lord, for letting this boy of mine go to school and learn some sense."

"Good going," I whispered to Granny, and she gave me a sly look.

AT THE END OF the week, when Betty Joyce still hadn't come to class, I stopped at the hardware to make sure her dad was keeping her out of school for good, that she wasn't sick or just working for a few days to help with the harvest business. I was afraid of going into the store, because Mr. Snow didn't like me hanging around and was liable to cuss me out. When I told Dad about that, he gave me two bits to purchase some washers, although he didn't need them.

When I went into the store, Betty Joyce and her mother were lifting a carton with a drawing of a big black bolt on the side. Mrs. Snow was frail, and she struggled with the box, almost dropping it. I wondered what kind of man Mr. Snow was that he would let his wife lift something that heavy. "Here, let me take your end." I grabbed the box. But Mrs. Snow glanced at the door in the back of the store that led into the Snows' living room and said she could do it. Mr. Snow was lying on an iron bed that had been moved into the center of the room so that he could watch what was going on in the store, and he rose up on his elbows. He was wearing an undershirt and hadn't shaved.

I knew he smelled bad, so I was glad he wouldn't expect me to go back there to say hello. The store smelled, too—of metal filings and mice and spilled oil that had seeped into the wooden floor. "How you, Mr. Snow?" I called. I didn't care how he was. I didn't even want to talk to him. I was just being polite.

From his bed, Mr. Snow could see past the counters on either side of the store, all the way to the front door. "What you doing here, girl? Can't you see Betty Joyce don't have time to jaw? Some of us has work to do." He breathed through his mouth, and I knew his yellow teeth were sharp like an animal's and had spaces between them. The way he looked at me always made me uncomfortable. I'd run into him walking down the Tallgrass road once, and I'd gotten the creeps being out there alone with him.

"Some of us," Betty Joyce muttered, so low that I could barely hear her. But I did hear her, and I knew she was worked hard, harder than a hired man. I remembered Darlene Potts and wondered what it would take for Betty Joyce to run off and marry some no-good boy, just to get away. Then I looked at Mrs. Snow and knew Betty Joyce would stick it as long as her mother was there. I thought, Maybe Mom could get the Jolly Stitchers to help, although a charity basket wasn't the answer.

"I came to buy washers for my dad, Mr. Snow."

"Is that right? How much you want?"

"Two bits' worth."

"Well, get to it then, Betty Joyce. Get her them washers so's you can unpack that shipment before the Second Coming."

Betty Joyce glanced at her father but didn't say anything. She and her mom set the box on the counter, and Betty Joyce moved to the front of the store, where her father couldn't see her in the gloom. The store was lighted by only two bulbs, which hung down on long cords from the ceiling, one over each counter.

"Aren't you going to school anymore?" I asked.

"What do you think?"

"I could bring your lessons to you until your dad's better. You could do them when you're not busy."

"Yeah, sure. If I had any extra time, he'd make me do something important, like count nuts." Betty Joyce had grown taller over the summer, and the dress under her apron was short and tight and dirty. Betty Joyce was dirty, too—her hands and her arms and her hair. I wished there was a girls' group like the Jolly Stitchers, whose members looked out for one another, and we could help Betty Joyce. But all she had was me, and I didn't know what to do.

"Besides, what makes you think I'll ever go back to school?" Betty Joyce asked.

"You can't just drop out," I said.

"Says who?"

I studied her, wondering how she could have turned so bitter in just a few weeks. Betty Joyce had always been funny, not sarcastic. I remembered thinking once that Betty Joyce and I were so close, we knew what the other thought without having to talk about it. Well, I was wrong about that. It had taken me a long time to realize how bad things were for her.

"Betty Joyce?" Mr. Snow called from the bedroom. He sounded agitated.

"Yes, sir."

"You get to them washers now."

"I'm looking for them." She said to me, "I have to go back to work. He's meaner than a rooster. It's the medicine." She grabbed a handful of washers out of a metal bin and, without counting them, thrust them into a paper sack. Her arm was covered with bruises. One of them was old and yellow, but another was fresh.

The bruises didn't come from bumping into anything, because they went around her arm.

"I'm sorry," I said.

"Don't be. It's just the way it is." She'd given up, and that was worse than if she'd been angry. Betty Joyce handed me the sack of washers and adjusted her apron straps. She was wearing the V for Victory pin that I'd given her, and the red rhinestone at the base of the V had come out. Betty Joyce noticed me looking at it and said, "I must have knocked it against something and lost the rhinestone. I looked all over for the stone so that I could glue it back in, but I couldn't find it."

I shrugged. "It doesn't matter. It was just a cheap pin."

"No, you brought it to me from Denver." Betty Joyce turned away and wiped her eyes against her sleeve. "That old man never gave me a single thing." She put her head on the counter and began to cry silently. Across the room, Mrs. Snow looked up from where she was writing in an account book laid out on the counter next to the box of bolts. She licked the end of her pencil. Glancing first at Mr. Snow, she looked at Betty Joyce with anxious brown eyes, turning her head from her husband to her daughter like a little bird watching a cat approach a nest and not knowing how to stop it. Then she sent me a pleading look, and I knew she wished I'd leave. She was afraid of Mr. Snow. What an awful thing to be scared of your husband. I couldn't imagine Mom being afraid of Dad. For some reason, I thought about Helen Archuleta and wondered if she would have become like Mrs. Snow if Bobby hadn't left her.

"How long's it take to sell washers?" Mr. Snow yelled from the back room.

"You have to go," Betty Joyce said, putting her hand over the pin. I should have brought her back another present from Den-

ver, one that was finer. I thought maybe I could give her something else now and say I'd gotten it on my trip and forgotten all
about it. But she'd think I felt sorry for her. I'd learned from the
way that Mom and the Stitchers had presented the charity basket
to Helen Archuleta, as well as how Mom had asked Mrs. Snow
to take some of the food people brought after we got the telegram about Buddy, that there was a special way you gave things
to people. You had to make them think they were doing you a
favor by taking them. I realized I'd have to think about how to
do that before I gave something to Betty Joyce.

Just then, the bell on the door jangled, and a man came in.
The light was at his back, and at first, I couldn't tell who he was.
Then he walked into the center of the room and took off his hat
and bowed slightly to Mrs. Snow. He was Japanese. "I'm need-
ing a hammer," he said in a quiet voice.

"What's that?" Mr. Snow called from the back room.

"He needs a hammer," Mrs. Snow said, so low that I thought
her husband would not hear her.

But he did. "Who needs a hammer?"

"I don't know. A man," replied Mrs. Snow.

His hand on one of the vertical bars of the iron bed, Mr.
Snow pulled himself upright, then leaned forward to peer into
the shop. "What man's that?"

"I don't know, Gus. Just a man."

"Well, he's got a name, don't he? Don't you got a name, whoever you are?"

The man took a few steps toward the bedroom and dipped
his head. It wasn't a bow. I think if Mr. Snow had been nice to
him, the man might have bowed. Instead, he nodded just enough
to be polite. "My name is Mr. Yamamoto. I understand you sell
hammers. I have come to buy one."

"Are you a Jap?"

"I am an American."

"You're a Jap is what you are. We don't sell to Japs. Can't you see the sign in the window? It says 'No Japs Wanted.'"

Betty Joyce looked at the window, then exchanged a glance with her mother, and I knew they had taken down the sign.

"I have money."

"Blood money's what it is. You Japs are killing American soldiers. You killed my boy over in the Pacific. Gut-shot him is what you did. You're nothing but a bunch of damn spies. I don't want your filthy money. Take it, and get the hell out of my store."

"Gus, it don't matter. We could use the sale," Mrs. Snow said.

"You deaf? You want a knock in the head?"

Mrs. Snow cowered back against the shelves, and Betty Joyce went to her and took her hands.

"I don't want no Japs in my store. Don't you remember nothing about Eddie getting killed by kamikazes, lying there with his guts spilled out? Don't you remember nothing about the Reddick girl? You want Betty Joyce to get that done to her by this man, this Mr. Japamoto? You want your own daughter raped and murdered, do you? You might as well send her off to live at Jay Dee's." Spit came out of Mr. Snow's mouth as he yelled, and he turned his head and wiped his face against his shoulder.

Mr. Yamamoto was frozen for a moment. Then with great dignity, he turned and slowly bowed to Mrs. Snow. Taking his time, he walked to the end of the counter and out of the store, holding the screen door so that it didn't slam shut. He waited until he was outside to put on his hat.

"Goddamn Nip. I wish I had a dog to sic on you! You ever come near my store again and I'll break your damn yellow neck!" Mr. Snow called. His face was so red with rage that I thought he might get out of bed and chase after Mr. Yamamoto. Instead, he let go of the iron bar and flopped down on the bed.

"Go," Betty Joyce mouthed. She was too beaten down by her father to be embarrassed. I wanted to say something to show I understood, but I didn't understand. My insides curled up as I thought of how that Japanese man must feel having those horrid words flung at him. Mr. Yamamoto seemed like a nice person who just wanted to buy a hammer. He didn't deserve the insults. If I'd been Mr. Yamamoto, I would have gone into the back room and pounded Mr. Snow.

Betty Joyce's father had always been surly, but he'd gotten worse since the mule had kicked him. I didn't know what to say, so I muttered, "I'll see you" to Betty Joyce, who nodded but didn't look me in the eye, and then I went outside, letting the door bang behind me. I took a deep breath to rid my lungs of the stale air of the hardware store, but nothing could get the insults out of my head.

Through the screen, I heard Mr. Snow call, "Tessie, you get yourself in here. Don't you know no better than to let some damn Jap put his hands all over Betty Joyce? You want a smack? Don't you know nothing? Betty Joyce, fetch my medicine."

OUTSIDE, BEANER AND DANNY were going through the junked auto parts in the yard behind the store. Besides hardware, Mr. Snow used to sell pieces off wrecked cars and trucks, but most of them had gone to the scrap-metal drives. Only a few lay near the store.

"You in there talking to 'Axel' Sally?" Beaner asked, kicking a broken axel from an old auto so that I got the joke, only it wasn't funny. Betty Joyce didn't have anything more to do with Axis Sally, who was the German version of Tokyo Rose, than I did.

Danny slapped Beaner on the back and said, "Good one."

I squirmed. Betty Joyce was now in a class with Darlene Potts, fair game for jokes from the likes of Beaner and Danny. So that they wouldn't say anything more about Betty Joyce, I told them, "Mr. Snow'll cuss you out if he sees you in his stuff."

"Let him cuss. That old jackass can't get out of bed. He doesn't care anyway. He's beholden to us," Beaner said.

"Yeah. Besides, he'd rather cuss the Japs."

"Not everybody's a Jap lover like your old man," Beaner said. "Course, maybe you like them squint-eyes, too. You and your sister. I hear she likes just about anything." His eyes slid over to Danny, and he punched Danny's arm. "With those Nips working on your farm, maybe you want what the Reddick kid got." Beaner leered at me, making me take a step backward.

"Maybe she already got it," Danny said.

I thought about what Miss Ord had told me about not arguing, even though Beaner had insulted my sister, and started to walk away.

"Where you going?" Danny called.

"That's for me to know and you to find out." It was a stupid thing to say, and I was sorry the instant the words left my mouth, because it was a challenge. I'd had to fight my way out of plenty of dumb remarks like that when I was a kid. Beaner had lost interest in me, however. He'd spotted something on the ground, picked it up, and put it into his pocket.

But Danny looked at me oddly. "How's that Jap girl you got working for you?" He winked and moved his tongue over his lips, then turned to Beaner and asked, "What's that you found?"

I hurried off down the Tallgrass Road before they could turn their attention back to me, and in a few minutes, I caught up with

Mr. Yamamoto. As I came alongside him, he touched the brim of his hat and changed his stride to match mine.

"Mr. Snow isn't a very nice man," I said, a little winded.

Mr. Yamamoto slowed to let me catch my breath and looked at me, not understanding.

"He's the man in the hardware store, the one in the back room. He got kicked in the head by a mule. That's why he's in bed. But that's not why he's a jerk. It's his nature."

"Ah, him." Mr. Yamamoto smiled.

"He yells at Mrs. Snow and Betty Joyce all the time. He's so mean that he won't let Betty Joyce go to school anymore. So you shouldn't take it personally."

"We're used to it. It is hard to lose a son."

I shook my head and explained that Eddie wasn't Mr. Snow's son. He was Mrs. Snow's nephew, and he worked in the hardware store until he got so fed up with Mr. Snow that he joined the navy. "And what Mr. Snow said about Eddie getting killed by kamikazes, that's hogwash. Eddie died of appendicitis. Eddie told me once hard times turned Mr. Snow into a drinking man, but everybody's been through hard times in Ellis, and not everybody's a drunk."

"I don't believe that man's just a drunk," Mr. Yamamoto said. I waited for him to explain, but Mr. Yamamoto only shrugged.

"I bet my dad would loan you a hammer," I said.

"There are hammers at the camp. I just wanted one of my own."

A truck came toward us, and Mr. Yamamoto stepped down into the ditch, pulling me with him. After it passed, he let go of me. "You never know what drivers do when they see us. Sometimes they swerve. . . . They might think you are Japanese, too." He seemed embarrassed and fanned the air with his hat to get rid of the dust that had boiled up behind the truck. "You're the Stroud girl, aren't you?" he asked. "I see you when I walk past your farm." I nodded.

"Your father is a good man. He was the first farmer to hire boys from the camp."

"Others do that now. Mr. Gardner's one." I wanted Mr. Yamamoto to know that we weren't all like Mr. Snow. "Plenty of people like the Japanese—Sheriff Watrous and Mr. Lee, who owns the drugstore. And there's Miss Ord, who's my history teacher this year. She knew a lot of Japanese in California. You'd like her."

He chuckled. "I do like her. She teaches American history at the camp on Saturdays. My wife and I are in her class." He leaned forward and smiled. "She told us about you. She said there are girls at your school who tried to hurt you because of your father. I will tell her I met you, and that you are a fine young lady." Then he grew very serious. "I know that the son of Mr. Stroud was captured by the Germans, and I am very sorry. I hope that he will be all right."

I wasn't sure what to say. People I didn't know were always telling me they were sorry about Buddy, but it surprised me that Mr. Yamamoto knew my brother was in a prisoner of war camp. "Thank you."

We walked on slowly now, because our drive was only a few yards away. I kicked a rock ahead of me, and when I reached it, I kicked it again. Then we came to the turnoff, and Mr. Yamamoto said, "I will also tell Miss Ord about the little girl in the hardware store who no longer goes to school." When I looked at him curiously, he added, "I heard you talking to her before I went inside."

He bowed, and I bowed, too, putting one hand in front of my waist and the other behind my back and bending in half like a sack of sugar.

DAD SLAMMED HIS FIST on the table. "Gus pret' near threw me out of the store, or he would have if he could have got out of the dang bed. By Dan, Mother, by Dan!" Dad stopped and took a deep breath and calmed himself. He didn't often get riled up like that. "I went in the back room. It smelled like a bunch of dead owls in there. I said to him, 'Gus, we've been friends a long time, since we were boys. That's too long for me not to speak my mind to you.'" Dad stopped and shook his head. "I didn't care much for him then, and I care even less for him now, but I didn't tell him that. I believe these days, where he walks, nothing grows."

"I didn't know he could walk just now," Mom said.

"Don't put too fine a point on it, Mother." Dad held his coffee cup in his right hand. The index finger of his left hand traced a rose on the oilcloth.

"I don't know how Tess and Betty Joyce have put up with him all these years." Mom absentmindedly picked up a spoon and stirred her coffee. But she'd given up sugar for the duration and had only coffee in her cup. "You want a cup of coffee, Rennie?"

I looked at her, surprised. I'd never had coffee. Mom always said it would stunt my growth. Besides, kids didn't sit around the kitchen table drinking coffee. Offering me a cup was almost like saying I was grown up. "Yes, ma'am," I said.

"You've been carrying a woman's load for some time now. I guess you're old enough to drink coffee." She got up and poured me half a cup of coffee and set it down on the table, pushing the cream pitcher toward me. She told me that I might want to doctor it some.

I tasted the coffee, which was bitter, and I didn't like it much, but I wouldn't tell her that for the world. Instead, I said it was fine the way it was. If drinking foul coffee was what it took to be an adult, I'd do it.

"I reckon coffee always tastes better with a cigarette," Dad said.

"Loyal, you watch it!"

Dad told me, "I guess you're not so growed up as your mother thinks." Dad took out the makings and rolled a cigarette, struck a match on his overalls and lighted up.

We waited while he took a couple of puffs and laid his cigarette in the ashtray. Dad hadn't gone to the hardware store right away. He'd waited more than a week after I'd stopped to see Betty Joyce, hoping maybe that it wouldn't be necessary for him to talk to Mr. Snow, that Betty Joyce might go back to school after all. Dad also wanted to give Mr. Snow a chance to settle down after Mr. Yamamoto's visit. There was no reason to step into a hornet's nest, he'd said. So he waited until Saturday morning, when he'd needed to go to the hardware to buy some wire anyway.

"You going to tell us what he said, or just come up with ways to lure your younger daughter into sin?" Mom asked, nodding at the cigarette that was smoldering away. She took a sip of coffee. Dad and I did, too, and we sat there, just like three old farmers. I saw the rest of my life stretched out in front of me, seventy-five more years of sitting at the kitchen table, drinking coffee. I was convinced those would be long years if I didn't develop a taste for the stuff.

Dad picked up his cigarette and smoked it down to the end, then snubbed it out. "I said, 'Gus, you had your time to finish high school, and it wasn't easy on your folks, 'cause they could have used you at home. But they wanted you to get an education. Betty Joyce is smart as a whip. You let her finish high school and maybe college, and she'll get a good-paying job and help you out in your old age, do it a lot better than selling saws and rakes.'" He picked up the tobacco bag and wound the gold drawstring around his finger. That sounded pretty good to me. I couldn't see how Mr. Snow wouldn't get the logic of it, except that he was crazy.

"Then what?" Mom prodded.

"Then Tessie says, 'She will, Gus. You know she will. She'll put us on easy street.' And Betty Joyce chimed in she would at that."

I sipped the coffee again. Mom pushed the sugar bowl toward me, and I took a spoon from the spooner in the middle of the table and stirred in a day's ration of sugar. I liked the idea of stirring coffee. This time, the coffee tasted better.

"And?" Mom asked. "I'll pick a Jolly Stitcher over you any day of the week for someone to talk to."

Dad nodded his head up and down, thinking. "He told Tessie to be still and said right back at me he thought he wouldn't take any advice from a Jap lover." Dad glanced at me and lowered his voice. "Then Gus said he guessed since we'd been friends so long, he could speak his mind, too, and he asked me what kind of a father I was that I let my daughter be around Japanese boys, who'd give her a dose of what Susan Reddick got. He said, 'My guess is that you wouldn't hinder them boys from what they wanted to do.'" That was an awful thing for Dad to have to repeat.

Mom got up then and went to the sink and stood there, her back to us. "Well, what do you expect?" she asked angrily.

"Now, Mary, we hashed this out a long time ago—"

"Oh, I'm not mad at you, Loyal. I'm just saying we ought not to have expected cream from a bull. That man just spreads iniquity." She turned around, her arms crossed, rubbing her hands along her forearms as if she were cold. "I'll be so glad when this war's over and the Japanese are gone and things are back to normal. I'd just like to sit down with my friends and sew again the way we used to, without arguing about the people in the camp all the time, without having to take sides. I get so tired of the meanness, the hatefulness. We've got a boy in a prison camp in Germany. Now that's something to worry about. But some people here only think about hate. Do you know, three Japanese women came to church last Sunday, and one of the elders told me he wished they wouldn't come back, because they might be spies. Now I ask you, what's there to spy on at the Methodist church? You think Tojo cares about the sermon? I couldn't hardly understand it myself."

Dad chuckled.

"I told Afton Gardner about how those three were treated, and she said she'd invite them to the Mormon church, if they had a Mormon church in Ellis, because the Mormons knew a thing or two about persecution. I never knew she was a Mormon."

"The Gardners are good people." Dad paused. "I don't see that things'll hardly ever be back to normal, not for a long time anyway. They've gotten worse, too, from when the Japanese people first arrived, and I can't put a reason to it. I thought folks would settle down after a bit, especially since so many of the men from the camp have joined up. That shows they're as American as we are. And every one of the Japanese boys who've gone to work on the farms around here has done a fine job. The farmers can't say enough good things about them. You'd think that would count for something. But it doesn't. I expect they'd try to storm the camp again if they weren't so afraid of you out there in your nightgown."

"Now," Mom warned him. She added, "People are upset because Ellis boys are getting killed, some of them by the Japanese.

And the people out at Tallgrass, they're the face of death. So it's easy to hate them."

"It's Susan Reddick, too," I added. "People still think one of the Japanese killed her."

Dad and Mom exchanged a look over my head, and Mom said, "She's right. Until Sheriff Watrous arrests a man, that murder hangs over Tallgrass."

"Maybe one of the Japanese really did kill her," I said.

"There's that, too." Mom went over to the stove and turned the gas knob, and fire flared up. She stared at the stove absently, then focused on the flame and shook her head. "Now, why did I turn on that burner?" Her hand slowly twisted the knob until the gas went off. "I don't suppose you did any good with Gus Snow."

"Not that I could tell. I probably did Betty Joyce some harm, and for that I sure am sorry. I don't imagine that old fool will ever let her go back to school now."

"At least you tried. What is it that makes people so stubborn?"

"You're asking me?"

Mom sat down at the table and put her hand over Dad's. "I never saw you stubborn when you weren't right about a thing."

I wasn't so sure about that. Once Dad made up his mind, he almost never changed it, even if you all but proved him wrong. Dad was as stubborn as a person could get. When I was in sixth grade, my class went to a Halloween picture show in Lamar that didn't end until midnight. Dad said I had to be home by ten. Mom talked to him, but he wouldn't change his mind, and I was the only kid who didn't go. I knew Dad felt bad about that, and he bought me a sack of licorice the next time we were in town. But he wouldn't change his mind.

"You remember your mother said that." Dad got up and poured us all more coffee. I'd managed to get down the first cup, but I groaned to myself at the thought of having to drink more. Still, now that I'd passed this ritual into adulthood, I wouldn't for anything admit I didn't like coffee. I gulped down as much as I could, then emptied the rest of my coffee into the sink, rinsed the cup, and set it on the drain board. I started for the stairs, stopping when Dad said, "There's something not right with Gus."

"He's a drunk is what it is. And even before that, he wasn't much to speak of. The Stitchers never could understand why Tess married him. I remember Bird Smith said at the wedding, 'How'd you like to go to bed with Gus Snow? That's the acid test.' It might be the only time I ever agreed with her." Mom glanced up and saw that I was still in the room and clamped her hand over her mouth. "Oh my stars!"

Dad laughed. "Like you said, Rennie's getting to be a regular woman."

"Well, I never intended for her to hear that."

"He could make me throw up. I don't even like being in the same room with him. He smells," I said.

"You can say that again." Mom exchanged a glance with Dad.

Dad told us he meant Mr. Snow had changed recently. "Maybe that mule did something to Gus's brain. Of course, that's assuming he's got one. I'm saying there's something not right in his head."

Mom thought that over and asked if Mrs. Snow and Betty Joyce were in danger.

"That's what I'm thinking."

Mom took a handkerchief out of her pocket and touched it to her eyes. Then she blew her nose. "I wish the Stitchers could do something. I've thought and thought about it, but you can't make a quilt for a person just because you don't like her husband. Of course, she could use it to smother him."

Dad shrugged and stood up. "And you can't go to the sheriff and have a man arrested because he talks back to his wife and daughter."

"Well, you ought to be able to. Maybe we could if men didn't make all the laws."

"Perhaps you should run for the state legislature, Mother."

Mom dismissed Dad with a wave of her hand and looked up at him, but Dad wasn't smiling. "I'll do that," she said, "right after chickens fly south."

I NEVER KNEW FOR sure how Betty Joyce returned to school, but I always wondered whether Mr. Yamamoto told Miss Ord what he'd overheard at the hardware store, and Miss Ord did something about it. Betty Joyce returned midway through the fall semester, after football season was under way.

There wasn't anything more important in Ellis than football, and it wasn't just the high school kids who got carried away with it. Everybody in town and the surrounding countryside went to the home games and drove to the other schools for out-of-town matches. Ellis had always supported its high school team, even when it wasn't very good, which was most of the time. This year, however, it appeared that Ellis High School had a chance at the championship. Not the state championship, of course—the Denver schools always won that—but the unofficial championship of southeastern Colorado. The Ellis Chiefs beat Lamar, our arch-rival, and Limon, which always clobbered us. And then we beat La Junta, whose team was the powerhouse in our part of the state.

People in Ellis went crazy with excitement. It wasn't just local pride; it was a way to forget the war. Stores put up signs supporting Ellis. Living room windows had pictures of the fighting

Chiefs wearing feathers of blue and orange, the Ellis school colors. Even Mrs. Snow and Betty Joyce strung blue and orange
crepe paper streamers across the front of the hardware store. A
farmer wrote "Go Ellis" in white rocks ten feet high on a bluff
just east of town. Another painted his tractor orange and put on
blue overalls and drove the tractor to town.

Tod Perkins, our quarterback and captain of the team,
who'd been set to join the Marine Corps when he turned eighteen on October 13, decided to wait until the end of football season to enlist. That was after a group of Ellis businessmen called
on his father at the Perkins farm and told him Tod would do
more patriotic good playing for Ellis for a few more weeks than
he could in boot camp. Dad thought there was an offer of next
year's fertilizer included. Folks said they'd have given Tod a
convertible automobile if there had been any cars available.
When Mr. Elliot announced to an assembly at school that Tod
was staying on, he said, "Tod, that's with one *d,* like God," and
everybody clapped. That's how important football was in Ellis.

Under Tod, the Ellis Chiefs won every game they played. We
didn't win by much—an extra point, a lucky interception. Still,
people saw it as the Lord's will, and they began to think the high
school might have a perfect season, which would have been the
first time in memory. It seemed there wasn't anything that could
beat the Ellis team—nothing, that is, except the Tallgrass Buffaloes, the team from the internment camp high school.

I thought it was too bad the government wouldn't let the kids
from the camp attend the local schools. Maybe we'd have all gotten along better if they had. Or maybe not. Still, if the Japanese
boys had gone to Ellis High, there's no question we would have
had the best football team in southeastern Colorado and maybe
even the state.

It was a shame Ellis High hadn't played Tallgrass at the beginning of the season. The game wouldn't have mattered much then, because nobody had expected Ellis to do so well. But we were scheduled to play the Buffaloes the last game of the year, when Ellis's perfect season was at stake. And by then, it was obvious that Tallgrass High School threatened to ruin it. That's because the internment camp hadn't lost a game, either, and the Tallgrass Buffaloes weren't just lucky; they were good. The Buffaloes were coordinated and tough and aggressive. They didn't make mistakes. They won their games not by a point, but by two or three touchdowns. Of course, I went to Ellis High and rooted for my school. Dad and Mom had gone there, too, and like everybody in Ellis, they were behind the high school team. Still, Dad always liked an underdog, and he said he admired the boys at Tallgrass for the way they played their hearts out. Dad and Carl had a two-dollar bet on the final game, and I figured Dad would pay off Carl no matter which team won.

A couple of weeks before that game, there were threats against Tallgrass. Signs went up saying Ellis High Remembers Pearl Harbor. Kids threw rocks at the Tallgrass team's bus, and people started talking about avenging Susan Reddick. Men who hung out at the feed store and the barbershop said it wasn't patriotic to play the Japanese. Mr. Tappan put the guards at the camp on overtime.

"How come my boy's to play football with the Nips when he's about to get drafted to fight them in the Pacific?" Lum Smith asked.

"It's un-American," Mr. Kruger added.

The Monday before the Saturday game, the two of them called a meeting of the parents of the Ellis High team. That night, seven fathers told the coach that their sons wouldn't be playing football against the Tallgrass Buffaloes.

The coach went to the school board, which called an emergency meeting and announced that the stadium was closed to Japanese players. On game day, the Ellis Chiefs showed up. So did the Tallgrass Buffaloes, but the school board wouldn't let them onto the field. Ellis claimed it won the game by default and declared itself unbeaten. The team went to the state finals, where it lost its first game. Ellis still claimed to be the football champion of southeastern Colorado, but that was unofficial, and there was always a taint to it.

Tod Perkins's father was not at the meeting, and Tod was not one of the seven who refused to play the Japanese. A few days after football season ended, Carl was at the camp when Tod walked out there and asked to see Jimmy Matoba, the captain of the Tallgrass team. "Dang, boy, I sure did look forward to that match. We would have whipped you," Tod told Jimmy.

"Nah, you'd have lost bad. We had you beat in a walk." Jimmy gave him a crooked grin, then kicked at the dirt with his shoe. "I heard you were joining up."

"I thought I might."

"Me, too. Maybe the army'll let us play against each other."

Tod considered that. "I was thinking maybe we could be on the same team."

"Yeah, how 'bout that?" And they shook hands.

BETTY JOYCE AND I had planned to go together to that game against Tallgrass. By then, she had been attending classes for nearly a month.

Betty Joyce had been out of school for three weeks when

Miss Ord asked me whether she had quit for good. I told her about Mr. Snow's accident and how he had kept Betty Joyce at the store, and then Miss Ord asked whether it would help if she spoke to Mr. Snow.

I shrugged. "He doesn't like people telling him what to do."

Miss Ord talked to him anyway, and Betty Joyce told me her dad was as rude to Miss Ord as he had been to Mr. Yamamoto. I don't know what happened after that, but a week later, I came home from school, to find Mom in my room, peering into my closet. "We'll have to make room in here and clean out one of your dresser drawers, too. You'll be having company."

"Marthalice is coming home?"

Mom shook her head. "Betty Joyce is going to be living with us for a while." She sat down on the bed. "Sheriff Watrous was here this afternoon. Your dad and I think you're big enough to know what's going on. Besides, you ought not to pester Betty Joyce about it. She can tell you if she wants to." Mom patted the bed, and I sat down beside her. Outside, the chickens clucked, but Mom was figuring out what to say, so she didn't even look out the window.

Finally, she said, "I guess I'll tell you all of it. Doc Enyeart and the sheriff went to see Mr. Snow this morning, and they found an illegal supply of morphine, enough to supply a whole bunch of dope fiends. Mr. Snow is a morphine addict. That's why he's been so cussed mean. Doc gave him a little bit of morphine right after he got kicked in the head by that mule, but he cut it off a long time ago. The sheriff says there's morphine been stolen from the camp, and he thinks somebody sold it to the person who sold it to Gus Snow. The Jack boy would be my choice for the middleman. It seems like when nobody's around, Mr. Snow beats up on both Mrs. Snow and Betty Joyce. I don't like

to think what they've gone through." Mom ran her hand across
the quilt—a Grandmother's Flower Garden that Granny had
pieced and the Jolly Stitchers had quilted. She stopped at a worn
place where the stitching had come loose and worried at the rav-
eled area with her finger. "Do you know what a dope fiend is?"

I nodded. I'd read about them in comic books and heard
about them on radio programs, and I was horrified that my best
friend had had to live with a father whose mind was crazed
from drugs. Dad had figured out that there was something
wrong with Mr. Snow's brain, but who would have thought he
took dope? Betty Joyce must have been scared all the time. I'd
been an idiot to think I could read her mind. "Did he hurt Betty
Joyce?"

"They'll both be all right, thank the Lord."

"Is Mr. Snow going to jail?"

"The sheriff told Mr. Snow he could do that or he could put
himself in a hospital and get help. Mrs. Snow is so worn-out,
she's going to her sister's place for a few weeks, until she's up to
running the hardware again—that is, if she wants to. The sheriff asked if we'd take Betty Joyce until her mother's recovered. I
said of course we would."

That afternoon, we drove into Ellis for Betty Joyce. Mr. Snow
was already gone, and we waited at the store until Mrs. Snow's
sister, LaVerne Booth, came from Pueblo for her. "If I'd have
known . . . Why didn't you write me, Tessie?" Mrs. Booth asked.
Mrs. Booth was a fat woman, and together, the two sisters looked
like Mr. and Mrs. Sprat.

"I was ashamed," Mrs. Snow replied, so softly that we could
barely hear her.

"But what about Betty Joyce? Didn't you think about her?"

Mrs. Snow didn't answer, only hugged her shoulders together.

"She couldn't help it," Betty Joyce said, talking to nobody in particular.

Mrs. Booth opened the car door and said to Mrs. Snow, "I want you to sit up here in front, honeypot, right next to me." After her sister was in the car, Mrs. Booth shut the door and told us, "No wonder she never figured out what was wrong with Gus." Patting Mrs. Snow's shoulder through the window, Mrs. Booth added, "Tess is awfully fine, but she's such a timid little thing. She don't know a morphine addict from a gum chewer."

9

AFTER THE SUPPER DISHES were done one evening late in the fall, we all went outside. Mom and Granny rocked on the porch swing, moving back and forth in the soft dusk, while Betty Joyce and I sat on the steps with our homework. Dad leaned against the railing, whittling a stick, telling Mom that she had fixed an awful good supper. He always said that when we had pie for dessert. The night was peaceful, the kind of evening we used to have before the war started, when Dad and Buddy played catch on the front lawn and Marthalice read while I cut out paper dolls. That seemed like a long time ago.

Dad stripped curls of bark off the wood for a few minutes, then looked up and stared off into the distance, down the road, where wooden telephone poles stood out against the darkening sky like crosses. After a bit, he said, "I believe that's Carl coming this way."

Mom stopped the swing and leaned forward for a better

look. Granny put down the remembrance quilt square of Sabra that she was piecing and peered over the top of her glasses. It was too dark for her to sew; just holding her piecework comforted her. "Yes, that's Carl," Dad said, closing his pocketknife and putting it away. He threw the stick into the yard and kicked the wood shavings off the porch with his high-top shoe. I got up and stood beside him. Carl had never been to our house at night.

He came down the road at a fast clip, low to the ground, his elbows to his sides, and leaped the fence instead of going through the gate. Carl ran across the lawn toward us, then stopped, winded, and walked a dozen yards before he picked up his pace again. When he reached the porch, he leaned over to catch his breath, holding on to the porch post. Dad went down the steps and put a hand on Carl's arm. "Son?"

Carl looked up at him. He'd been crying. Behind me, I heard Mom barely whisper, "Daisy?" I put my hand on top of Betty Joyce's.

Carl didn't hear her. "Mr. Stroud." He gasped and breathed deeply, filling his lungs with air. "It's Harry, sir. He's dead."

"Oh," Mom said, the breath going out of her. She stood up and walked over to the railing, putting her hand on my shoulder. "Oh, Carl."

"Who?" Granny asked.

"Harry. Our friend," Mom told her.

"That nice boy?"

"I sure am sorry to hear that." Dad helped Carl sit down on the steps. I went inside and came back with a glass of water. We watched Carl drink it while we waited for him to tell us what had happened.

"It was some damn jeep accident." Carl had covered up his sorrow with anger now. "The jeep blew a tire and turned over or something. Harry didn't even have a chance to get killed in the war. It was just a dumb accident." Carl handed the glass to me, and I went inside and refilled it. He waited until I returned. "Harry's folks got a letter. I guess they don't send telegrams if your son's Japanese." He made a fist with his right hand and socked it into his left palm. I'd never seen him angry before.

"Maybe the telegram went astray. Or they didn't know where to send it," Mom volunteered.

"They sure as hell knew where to send us." Carl put his elbows on his knees and rested his head in his hands.

Maybe Dad agreed with Carl, because he didn't argue with him. Instead, he said, "Harry was as fine a young man as I've ever known, a hard worker, too." There wasn't any better compliment Dad could give a man than to say he was a good worker.

"He was going to show everybody, show them he was a better American than they were, better than those damn boys that hang around Ellis. He was going to be a war hero. He didn't care if he got killed. Harry said he was a one hundred and fifty percent American. Now he's dead in an accident. It's not fair, Mr. Stroud." Carl didn't look up, and his voice was muffled.

"I don't reckon anything about this war's fair," Dad said. "But you already know that, Carl."

"Yes, sir."

"I hate this war," I said. Mom didn't like my saying I hated things, and sometimes she told me to use the word *dislike* instead of *hate,* but this time she nodded in agreement.

"We loved Harry as much as if he'd been one of Bud's friends," Mom said.

"Yes, ma'am."

Mom asked how Harry's folks were doing.

Carl looked up at her then and slumped back against the porch steps. "They're pretty broke up."

"And Daisy?"

"She's broke up, too." Carl began to cry, and Dad sat down on the steps next to him, putting his arm around Carl's shoulder. We were all silent, listening to Carl's sobs, which were ragged, like a piece of machinery that wasn't hitting right. After a few minutes, they slowed and stopped, and we stayed quiet.

I wished I could think of something to say, but nothing came to me then. I knew it probably wouldn't until after Carl had gone home. Harry was always a little disdainful, and I'd never been sure how much he liked me, but he was nice. He'd brought me a bird's nest that the wind had blown out of a cottonwood tree, and after he heard me tell Daisy I'd lost my pocketknife in the barn, he'd spent an hour after work looking for it, finally finding it in the straw under the milking stool. Although other Ellis boys had been killed in the war, Harry was the one I knew best. It struck me as odd that I thought of him as an Ellis boy, not as someone from the camp.

I touched my cheek and realized I was crying. Harry's death made me feel lonely, although my family was there, and in the distance were the sounds I had heard all my life—horses moving around in the corral and chickens squawking. Mom would go out later with her shotgun, because a coyote might be hanging around. She wouldn't think twice about killing a predator. I wished she would shoot every dang coyote in the county and everybody who was responsible for the war, too. I smacked the fist of my right hand into the palm of my left, too.

A breeze came up. It was too late for lilacs and honeysuckle, but the fall wind brought the smell of the fields. That scent made me think of Harry, how in the spring he brought the smell of freshly turned earth when he came into the kitchen to talk to Daisy.

Mom took a handkerchief from her apron pocket and wiped her eyes. "I'd like to call on Harry's people, but I don't know your customs, Carl. Would that be all right?"

"Yes, ma'am. I think they'd appreciate that. There's just Mr. and Mrs. Hirano. Harry's got a brother, but he's at that Manzanar camp in California with his wife."

There didn't seem much to say after that, but it wasn't awkward. Carl was comfortable with us, especially with Dad. After a while, he stood up. "I don't know exactly why I came, Mr. Stroud. It just seemed like I should."

"We're glad you did, Carl. You knew we'd want to know about a thing like that. Harry was our friend, too. He was a good man, a fine American."

"Yes, sir."

"Damn war," Dad said.

"Yes, sir. Damn war."

After Carl left and the others went inside, Dad and I sat on the porch in the dark. I thought about the Japanese being forced into the camp and the government making Harry join the army, and Harry getting killed before he could even go overseas. He'd never get a Purple Heart or any other medal. "Carl's right: It's not fair," I said.

"Not fair at all, Squirt. But then I never heard of a war that was."

THE NEXT MORNING, MOM baked a chocolate cake, using our chocolate and sugar rations. She'd thought about making divinity

because Harry had liked it, but cakes were what she always took
to the neighbors when somebody died, and she didn't see why
she should treat the Hiranos differently just because they were
Japanese.

"Are you sure you're doing the right thing, Mary?" Mrs.
Rubey asked her. She'd called that morning and found Mom in the
kitchen by herself. Carl had told us that he and Daisy and Emory
wouldn't be coming to work for a couple of days. "Mightn't you
just be better off letting them grieve in their own way? After all,
you do run the risk of offending those people."

"*Those people?*"

"Oh, dear, now what have I gone and said?"

"You haven't said anything. It is hard to know what's right.
But Carl said Harry's people would appreciate it. I prayed about
it some last night, and it came to me that all I can do is what I
think is right. I have to hope that if I offend them, the Hiranos
will know I acted in good faith and forgive me."

"Just like folks in Ellis would." They both laughed.

When the cake had cooled and Mom had iced it and put it
into the metal cake carrier, she dressed in her good clothes and
put on a hat. She made Dad put on his suit and a tie and told me
to wear my Sunday dress. Then the three of us walked to the
Tallgrass Camp to call on the Hiranos. Betty Joyce stayed behind with Granny.

I'd never been inside the camp before, and although I'd
passed it dozens of times, I was surprised at all the rows of
wooden barracks, which were lined up as straight as the furrows
in our fields. The streets weren't as barren as Dad had described
them in the beginning. A little more than a year after the first
Japanese had moved in, saplings and grass grew in the dirt, and
a pretty garden with a dozen kinds of flowers and a still pond

with a bridge lay behind a little fence. "Somebody's made the desert bloom," Mom observed. "And they've done it better than I ever did."

We stopped at one of the long buildings, and Dad knocked on the door frame because the door was open and there was no screen door. The murmuring in the room stopped, and a man came to the doorway. Dad took off his hat and said, "Stroud's my name. This here's my wife and daughter. We've come to pay our respects to the Hiranos."

There was a stir in the room then, and Carl came forward and shook Dad's hand. Carl wore a suit and a tie, and I knew Mom had been right to make Dad dress up. "Come on in," Carl said. Mom and Dad stepped inside, and I followed them reluctantly, suddenly feeling like an intruder. Maybe the Japanese don't want us here, I thought. After all, white people had sent them to Tallgrass. I didn't care to be someplace where people resented me. But then I realized that maybe Mom was right and they would appreciate our good intentions, even if those intentions came out wrong.

The Japanese opened a pathway between the door and a cot, where a man and woman sat, and we walked to them. Carl introduced us to Mr. and Mrs. Hirano, who stood and bowed.

"We are honored," Mr. Hirano said.

"We're so sorry. Harry was a fine young man," Mom told Mrs. Hirano, who nodded solemnly. Her face was white, and her dress was a shade of pink so pale that it was almost white, too.

"A good worker," Dad added.

The Hiranos looked at me, waiting for me to say something. I glanced around and saw a girl about my age, who gave me the wisp of a smile. I smiled back. "He always teased me."

"Ah," Mr. Hirano said. He smiled, and the corners of his wife's mouth turned up the tiniest bit. Behind me, someone laughed. I should have said what a nice boy Harry was, and I flushed with embarrassment. But people began to whisper and then to talk again. "He liked to tease the pretty girls," Mr. Hirano said, and there was quiet laughter. I looked at the girl again. She was small, with sleek black hair and smooth skin. With my scraggly hair and washed-out suntan, I felt awkward. I watched as the girl glided out the door, thinking that in a hundred years of practice, I could never move like that.

A man brought chairs for us, small, rough, hand-fashioned chairs that might have been made at the camp, and Mom gave Mrs. Hirano the cake. "Chocolate," Mrs. Hirano said. "Harry liked your cooking. He said the first day he went to work for you, you made special white candy."

"Divinity. I almost brought some."

"Chocolate cake is good." Mrs. Hirano handed the cake to a woman, who placed it on a table that was covered with a white cloth. Other food was spread out there—Japanese food, I knew, because it was strange to me. Some of it was almost too pretty to eat. At the back of the table stood a tall white vase with three odd-shaped flowers on long stems. Daisy emerged from the side of the room with tea in tiny white cups like eggshells. She gave them to us without speaking.

Mrs. Hirano told Mom she was sorry about Buddy being taken prisoner by the Germans, which brought tears to Mom's eyes. "Imagine, in her own grief, she thought of us," Mom said later.

Mr. Hirano asked Dad how his sugar beets were doing, and the two of them talked about crops. Then Mrs. Hirano told Daisy to get out a piece of needlework to show Mom. "It has been in my family for several generations. Daisy says you make many beautiful quilts with your needle."

Daisy pulled a suitcase from under another cot across the room and took out a silk bag and gave it to Mrs. Hirano, who carefully removed a white silk cloth and opened it. The cloth was an embroidery of birds done in blue and white, and it was so beautiful that Mom drew in her breath. "Oh my," Mom said as women on either side of her peered over her shoulders to admire it. Mrs. Hirano handed the embroidery to Mom and gestured for her to take it to the single lightbulb that hung in the center of the room, so that she could see it better. The women gathered around Mom and muttered signs of approval. After she examined it, Mom folded the cloth, making sure she did not fold it along the old lines, and handed it back to Mrs. Hirano. "Some of those stitches are as small as poppy seeds. I never saw anything so nicely made. It's a treasure, a sure enough treasure. You're smart to protect it from all the dirt around here."

"Yes." Mrs. Hirano returned the cloth to its bag and handed it to Daisy. "It is too dirty here for us to leave it out." I looked at the windowsill and saw a film of dust, and I knew that no matter how often Mrs. Hirano cleaned, there would always be dust in the room.

Mom asked then if the Hiranos were planning a service for Harry, admitting she didn't know Japanese customs.

"He was buried at the camp where he died, but we had a service here this morning at Tallgrass. We are Methodist, not Buddhist," Mr. Hirano told us.

"The Methodists in town didn't want us," a woman said, and there were shushing sounds. Mrs. Hirano looked embarrassed, as though the woman had been impolite.

Mom ignored the remark and said, "I'm sorry we didn't know. We would have attended to show our love for Harry."

"Thank you," Mrs. Hirano said. "Harry liked his work with the sugar beets. There is dignity in work."

We finished the tea and a little plate of Japanese food—crackers and something made with rice and raisins. "Real raisins," Daisy whispered when she handed the plate to me, and I knew she remembered a story she'd told me. When the camp was opened, a cook had fixed a vat of what the Japanese thought was rice pudding, which was placed outside on a huge table. "When we got close, we found out what we thought were raisins were really dead flies," Daisy said. "We were so hungry, we picked them out and ate the rice."

Then Mom and Dad stood and told the Hiranos again that they were sorry about Harry. We went back through the crowded room, Dad nodding at one or two of the men he had met somewhere. At the door, he shook hands with Carl, who thanked us for coming and handed Mom her cake carrier.

As soon as we were on the street, Dad took off his suit coat and loosened his tie. He said he didn't know how people could stand to live in a room like sardines in a tin can, without so much as a breath of fresh air. "You'd think the government had never heard of cross-ventilation," he said. "Or screens."

"I understand that saying about a bull in a china shop," Mom told us, fanning her face with her hand. "I never felt so awkward in my life, putting my sweaty, chapped hands on that beautiful piece of silk. It was as fine as a cobweb. I was afraid I'd snag it with my rough skin."

"Do you think they gave us more comfort than we gave them?" I asked.

"I reckon that's so," Dad said. "And we're supposed to be the civilized ones."

THE BEET HARVEST WENT smoothly that fall, although Dad
worried about some of the Ellis boys interfering with our Japanese
hired hands. Carl selected a crew of boys from Tallgrass to dig the
beets and top them and throw them into the wagon. Then Dad
drove the wagon into town to the sugar factory. The first day the
Japanese crew was there, Betty Joyce and I stood in the doorway
of the house, looking at each boy to see if one of them might be
Susan Reddick's killer. But there was no way to tell. They were all
young boys, not much older than we were, and polite. They didn't
look any more like killers than Carl did, and after a day or two,
we stopped worrying that one of them was waiting to murder us.

The boys worked as hard as Carl, Emory, and Harry had
during spring planting. Dad never had to teach them a thing
twice, and they never loafed or goofed off. They weren't surly
the way some beet workers were, but seemed grateful to have
jobs that took them out of the camp. And after visiting Tallgrass, I knew why those Japanese boys were glad to be on the
other side of the bobwire.

Sometimes, on the way back to the farm with the empty
wagon, Dad passed Beaner, Danny, and Pete leaning against the
fence, watching the crew. Dad always waved and was friendly,
and sometimes he stopped and exchanged a word with them. If
they ever said anything nasty about the Japanese, Dad didn't tell
us. But he kept an eye on those three, and he told Carl to let him
know if they didn't behave. Carl grinned and said that with
their big beet knives, the Japanese crew could handle themselves. Dad told him that was what he was afraid of. He didn't
want trouble, even if our boys were in the right.

"All we need is one little incident to set off this town. It won't matter who's at fault. Beaner Jack could jump one of the camp boys, but if Carl or Emory or one of the others turned around and fought back, we'd have Pearl Harbor in reverse right here in Ellis," Dad predicted one afternoon as he dried himself with a towel we kept next to the pump. He'd pumped water over his head to cool off.

Dad told our boys to walk from the camp in a group. They weren't to be alone, because somebody could treat them like prey. Other farmers who hired Japanese crews drove them to and from the fields so that they didn't have to walk along the roads, where Ellis men called them dirty names or tried to start fights. Japanese people didn't go into town much now, and when they did, they went in groups.

"They don't understand it out at Tallgrass," Dad told us. "Sheriff Watrous says in towns near the internment camps in California and up north in Wyoming, people are getting along all right now. Why do things have to be so bad in Ellis?"

"It's Susan Reddick's death. Folks just won't stop talking about it. It's the older Elliot boy getting killed in the South Pacific, too," Mom replied, and Dad thought it over and guessed she was right.

Fred Elliot, Pete's brother, had joined the Marine Corps, and he'd been sent to the South Pacific. In early fall, about the time football season got under way, word came that he'd been killed. The telegram asked the Elliots not to divulge where Fred had been fighting, because it might aid the enemy. But Mr. Elliot did. He stood up in church and asked for prayers to beat the Japanese. "Fred was fighting the Japs in New Guinea. It's my belief we got spies out at the Tallgrass Camp giving information to their relatives in Japan, and we ought to go out there and kill a dozen of them for every one of our boys they murder."

Mrs. Elliot tugged at her husband's sleeve to get him to sit down, and a few of the men coughed and looked embarrassed. The minister scrapped his regular sermon and preached about forgiving our enemies, which caused more foot shuffling. But after church, several men clapped Mr. Elliot on the back and said, "You told it for us." One of the deacons said, "We know the Lord's on our side in this war, but sometimes it seems like He sure has a funny way of showing it."

Another added, "Those mysterious ways He works in, I sure don't understand 'em all the time."

Fred getting killed gave Pete an importance he'd never had before. He went around saying the Japanese at Tallgrass were nothing but a fifth column. He'd claimed that before, but now people paid attention to him. Danny and Beaner nodded and said, "You got that right, Pete."

Things were tense even for the kids in the camp who never came in contact with people from Ellis. Little boys there played war games, just like the boys in Ellis. Daisy told us she'd watched a group of Tallgrass kids pretending they were fighting in the South Pacific and heard one complain, "How come I have to be the damn Jap all the time?"

"We're just a tinderbox," Dad said. "All we need is for some fool to strike the match. Maybe it's a good thing we didn't play football against Tallgrass. Can you imagine what would have happened if Ellis had lost to those boys?"

Carl no longer let Daisy walk to and from our farm by herself. Carl and Emory and the other boys from Tallgrass who'd come to work for us brought Daisy and the two Japanese women Mom had hired to help with the cooking to our back door each morning. Mom was feeling better, but Dad told her if he had a crew to help him with the beets, she ought to have one to help her in the kitchen, and Mom didn't argue too much about it. I was glad, because Mom worked hard just keeping up our spirits, never complaining and always being cheerful. I knew it wasn't easy for her. Sometimes, when Daisy was outside, I'd go into the kitchen, tiptoeing so that I wouldn't wake Mom, and I'd hear her crying. I'd sneak back to the door and slam it to let her know I was there. By the time I got to the bedroom, Mom would have dried her eyes, and she'd be smiling.

So Mom stayed in her bedroom and turned the harvest work over to Daisy. Mom made up the menus, and Dad shopped in town for what we didn't grow ourselves.

Betty Joyce and I did our part, fixing breakfast and supper for the family and making sure coffee was ready for the boys before we left for school in the morning. One day, Daisy sent word that she was too sick to work, so Mom let us stay home from school to help cook for the crew.

"When's her baby due?" Betty Joyce asked me as I rolled out piecrust on the floured oilcloth on the kitchen table. Four of the five pie plates in front of me already had crusts in them. Betty Joyce was peeling the apples, cutting them up, and dropping them into big mixing bowls filled with cinnamon and honey, since we were trying to stretch the sugar rations. The two women Mom had hired were outside. One was sitting in the sun snapping green beans, the other peeling potatoes and dropping them into a pan of water. We could hear them talking in Japanese. Granny sat with them, her piecing in her hands, nodding every now and then, as if she understood what the women were saying.

"Whose baby?" The piecrust tore, and I dipped my finger into a tumbler of water on the table and smeared the water over the ripped part, patching it back together. I wondered if ever in my life I'd make a perfect piecrust. Mom said men never paid attention, so

I shouldn't waste time on the looks, that only the taste counted, but women noticed. I'd heard them comment at church suppers and bake sales and knew that to them, the way a pie or cake looked was just as important as the taste. I knew if I ever became a Jolly Stitcher, I'd have to make a perfect piecrust, but that wasn't a big worry. I'd run off and join the WAVEs before I ever became a Jolly Stitcher.

"Daisy's."

"Daisy's not even married." I thought of wrapping the piecrust around the rolling pin the way Mom did and then unrolling it onto the pie plate, but I didn't dare. The crust would tear in half and fall off, and I'd have to gather it up and roll it out again, and a reworked piecrust tasted like cardboard. Even a harvest crew would notice that. I sifted flour onto a spatula and edged it under the crust, then folded the crust in half and slid it onto the pie plate. It was a little off center, and I considered pulling it into place, but I didn't want to rip it, so I left it alone. "That's the last one. You can start filling these if you want to."

I glanced up at Betty Joyce, who was standing with her hands on her hips, the big metal spoon grasped in one fist. "Don't try to fool me," she said. "You don't have to be married to have a baby."

Reaching into the bin, I took a handful of flour and spread it on the table. Then I patted out dough, picked up the rolling pin again, and began to roll the dough to make lattice strips for the tops of the pies. The rolling pin was white ceramic and had green handles. As I began rolling the dough, a tiny flake of green paint came off. I stuck my fingernail into the dough beneath it and picked out the speck, wiping it on my apron. Then I looked up at Betty Joyce.

The springs in the bedroom moved, which meant Mom was listening.

"Well, Daisy's pregnant, isn't she?" Betty Joyce scooped out bits of butter and flicked them on top of the apples she'd put on the piecrusts.

I set down the rolling pin so hard that I almost broke it. "Well, what if she is?" I'd hoped that if I didn't pay attention to what she was talking about, Betty Joyce would drop it.

From the bedroom, Mom called, "Girls, those pies ought to go into the oven pretty quick now."

"Yes, ma'am," Betty Joyce said.

I cut thick strips of lattice with a knife, thinking hard about Daisy and not caring how irregular the strips were. Of course, I knew she was pregnant. At first, I'd worried that Daisy was sick, because she threw up so much. I'd thought she was getting fat and that was why her skirts were so tight. Then one day, she wore a big, loose blouse, and I just knew she was going to have a baby. And, of course, she wasn't married, because the father of her baby had been killed in an accident at boot camp. A couple of times, I'd asked Daisy how she was doing or if she was feeling all right, thinking she might want to talk to me, but she'd replied, "Fine," so she hadn't wanted to say anything, at least not to me. Why would she want to talk to me anyway? I wondered. Some help a ninth grader would be. She might have spoken to Mom. She probably had, because a couple of times, the two of them had broken off their conversation when I'd walked into the room. Nobody said anything to me, and I guess I hoped that if I ignored her condition, it might just go away. I hadn't even written to Marthalice about it.

I crisscrossed the lattice strips over the apples, then folded the ends under the crust and pinched the edges with my fingers. I picked up the sifter and sprinkled sugar on top of the lattice-work. As Betty Joyce and I put the pies into the oven, the two women from the camp came back into the kitchen, chattering in Japanese, occasionally slipping into English when they said something they wanted us to hear. They put the potatoes and beans on to boil and began frying the meat for dinner.

Betty Joyce and I went outside to set up the tables. "I'm right, aren't I?" Betty Joyce asked as we set a plank on top of two sawhorses and shook out a tablecloth and arranged it on top.

"How would I know?" I set rocks on the corners of the table to keep the cloth from flying off in the wind and then went back into the house for the plates.

"Hey, I just asked." Betty Joyce passed me as I came back outside. She was going in for the silverware. The Japanese women began carrying out dishpans full of sliced bread and pitchers of iced tea.

When everything was ready, Mom called to me to ring the dinner bell to bring the workers from the field. I opened the oven to peek at the pies, which had begun to brown. The juice was seeping over the crust, and you couldn't tell where it had broken or where the strips across the top were different sizes.

"Ah," one of the women said, looking over my shoulder. "Japanese men always like apple pie."

After a while, the men came in from the far field, talking, laughing, pumping water to wash up, then sitting down at the table as we hurried out with platters and dishes of food. We were so busy that Betty Joyce and I didn't have time to talk about Daisy. When the men were finished with the main course, we took the pies from the oven and cut big slices. "What did I tell you? We eat good here," Carl told one of the workers. "My mom never made an apple pie like that."

"Your Mom never made any apple pie." Emory punched him.

When they finished eating, the crew lounged in the shade under the big cottonwoods and talked and laughed. Some of them smoked, not roll-your-own cigarettes like Dad's, but ready-mades. Carl and Emory joked with me and sometimes Betty Joyce, but the others didn't look at us and always grew quiet when we got near them. I tried to be friendly and asked one boy where he came from, but he stared at the ground and mumbled, so I gave up. His friend said something to him in Japanese, and the boy swatted him, so I knew I'd embarrassed him. After that, I didn't talk to the boys I didn't know.

The crew was about to go back to work, when a truck drove into the yard and parked, the engine idling. Before Beaner could step down out of the cab, Dad got up and went over to him. Dad didn't hurry, but he walked with a purpose, his head up, as if Beaner had stopped for a reason, not just pulled into our place because he was passing by. The boys stopped talking and sat up. One put his hand on his beet knife. They knew who Beaner was. Only the Japanese women ignored the truck.

"Afternoon, boys," Dad said, putting his heavy work shoe on the running board of Beaner's truck. Bits of dried mud came off his shoe and lay on the rubber tread. Dad gripped the window frame with his right hand. It was an easy gesture, but Beaner couldn't open the door with Dad's hand there.

"Howdy, Mr. Stroud," Beaner said.

Danny opened the passenger door and stepped out. He raised his elbows, flexing his arms, then looked around the yard. When he spotted me, he grinned. I looked away, sorry they were there, because they had spoiled the easy manner of our crew. The Japanese were serious now, watchful. Beaner and Danny always ruined things.

"Is there something I can do for you fellows?" Dad asked.

"Anything wrong with a little neighborly visit?" Beaner didn't look at Dad when he spoke; instead, he caught his reflection in the side-view mirror and raised his chin, looking pleased with himself.

"We're a little busy right now with the beet harvest. Say what you came for," Dad told him. His voice was calm, but there was an edge of steel to it. I knew never to cross Dad when he spoke like that.

"We're not looking for trouble," Beaner told him.

"I didn't say you were." But I knew they were, and I expect Dad did, too.

Danny took a few steps toward the house, looking around. Betty Joyce sucked in her breath, and I whispered, "They have to get past Dad and a crew of beet workers to get to us." That was a silly thing to say, I thought. Why would Beaner and Danny go after us? Still, from the way Betty Joyce drew back, I wondered if they had tormented her at the hardware store and she was afraid of them. I figured she'd be glad the crew was between her and those two. Shoot, even I felt safer knowing there were all those beet knives in their way.

Dad didn't move, but he told Danny, "Son, I advise you to get back into the truck."

Danny didn't do it, but he stopped walking and hitched up his pants.

"State your business, and then move along," Dad said sternly.

Carl and Emory had stood up, their beet knives in their hands, watching Dad to see if he needed them. The others were squatting on their heels. The Japanese women knew something was wrong now, and they moved closer to the house, their hands wrapped in their aprons, just like regular farm women. Mom had gone to the bedroom window when she'd heard the truck pull in.

Beaner jutted out his jaw and said in a loud voice, so that the Japanese boys would hear, "Somebody's stole my spare tire, stole it right out of my truck."

"I'm sorry to hear that," Dad said. He wasn't looking at Beaner. Instead, he was watching Danny, who had started walking toward the house again, his hands on his hips.

"Yeah. I'm betting it was one of your Japs."

"And when would they have done that?" Dad asked.

"Maybe at night."

"Sneaked onto your farm, right past your dogs and all your people?"

"Could be."

"You have proof of that, do you?"

"Maybe."

"Then I advise you to take it to Sheriff Watrous."

"Yeah, I thought that's what you'd say."

Dad couldn't help but chuckle. "That's the way the justice system works in America."

"Well, these here ain't Americans, are they?"

"They are on this farm." Dad stepped away from the truck and made a circling motion with his arm. "You just swing on around now and go out the way you came. Danny, get back in the truck. We're not looking for trouble here."

Danny stopped but didn't turn around, until Dad said again, "Danny." His voice was as hard as it ever got, which was pretty darn hard.

"Yeah?" Danny said over his shoulder.

"I believe you heard me."

"You wouldn't be fixing to throw us off your property, would you, Mr. Stroud?" Beaner asked. "I got a couple of brothers could take on any Japs you got."

"You go on about your business, Beaner. You're not wanted here," Dad said. "Danny, I advise you again to get into the truck." Then, as if Beaner had come into the yard just to shoot the breeze, Dad turned and walked toward the house.

After a moment, Beaner said, "Spano, what the hell are you doing out there? Get in the damn truck." Danny tried to look nonchalant, but he did what Beaner told him to. Beaner turned the truck around and sped out onto the road.

"Wow, Mr. Stroud. He could have hurt you," Emory said, watching the truck disappear behind a wave of dust.

"Not when I had all you boys backing me up," Dad said. "Now, come on, there's beets to harvest."

"He's still pretty brave," Betty Joyce whispered to me, and I nodded. I didn't tell her how scared I'd been. Dad could have handled them in a fair fight, but Danny and Beaner weren't fair. Beaner might have run down Dad in his truck, or Danny could have sneaked up behind him and punched him.

After the crew returned to the fields, Dad went over to Mom at the window.

"What was that about?" Mom asked.

"Those two were all liquored up. But even full of whiskey, a Jack isn't fool enough to take on a crew armed with beet knives. I don't think we have to worry about them." But he told Betty Joyce and me that if Beaner came back, we were to ring the dinner bell and that he and the boys would come running.

After Dad went to the fields, I took a plate of food to Mom; then Betty Joyce and I sat down at the table with Granny and the Japanese women and ate our dinner. Afterward, we washed the dirty dishes.

"One day, we make Japanese food for those boys. You ask your mother. Daisy will tell you what to get," one of the woman said.

"That'd be swell," I told her.

"No apple pie," the other said, pretending to look sad. They both laughed.

When we had finished cleaning up, Granny went outside with the Japanese women, who took out their knitting and waited for the boys to walk them back to the camp. Betty Joyce and I got out homework and spread it across the kitchen table. We were still learning diagramming in English class, and without Daisy to help us, neither one of us was very good. "Okay, we'll start with a declarative sentence. Give me an example," I said.

"Daisy is pregnant." Betty Joyce giggled.

The springs in the bedroom squeaked, and we heard Mom get out of bed. I kicked Betty Joyce, who pantomimed "I'm sorry." We both waited while Mom put on her slippers and her housecoat, then came out into the kitchen. She told us we'd done a good job and that she was sorry to have left us with all the work. Then Mom sat down at the table next to me, across from Betty Joyce.

Betty Joyce told her she didn't mind. "You want some iced tea, Mrs. Stroud? I'll get it for you." Betty Joyce might have been hoping to get Mom's mind off what she'd just said about Daisy, but I knew there was no use. You never got Mom's mind off a thing once it was fixed on it.

Mom shook her head. She picked up the saltshaker, a Dutch girl. The pepper one was a Dutch boy, and if you put them together just right, it looked as if they were kissing. I never put them together. Mom twisted the shaker in her hand and set it down. She told us she had to make up a menu for the next day so that Dad could stop at the grocery after he took in the last load of beets. I knew this would be torture. Mom would go through the whole meal before she'd get around to Daisy. She asked me for a piece of notebook paper and picked up my pencil. "I thought hamburg steak, mashed potatoes." She droned on, writing down the items. "What kind of pie? I guess you'll get to be a champion pie baker before harvest is over, Rennie. What about lemon? Your dad can pick up some lemons. There ought to be lemons at the store."

"You can use vinegar. It tastes the same," Betty Joyce said.

Granny came into the kitchen then, catching the screen door with her foot. "Vinegar pie!" She wrinkled her nose. "Not in this house. We've never been so poor we had to serve vinegar pie." She went into the dining room and came back with a spool of thread. "No vinegar pie in this house."

"I guess that's our answer. Lemon," Mom said. When she had finished the menu, she wrote a grocery list at the bottom of the page, then folded the page and tore off the list and set it aside for Dad. "Do you girls know how to make meringue? If you don't, Daisy can show you. She ought to be here tomorrow."

"I know how," Betty Joyce said.

I didn't say anything. Mom had brought up Daisy's name. Now we were about to get it.

"You girls should know that Daisy being pregnant is her business. It's not ours." Mom looked straight at Betty Joyce.

"Yes, ma'am," Betty Joyce said.

Mom turned to me.

I thought that over and wasn't so sure. "Maybe it is our business. After all, she works for us, and people are going to talk. They'll ask us about her," I said.

"I don't know who that would be, unless we tell them."

"They've got eyes. If we can see she's going to have a baby, so can everybody else."

Mom sighed. "Yes, I suppose it's wishful thinking to believe we could keep it quiet."

"Maybe she got married and didn't tell you," Betty Joyce said. I'd never told her about Daisy and Harry.

"No, she didn't."

"Why doesn't she get married, then?" Betty Joyce asked. "Darlene Potts did when she got pregnant."

I didn't know that. "I'd rather have a baby and give it away than marry a Jack," I said.

Outside, the Japanese women laughed at something, and we all looked out the door, surprised to realize they were still there. Betty Joyce lowered her voice. "I thought Japanese people knew about ways to get rid of babies, herbs and stuff like that."

Mom gave a sad laugh. "As a matter of fact, I did, too." She picked up the pepper shaker this time, wiped a few black grains off the top, and set it down so that the two shakers were back-to-back. "Girls, this is hard on Daisy. In the Japanese culture, it is a very bad thing to bring disgrace on your family."

"It isn't such a great thing if you're a white person, either," Betty Joyce said.

"No, I suppose not," Mom replied. "But it's even worse if you're Japanese. People at the camp can be cruel to Daisy. That's why she wants to keep on working here, to be away from Tallgrass for a few hours a day. I don't suppose Ellis people will be much better. If any of the Stitchers remark on it, I'll just tell them to mind their own business. Can you girls handle it if anyone at school says something to you?"

"Nobody at school knows anything about Daisy. They don't know if she's married or not," I said. "Would you really tell the Stitchers to mind their own business?"

Mom gave me a stern look that said, Don't be smart, and turned to Betty Joyce.

"I've had worse said to me. Don't forget my dad's a morphine addict," Betty Joyce told her. I wondered what hurtful remarks kids had made to her. They hadn't said them about her to me, maybe because they were too busy calling my dad a Jap lover.

Mom's eyes got teary, and she reached across the table for Betty Joyce's hand. Then she took my hand.

After a moment, I had a great idea. "Why don't we say Daisy married Harry right before he joined the army?"

"That would be a lie," Mom said.

"But it would make things a lot easier for Daisy. You could tell the Jolly Stitchers they got married in secret and then her husband was killed, and they'd make her baby clothes and be real nice to her because she's a widow."

"That doesn't make any difference." Mom's voice was as firm as Dad's when he'd spoken to Beaner that afternoon. "It would be wrong. It would be a lie." She got up and went into the bedroom.

Betty Joyce frowned. "I think that's a great idea. What's wrong with it?"

"It's a lie," I said.

"But people lie all the time." She gave a grim laugh. "We did."

I thought about what a terrible thing it was to have been brought up in Betty Joyce's family, where lying was as ordinary as telling the truth. Betty Joyce lied so that people wouldn't know what went on at home. Mrs. Snow lied to protect Betty Joyce from Mr. Snow. And Mr. Snow's whole life was a lie. But things were different in our house. "Our family never lies," I said.

WHEN THE HARVEST WAS finished, the Hiranos came to call. We knew we had company, because they came to the front door. It was a Sunday, and we were in the dining room after dinner,

Mom and Dad reading the newspaper while Betty Joyce and I lay on the floor listening to the Philco that we'd bought with the 1940 beet money. Dad and Mom exchanged a glance at the knock before Dad got up in his stocking feet and opened the parlor door. "Come on in, folks," he said. The Hiranos followed him back to the dining room.

I stood up and motioned for Betty Joyce to get up, too. Dad sat down on the footstool to put on his shoes, the ones with the elastic gussets in the sides that he'd picked out of the Montgomery Ward catalog. Mom switched off the radio and gathered the newspaper sections and folded them together. She straightened the starched doily on the table next to her rocker and glanced around the room to see what else was out of place. Then she smiled at Mrs. Hirano and held out her hands. "What a pleasure to have company on such a blustery day." We'd been lucky the weather had held until after the harvest, but now it was snowy and so dark at midday that Dad had turned on the floor lamp, which sent out a circle of yellow light.

Mrs. Hirano squeezed Mom's fingers with her own tiny hands, which were protected from the cold by gray kidskin gloves. She wore a gray wool coat and a scarf made from some dead animal. Its legs hung over her shoulders, and its eyes must have been replaced with glass beads, because I'd never seen an animal with eyes like that. She wore high-heeled rubber boots that snapped on the sides and came up over her ankles. Mr. Hirano bowed and said, "We came to thank you for your kindness." When Mom looked confused, he added, "The cake," and handed her back her cake plate.

"It was nothing. There was so little we could do," Mom said.

"You called. You were the only ones from the town. And you gave Harry a job," Mr. Hirano said.

Mrs. Hirano stood very straight and touched the tip of a tiny gloved finger to her eye. "Thank you." Her way of saying it seemed to tell us she did not want to talk about Harry. People were funny about the dead. Sometimes they couldn't stop talking about a friend or relative who'd passed on, but other times they couldn't stand even to hear the person's name.

After a pause, Mom asked, "Will you have coffee? We don't have loose tea, just tea bags, which Daisy says are Japan's revenge for sending missionaries to—" Mom got a horrified look on her face, but the Hiranos smiled at the joke.

"We like coffee," Mrs. Hirano said. She took off the gloves, straightening each finger, then folded them together and put them into her pocket.

Betty Joyce and I made the coffee and took it into the living room. The men were already in the corner, talking about beets, and we joined Mom, who was sitting at the dining room table with Mrs. Hirano. Granny sat next to them in her rocker, sewing together two sections of a quilt square with a design called Soldier Boy, which was made up of squares and triangles and rectangles.

"May I?" Mrs. Hirano asked, nodding at the pieces of the square that were pinned together in Granny's sewing basket.

Granny smiled, and Mrs. Hirano unpinned the cut shapes and laid them out on the table, carefully fitting them together like the pieces of a puzzle to make a soldier. When she was done, she clapped her hands.

Mom said, "Nothing brings women together like sewing. You don't even have to speak the same language. It's like men and crops. Have you ever seen two men smell the earth?"

"Yes, you are right," Mrs. Hirano said. "Sewing is like that for women. That's why I've brought you this." She reached into her handbag and took out the silk bag that held the needlework of the birds. "It would please me if you would accept this. I would like to know that each time you look at it, you remember Harry."

Mom's face went pale, and she said, "Oh, Mrs. Hirano, I couldn't. It's a family heirloom."

"Please," Mrs. Hirano said.

"She wants you to have it," her husband said, watching from across the room. "Please."

Mom looked at Dad, who nodded once. "It would be an honor." Mom's voice broke, and she took a moment to compose herself. "I will treasure it in remembrance of Harry," she said, as if she were reading Scripture. "And one day, I will pass it on to Rennie. She valued Harry's friendship, too. It will be our family's heirloom now."

The Hiranos turned to me, and, not sure what to say, I could only smile at them and mumble, "Thank you." I was overwhelmed, too, because, like Mom, I knew what it meant for a woman to give away a piece of needlework she prized. Women treasured the things the womenfolk in their families made with their needles. Granny had quilts folded up in pillowcases that were promised to Marthalice and me when we married. Granny's mother and grandmother had made them a hundred years ago. When I was little, I'd told Mom that if there were a fire, I wasn't sure whether Granny would save me or the quilts. Mom had warned me to be careful with matches.

Sleet had begun falling by the time the Hiranos went home, but that wasn't the reason Dad insisted on driving them back to camp. He didn't want them walking down the road alone. As they left, Mom said softly to Mrs. Hirano, "Are you sure this needlework shouldn't go to Daisy?"

"Daisy?" Mrs. Hirano looked confused for a moment. She touched the pearls at her throat, pearls the color of milk frozen in a bucket. "Oh, you mean Daisy Tanaka?" She frowned.

When the Hiranos were gone, Mom said to me, "Wasn't that odd? It was almost as if she'd forgotten who Daisy was. I'd think Daisy would be precious to them. My goodness, that baby is all they have left of Harry."

10

EMORY ENLISTED IN THE army at the end of 1943. Carl wanted to join, too, but he told Dad he would keep working for us so that he could look after Daisy, at least until the baby came. I was glad he stayed on, because things were hard for Daisy at Tallgrass, just as they would have been for an Ellis girl who was unmarried and pregnant. Daisy didn't complain, not to me anyway, but she was quiet, and she liked to have Carl around her.

I liked him, too. Betty Joyce said I had a crush on him, which wasn't true. But he was nice to me and never treated me like a little kid. He made me feel safe, too, the way Buddy and Dad did. And with Susan Reddick's killer still out there somewhere, I needed to feel safe.

During the winter, Carl and Dad repaired the tractor and the truck. They rebuilt the beet drill, improvising on the parts, because with the war on, we couldn't get them. Dad made a list of what needed to be done around the farm before spring planting—reroofing the south side of the barn, replacing corral posts, tearing out the chicken coop and rebuilding it. There was enough work for a dozen men, but then, there always was. Betty Joyce gave Dad the key to the hardware store, which had been locked up since Mr. Snow went to the hospital, and Dad kept track of the supplies he took.

Daisy continued to come to the house every day, too, helping with the cooking and light housekeeping, since Mom wouldn't let her do heavy work. With Betty Joyce and me there and Mom feeling stronger, Mom didn't need full-time help, but she knew Daisy didn't want to spend her days at the camp. Besides, Mom had grown used to Daisy's company. When their work was done, the two of them made baby clothes—knitting vests and soakers, caps and booties and cunning little sweaters with duck buttons that Mom found in her sewing basket. Or they stitched flannel jackets and gowns and embroidered them with chickens. Mom taught Daisy how to quilt, too, and Daisy made a square with a sugar beet appliquéd on it for the remembrance quilt.

For Mom, it was a little like having Marthalice around. Sometimes I'd hear her talking about Buddy, although not about Buddy being in the prison camp. She told stories of when Buddy was a boy. He'd cut off the mane of our horse Pumpkins to make himself a beard for Halloween. And the first time he drove, he put Red Boy into reverse by mistake and backed into the chicken coop. When she could laugh about the foolish things my brother had done, Mom felt Buddy was all right.

Mom made Daisy feel all right, too. One afternoon when Daisy was blue, she asked if people would ever stop hating the Japanese at Tallgrass and whether she'd have to spend the rest of her life at the camp. Mom took out her Bible and opened it to Psalms and read, " 'Thou hast brought a vine out of Egypt; thou

has cast out the heathen, and planted it. . . . The hills were covered with the shadow of it, and the boughs thereof were like the
goodly cedars.'

"If you ask me, the Lord is talking about the Japanese right
there in Psalm Eighty. He intends to give you that vine out of
Egypt before long," Mom said. "He'll open the gates of Tallgrass and make a home for you and your baby, and for all the
other folks who are in the camp, too."

"Do you think so?" Daisy asked.

"I do. I surely do."

I thought the Lord was a little poky about it, just as Dad said
He could be late with the rain, but I never doubted Mom when
she quoted the Bible. Even Dad wouldn't do that.

DAISY'S PREGNANCY DIDN'T ESCAPE the notice of the Jolly
Stitchers. Mrs. Larsoo stopped by and remarked to Mom in a
loud voice about fallen women, raising an eyebrow and narrow-
ing her eyes at Daisy's stomach to make sure both Mom and
Daisy got the point. Mom asked whatever did she mean, then
stared Mrs. Larsoo down, so that the old biddy looked away,
which Mom considered a triumph. At a Jolly Stitchers' quilting,
Mrs. Smith said in her pinched-nose way that maybe they ought
to put together a charity basket for poor unfortunate Daisy.
Mom asked why would they do that when Daisy had everything
she needed. When Mom told me that story, I thought about how
Helen Archuleta had almost turned down the Jolly Stitchers'
basket, because of her pride. Mom was too proud to let Daisy
take charity.

There were kindnesses, too. Mrs. Gardner brought by a crib
blanket she had knit. It was so frothy and light, you could hold

it up with your little finger. It was wrapped in tissue and tied with a gold ribbon, and she laughed when Daisy opened the package. "You'll have to forgive a foolish woman, Daisy. When I saw that purple yarn, I said to myself, Now why's a baby have to wear those silly pastels?"

"If Daisy's baby was to have mousy brown hair like most of the little ones around here, it would look all washed out in purple. But it'll have black hair like Daisy and will look right smart in this," Mom told her.

Then Helen Archuleta stopped by with little Susan and a flour sack of clothes and baby blankets that Susan had outgrown and asked if Daisy would please take them because they'd hardly been used and it would be a shame to let them go to waste. "It would make me feel good to see a baby in these things," Helen said. She was so gracious that I wondered if she had learned something from the way the Jolly Stitchers had given her the charity basket little more than a year before. Helen said she hoped Daisy would understand why she'd kept the quilt with the square that her sister had made. The two of them giggled about how it was just like falling on top of a basketball when you turned over on your stomach at night in the last months of pregnancy. I was glad Daisy had someone to laugh with, someone who didn't care that she had no husband. But then, Helen didn't have a husband, either. She hadn't heard a word from Bobby since the baby was born, Mr. Lee told Dad.

Edna Elliot and her friends made a couple of nasty cracks at school about us running a home for loose women, but I'd learned that Miss Ord was right: I just walked away, and pretty soon they ignored me. Maybe they talked behind my back. They probably did, but Betty Joyce didn't tell me about it.

Once, Danny passed me on the Tallgrass Road not far from our farm and offered me a ride in the Spanos' old rust pot. I'd seen Danny driving that truck down the road before, riding in it by himself now that Beaner had a job at the sugar company. Dad said the refinery was so hard up for workers that it had hired a one-legged man and two wooden-headed women, so it wasn't any surprise that it had employed a no-good like Beaner.

When I turned him down, Danny ran his hand through his greasy hair and asked me if I thought I was too good for him. I didn't reply, just treated him the way I did Edna Elliot and kept on walking. "You're not too good to talk to some Jap girl that's got herself knocked up," he said, and laughed. When I still didn't reply, Danny sneered at me. "You're just as stuck-up as your sister." He took off then, swerving toward me so that the running board of his truck rubbed against my leg, and I jumped into the ditch. Danny looked at me in the rearview mirror as he hightailed it down the road, and I could see him laughing. At the crossroads past our farm, he made a U-turn and came back toward me, fishtailing back and forth across the road, but by then, I'd reached our property, so I climbed the fence and went across the fields to the house. Danny peeled on by, honking and shouting something I didn't catch. When I got home, Mom looked up from where she and Daisy were sewing and asked what all the noise was about. I told her it was just Danny Spano being a smart aleck.

"Stay away from him," Daisy told me, but she didn't have to warn me about Danny Spano.

THE DAY DAISY'S BABY was born, we thought she and Carl had stayed home because of the blizzard. The snow was bad—so bad that Betty Joyce and I didn't go to school. The storm started in the evening, just after chores, and kept up all night. By the time I woke up the next morning, I could tell it was still snowing, because the light through the white curtains was pink.

"Prettiest snow I ever saw, just like Lux flakes coming down," Mom remarked when she came into my bedroom to say that Betty Joyce and I wouldn't be going to school that day. She told us to go downstairs and dress by the oil heater, since Dad was out milking. "We'll have corn cakes with brown-sugar syrup and cocoa. Dad said he might get out that old sleigh and take us for a ride when the snow stops."

The snow didn't stop for two days, so we played checkers and worked a puzzle by a kerosene lamp on the kitchen table, because the wires were down. When we got bored, Betty Joyce and I decided to make a quilt for Daisy's baby. Granny helped us cut out squares for a Nine Patch design, which was the simplest quilt you could make. We pressed the seams to one side with our fingers, since there was no electricity for the iron. When we finished the top, we cut the batting and backing and took turns quilting the layers together. Then we edged it with bias tape. By the time the storm was over, we had finished the little quilt.

"It will keep the baby warm," Mom said.

"Every stitch taken with love," Granny added. Her mind was working fine that day, and she had entertained us with stories about people being snowbound, not just long ago but as recently as last year, when Mr. Jack had had to spend the night in the barn during a blizzard because he couldn't see his way to the house. None of the Jacks had even missed him.

Neither Mom nor Granny said a work about the workmanship

on the Nine Patch, but we knew Daisy would be pleased, and we were, too. We laughed when we looked at the quilt up close and saw how crude it was. "We ought to call ourselves the *Folly* Stitchers," I said.

After the snow stopped, Carl came to our house. The big snowplows had made a path down the center of the road so that supply trucks could get to the camp. Still, Carl looked like a snowman because he'd had to make his way through the drifts from the road to the house. We all jumped when he stamped his boots on the side porch, and Mom got up and wrapped her hands in her apron when she saw who it was. "Daisy?" she asked, worry spreading across her face.

Carl grinned. "I'm an uncle."

"By Dan, isn't that fine! Take off those galoshes and sit right down," Dad said. "Boy or girl?"

"Slow down. You tell us how Daisy is first," Mom chided.

"Oh, she's swell," Carl said. "Girl. Cutest girl in the whole world."

"Girl," Mom said, sitting back down next to Dad at the table, where we were finishing breakfast. "Oh, I was hoping for a girl, a girl or a boy."

Dad reached over and slapped her on the knee. "I'll bet if it wasn't a girl, it would have been a boy."

Mom swatted his hand. "Oh, go on with you."

Dad stood up. "I think we have a bottle of whiskey here somewhere."

"Loyal! It's eight o'clock in the morning!"

"This young man came through four-foot of drifts to bring us the news. You don't expect me to give him a cup of coffee, now do you?" Dad went to cupboard and took down a bottle of Four Roses and two glasses. Then he asked, "Mother?"

She nodded, and I exchanged a look with Betty Joyce. I'd never seen my mother drink liquor before. "I'll tell the Jolly Stitchers," I said, kidding her.

"I wouldn't care if you did," Mom said, although I knew she would care, just as she knew I'd never tell.

Dad removed the ice tray from the refrigerator and put a cube into each glass, then poured a half inch of liquor into the glasses and passed them around. He held up his and said, "To Daisy." They sipped.

Then Mom held up her glass and said, "To Amy Elizabeth."

"Amy Elizabeth?" Dad asked.

"Isn't that what Daisy named her?"

"How'd you know?" Carl asked.

"Daisy told me Amy Elizabeth was a teacher she had in California, the finest woman she ever knew, and she thought that Amy Elizabeth was the prettiest name she'd ever heard. I don't imagine she'd pick the second-prettiest name for her baby."

"It doesn't sound Japanese," Betty Joyce said.

"It sounds American," I told her.

Later, Dad hitched our horse Nancy to the sleigh. Carl had changed into some of Buddy's dry clothes, and Mom heated bricks in the oven and wrapped them in burlap bags for our feet, because, while the snow had stopped, the temperature was below zero and the wind was up. Then we all climbed into the sleigh and covered ourselves with quilts and Dad drove us to the camp to see Daisy. The doctor wouldn't let us go inside the infirmary, so we sat in the sleigh and waved to Daisy through the window. Carl had given his sister the quilt Betty Joyce and I had made, and she wrapped the baby in it and held her up. Her face looked like a giant walnut.

"Prettiest baby I ever saw." Granny sighed.

"Told you," Carl said.

MOM AND BETTY JOYCE had taken Granny into the house, and Dad and I were rubbing down Nancy when Sheriff Watrous came into the barn. He must have parked on the road and walked in, because we hadn't heard his car. "Mr. Stroud," he said, then touched his hat to me as if I were a grown woman.

"That's some snow we had," Dad said.

"It surely is. I see you got your old sleigh out. I always liked a sleigh ride, especially with a pretty girl." He smiled at me.

"Beats a gasoline vehicle in a storm like this."

"Oh, it's not so bad where it's plowed. I put the chains on. I'd like to shake the hand of the man who invented the automobile heater and give him an Oh Henry bar. You taken yourself on a joyride, have you?"

"We've been out to the camp. Daisy had her baby, a girl."

"Well, ain't that fine. They come through all right?"

Dad nodded. "I don't suppose you came out in this weather on a social call, Sheriff. You here on business?"

"I am."

Dad turned to me. "Rennie, go ask your mother to make some coffee."

Sheriff Watrous held up his hand. "You might ask the girl to stay a minute. This concerns her."

Dad and I exchanged a look, and I thought about Susan Reddick. She'd been killed during a snowstorm. I thought, Maybe some other girl had been killed. I wondered if I'd ever quit thinking about Susan Reddick's death, if I'd ever stop checking the locks on the doors or looking out the window when something woke me in the night.

"Wait just a bit," Dad said. He was a farmer, and with farmers, animals always come before anything. He and I finished rubbing down Nancy, and Dad led her to a stall. I filled a bucket with water and hung it up for the horse, then went back and waited with the sheriff while Dad got grain. Sheriff Watrous blew on his mittened hands and stamped his feet until Dad finished and climbed into the sleigh, which was sitting in the middle of the barn. I edged in next to him. "Now, Hen, what can we do for you?" Dad asked.

"Gus Snow showed up in town this morning," Sheriff Watrous said, leaning against a post and crossing his feet. He chuckled a little. "Two 'snowstorms,' I guess you could call it." He shook his head. "'Taint funny, McGee,' as the feller says on the radio." He pronounced the word *raad-e-o*.

"He's doing all right, is he?"

The sheriff shook his head. "I wouldn't know. I'd heard he didn't stay in that hospital but a short time, just kind of disappeared. But as long as he didn't turn up here, it wasn't any of my business. He did turn up this morning, however, just like a bad penny. He asked me where his girl was." The sheriff took off his hat and slapped it against his leg to get rid of the snow before he put it back on his head. "I told him I didn't tend kids."

"I don't suppose it will take him long to find out where she's at."

"No, not too long. And when he does, there's nothing I can do to stop him from taking Betty Joyce. Mrs. Snow never did take out a restraining order or nothing. He hasn't been here?" The sheriff removed the mitten from his right hand and took a cigar from his inside coat pocket and put it into his mouth. He didn't light it.

I trembled, not from the cold, but from the idea that Mr. Snow could just take Betty Joyce. She'd have to go back to the hardware store, where he'd yell at her and hit her, and her mother wouldn't be there to protect her. I realized even if we could hide her on our farm, she wouldn't be able to attend school, because Mr. Snow would show up there and make her go home with him.

"No, he hasn't been here yet, not in this storm," Dad replied.

The sheriff turned to me, and I shook my head. "Not unless he came while we were at Tallgrass."

"You didn't see any sign of anybody, Mr. Stroud?"

"Didn't look." Dad shifted in the sleigh. "Is Gus still on the morphine?"

"That, I couldn't tell you. He looked all right to me, but I don't know much about those things."

I wondered if Mr. Snow would make Betty Joyce go to work to earn money to buy him drugs. If Mr. Snow had gotten morphine from Beaner Jack, as Mom suspected, then Betty Joyce would have to be nice to Beaner. I was worried that Mr. Snow would make her marry one of the Jacks, and then she'd be just like Darlene Potts. I thought of the way Betty Joyce had been just before she came to live on our farm, tired and beaten down. She'd been so happy since she'd moved in with us, but I knew it wouldn't take much to turn her into her mother. "Couldn't she go live with her mom?" I asked suddenly.

"That's what I'm thinking." Sheriff Watrous chewed on the end of the cigar for a minute. "But with the wires down, I can't even telephone to her."

Dad asked when the lines would be fixed, and the sheriff said he thought it wouldn't be for a day or two.

"Mr. Snow could find her by then," I said.

"I kind of hate to wait that long myself," Sheriff Watrous said.

"Maybe Mrs. Stroud could take her to Pueblo," Dad suggested.

The sheriff nodded. "I was hoping you folks'd see it that way." He took the cigar out of his mouth and looked at the end, which was soggy.

"Will it be all right, Betty Joyce just showing up like that?" I asked.

"It will," the sheriff replied. "LaVerne Booth—that's Mrs. Snow's sister, I think you know—she's an odd one, but she's got a soft spot for a hard case, unless it's Gus Snow. She takes in stray dogs, cripples, widows, orphans. She don't know a stranger." He put the cigar into his pocket.

"I guess we'd better go talk to Mrs. Stroud. They'll be wanting to leave pretty quick, before Gus comes here." Dad stepped down from the sleigh and held out his hand to me, and we went into the house.

Mom and Betty Joyce were waiting for us in the kitchen, and when the sheriff told Betty Joyce that her father was in town, she clasped her hands together until they turned white. Then she moved behind Mom. I went over to her and pried one hand loose and held it, whispering that everything would be all right. We'd become almost sisters in the time she'd lived with us, and I hated to see her leave. It would be just like Marthalice going away. But there wasn't any choice. I couldn't ask her to stay on with us if there was danger of her father coming for her and taking her away.

"I like it here. I've never been with a real family before," Betty Joyce told Sheriff Watrous. "I'm scared of him." And I thought again what a terrible thing it was to be afraid of your own father. Betty Joyce said she'd run off before she'd go back to him.

"You don't have to do that, sis. I think we've got a plan," Sheriff Watrous said. He turned to Mom and asked if she'd be willing to take Betty Joyce to her mother in Pueblo. He'd drive the two of them to Lamar on the hard road, which had been plowed, and they could catch the train there. That way, they wouldn't chance running into Mr. Snow in Ellis. I helped Betty Joyce pack her few things, and I pinned the new V for Victory pin onto her coat. I'd sent money to Cousin Hazel to get a second one and had given it to Betty Joyce for Christmas. An hour later, Betty Joyce and Mom were gone.

Before they left, Dad gave Mom a check for Mrs. Snow, to cover the items Dad had taken from the hardware store. When I asked him why he did that—because, after all, Betty Joyce had lived with us since fall and Mom was paying for their train tickets—Dad replied, "It wouldn't be right not to."

Mr. Snow never came to our farm. He stayed around Ellis for a week or two, living in the hardware store, although the heat and lights were turned off. He sold everything in the store that was worth a nickel, the stock as well as the furniture and Mrs. Snow's dishes and silverware, even her old shoes and aprons. Mr. Snow spotted me in town once and yelled, but I ran into the Lee Drug, and he didn't follow me. Mr. Lee said I could go out the back door and that he'd drive me home, but Mr. Snow wandered off toward Jay Dee's and disappeared.

Not long after that, Mr. Snow went on the tramp. For a time, people thought he'd turn up, asking for a handout, whining about his luck. I worried that he'd blame us for what happened to him, that some night when it was darkest, I'd go into the barn and he'd be waiting there, crazed on morphine, and push me into the tack room and kill me. But that didn't happen. After a while, Dad decided Mr. Snow had just drifted off, maybe froze to death on the prairie or died in a hobo jungle.

DAISY CAME BACK TO work for us a couple of weeks after Amy Elizabeth was born. "I'm as strong as a tractor. I feel like a million," she insisted. When Mom told her it was too soon, Daisy said, "Here's the dope: I can come here and be useful, or sit in that darn barracks and go crazy. Now that's the straight stuff." She sounded like the old Daisy. And she was the old Daisy. Maybe it was having the baby to live for that had restored her.

While Daisy worked, Amy Elizabeth slept in our family cradle, which Dad took down from the hayloft and set up in the living room. Mom scrubbed it and fitted it with a new mattress, and Granny worked a couple dozen baby quilts for it. But Daisy said her favorite was the one that Betty Joyce and I had made.

When Daisy hung up laundry or worked in the yard, she carried Amy Elizabeth around in a sort of sling across her chest. Daisy chattered to the baby all day long or put records on the phonograph and jitterbugged around the living room with Amy Elizabeth in her arms. "She's the nuts," Daisy said. The little girl had inch-long black hair that stuck out all over and eyes as black as currants. Amy Elizabeth hardly ever cried, and she smiled before she was a month old, and after she stopped looking like a walnut, she really was pretty.

Dad worried about Daisy, Carl, and the baby coming to the farm by themselves in the mornings. He offered to pick them up in the truck. "You can't carry the baby all the way from the camp, especially in this weather," he told Carl.

"That baby doesn't weigh any more than a sack lunch," Carl told him, and he refused Dad's offer of a ride.

Still, some mornings when he heard a truck or a car going down the Tallgrass Road toward the camp, Dad went out on the porch and watched for Carl and Daisy. He said he'd feel better when spring came and Carl hired boys from Tallgrass to help with planting. It wouldn't be long now. Carl and Dad were spending more and more time preparing the fields instead of re-pairing equipment and working in the barn.

One Friday morning, when school was closed for a teachers' conference, Mom asked me to go with her to town. A storm was threatening and she'd run out of her medicine. The winter had sapped Mom, who was feeling weak again and was glad that Daisy had taken over the heavy work. Mom didn't like driving the big, awkward truck. But Dad was off at the sugar refinery with the team and wagon, and she didn't want to wait until he returned. It was too cold for me to walk into town, Mom said, and she'd feel safer if I drove along with her. "I just don't know how I could have let a thing like this slip my mind, but I hate to go without those pills," she told me. Daisy, with Amy Elizabeth in the sling, was hanging out the wash when we left, and Mom called to her and said we were going into Ellis.

She pulled out onto the Tallgrass Road and drove with both hands clutching the wheel, staring straight ahead, barreling along at five miles an hour. We could have walked faster. When a beat-up truck passed us, going the other way, she slowed down. "How those boys do speed," she complained. We hadn't gone far when a dog came out of the field and ran alongside us in the ditch, unnerving Mom. She used to be just fine driving Red Boy, but since she'd been sick, she'd lost her self-confidence along with her strength. Mom slowed, glancing at the road, then at the dog, her head going back and forth. Finally, she stopped to let the dog cross in front of us, but it only continued along in the ditch. So Mom started up again, and in a minute, the dog disappeared into the field, and she breathed a sigh of relief and stepped on the gas.

At that moment, a jackrabbit darted in front of the truck, and Mom turned the wheel hard, too hard. She corrected, turning the wheel in the opposite direction. Red Boy jerked one way, then the other, and the right front wheel plunged into the ditch and we came to a stop. "Well, darn it all!" Mom said. We were going so slowly that she barely hit her chest against the steering wheel. "Rennie, are you all right?"

I'd put out my hands and caught myself against the dashboard. "Yeah." I blew out my breath and looked at Mom and almost laughed. We were no more hurt than if she'd stopped at a red light. I opened the door and got out and looked at the front wheel, which was all the way down in the ditch. I climbed back in and told Mom the truck was all right, too, but there was no way we could back it out. "Dad and Carl will have to bring the horses and pull it out."

"Well, that's a heck of a thing," Mom said. "What's your Dad going to say about that?"

"Probably 'Thank the Lord you're both okay.'"

Mom reached over and squeezed my hand, and there were tears in her eyes. Dad was the only man in the county who wouldn't blow up at his wife for running his truck off the road. "I guess we'd better get out and start walking," she said.

As we started back up the frozen dirt road, it began to sleet—hard little granules of snow like clumps of sugar that hit our faces and necks. After a minute, they turned into snow. "I hope your Dad can get the truck out in time to drive the Tanakas back to camp tonight. I don't like the idea of them walking home in this storm with that dear little baby," Mom said. We shivered as we walked along, and Mom drew me close to her to keep us both warm. For a few minutes, we sang "Onward, Christian Soldiers," marching along in tandem. We finished the last verse but kept on taking big steps together until we reached our driveway. As we turned in, Mom stopped and scanned the yard, frowning as she looked at the clothesline. A sheet was half-pinned to the line, and the clothes basket was turned over. "Where's Daisy?" Mom asked. She sounded confused more than worried.

"She probably went into the house to check on Granny. Or maybe she's putting Amy Elizabeth in the cradle," I said. But the door was closed, the storm door shut tight, just as we had left them. If Daisy had gone inside for just a minute, she wouldn't have bothered to secure the doors.

Then I pointed to the rusted old truck that had passed us on the Tallgrass Road. It was parked by the side of the barn, the engine running, the driver's door open. I knew that truck. Mom and I started running. As we got closer, we saw the wind whipping one end of the sheet back and forth across the ground. Daisy wouldn't have left it like that on purpose, one end pinned to the line, the other loose, because now the sheet would have to be washed all over again. Beneath the line, the wet clothes from the laundry basket were spread over the dirt.

"Daisy!" Mom called. She looked around frantically. From somewhere we could hear Sabra and Snow White barking, but the wind had picked up, and I couldn't tell where the noise was coming from.

I grabbed Mom's arm and showed her the clothespins scattered in the dirt. Most were under the sheet, but a few lay beyond, as if Daisy had dropped them as she ran away from the clothesline. "The barn. She's in the barn," I said.

"Daisy!" Mom called as loudly as she could so that not just Daisy but anyone in the barn would hear her, but the wind drowned out her words. "Daisy!" It was almost a shriek. We started for the barn, both of us running.

When we reached it, we stopped at the door, letting our eyes adjust to the darkness inside. All I could see at first were big black shapes in the light that sifted through the roof. On one side, bales of hay were piled halfway to the ceiling. On another were the stalls for the horses. From the hayloft came the sound of the radio turned up loud. As my eyes adjusted, I saw Daisy backed up against the hay. Amy Elizabeth was still in the sling, but Daisy was clutching the baby against her chest, protecting her. Danny Spano stood in front of her, a beet knife in his hand. Neither of them saw us.

"I'm not telling you again. Give me the baby," Danny said.

Daisy didn't reply, only held Amy Elizabeth tighter.

"She's mine, and my kid ain't growing up in no damn camp. I'll take her, and you'll never see her again. She's a Spano, not some dumb Jap."

"She's not yours."

"I'm her father, ain't I?"

I turned and looked at Mom, who had a stunned look on her face. I mouthed, "Is he?" But he couldn't be, I thought. Daisy wouldn't have had anything to do with Danny Spano. Harry Hirano was Amy Elizabeth's father.

"You don't give her to me, I'll take her. I'll kill you if I have to. Wouldn't bother me."

"Call the sheriff," Mom whispered, her voice so low that I could barely hear her above the noise of the radio. I hesitated only a second before I backed away and raced for the house, covering the ground in seconds. I yanked open the storm door and was twisting the knob of the back door, pushing it open with my hip, when I heard the scream. It didn't seem like a human scream, and it was so loud that it carried through the wind. The closest thing to it that I'd ever heard was the sound of a pig being butchered, the high-pitched squeal of fear at the instant of death. The sound from the barn chilled me like nothing else I had ever heard. Daisy, I thought. I turned and retraced my steps as fast as I could, stumbling and pitching forward onto the frozen ground and scraping my knees. I scrambled to my feet and ran on, moving, it seemed, as if in a dream where no matter how fast I tried to go, I stayed in place. But at last I reached the barn and stopped where Mom and I had stood, not sure what I would find.

Mom had gone inside the barn. Slowly, I made out her figure standing next to Daisy. And Carl was on the bottom step of the ladder that led to the hayloft. They were all three frozen in place, silent. The only sound and movement came from Amy Elizabeth, who cooed and swung her little arms back and forth from the sling on Daisy's chest. Then I saw Danny Spano sprawled on the floor, a beet knife sticking out of his stomach. I crept up to Mom and looked down at Danny. His eyes were open and glassy. Mom, still staring at Danny, reached out her hand to me, and I gripped it.

"Is he dead?" I asked.

"Yes," Mom whispered.

No one spoke after that, not for the longest time. We just stood there and stared at the body. I couldn't move. Even my eyes wouldn't move. All I could do was look at Danny. Then Daisy began to shake. Her body jerked violently, her arms going in all directions, her chest heaving, her head swinging back and forth, her teeth chattering. She shook so hard that I thought the baby would fly out of the sling. Carl stepped off the ladder and took off his jacket, putting it around Daisy and holding her tight. "It's okay, Dais. It's okay," he said. "It's okay." He held her, repeating over and over again that everything was okay, and after a bit, Daisy quieted down.

"Where did you come from?" I asked Carl.

He gestured to the haymow. "Up there. The radio was on. I thought that was Mr. Stroud talking to Daisy."

Nobody said anything, until I asked, "Was Danny really Amy Elizabeth's father?"

"Hush," Mom said.

"He's the one who raped you, isn't he?" Carl asked, and Daisy nodded. He released Daisy then and spit on the barn floor next to Danny.

Mom's hand went to her mouth, and she said, "Oh, Daisy." I opened my mouth, but no words would come.

Carl turned to Mom and said, "When Daisy was walking home by herself that time, that boy caught up with her in the arroyo. She tried to fight him off. I should have been there to—" Carl broke off, slamming his right fist against a wooden post. I sucked in my breath, thinking that something terrible had happened to Daisy on our farm, and we hadn't even known about it. She had been ravished, just like Susan Reddick. The same horrid thing had happened to her, and she'd kept it to herself. She'd let us think Harry was Amy Elizabeth's father, when all along it was Danny Spano.

"I would have killed him," Carl said. "Harry and I would have killed him, but Daisy wouldn't tell us who he was. I didn't know till now."

"And of course you didn't know then you were pregnant," Mom added.

"Is that when you said you fell in the shower house?" I asked. "Is that when you broke the compact?"

Daisy nodded and looked at Amy Elizabeth. I sneaked a look at her, too, but I couldn't see that she looked like Danny Spano.

Daisy began to sway, and Mom took her arm and made her sit down on a bail of hay.

"You didn't tell the sheriff," Mom said.

"Who'd believe her?" Carl asked angrily. "Nobody'd believe a Japanese girl, even about Danny Spano."

"No, I don't suppose so," Mom said.

"I would." The voice came from behind us—small and quiet, but clear—and we all whirled around. No one had heard Granny come into the barn. She stood a few feet behind us, a tiny figure, her head high, her hands clasped in front of her in her apron. I wondered how long she'd been there and if she understood what she'd heard.

"Granny," Mom said. "Rennie, take Granny—"

"No, Mary," Granny said. "My mind is clear. I believe Daisy. I know that boy did that bad thing to her."

"Well, of course, Granny. Now don't you worry."

"Don't baby me," Granny snapped. "Don't you doubt that girl. I saw that awful boy in here with Marthalice, too."

Mom drew in her breath, then asked in a sharp voice, "What are you talking about, Granny?"

"Sometimes at night, when I was in the yard, I'd see Marthalice sneak out and go into the barn. I followed her once, and she was with this boy." Granny pointed at Danny. "They were doing things. . . . Marthalice was crying." Her voice trailed off. "I'm sorry, Mary. I didn't know what to do. Marthalice wouldn't like it if she found out I'd snooped, but I didn't want you to be angry with her. I was so confused, and then I forgot about it. Maybe he's the reason Marthalice went away. . . ." Granny's voice trailed off and she sat down next to Daisy, reaching out her finger so that Amy Elizabeth could grab it with her little fist.

"Is he the reason?" I asked.

Mom put out her hand and closed her eyes. "Be still, Rennie. We'll talk about that later. Let me think." Mom stood silently for several minutes—whether thinking or praying, I didn't know; probably both—while we all watched her, waiting. When she opened her eyes, she was calm, and she spoke quietly but firmly. "Carl and Daisy, you are to go back to the camp right now. You are to say you left when the storm started, which was just as Rennie and I went to town. You didn't see Danny turn in at the farm. You didn't even see him drive down the road. You don't know he's dead. Do you understand?"

Carl and Daisy exchanged glances. "I guess so," Carl said.

"Daisy?" Mom asked.

Daisy nodded.

"This is very important," Mom said. "You left when the storm started. You never saw Danny," Mom repeated.

"Why?" Daisy asked.

"Because if we tell what really happened, nobody will believe us, and I'm afraid there could be trouble about the baby."

Daisy clutched Amy Elizabeth to her, and Carl asked, "Are you going to call the sheriff?"

Mom nodded.

"What are you going to tell him?"

"I don't know yet. I just know that when somebody tells you the Spano boy's dead, you're to act surprised. Do you understand?"

Carl started to say something, but Daisy touched his arm, and they both nodded.

"Go now," Mom said. "Go across the fields. It's better that nobody sees you. We'll give you a few minutes before we call Sheriff Watrous. Go. Run." They started off, and we watched them from the barn door until they disappeared.

Then Mom turned to Granny, who was playing with her fingers. "Granny, would you go upstairs and get out your piecing?" Granny smiled. Her mind had already clouded over.

Mom waited until Granny was inside before saying, "I'll call the sheriff now. You pick up the laundry on the ground and take down that one sheet, Rennie. It'll all have to be washed again. Somebody's bound to wonder why it's dirty." I thought it was strange that in a time like that, Mom would think about laundry, but she was right. If one of the Jolly Stitchers came by, she'd notice first thing the washing lying in the dirt.

MOM TOLD THE SHERIFF only that we had an emergency and to come as quickly as he could. She didn't want anybody who was listening in on the party line to know what had happened. We waited in the house, Mom pacing back and forth and biting her fingernails. "I wish I could put in that laundry," she said a dozen times, "but the sheriff would wonder why I'm washing sheets at a time like this."

I offered to make coffee then, but Mom said coffee would only make her nervous, so I fixed tea, and we drank it with milk and sugar at the kitchen table. Then I asked about Marthalice, and Mom sighed and stopped playing with her hands and folded them on the oilcloth. "I guess you have the right to know now. Marthalice got pregnant a few months before she graduated from high school. She went to live with Cousin Hazel for a while. Then Cousin Hazel arranged for her to stay in a home for unwed mothers in Denver. That was why I went to visit her so sudden fall before last. The baby came. After that, Marthalice didn't want to move back home, and we didn't blame her. So she got a job and stayed on in Denver."

I bit my knuckles. My sister'd had a baby, and nobody had told me. Dad would have known, of course, but had they told Buddy? Probably not, because he had joked about Marthalice going to Denver and meeting lots of servicemen. Mom and Dad had kept the baby a secret from both of us. "Didn't she tell you Danny Spano was the father?"

Mom shook her head. "She wouldn't tell us. We assumed he was Hank Gantz, because Hank joined the army so sudden, just as if he was running away from getting married. Marthalice had a wild streak. Once, your Dad . . ." Mom looked at me and didn't finish. "But Danny Spano? Our poor girl." Mom put her head down on her hands and began to cry. But she steadied herself and shook her head. "I can't think about that now. You musn't ever let on to Marthalice that you know. She'd be shamed. Promise me that."

I wouldn't tell for anything. No wonder Marthalice had changed so much. There couldn't be anything worse than having Danny Spano's baby. I wondered if Danny had known Marthalice was pregnant, but of course he hadn't. He'd have bragged about it. And maybe he'd have claimed the baby, just as he had Daisy's. It would be horrible to raise a Stroud baby as a Spano.

Mom said, "These are awful burdens for you to carry, Rennie."

"You, too, Mom."

She picked up her cup and looked at it, then set it back down. "I never liked tea too much."

"What if Granny tells?"

Mom gave me a sad smile. "She forgot about Marthalice. I expect she forgot about Daisy before she left the barn. Don't you?"

I thought that over and agreed. "What happened to Marthalice's baby?"

Mom brightened for an instant. "That nice little girl from Mississippi you played with at the Varian house next door to Cousin Hazel, the Brown girl? The baby's her new sister. Her name is Alice, for Mrs. Varian's mother and for Marthalice, too. They're a nice family. Cousin Hazel arranged it."

We heard the sheriff's car then and went to the door. Mom gripped my hand hard and asked, "Ready?"

"I think so." I wasn't, but if Mom, who could hardly stand up in the wind, was strong, I could be, too.

"You let me do the talking."

We took our wraps from the hooks beside the door and went outside, waiting for the sheriff to get out of the car and come to us. He touched his hat to Mom but didn't say anything, just waited for her to speak. She took a deep breath. "We've had a terrible accident, Sheriff Watrous. The Spano boy's dead. He's in the barn with a beet knife in his stomach."

"Is that so?"

Before she could continue, there was the sound of a team and wagon, and Dad drove into the barnyard. "Oh, thank God," Mom said. She sagged against me, and I wondered how her heart could hold up under all the strain.

Dad pulled the team to a stop beside the sheriff's car and got down off the wagon seat, tying the reins to the fence. He looked from Mom to the sheriff, waiting for an explanation. It was the sheriff who explained. "Your wife says the Spano boy's dead in your barn with a beet knife sticking out of him."

"Mary?" Dad asked.

Mom nodded, and Dad came to stand beside her and put his arm around her. She leaned against him, and the two of us held her up. "It's my fault, Loyal. I did it." Mom began to cry.

"What?" I muttered, although nobody paid attention to me. Until that minute, I didn't know what had happened to Danny. I hadn't asked, and nobody had told me. I'd just assumed Danny had killed himself, that he'd fallen or something. How could Mom have killed him? She'd never hurt anything in her life, except a coyote. I tightened my arm around her.

"Why don't you tell us what happened, Mrs. Stroud." The sheriff's voice was kind, but it was firm.

"Just let her get a grip on herself," Dad told him.

"No, Loyal. Let's get this over with." Mom took a deep breath. The wind picked up and blew Mom's coat about her. Snow swirled around us, and Dad asked Mom if she wanted to go inside, but Mom said no. I think she liked the feel of the cold. Maybe it numbed her the way it did me. "You remember when Daisy fell at the camp last summer and didn't come to work for a couple of weeks?" Dad didn't answer, and Mom continued. "Well, she didn't fall. The Spano boy raped her on the way home from our place. That's how she got pregnant. It's his baby she had, not Harry's. Loyal, she didn't even tell us what happened." Mom's voice broke, but she swallowed and took hold of herself.

She looked from Dad to the sheriff to make sure they understood. "Danny's been driving back and forth on the Tallgrass Road lately. I've seen him in that rusted-out truck of the Spanos. He must have known you were off with the team, Loyal. So when he passed Rennie and me on the road to town this afternoon, he figured this was his chance to get Daisy alone. But I ran the truck into the ditch. It's down there half a mile. Red Boy's all right, but you'll need a chain to get it out." Mom stopped and blew out her breath. "Rennie and I walked back to the farm, and when we got here, we knew something wasn't right. The sheet was half-hung up on the line and trailing on the ground, and the laundry basket was upended and the wash all in the dirt. When we got to the barn, Danny was there, holding a beet knife on Daisy." Mom paused and took a deep breath, willing herself to continue. "He said he'd kill her if she didn't give him that baby. I think he meant to do it. I truly do."

Mom stopped, her eyes closed, as if reliving that scene. "I don't know what he'd have done with that little girl, but he surely did mean to take her." She opened her eyes. "He didn't hear me. I got behind him and tried to snatch the knife, but I didn't do much of a job of it. My hand slipped, and Danny turned, and, oh, I don't know how it happened." Mom swallowed and put her face against Dad's shoulder. She mumbled, "I expect you can guess the rest."

The sheriff turned to me. "Is that about how it happened?"

I held tighter to Mom. "I don't know. I'd started for the house to call you. Then I heard a scream, Danny's scream, I guess. Dad, he sounded like a pig."

"Where's your Japanese people at?" the sheriff asked.

"I told them to go on home," Mom said. "You know what would happen if people's to find out they're involved in this."

"You shouldn't have done that, Mrs. Stroud," the sheriff said.

"Maybe not, but I believe it was the right thing. I had to think about them and that baby. Somebody else might be hurt if people got riled up. It's well over a year since Susan Reddick was murdered, and folks still blame the Japanese. You know what'll happen if they think one of our workers had a hand in Danny's death."

The sheriff mulled that over for a moment. "That's a fact. We best take a look at the scene." He indicated me and asked Dad, "You want your daughter mixed up in this?"

Dad glanced at Mom, who replied, "It appears she already is."

I wasn't surprised she'd said that. After all, Mom and Dad hadn't protected me from Susan's murder or Mr. Snow's morphine addiction. With Mom between Dad and me, the three of us walked to the barn with the sheriff. On the way, Dad stopped to turn off the motor of Danny's truck. We'd left it on all that time.

"Did Danny kill Susan Reddick?" I asked suddenly.

"Oh, I hadn't thought about that," Mom said, turning to Sheriff Watrous.

The sheriff rubbed his wrist across his forehead. "I wished I could say he did, but I don't have the proof of who done it. It'd sure make things easier around here if I did."

By then, we had reached the barn. Mom told me to wait just inside the door while she showed Dad and the sheriff the body. The two men walked around Danny a couple of times, then squatted beside him, talking in low tones. After a while, Mom came back to me, and the two of us sat down on a bench in the late-afternoon light that came through the door. The snow had stopped. It hadn't been much of a storm, but the sun hadn't come out, and the air was cold. It looked like the snow might begin again. I started shaking, and Mom put her arm around me and drew me close to her.

Dad and the sheriff talked in low tones for a long time. Finally, Sheriff Watrous leaned over and slowly pulled the knife out of Danny's body and laid it alongside him. Then the two of them came over to us.

"You're telling me this was an accident, Mrs. Stroud?"

"Of course it was," Mom said. "You don't think I killed Danny on purpose, do you?"

"No, it's not probable."

"She's a good woman, Hen," Dad said.

"Never said she wasn't, Mr. Stroud. Your wife makes a good point that if it gets out that your Japanese people was involved, it's likely to cause a lot of bitterness in Ellis, and that could lead to trouble we don't need. I wouldn't like to see that happen. There's no sense in it." He stood with his feet apart, leaning forward. "I don't understand myself why Danny would want that baby except out of little-hearted meanness. And if they find out Danny sired it, the Spanos are just mean enough theirselves to hire a lawyer to claim it. With that baby half-white and the way the courts are, they'd likely get her, too. Then what'd become of the poor tyke?" The sheriff looked from Mom to me to see if we followed him, and we nodded. We knew it would be a terrible thing to turn Amy Elizabeth into a Spano.

"Now, what if there was to be a trial and you were charged with something, Mrs. Stroud?"

Mom shivered then and began buttoning her coat.

"Of course, nobody'd find you guilty of anything for trying to get that knife away from Danny Spano," he added quickly. "So what good would a trial like that do anybody, and it would just cost the county money."

Mom started to say something, but the sheriff held up his hand. "You say your truck ran into the ditch?"

"Halfway to town."

"Anybody see you after that?"

"No."

"Then it looks to me like Danny Spano came along and picked you and your girl up and offered to pull out your truck, maybe offered to do it for a couple of dollars. He went into your barn to get a length of chain Mr. Stroud keeps in there, and he fell in the dark and ran that beet knife through hisself. Somebody must have left it there on a bail of hay."

Mom looked from the sheriff to Dad, then back to the sheriff. "Is that about right?" the sheriff asked.

"I wouldn't want to lie about it." Mom hesitated.

"I never knew her to tell a lie," Dad said. "I think maybe you'd rather step on baby chicks than lie, wouldn't you, Mother?" Dad asked, uncertain.

Mom picked up a piece of hay and broke it into pieces and dropped them on the floor. "I suppose there are worse things than lies. The Spanos raising Amy Elizabeth is one of them."

"I don't see the harm in covering this up, but I wouldn't want you to go along with something you don't feel right about," the sheriff said. "Make your own choice."

Mom thought that over. "It would be a terrible thing for Daisy to have to tell what Danny did to her."

"Yes, it would," Dad said. "No sense to it."

"And who knows what people might do to the Japanese at the camp, even though it's not that poor girl's fault."

"There's that," the sheriff said.

I looked from one to another as the three of them talked, spinning the conversation around. I didn't dare speak and destroy the way they'd convinced themselves there was nothing wrong in what they were doing. And there wasn't. Maybe it was a lie, and maybe it was wrong in the eyes of the law. But in the light of human kindness, as Mom would have said, they were making the right decision. Those three were good people, and they were doing a good thing.

Mom turned to me. "Rennie?"

"Danny Spano was a predator."

Mom's eyes opened wide. "Why yes, he was. Yes. Danny was a predator." She smiled at me.

"What about Daisy and Carl?" Sheriff Watrous asked.

Mom released me a little. "They won't know Danny's dead until someone tells them. We agreed to that."

"You what?" The sheriff, who had turned to look at Danny's body, jerked his head around at Mom, his eyes wide, and stared at her for a long time. Then he shook his head. "Yes, ma'am, I believe you can handle this," he said with a rueful smile. He'd just realized that Mom had known all along he'd come up with the story he had. "Now are we all agreed, before I help get that truck out of the ditch?" He looked to Mom, then me, then Dad.

"We ask no odds of you, Hen," Dad said.

"None given," the sheriff replied.

BY MORNING, EVERYONE IN Ellis knew what had happened, and the Stitchers began showing up at our farm. Although it was cold outside and there was an inch of snow on the ground, Dad stationed himself outside the back door and wouldn't allow any of the women to go inside. He took their food and thanked them and told them Mom was in bed, under doctor's orders not to see anyone.

"I'm not just anyone, as you can plainly see, Mr. Stroud," Mrs. Larsoo said.

"I *can* plainly see that," Dad told her, not moving away from the door.

"Well?"

"Well what?"

She turned and marched back to her car, and Dad remarked that he'd never seen anyone leave in such a huff. Then he added, "I believe a huff looks something like a Dodge automobile."

The only person Dad let inside the house was Miss Ord, because she came to see me, not Mom. "I don't have any idea what happened, and I don't care to know, Mr. Stroud. I'm just concerned that your daughter is all right," she said.

Dad turned to me and asked, "Are you all right, Squirt?"

"I'm okay." I wasn't, however. I was sad and confused and mad all at the same time, and I wanted to tell someone. But I couldn't tell anyone, even Miss Ord.

"I have an idea this could have become an ugly thing if it hadn't been for your wife and daughter. I don't know Mrs. Stroud, but Rennie's a fine young woman."

"Oh, she'll do," Dad said.

"Well, if you ever give her up, I'd take her."

"I guess we'll keep her."

Late in the afternoon, Mr. and Mrs. Spano came with one of their boys, who got into the old truck and drove it off. Dad had started to put gasoline into the tank, because the truck had run for an hour in our barnyard, and he didn't want it to run out of gas on the way to the Spano farm. But the tank was almost full, and Dad had remarked he guessed he knew who'd been siphoning gas out of cars around town.

Dad invited the Spanos into the house, but they shook their heads. "We're sorry as we can be about this," Dad said. "Mrs. Stroud's taken to her bed just now, but we both give you our condolences."

"There wasn't a finer boy in this town," Mr. Spano said. "We'll have you know we don't like this, Stroud. There's something not right about it. I don't believe Danny would have charged your wife to pull your old truck out of the ditch. No sir." He folded his short arms across his fat chest.

Mrs. Spano only sobbed, wiping her eyes on the sleeve of her coat.

I thought about Susan Reddick dying and how Mrs. Reddick had cried, and I felt a little sorry for Mrs. Spano, but not very much, because she was better off without Danny. Everybody was, especially Daisy and Marthalice.

"It was an accident. I wish I'd been here. I wish I could tell you exactly how it happened," Dad said.

"Could be you'll understand how I feel if your boy don't come back. Might be a case of turnabout being fair play."

I felt Dad stiffen. In another time, he'd have slugged Mr. Spano for saying that. It was a measure of his compassion for another man's loss that he didn't respond. Dad stood there mute for a minute, getting his anger under control. Then he asked when the service would be held.

"We don't hold with that," Mr. Spano said, and his wife let out a sob, and I knew he might not hold with it, but she did. "The wife would like to see where he died."

Dad nodded. He told me to stay inside the house, then led the Spanos to the barn. They were there only a few minutes. After they left, Dad came into the house and took out the bottle of Four Roses and poured himself a drink. Dad had never gotten that bottle down for anything except to celebrate births and weddings. "It tears me up inside to think Amy Elizabeth might have been raised by such as that," he said. "Your mother did the right thing."

THE NEXT DAY, AFTER we had finished breakfast, Mom went into the bedroom, then came out all dressed up. She had her hat on, too, the one Cousin Hazel had bought for her in Denver. She wore it when she wanted to look her best. "Where do you think you're going?" Dad asked.

"It's Sunday. If I'm not mistaken, it's the day I go to church."

"I thought you were staying in bed for a few days, doctor's orders."

I thought so, too, and I was disappointed she wanted to go to church, because I wanted to stay home in the worst way.

Mom sighed. "I'd like to. My head's an awful muddle. But the longer I wait to face people, the worse it's going to be. Best to get it over with."

"Can't it wait a week?" Dad asked.

"The gossip'll just go on and on," Mom said. "You know how folks talk."

"Is Marthalice coming to church?" Granny asked.

"Marthalice lives in Denver," Dad told her.

"Oh," Granny said, and I thought Mom was right about Granny forgetting what she'd seen in the barn.

Mom sat down at the kitchen table and rubbed her hands over her face, which was gray from lack of sleep. I hadn't slept much the past two nights, either, because I'd been crying. If somebody had to die, I was glad it had been Danny instead of Carl or Daisy. But I didn't want anybody to die on our farm. I'd cried because Daisy had been raped, and Marthalice had been wild and she'd never come back to Ellis for fear of what people would say about her. Life was so awful—Susan murdered, Buddy captured, Mom sick, Harry dead, Daisy and Marthalice forced to have Danny's babies.

My bedroom was over the kitchen, and as I lay there awake, I'd seen the light come on downstairs through the grate in the bedroom floor. Mom was moving around. Then Dad came in and told her to go back to bed, and Mom replied, "What's the use?"

"You want to talk about it?" Dad had asked.

"I've told you all I'm going to. Right or wrong, I don't want us ever to talk about it again. I don't want to talk about it, and I don't want you to talk about it, and I don't want Rennie to have to talk about it." And we never did. It would have been easier for me if we had. There was so much I wanted to ask Mom, but I couldn't. And I couldn't talk to anyone else, because what had happened was a secret. So I just kept everything bottled up inside me. People back then thought that if you didn't speak about a thing, you'd forget about it. But that wasn't true. I never forgot one instant of that day. Still, Mom did what she believed was best for me, and I never faulted her for it.

Now Mom's face was lined, and there were black half circles, like smudges, under her eyes. "What's people to say if I don't show up at church?"

"What do you care?" Dad asked, but that was just it: She did care. And she was right: It would only get worse for her if she waited. And for me, too, although I dreaded going to church as much as she did.

Mom took a deep breath and stood up. "All right. Let's go. Granny, come along. Rennie, where's your Bible? Loyal, get the truck keys." Dad usually drove us to church, then went to the drugstore to jaw with Redhead Joe Lee until it was time to pick us up. Mom gripped the table. I knew this would be a hard morning for her, with people watching and asking questions, demanding details, giving her little pats of sympathy. She'd be the center of attention, with nobody but Granny and me to protect her, and Mom would hate that. It would be hard for me, as well. I didn't want people turning around in their pews to look at us, kids asking me what had happened. What if I slip up and say the wrong thing and get Mom into trouble? I thought.

Dad pushed back his chair and stood, telling us to wait until he changed his shoes and put on his jacket, and he went into the bedroom. Mom looked at her watch and sighed and said if he took any more time, we'd be late and have to sit in the front pew. "Hurry up, Loyal," she called.

"Fine and dandy," Dad replied.

Mom had her back to Dad when he came out of the bedroom, and she didn't see him until he put out his hand. It must have been when she touched his sleeve that she realized he wasn't wearing his old jacket, because she turned around, and her mouth dropped open. Dad was dressed in his suit and his good shirt, and he was even wearing a tie. "Why, what's this, Loyal?" Mom asked.

Dad shifted the truck keys from one hand to another and gave her a dopey grin as he took her arm. "By Dan, I reckon I can go to church with my wife if I want to."

||

FOLKS SAID WHAT A sorrow it was that Danny had been killed, what a shame for a young man to be taken in the prime of life. The women brought the Spanos enough food to feed them for a month, more food than normal, because they felt guilty that they were relieved Danny wasn't around anymore. The Spanos and Beaner were the only ones who mourned him. A few people muttered that Danny was mean enough to murder Susan Reddick. The sheriff told Dad, however, "Danny was home that night. It's a fact. I couldn't find no tracks in the snow around the Spano place to show he left."

"She must have been killed by somebody coming in off the hard road. I expect we'll never know," Mom said. "Now why won't this butter gather? It must be the weather."

She was in the kitchen with Mrs. Yamamoto, who said, "Let me try." Mrs. Yamamoto worked for us now that Daisy had moved to Pueblo. The government allowed evacuees with jobs to leave Tallgrass, so Mom had written Mrs. Booth in Pueblo and asked if she could find work for Daisy. Mrs. Booth wrote back by return mail, saying there was plenty of work in Pueblo, and she invited Daisy and the baby to live with her and the Snows. So Daisy and Amy Elizabeth took the train to Pueblo. I cried when she left, because Daisy had been like a sister to me, but I knew it was best for her to move on. The next day, Carl joined the army. "Maybe it is good we don't know who killed the little girl. It would stir things up again. There is not so much unpleasantness now," Mrs. Yamamoto said as she turned the butter paddle.

"That's because without Danny around, Beaner isn't causing trouble," I told her. Whatever the reason, things had indeed improved for the evacuees. Signs with cartoons of Japanese faces had disappeared from the stores; even the Elliot Drug had taken down its sign saying Japanese weren't welcome. More evacuees came to town to shop now, ordering Cokes at the Lee Drug soda fountain and taking in the movies at the Roxie. The evacuees smiled and said hello to people on the streets, and sometimes when Dad was in the fields, the evacuees walking down the road from the camp leaned on our fence and talked to him about crops. More and more farmers were hiring Japanese boys for spring planting.

Mrs. Yamamoto nodded, adding slyly, "And you people don't mind taking credit for our victories." She was right about that. The 422d Regimental Combat Team, made up of Japanese-American soldiers, was in the newspaper all the time because of the battles it had won in Europe. Some of those soldiers were Tallgrass evacuees, and Ellis always did like to claim winners.

A few weeks after Mrs. Yamamoto came to work for us, Mom took the train to Denver. After Danny's death, she'd been quiet, melancholy even, and Dad had worried about her. "You ought to go stay with Hazel for a time. That'll whistle away your sadness," he'd told her.

"Oh, I couldn't leave. You've got to break in a new crew for planting."

"I can do that, Mother," he said. "I reckon Marthalice would be glad to see you."

What he meant was that Mom and Marthalice needed to talk. "You understand why I can't take you?" Mom asked me as she was packing, and I did. I hoped Marthalice would tell me about the baby one day, but until then, I'd never let on that I knew why she had moved to Denver.

Mom was still at Cousin Hazel's the day Dad and I walked into Ellis carrying a box of things we had put together for Buddy. I'd saved up a month's worth of "Terry and the Pirates," and Mom had left behind a cap and vest she'd knit for Buddy. Dad put in some books, a carton of cigarettes, and a little sack of licorice. "I imagine he's hungry enough just about now to like it," Dad said.

"If some German doesn't eat it first," I told him.

"I've been thinking a lot about that lately. Maybe your mother's right; we have to believe that Buddy will get this box."

After we mailed the package, Dad gave me a nickel for a Coke before heading for the feed store. I went into the Lee Drug and sat down at the counter, where Helen Archuleta was the fountain girl now. She wore a white uniform with a green collar and a little white paper hat like a soldier's cap. She looked as smart as a WAVE, and I told her so.

Helen saluted me. "You hear anything from your brother?" She put crushed ice into a glass and filled it with Coke. Then she squirted in a dash of cherry syrup, placed a napkin on the counter in front of me, and set down the drink.

"Dad says it's good news if we don't hear until the war's over. That means Buddy's probably okay." I wasn't sure Dad believed that, but it was a nice way of explaining why we'd received no letters.

"I hope so. I always did like Bud. . . ." Helen stopped, and her mouth turned into a thin, straight line.

I took a straw out of the round glass container and put it into the Coke and sipped. When I looked up, Helen was still staring past me.

"What do you want?" she asked. I wondered if one of the evacuees had come in. Some people in Ellis were still scared of them, although it would have surprised me if Helen was among them. After all, she'd given Daisy Susan's baby clothes.

I turned around. Helen wasn't staring at an evacuee. Bobby Archuleta stood behind me, grinning. He was still good-looking, although he was older, his skin less baby-fine. A scar ran from the corner of his eye almost to his ear. He had a little moustache, and smiling at Helen, his eyes glinting, he looked like Clark Gable. That smile could unhinge a beet drill. I thought it was romantic that Bobby had come back even though I knew he was no good. I wondered if Helen thought so. After all, she'd loved him enough to give up her family for him. He might have changed. I thought maybe he wasn't so bad after all. "Hey, Helen," Bobby said, his black eyes crinkly.

Helen looked at him as if she'd just tasted sour milk, and she didn't reply.

Bobby pretended to pout then. "Come on, you're not sore, are you, honey?"

Instead of answering, Helen picked up a rag and began to wipe the counter with it.

"Come on, baby," he said.

Helen threw the rag into the little sink behind her. "What do you think? You ran out on me, Bobby. You left me all by myself."

Bobby looked like a naughty boy now. "Okay, that was a dumb thing to do, but I didn't want to get drafted. Besides, I come back, didn't I?"

"Maybe you shouldn't have. Maybe you should have stayed away."

Bobby shrugged and said softly, "I didn't want to get killed in no war. You wouldn't want me to get killed, would you?" When Helen didn't answer, he added, "Besides, I couldn't come back. I was in the pen in Iowa, up at Fort Madison."

"What for?" I blurted out. When the two of them looked at me, I was mortified that I'd spoken.

Bobby saw me for the first time and asked, "You think this is your business? Get lost."

The way Bobby looked at me scared me, and I knew he hadn't changed. Although I hadn't finished my Coke, I swung around on the stool to leave. But Helen put her hand on my arm and said, "Stay." She might have been afraid of Bobby, too, and felt safer with me there. The only other person in the store was Redhead Joe Lee, but he was on the phone in the back and couldn't hear Bobby and Helen. I turned back to Helen, watching Mr. Lee in the mirror behind the soda fountain, wishing he'd come over. But Helen and Bobby were none of his business. Or mine, I thought as I stared at the scratches on the Coke glass, embarrassed at being caught between them. I hoped Dad would come soon.

Bobby acted as if I weren't there then, and said, "Hey, I brought you something." He held out a box to Helen, but she wouldn't take it. He set it on the counter. "It's a bracelet, real gold. You like gold, don't you?" He had such a pleading look on his face that I was surprised Helen didn't give in.

"Aw, come on, Helen. You can't be mad forever. Let's get out of here, maybe go to Denver and have us a good time. You always did like a good time." The look he gave her was a leer.

"I'm not like that anymore, Bobby. I have to think of the baby now." Helen didn't look at him. She kept glancing at the door, as if she were hoping someone would come in. There still was no one else in the store except for Mr. Lee, and he didn't seem to be paying attention.

"Yeah, I forgot about that." Bobby raised his chin and flexed his arms. "So I'm a father now. What's his name?"

"*Her* name. The baby's a girl. I named her Susan."

Bobby frowned. "Susan, huh?"

"After my sister."

"Yeah, I'm real sorry about that."

"Are you?" Helen's answer was so sharp that I felt the hair rise on the back of my neck.

Bobby ignored her tone and asked, "So where's the kid?"

"Where you'll never see her." Helen glared at Bobby then. She didn't seem afraid of him anymore.

Bobby narrowed his eyes and leaned forward, his heavy arms on the counter. "I asked you where she's at." He reached out and grabbed Helen's arm.

In the mirror, I saw Mr. Lee start forward, but just then, Sheriff Watrous came into the drugstore and walked up behind Bobby. "Let go of the lady's arm, bub."

"Don't you 'bub' me. She's my wife."

"No, I don't believe she is. I believe she's your former wife. Is that right, Helen?" The sheriff stood a little behind Bobby, his legs apart, rocking back and forth.

Helen nodded. "I got a divorce. We aren't married anymore, Bobby."

"Since when?" Bobby loosened his grip on Helen, and she pulled away, rubbing her arm.

"Since last year," she said.

"You can't do that unless I say so." Bobby flexed the muscles in his arms, which were as big as truck tires. There was a tattoo of a naked lady on one.

"She can, and she did," the sheriff said. "She's an independent lady with a job now."

"Doing what, working nights for Jay Dee?" Bobby asked it in such an ugly way that I was embarrassed for Helen. She worked hard at the drugstore to provide for Susan, and she stayed home at nights, although plenty of men would have taken her out dancing and drinking.

"You keep a civil tongue," the sheriff said.

"And you butt out of this, Sheriff. This ain't your business. It's between me and Helen."

"What did you say?" The sheriff held his arms out a little from his sides, and he had stopped rocking.

"I said keep your nose out of it. I'm not afraid of any hick sheriff. Maybe you ought to be afraid of me." Bobby jutted out his jaw and gave Sheriff Watrous a nasty smile.

"I guess that's about right. Me and the whole town's been afraid of you, but not anymore. You best come along with me now."

"Why's that?" Bobby clenched and unclenched his hands as if he were about to punch the sheriff. But before Bobby could move, Sheriff Watrous yanked a pair of handcuffs out of his pocket and slid one end over Bobby's right wrist. Then he pulled Bobby's cuffed hand behind his back and placed the other cuff over Bobby's left wrist. "What the hell!" Bobby said.

The sheriff gripped Bobby's arm so that he couldn't move.

"Shut up, Bobby. You're under arrest. . . ."

"What'd I do? You can't arrest me for talking to my wife."

"This isn't about Helen. I'm arresting you for the rape and murder of Susan Reddick," Sheriff Watrous said. "You can come along peaceable, or you can make a lot of noise, so that the men of this town know why I'm taking you in. I expect it wouldn't be too hard for them to overpower me. Helen, I'll call on your folks and tell them we caught the fellow who did it."

"*He* killed Susan?" Every single day for more than two years, I'd thought about who'd killed my friend. Each time I saw a Japanese man, I wondered if he'd done it. And despite what the sheriff had said, I'd still suspected Danny was guilty. But I'd never even considered Bobby Archuleta. He hadn't been seen around Ellis since he ditched Helen. I slumped on the stool and laid my head on the cool marble counter.

"That's about right, Squirt," Dad said. He'd slipped into the store without any of us seeing him. He turned to Sheriff Watrous then and told him, "I heard at the feed store that Bobby just got into town and was asking about Helen, so I came right over here, but I reckon you've got things under control."

"I thank you for it anyway. He's a mean one."

The sheriff led Bobby away, and Mr. Lee came over and patted Helen's shoulder and asked, "You all right, honey?"

Helen's arms were covered with goose bumps, and she folded them over her chest. "I'm glad he came here instead of the house. I saw you call the sheriff."

"We figured he'd want to swagger a bit. It's a good thing we were right."

"Bobby Archuleta killed Susan?" I asked again. "Did you know that, Daddy?"

Dad nodded. "I'm afraid so—the sheriff, Mr. Lee, Helen, me. We were the only ones. Even the Reddicks didn't know. If the word got out and Bobby heard we were onto him, he wouldn't have come back. We figured he'd show up one of these times."

"How did you know it was Bobby?"

Mr. Lee looked at Helen. "You up to telling her about him?"

Helen moved away from Mr. Lee and stared at the counter, touching a wet spot with her fingers, then making a circular motion as she swirled the water around. Without looking at me, she said, "Bobby hit me all the time. The night he left, he beat me up bad. He said if I told anybody, he'd kill me, kill my family, too. I don't know why he hurt Susan. Maybe he was drunk and went there to threaten Dad. Bobby hated him because Dad called him 'a no-good Mexican.' When I heard about Susan, I knew it had to be Bobby, but I was afraid to tell the sheriff. I thought Bobby would come back and kill us. Besides, why would Sheriff Watrous believe me? He'd just think I was trying to get even because Bobby ran out on me."

Helen set her hand down flat on the wet spot and began to rub it again. "Last winter, Bobby wrote me a letter from Iowa. He said he was coming back, and that if he found out I'd been carrying on with another man, I'd end up in a haystack just like my sister. That was a dumb thing to write, because how would he have known what happened to Susan if he hadn't done it? I mean, somebody could have written him or something, but Bobby didn't have any friends in Ellis. And he never read a newspaper in his life. That's when I went to the sheriff."

"By then, Sheriff Watrous was pretty sure it was Bobby," Dad said. "But there wasn't any proof until Helen gave him that letter. I had a hunch about him, too, because Bobby'd worked the beets for me. I knew Bobby had a cruel streak, because he once took a knife to a beet worker's wife."

"Both the sheriff and your dad believed from the beginning that whoever killed Susan went to our farm on purpose," Helen added.

Mr. Lee put his hand on top of Helen's wet fingers to quiet them, and she leaned her head against his chest and began to cry.

There wasn't any trial. Bobby's lawyer told him that people in Ellis were so angry about Susan's murder that if he were put on trial, he would get the electric chair; it wouldn't matter if he'd killed Susan or not. So Bobby confessed and was sent to the penitentiary in Cañon City for life.

He said he was driving to Ellis from Denver in the storm, drinking rye whiskey and smoking marijuana cigarettes, when he decided to rob the Reddicks, because he knew that Mr. Reddick kept his money in a drawer of the Hoosier cupboard in the kitchen. Bobby pulled off the hard road, intending just to sneak into the house. He figured nobody'd know he'd even been there until Mr. Reddick went to get his money, and then he'd probably blame his wife or daughter for taking it. He forgot that Susan slept next to the kitchen. When she woke up and saw him, Bobby lost his head and stabbed her. He carried her outside, where he raped her and slit her throat. Then he got into the car and drove back to Denver.

You could almost see the relief in Ellis after Bobby confessed. People said all along they knew it wasn't any of the Japanese. But nobody was as relieved as Helen. After Bobby was sent to Cañon City, Helen married Redhead Joe Lee.

EPILOGUE

I HADN'T SPOKEN TO Daisy in a long time, until the day in 1974 when Mom's heart finally gave out. I called Daisy, who was living in California with her husband and two daughters, to tell her that Mom had died. Daisy, along with Carl, who owned a sugar beet farm in Idaho, came for the funeral. Dad kept the casket closed, since Mom never liked people staring at her, and I spread Buddy's remembrance quilt and Mrs. Hirano's embroidery over it, because Mom had prized them both. The church was filled; people were even standing in the aisles. Mom drew a crowd of nearly two hundred. She would have been pleased.

A few of the Stitchers were still around, although death and ill health had decimated their ranks, and younger women like me weren't interested in quilting. The Stitchers who were left had long ago forgotten the rancor of Tallgrass. Now, they fussed over Vietnam and Nixon and hippies. But they still pulled together in times of trouble, and those who could walk came by the day of the funeral, along with the farm women of my generation. Bringing covered dishes in a time of sorrow was a tradition that never died out. So the kitchen was filled with food, and we invited Carl and Daisy to stay for supper with the family.

Afterward, Dad drove the two of them down to the Tallgrass site, which was now just dirt roads and a few concrete slabs. Yucca and sagebrush had taken over where buildings once stood. "I wouldn't have recognized it," Carl said. It struck me that neither Carl nor Daisy was bitter.

Later on, Dad, Carl, Bud, and my husband, Mike, walked out into the fields. Bud had survived the German prison camp and come home, but he'd changed, and he didn't want to be tied to a place. Since Marthalice, who'd never married, wasn't interested in returning to Ellis, the place came to me after all. Mike had grown up on a wheat farm in Kansas and loved the rhythm of the growing seasons and the open sweep of the plains as much as I did. We built a house next to the folks' place, and Mike went to farming with Dad. After about ten years, Dad said, "I reckon one of these times, you might make a beet farmer." Mike said that was one of the best days of his life.

While Marthalice went inside to box up the Persian lamb coat that Dad had bought Mom after the war, Daisy and I sat in the yard, remembering when the beet workers had once rested under the cottonwoods and pointing to the spots where the pump and the clothesline had stood. "We've got a dryer now," I told her.

"I should hope so," Daisy said. "I remember how your grandmother used to quilt. Your mom taught me, you know. I've gotten pretty good at it."

"I haven't," I said, and we laughed. Daisy said she still had the baby quilt that Betty Joyce and I had made for her.

"Betty Joyce was at the funeral. She's married to our doctor. Did you see her?"

Daisy laughed. "If she hadn't introduced herself to me, I wouldn't have recognized her. She must weigh twice as much as she did when she was a girl." Daisy leaned back in her lawn chair and raised her face to the sky. Then she remembered something. "Bea Yamamoto sends you her condolences. Bea's my neighbor, you know."

"I'd forgotten all about her." I chuckled, recalling how just after V-J day, Miss Ord had stopped by our farm, and said, "Do you remember I told you I'd let you in on a secret? That was the day the Elliot girl picked a fight with you." Her silver eyes sparkled. "Here it is. I'm married to the Yamamotos' son, Jim. He's in the army. After his folks were sent to Tallgrass, I took the teacher position in Ellis so that I could watch after them. Of course, I'd have been fired if anybody had found out. Are you surprised?" I was. Nobody had suspected she was even married, let alone the wife of a Japanese man.

When we heard the men coming back to the house, Daisy touched my arm and grew serious. "Your Mom once read me a passage from the Bible about the Lord giving His people a vine out of Egypt. She said it wouldn't be long before He gave a vine to Amy Elizabeth and me. I thought about that Scripture during the hard times. I couldn't help but believe it, because your Mom was so sure about it." A car drove past on the Tallgrass Road. The driver honked, and I waved, although I couldn't recognize him. Daisy waited until the car had disappeared. "Not a day goes by that I don't remember your mother, that I don't think how much I owe her. I want you to know that."

After Carl and Daisy drove away, Bud went with Mike to do chores while Dad and I sat on the porch of the folks' house, the way we used to in the old days, after the supper dishes were done, looking down the Tallgrass Road. The road had been widened and paved and now was a four-lane highway. I liked it better when it was dirt.

"Carl and Daisy don't look that much older, just a little grayer," Dad said. "I wonder how that happened."

"How did you get bald?"

He chuckled. "What would I do without you, Squirt?"

"I expect you'd sell the farm and live the life of Riley."

"Oh, I guess I wouldn't do that. I'm as much a part of this place as a fence post."

We were quiet, listening to the evening sounds—the kids' horses moving around in the corral, a tractor working off near the old Reddick place, the rumble of voices inside, where Marthalice was watching TV. Then I said, "I suppose you know Daisy named her girl Mary, after Mom."

"Your mother liked that."

"She owed Mom. She just told me so," I said.

"That's about right."

Dad had always been comfortable with silence, and we moved back and forth in the swing, not talking. After a bit, Dad said, "I was looking at Daisy just now, Squirt. She's still as strong as a horse, always was, even after that first baby of hers was born—Amy Elizabeth. And you remember how weak your mother was back when she had that heart trouble. She couldn't hardly heft herself." He reached into the pencil pocket of his overalls and pulled out a licorice stick, which he handed to me.

I peeled off the cellophane wrapper and bit off a third of the licorice. A truck sped down the road, reminding me of our old truck. Dad had forgotten to put the emergency brake on Red Boy twenty years back, and it had run down a hill and crashed into an arroyo, where he'd left it. Kids played in its rusted-out carcass now. Dad replaced the truck with a new one, but I never felt the same way about Red Boy Junior.

Dad spread out a little on the swing and put his arm on the back of the seat behind me. He chuckled. "I always wondered if that sheriff was fool enough to believe your mother when she said she'd stabbed the Spano boy? Or do you think Hen Watrous knew all along that it was Daisy?"

"I didn't know that." I leaned forward and turned to look at Dad. "I never knew for sure whether it was Daisy or Carl. I thought most likely Daisy, because Carl was on the haymow ladder when I went into the barn. But I never was sure." I smiled at Dad. "You know, it was almost a week before it hit me that Mom wasn't strong enough to push any beet knife into Danny Spano, that there was no way she could have killed him."

Dad thought that over, rubbing the back of his hand over his forehead. "Your mother was sorely tested by having to tell that lie. Lying wasn't part of her nature, any more than killing was. All she ever wanted was to live an ordinary life."

"Well, she wasn't an ordinary woman, Dad." I leaned back in the swing and moved in rhythm with my father. I added, "She was a good woman."

"By Dan, I reckon she was." He looked off down the road in the twilight. "An awful good woman."